More TRICKS

HIDDEN EMPIRE 4

ELIZABETH KNIGHT

Copyright 2022 © Elizabeth Knight

All rights reserved.

This is a work of fiction. Names, characters, places, and incidents are either the product of the author's imagination or are used fictitiously, and any resemblance to actual persons living or dead, business establishments, events, or locales is entirely coincidental.

All rights reserved. No part of this book may be used to reproduce, scan, or be distributed in any printed or electronic form in any manner whatsoever without written permission of the author, except in the case of brief quotations for articles or reviews. Please do not participate in or encourage piracy of copyrighted materials.

Knight, Elizabeth

More Tricks

Editing: Swish Editing

Cover artist: Dazed Designs

Formatting: Creative Wonder Publishing

It's okay to ask for help every once in a while...

even a badass needs accomplices to hide the bodies

Contents

1. Dax — 1
2. Cognac — 13
3. Dax — 24
4. Dax — 37
5. Dax — 50
6. Dax — 66
7. Eagle — 81
8. Dax — 95
9. Dax — 106
10. Dax — 122
11. Dax — 137
12. Sprocket — 148
13. Dax — 159
14. Dax — 169
15. Weston — 180
16. Dax — 194
17. Dax — 207
18. Dax — 222
19. Dax — 234

20.	Void	246
21.	Dax	258
22.	Dax	272
23.	Dax	284
24.	Picasso	295
25.	Cameron	312
26.	Dax	323
27.	Dax	335
28.	Dax	347
About Author		355
Also By		356

Chapter One

Dax

Stepping out of the shower in Eagle's room, I toweled off and looked at myself in the mirror. I flinched at the bruises on my face that I'd gotten in the fight with Mastiff. The bastard hadn't held back, but then again, neither had I as I stabbed him far more times than I needed to. At that point, I'd needed the reassurance he was well and truly dead and wouldn't keep popping up like a bad penny.

The Mad Dogs were finished. The battle that happened earlier today had seen to that. A group mixed with my people and the Saints had gone out and made sure any stragglers wandering the desert had been dealt with. Cam had called the FBI and let them know we had a massive cleanup that needed to be handled. If I'd known how helpful having a Fed as a boyfriend would be, I would have done it sooner.

"Beautiful, as much as I love seeing you wander around the house naked, the FBI is almost here," Cam informed me.

Speak of the devil—he always seemed to know when I was thinking about him.

I cocked a hip and raised a brow. "I didn't realize a bedroom was a whole house? Have they started giving their agents X-ray vision or something?"

Cam stalked over to me, crowding my space until my back hit the bedroom wall. His fingers curled around my neck and gripped tight enough that I knew he wasn't joking around. "Beautiful, as much as I love that sharp tongue of yours, the way it can eviscerate people where they stand, you've forgotten something important."

"What would that be?" I asked, holding his golden-brown gaze, not backing down from his challenge.

He leaned in and kissed me ruthlessly, nipping hard enough at my lip, I actually tasted blood. "You're grounded, and I was put in charge of you for the day," Cam whispered against my lips, then licked the blood that seeped out of the corner of my mouth and moaned. "I forgot how good you tasted."

I smirked at him. "Did you really think I was going to let the grounding stand? I'm well aware that you're all pissed at me, but that doesn't mean you all get to rule my life. How quickly you forget that I created the Hidden Empire, fought tooth and nail for it so I could be the top dog."

"Hmm, I love it when you get feisty," Cam murmured into my ear, pressing his whole body to me so I could feel how turned on he was. "But, now is not the time for us to play our favorite game. You still have to call Dani so we can speak with Eagle and catch him up on events. Then the FBI will have questions that we need to skirt around, all the while with you attached to my side." He pulled back, pressing a kiss to my forehead. "Now get dressed, Weston made dinner, and we wouldn't want it to go to waste. If I find you still not dressed in five minutes, there will be punishment and not the kind you enjoy. Don't forget. I know all your secrets, Dax, so be a good girl."

I stood there stunned that Cam had just ignored everything I'd just said, threatened me, and walked out, leaving me a panting mess. *God, I was fucked in the head if that was one of the sexiest things he's done in a long time.*

Yanking open the drawer Eagle emptied for me to hold my stuff, I realized I'd left a ton of stuff back at the ranch house. "I seriously need to stop losing all my shit after each of these battles. No cell phone, no smartwatch, lost my favorite guns... again. Fucking hell, just when I didn't think Marco would make me even more pissed at him," I grumbled to myself as I pulled on clothes.

Bless Tilly for having good taste and knowing what basics a woman like me needed. I wriggled into my jean shorts and pulled on a T-shirt with a classic rock band name on it. It was a little big, but with how tiny I was, that wasn't unusual, so I tied a knot in the front and called it good enough.

Padding out into the living room, I found Wes sprawled out on the couch, arm over his eyes. He had one bare foot up on the leather cushion and the other planted on the floor.

Silently, I walked over and ran the edge of my nail up his foot, knowing how ticklish he was. "Motherfucker," he roared, shooting up into a sitting position but flailed and landed on the floor in a heap. "*Dax.*"

I grinned at him sheepishly. "Damn, I didn't think you'd freak out that bad," I commented as I reached down to help him up. "Just figured I would startle you, not send you into cardiac arrest."

"Well, shortcake, it might not have been so dramatic if we hadn't just been fighting for our lives all day," Wes muttered as he sat back on the couch, hauling me into his lap.

He nuzzled his face into my neck, trailing little kisses down to my shoulder, then back up behind my ear. I yelped as he bit the tip of my ear with a grunt of pleasure. "Serves you right after all the shit you pulled today. I ought to do what I did in the beginning days of the Empire when you got out of hand."

"Don't you even think about it," I gasped, looking at him in horror.

"Sounds like this is something we should know if it makes her that worried," Sprocket interjected. "Nothing we've come up with so far has made her bat an eyelash, yet a simple implied threat from you, and she's panicking."

Wes grinned at me, tightening his hold as I tried to squirm out of his grasp. "Should I tell him?"

"You do, and I'll chop off your balls," I snapped. "There are some things that should stay just between the two of us."

He tilted his head, considering me for a moment, then looked over at Sprocket. "I'll keep it to myself for now, but if she doesn't take this grounding seriously, I'll play whatever cards I need to." Then he looked back at me. "No matter how mad it makes you at me. You've been warned, shortcake, we're serious about this."

I opened my mouth to rip him a new one, but when I saw the determination in his gaze, I knew nothing was going to change his mind. "Fine, I've been warned and am fully aware of the fallout if I don't play nice."

A hand slid up to cup the back of my head, and he caught me in a demanding kiss. He wasn't as aggressive as Cam had been, but that wasn't Weston's style. No, he was dominant and liked to be in control in the bedroom, but he gave as much as he took. Our tongues tangled together as we lost ourselves in the moment. Since Cam had already gotten my engine running, this wasn't helping the situation in the least.

When a throat cleared, we broke apart to see the rest of the guys showered with matching expressions of exhaustion and heat. They wanted me, but it would seem none of us had the energy to do much about it.

"Someone said dinner was ready? I didn't realize you were talking about *loba*," Cognac teased, giving me a flirtatious wink.

Wes gave me a quick kiss, then pushed us both to our feet. "While I'm sure none of us would argue she's rather tasty, I do have actual food made. Hope you don't mind a simple meal. It's all the energy I had in me. There are noodles and you can choose between meat sauce or alfredo to put over it."

Like ducks following their mother, we trailed after him into the kitchen with a chorus of rumbling bellies. "Fuck, man, anything sounds good right now," Void said as he grabbed a plate and dumped a massive pile of noodles on it.

"Ah, did you want to leave some for the rest of us, big guy?" I asked with a chuckle.

He paused and looked at his plate, then me with a wicked grin. "Then I guess you're just going to have to sit on my lap and share this with me, little demon."

"Guys, I made plenty of pasta for everyone. I know you're all bottomless pits," Wes cut in, opening the lid to another pot full of pasta. Void glared at Wes, but to his credit, my best friend didn't flinch, just handed him a ladle for the sauce. "You might want that to make sure you have enough to cover all those noodles."

I snorted, turning away so they couldn't see me laughing. Never did I think a group of alpha males like this could become this hodgepodge family we've seemed to have created. While they came from all different walks of life, somehow, they each felt it was worth putting up with the others to be with me. It blew my mind, and I tried not to dwell on it too much, but the facts remained the same. I was dating and in love with seven men and they were in love with me— go figure.

"What are you laughing at, spitfire?" Picasso whispered, coming up behind me.

I shook my head and wrapped an arm around his waist, to which he automatically pulled me closer. "That you're all friends. Seriously, how crazy is that?"

"Yeah, about that, I'm still not sure about this guy," Cognac said, jerking his thumb at Cam. "He still seems a little too assholish for my liking."

"You met his dad. There's no way that wouldn't have happened," Sprocket remarked. "That man is drama and a half. Speaking of the shifty bastard, where is he?"

"He's still showering," Picasso muttered. "Thank God, Cam warned me to shower before he did. I'm not sure we're going to have enough hot water for him at this point."

"Oh, he's out of the shower. It's his skincare routine that takes a million years," Cam explained. "As for the asshole comment, one can only do so much with the personality the Lord has blessed me with." This caused all of us to give him a baleful look that caused him to toss up his hands in surrender. "Message received. I'll work on it."

"Leave the black knight alone. He's exactly who we needed in this group," Void scolded the others. "He is the only one who can keep up with the devious nature of my little demon. With him around, we might be able to keep her alive a little longer."

My jaw dropped at his words. "What does that mean?"

"Really, little demon, do you think we're all mad at you for no reason?" Void asked, giving me a deadpan look. "You are smarter than that. Take a moment to think it over and let me know when you've managed to see our point of view."

Fuck, if Void was upset with me too about what happened earlier, then maybe I did go too far.

Wes seemed to follow my train of thought as he snapped out an arm to block the giant man. "Hold up. How are you mad at her when you were right on her heels, running into battle?"

Void looked completely confused by the question. "You would rather I let her go alone? My little demon is many things, but bulletproof, she's not. I'd rather enter the fires of Hell beside her than send her off to fight alone. There is always better luck when you have backup."

Wes tried to come up with a rebuttal but couldn't. *Damn, my man, Void, is the best kind of crazy, no wonder he believes we're soul mates.* While he made a good point about why he went running off into danger, I, on the other hand, didn't have one other than being an impulsive adrenaline junky. It was simpler to just deal with things head-on, get to the root of the problem, and be done with it.

Once everyone took a seat and dug into our meal, we fell silent, mouths too full to harass me about my life choices. I was gonna need to fix this, though, because being grounded was *not* gonna happen. Just as we all started to relax, the sound of vehicles pulling up and headlights flashing in through the windows alerted us to the arrival of the FBI. Cam shoved back his chair, tossing his napkin on the table angrily as he went to greet them.

"So, did you guys already discuss what we're telling them?" I asked, leaning back in my chair, sipping at my beer.

"We stick to the same story Cam told them when they got to the site of the explosion," Sprocket explained.

"Great…" I said cheerfully. "Anyone want to tell me what that is? I was a little kidnapped at the time."

This seemed to snap them all to attention as the realization that I had no idea what our cover story was.

"Right, well, part of it was the sneaky plan you cooked up with Cam behind our backs," Picasso started, letting me know how he felt about that. "As you instructed, the FBI was notified that we were in the works with a sting operation and we were helping."

"Huh," I mused. "That was simple and to the point of him, now, wasn't it."

"You didn't tell him to say that?" Cognac asked.

Shaking my head, I took another swallow of my beer. "Nope, I told him to do whatever he needed to, so we had backup since I had no idea how procedure works within the FBI. Seems like it did the trick since none of us are in jail."

"Yet, none of us are in jail *yet*," Wes corrected. "Don't forget we have a massacre out there that we need to have a damn good story for."

"Why do we need a story? They attacked us. We defended ourselves, plain and simple," I reasoned, twirling my fork in my pasta. "They would have come lights a blazin' if they were going to ship us off to jail. This seems too friendly in my book, and I don't think the FBI is *that* good at infiltration on a large scale."

"I just love your optimism, *loba*," Cognac said with a grin. "Here you sit, calm as can be, while the iron fist of the government is sitting on our lawn."

"Oh, my sweet, sweet, summer child," I teased. "Don't you know the guiltier you act, the easier it is for them to believe you are? One of the biggest reasons I haven't ended up in jail for the rest of my life is purely because I have *zero* guilt about what I've done."

Void just smiled and continued to shovel his face full of food, understanding what I was saying far more than the others. We paused when the front door opened, and Cam walked in with Agent Egger, who did not look any more thrilled to see me than when we first met. At least this time, I wasn't covered in blood. That should count for something.

"Hello, agent," I greeted, waving my fork at her. "We have more left if you're hungry."

She just looked at me like I'd lost my mind. With a shrug, I went back to my meal, not remembering the last thing I ate. Feeling the gnaw of hunger in my belly wasn't something I enjoyed. It reminded me of days I'd rather forget.

"How can you all just be sitting there eating like nothing happened today?" Egger blurted. "There is a wasteland of dead bodies out there that you created."

Setting my fork down, I turned in my chair to face her. "Do you know what would have happened if we hadn't killed them?"

"I don't care. You should have waited for the authorities to handle this matter," she argued.

Crossing one leg over the other, I cocked my head at her. "So it's fine with you if the cops kill them all, just not us? What about the women and children they would have slaughtered while we waited for said authorities to arrive? Were we just supposed to tell the people that call this home to cut their losses and run? If that's that case, then arrest me because I will never regret doing what was necessary to keep them safe," I dared, holding out my wrist, ready for her to cuff me.

Cam charged over to me and batted my hands down. "Would you please stop being so dramatic? She isn't going to arrest you because everything we did was in self-defense. There is even video to prove that everything that was done is justified."

Shoving to my feet, I brushed past Cam and stood right in front of Agent Egger. "I still want to know your answer. Would you, in their position, wait for the police to come or stand your ground to protect your home and family?"

Egger looked me dead in the eye, but I watched as when she truly thought about it, she wasn't so sure. "I... I am an FBI agent. I swore an oath to uphold the law—"

"Err," I yelled, cutting her off. "You swore an oath to uphold the constitution, and within that archaic document is the right to bear arms, and since you brought up the law, then there's something called the Castle Doctrine, which states I can defend my home and the people within it without fear of prosecution. They came on our land, breached our fences, and attacked us. Damn, Egger, you're one hell of an agent if you would tell me I'm wrong."

Knowing that I was too pissed off to talk to this woman reasonably, I stormed out of the house. Footsteps quickly followed, telling me they really weren't going to let me go off on my own.

"*Loba*," Cognac called after me. "Damn, you are fast for someone with such short legs," he said as he jogged up next to me.

"It's all a fucking joke." I snarled.

Cognac grabbed my arm and pulled me to his chest. "I know, *loba*, fucking hell do I know how true that is."

"They come here acting like we are the bad guys when if we didn't fight, so many innocents would have been lost," I fumed. "How can they see what happened and only see the black and white of it all?"

"Because that is how they were trained. The world is a set of rules, good and evil, while we live in a world of gray. Things are never cut and dry when you look under the surface, but they don't have the autonomy to do that," Cognac shared, running his fingers soothingly through my hair that was getting far too long for my liking.

"How the fuck did Cam make it through their training? He is the most gray person I know," I rambled, trying to keep from getting too emotional. I'd cried once today after finding out Eagle was alive. I didn't need to do that shit again because of some stupid FBI agent.

"Do any of us really want to know the answer to that? I feel like out of anything we know that could get us arrested or thrown in jail," Cognac said with a chuckle. "Come on. I have an idea of what might make you feel better."

"Is there someone you have tied to a chair I can stab?" I mumbled, letting him lead me by the hand into the darkness behind a garage.

Cognac let out a bark of laughter. "Yeah, I suppose that would make you feel better, but this idea is a little less… messy."

"If you say so." I sighed.

We didn't have to go far before I spotted what he wanted to show me. It reminded me of when I'd first arrived and found out they had a pool. A smile grew on my lips and as the soft light from within the water glowed invitingly, begging me to jump in.

"I'm not skinny dipping," I warned as I shoved my shorts down.

Cognac's face turned serious for a second. "Damn straight you're not showing off that hot little body of yours to anyone but us. Fuck, if the others found out, I'm not sure what would happen."

"And we'll never find out because I'm in enough trouble with them as it is," I pointed out and dove into the water.

Chapter Two

Cognac

Watching Dax glide through the water wearing a T-shirt and underwear was mouth-watering and tortuous in the best way possible. My *loba* was so full of passion, and she didn't even realize it. As she bitched out that agent, all I could think about was how proud I was that she was our woman. Dax, the fierce queen that she was, submitted to no man, woman, government, or evil that stood in her way from keeping her people safe. It was mesmerizing to watch, and I wanted to see it for the rest of my life.

People like Sally back at the hospital might not understand why we all choose to love the same woman, but it was easy for me to see. Who wouldn't love someone filled with fire, willing to run into battle without fear, just to ensure the enemy was vanquished? That was the woman I held in my heart, even if she was batshit crazy and tended to stab first, asking questions later. Who didn't like a little danger in their romance?

"Are you just going to stand there and stare at me, or are you getting in?" Dax asked, her voice bringing me back to the moment.

I flashed her a sultry smile and grabbed the back of my shirt. "Can you blame me for getting distracted seeing my woman all wet and waiting for me?"

She groaned and rolled her eyes, acting like she didn't enjoy my flirting. "Just make sure you keep your boxers on. No one gets to see the goods but me."

"Oh, would someone get jealous?" I asked, slipping into the pool. "What would have happened if I didn't wear boxers?"

She swam up to me and wrapped her legs around my waist, a dangerous look in her eye. "Well, either you'd be swimming in your jeans, or I'd be plucking out someone's eyeballs."

"Even after you just saved them?" I pressed, curious how far she would take this.

Her lips pressed against mine in a whisper of a kiss. "In a heartbeat," she murmured. "I don't share what's mine no matter what the circumstances are. Think you can live with that?"

A growl erupted from my throat, and I caught her bottom lip with my teeth and sucked it into my mouth, running my tongue over it. "I love when you get possessive. It's fucking hot," I shared. "You own us as much as we own you. What more could a man ask for?"

"I'm not sure what a man would ask for, but I know what I want right now," she said, rubbing her pussy over my rock-hard cock, only our underwear separating us. "Question is... how bold are you?"

"Oh, *loba*, that is not a challenge you want to make with me," I said, sliding a hand up the front of her shirt, palming her breast. "How far are you willing to let me go?"

"I suppose we'll just have to find out, now won't we?" she challenged, dropping a hand into the water to push down my boxers and let my cock free.

I groaned as she gripped it tightly in her hand, not moving it, just applying pressure around the tip, grinning at me. "Two can play that game, you know." Her head fell back as I pinched her nipple, pulling it until her skin stopped giving to my efforts. "Do you like that, *loba*, the bite of pain as pleasure floods your body?"

"Yes." She gasped as I let her nipple slip through my fingers and tugged harder.

Shoving up her shirt, I dipped my head to capture the other breast in my mouth, using my teeth to scrape along the raised bud. Then I locked my lips around it and sucked sharply, wondering if I might be able to make a hickey around her nipple. Dax's hold on my cock got tighter, and her nails dug into my back as she thrashed under my lips. Curious just how far I could push her, I tugged on her other nipple with my free hand.

"Fuck yes," Dax yelled, her hips grinding into me as her body instinctively knew what it needed. "More, I need more," she begged.

I lifted my head and smirked at the beautiful purple mark I'd left behind. Then I met her silvery-blue eyes, hazy with lust, and nipped at her chin. "Only good girls get to come, and you've not been good at all."

Indignation flashed over her face as she tugged on my dick, reminding me she still had it in her hands. "Are you sure that's the game you want to play, Juan? It could end poorly for you if that is the path you want to walk down."

"*Loba*, you don't scare me. You might intimidate the world, but I know better. You love me and my cock too much to rip it off my body," I pointed out, knowing it was the truth. "What I want from you is a promise."

Her face scrunched up. "A promise? For what?"

"That you will be honest with us. We are your partners in life, love, and business. As such, don't you think it would only be fair to let us know what the fuck is going on in that brain of yours? You told Cam your plan but not us. I won't lie to you and tell you that didn't fucking sting," I stated bluntly. "If you can tell an old flame who hasn't been by your side since this all started, then why couldn't you do the same for the men you claim to love?"

She opened her mouth to speak, then paused as if she was considering my words. Seeing that I hadn't hit the mark yet, I tried a different approach.

"Let's say we had a plan for getting Eagle's niece back and only told you half of it then told the most important part to Harper. When things go down, you find out from her that we'd planned this whole thing all along, leaving you in the dark and possibly wounded. Imagine how fucking pissed you would be at all of us, so maybe try to understand why today has us all with our hackles up regarding your judgment."

Dax brought a hand up to her face, wiping it with the cool water of the pool as understanding finally broke through the thick, stubborn skull of hers. "Goddammit, why in the hell are you the one using mind manipulation on me? That's Sprocket's specialty."

I flashed her a grin. "Ah yes, it is indeed but just think about how often he's used it on us. Let's just say I've picked up a thing or two from him along the way. Now about that promise?" I reminded with a raised brow.

"Ugg, yes, fine, alright. I get it. I'll be better about making sure to talk to each of you guys about things. You're just going to have to be patient with me about it. I've spent so long keeping things close to my chest it's hard to untrain yourself."

"Silly, *loba*, you already know we will do that. We love you," I said, rubbing my nose along hers before kissing her. "Don't you know by now that we'll do anything for you?"

"Have to admit that's hard to believe," she admitted.

I was proud of her for saying it. She never liked to confess her failings or fears. "Then we will do our best to remind you whenever you have doubts. We are learning how to be what you need too. This isn't about us wanting to change you, Dax. We love the fuck out of how batshit crazy you are. All we want is to be looped into the chaos so we can keep up and make sure you stay alive."

"How is that one of the most romantic things anyone has said to me?" she asked with a chuckle.

My lips caught hers, and I took my time with her mouth tasting, exploring, and making her sag in my arms as she trusted me to keep her from drowning. When I released her, I reached down and slid her panties to the side, lifted her, my hand gripping her ass, and slid inside her. Her sigh of relief was like air to my soul, knowing that she felt this as strongly as I did. Now wasn't the time for words. It was a time for action.

Letting her hold herself to me with her legs, I slid my hands to the middle of her back and laid her on top of the water as I slowly pulled all the way back and slammed into her time and time again. The water around us undulated, making it clear what was happening, but I knew no one would say a goddamn word about it. If they did, there was no telling which of us would come after them.

"Look at you taking my cock like the goddess of war that you are, *loba*. You look just as stunning here in my arms as you do covered in the blood of our enemies," I whispered as I kissed up her body, my thrusts shorter and faster, using my grip to pull her down on me as my hips shot forward. "I know you think there will be a day that you go too far, that your darkness will win, and it will scare us off. Only, you're forgetting we aren't the heroes in this tale either. We have souls just as black as you do. Some of us just hide it better than others."

I needed her to hear me, feel me, and know that what I was saying was the God's honest truth. None of us were free from blood on our hands. Each of us had chosen time and time again to survive in this criminal world, and we'd come out on top. That didn't happen and leave you innocent and in rose-colored glasses. It pulled away the façade of the world and revealed to you the underbelly we all choose to ignore.

"Your soul captured us the moment we found you at that party," I shared, letting my mind wander back to that moment she was grinding on my leg, taking what she wanted from our interactions. Unashamed of her need and ignorant of the eyes that watched her filled with jealousy and lust. "Let's be honest. You marked me as yours right there on the dance floor, rubbing that weeping pussy all over my leg."

"Oh God, shut up and fuck me," Dax growled, her heels digging into my ass, urging me on.

"I'm sorry, was I getting too emotional for you?" I asked as I pulled her back up against my chest. "Forgive me. I forget how that makes you all squirrely."

Walking us over to the steps, I pulled out of her, turned her around, and bent her over in front of the railing. "You're gonna want to hold on for this," I warned.

Without question, she grabbed the railing with both hands as I ripped out the crotch of her underwear. "What—"

She didn't get to finish her question as I slammed balls deep into her, shoving her forward with the power behind it. Slapping her ass, she moaned. "Pay attention," I chided as I took a firm hold of her hips and hammered into her, grunting with the effort along with how good it felt.

Once she got the gist of things, she was shoving back on me, the sound of slapping skin, moaning, and churning water filled the night air. "Yes, fuck, just like that," Dax shouted as I slipped a finger in her ass, teasing at the tight bud.

We all knew how much she loved her ass being played with, and it was erotic. Not many women embraced that part of sex or didn't enjoy it, but our woman couldn't get enough of it.

"What do you think, *loba? S*hould we see if we can fill you up with a cock back here too? Or maybe two cocks filling this needy hole of yours? I'm sure I can talk one of the guys into sharing space with me to make you scream," I taunted as I spat on her ass and worked another finger in. "Just think of how full you'd feel, one in your dripping pussy and two of us in your ass, maybe another in your mouth?"

Her pussy clenched around me as I talked, letting me know she liked the idea as much as I did. Just picturing the scene in my head had me almost coming. Taking my free hand, I reached under and pinched her clit. "I asked you a question, *loba*. How am I to make things happen if you don't tell me you want them?"

"Fuck yes, I want all my holes filled with as much cock as they can take," she managed to get out between breaths as I could feel her climax building.

"That's a good girl," I praised. "Remember what I said good girls get?"

"We get to come," she cried as I thrust into her and pinched her clit once more.

The walls of her pussy clamped down on me. There was no way I could resist my own finish. She milked me until I had nothing left to give, filling her with every drop of my cum as I slumped over her back, wrapping my arms around her. "Fuck, *loba*, the things you do to me are inhuman."

She let out a huff of laughter as we both took a moment to catch our breath. "You're not so bad at this yourself."

"Feel ready to go back in and deal with the bitchy agent?" I asked, kissing her neck.

With a sigh that seemed to come from the depths of her body, she nodded. "Yeah, better to just get this over with. Picasso and I still need to catch Eagle up on things too. I'm sure he's screaming at everyone, mad we haven't called yet."

I eased out of her and the smug satisfaction of seeing my cum covering her pussy was immense. "God, now I have to know all night that only your shorts are keeping everyone from knowing what I just did to you."

She looked over her shoulder with an exasperated look. "Right, and the fact that both of us were grunting like pigs and yelling, fuck yes, wouldn't clue them in."

Shrugging, I smiled as I followed her out of the water, slapping her ass playfully just to watch it jiggle before she put her clothes back on. "At least they'll know I did a damn good job."

"I can't with you," Dax said with a laugh echoing in her words. "You are such a cocky bastard."

"Yes, yes I am and one that you just so happen to love to fuck," I pointed out, booping her on the nose.

There was a plastic cabinet that we kept towels in since many of us jumped into the pool at random times without thinking to bring one with us. Shaking one out, I wrapped up my woman and secured another around my waist, leaving my shirt off. I caught her hand, and we headed back to the house, ignoring the eyes of the agents who were waiting for orders in the center of the compound.

Oops, guess I forgot about them.

True to who Dax was, her shoulders were back, head held high, and she gestured to the world to fuck off when one guy dared to whistle at her.

"Thanks for the entertainment," one guy taunted.

Ah hell, why couldn't they just keep their mouths shut?

Dax was on him faster than he could blink, pulling the agent's gun from his holster and shoving it under his chin. "I'm sorry, what were you saying?"

"Nothing, ma'am, nothing at all," he answered, eyes looking like they were going to pop out of his head.

"Learn how to keep your fucking mouth closed, and you might live to see if you get the chance to reproduce," Dax snarled as she pulled the front of the agent's pants forward and shoved the gun there instead of the holster. "Let's keep that there until you can learn to respect women and their sexuality, okay?"

The agent bobbed his head up and down, turning a little green around the edges. I wrapped my arm around her shoulders and turned her back to the house. "I'm sure they've all learned their lesson. Let's get you inside before someone actually gets stabbed or shot."

"She wouldn't dare. We're FBI agents. She would get put in jail in a heartbeat," another agent blustered.

"For fuck's sake, can you just let me keep you all alive and get her into the house?" I muttered as my *loba* slipped out of my grasp. "Void," I bellowed. "I need backup."

Out of anyone who could get her to retract her claws the fastest, it was the other bloodthirsty member of our odd family. Seconds later, the front door was tossed open, and the devil incarnate flew down the steps and scooped our woman up, tossed her over his shoulder, and marched back the way he'd come without saying a word. Dax, on the other hand, had quite a few things to say.

"Put me down, Void," she ordered. "That idiot has no idea who he's messing with. They think they can come onto my turf and start shit?" She raged until the front door cut off her words.

I looked at the man who she'd attempted to go after, and he didn't look as confident as he once had. Meandering over to him, I put my hands behind my back and leaned in to tell him a secret. "You really should thank me for saving your life. One thing I can promise you is never call her bluff or any woman for that matter. You. Will. Lose." With a wink just to throw him off, I spun on my heels and headed back into the house.

Fucking her senseless had only taken the edge off her temper. What she needed was sleep, but that was going to be harder than it sounded to make happen. She'd been running on fumes for two days now, but with Eagle in the hospital and the FBI running around, convincing her to pass out for a few hours was never going to happen. Best we get shit settled so we can cuddle our woman into submission and all of us can get some rest.

Chapter Three

Dax

Void dumped me on Eagle's bed and started to unwrap the towel from my body. He peeled off my shirt, ripped the last of my underwear off, and started to dry me. When he got to my legs, he looked up at me with hunger in his eyes, knowing whose cum was still leaking out of me.

"Even he couldn't fuck the temper out of you, I see," Void mused. "Are you still hungry? You've hardly eaten all day."

"Are you treating me like a toddler trying to find out what I need so I stop crying?" I asked, trying to hold back my laughter.

Void eyed me wearily before he nodded. "You've killed, had sex, had some food, and I know you won't sleep, so I was trying to see what other options there were."

"God, I fucking love you," I blurted as I grabbed his face and yanked him down to kiss me.

While Void was one scary motherfucker, the beast who lived inside him purred for me. He was right when he called us soul mates because I don't think there was another person on this earth who could possibly be as perfect as he was. If I were being honest, I would say that about all of them. None of them were perfect, but together, they filled in where another lacked, and it took all seven of them to keep my insane ass alive.

Void's large hands wrapped around my ribs, holding me still as we devoured each other. Sure, we'd already had sex on the battlefield earlier today, but I'm not sure I'd ever get enough of these men. Eventually, he pulled back with a quick sweet kiss on my lips before he resumed drying me off and cleaning up the mess Cognac left behind. No one could ever argue these men weren't secure in themselves when one was cleaning up another man's cum from between my legs.

"Ice cream," he announced.

"What?" I asked, not following his train of thought.

"You need ice cream and cuddles."

His suggestion had me perking up. "Does Eagle allow ice cream in this house? I know how he feels about junk food and things that aren't made from scratch."

Void gave me a toothy grin. "Our beloved president has a large soft spot for frozen milk flavored with pecans."

"Of course, he would like the grandpa flavor," I muttered. "Got something else to offer?"

"My personal favorite would be death by chocolate, and I know for a fact there is a tub of it in the freezer," he shared.

"Yup, you are absolutely getting a blow job later," I assured him as I rolled off the bed and grabbed a pair of Eagle's boxers.

If they were going to keep ripping my underwear, then I was going to start wearing theirs instead. Slipping one of his T-shirts on, I was comforted by the smell of him still attached to it. It was then I realized part of my agitation was the fact that he wasn't here with us and that I had to leave him behind in Vegas.

"Can I have your cell to call Eagle?" I asked.

"Of course, you can, little demon," he said, offering it to me. "Do you want me to stay, or would you rather talk to him alone?"

"I'll come out after I'm done talking to him. We all know he'll want a report from Picasso, the control freak that he is," I answered.

Dropping a kiss on my head, he left me to curl up in Eagle's chair, and I dialed his phone. I wasn't sure he had it, but it was worth a shot. If he didn't answer, then I would call Dani and have her hand it over.

"It's about goddamn time you called, you ugly bastard." Eagle snarled into the phone.

I couldn't help but snort at that. "If that's how you talk to him on the phone, it's a wonder he calls you ever."

"Little hellcat." He purred into the phone. "Fuck, I miss you."

"It's only been a few hours since I saw you, and you're not the one who believed you might be dead for half the day," I shot back.

"Dax," Eagle countered in a knowing voice. "What happened?"

"What didn't happen," I grumbled. "The guys are pissed at me, you're in the hospital, the FBI is here passing judgment, and I just can't deal with it all right now."

"In other words, you hit your limit on shit you can handle all on your own," Eagle stated, making me cringe at how right he was.

Kicking my feet over the armrest, I leaned into the back of the chair. "I don't like them mad at me, and I don't know how to fix it. Well, okay, Cognac basically told me how, but he makes it sound so simple. You understand, as leaders, we do what is best for our people regardless of how they will feel about it later because they're still alive to bitch about it."

"Well, I'll be damned, is Two Tricks coming to me for advice on how to deal with people?" Eagle teased.

"No, your wife is," I shot back, then paused, realizing that I actually liked saying that.

"Yup, I'm gonna need to make that happen really quick because fuck, do I love the sound of that coming out of your mouth, little hellcat," Eagle commented to himself.

"Enzo," I warned.

"Hey, now, no name calling," Eagle shot back. "Tell me everything from the moment you got taken, and I'll see what advice I can offer when it comes to the guys."

So that's exactly what I did, explaining how I took out Mastiff, the drugged girls, then the bomb.

"Back up one sec," Eagle cut in. "Did you just say that you took an ax to an electrical panel wiring?"

Rubbing my forehead, knowing this was gonna go downhill, I nodded as I answered, "Yeah, that's what I did."

"Of course you did. Then what?" Eagle acknowledged and moved on.

Next, I covered the guys and the FBI showing up, dealing with the women, going to see him, and taking the helicopter to the compound. He was oddly quiet after I shared my epic takedown of the machine gun on the back of the truck, not at all as impressed as I was. Then there was the live-action laser tag with Void. I shared about Pinky being a mole but left out the fact his nephew was part of this too. That was Picasso's deal once we got Eagle back home.

"Now the FBI is here to deal with the litter of dead bodies. I suggested we just burn the bastards, but Cam said that would cause more problems," I finished with a sigh. "So what do I do? How do I make them stop being mad at me?"

"You're absolutely not going to like it," he responded.

Sitting up, I swung my feet forward and leaned my elbows on my knees. "Just tell me."

"Part of why you're feeling the way you are right now is because I'm here in a hospital after you thought I was dead. My guess is you want to be near me as much as I want to have you wrapped up in my arms," he explained. "This is how the guys feel right now with how many death-defying moments you've had. All they want is to keep you in their sights so they know, without a doubt, you're alright. Give them a day or two to calm down. I'm sure the grounding won't stick. They know you'll never let that stand, *but* giving into it even for a short while will show how much you care and respect their feelings."

I groaned. "God, everyone is getting all Dr. Phil on me tonight. I get what you're saying, though. Today has been a lot for us all, and the day just won't end."

"Promise me you will get some sleep. The doctors said if I'm as stable as I have been, they'll let me go home since we have Dani looking after me," Eagle informed me. "You should see that woman in action. She is kinda scary when she gets all boss-ass nurse on your ass."

"Tell me about it. That's why I hired her," I agreed. "I'm assuming you want to talk to Picasso?"

"Nah, you gave me the four-one-one, and my pain meds just kicked in, so I'm gonna be useless in about five minutes. Get some sleep, hellcat. You've done good, and I love you," Eagle reassured.

"Love you too," I whispered back before hanging up.

Running my hands through my hair, I got to my feet, and prepared to deal with whatever was still going on with the FBI. When I went back out to the kitchen, there was no one there.

The plates were left on the counters where they were eating, so I assumed they'd be coming back. I heard voices on the porch, so I opened the front door to find them all at the foot of the stairs pointing out an area on a map for the agents.

"We'll have a team head out there with flood lights now and start tagging bodies. I don't want to leave them for the animals or the heat of the day to start them rotting," Agent Egger said, her face scrunched in disgust.

Cognac used a red marker to draw around an area. "The land mines are here, here, and over here. They knew just where to hit us because it's not a large gap, but we needed a space to be able to evacuate if other options were cut off. Just take care of the bodies and let us move everything else. A bunch of them ended up in the minefield."

"Are all you people out of your mind?" another agent asked. "Why would you even need to have a minefield in the first place?"

I snorted. "Really, that is a stupid question since you're cleaning up the attack we'd been prepared for. Being on the defensive means careful planning to ensure when shit goes down, you're not caught unaware. Or did they not teach you that sort of thing at Quantico?"

"Little demon, you can come out here if you're going to play nice. If not, go back inside," Void warned, giving me a look that told me he wasn't playing around.

Remembering Eagle's advice, I sighed and went back into the house to let the others deal with things. If they felt it was best for me to stay out of the situation, then I'd just find some other way to occupy myself.

"Honey child, what's got you all glum?" Dante asked, coming down the stairs and adjusting his teal-colored suit.

Gone was the makeup and prosthetics to hide his features. I noticed he'd let his perfectly styled hair go pure silver with some sprinklings of his once all-black hair like his son. Cam got his lighter golden eyes from his mother while Dante had rich, dark chocolate-colored eyes that didn't miss a detail. The man was a silver fox for sure, and it was no wonder he could sweet talk his way in or out of any situation. He had long legs, fine-fingered hands, and looked after himself more than most women did.

"You do know it's like eight o'clock in the evening after a battle for our lives, right? I doubt there will be any soiree for you to attend," I pointed out, a smile tugging at my lips.

Dante clicked his tongue at me. "Just because you're in a bad mood doesn't mean you get to be nasty." He glided over to the couch and patted the seat next to him. "Now come sit down with me and tell me what in the blue blazes is going on. Why are the FBI here so late?"

"That would be because your son called them, explained what happened, and they felt the need to take over since they dealt with the first part of this ridiculous day," I answered, flopping down on the couch.

"Hmm, that does sound like him," Dante agreed. "That doesn't explain why you look as thrilled as a wet hen in a rainstorm."

Oh God, I almost forgot how dramatic Dante could be and how hard it was to keep a straight face.

"Eagle, one of my men and leader of the Phantom Saints, is back in a Vegas hospital. The guys are grumpy at me, and we jumped over one hurdle only to find out a bigger one is coming before we can even see the finish line," I griped. "Do you have any idea how much harder it is to take down Diego De León and his cartel? They don't rule the East Coast by being idiots."

"My sweet child, you are looking at this all wrong," Dante scolded, patting my knee. "What do they say about eating the elephant?"

"Why would I be eating an elephant?" I countered, not following this man's crazy tangent.

He gave me a look that told me I was being a brat and continued, "If you want to eat an elephant, you do it one bite at a time. First things first, we need to get all your delicious eye candy back under one roof, then we can start to figure out how to deal with the De León issue."

"I think I need another beer." I sighed, shoving to my feet. "Do you want anything?"

"Don't happen to have a nip of brandy about, would you?" Dante asked, craning his head to watch me in the kitchen.

Feeling that sounded better than a beer, I opened the cabinet they kept all the liquor in and took a gander. "Looks like we're in luck," I answered, grabbing a bottle off the shelf.

"Hey now, spitfire, you're not planning on drinking all of that yourself, are you?" Picasso asked as he spotted what I was holding.

Rolling my eyes, I set it down, grabbed two short glasses, and turned to Dante. "You want it neat or on the rocks?"

"On the rocks," he called in answer, then spotted his favorite person to torture walk in the door. "Oh, Westin, come sit. We have so much to catch up on, now don't we?"

I'd warned Wes a long time ago that I wasn't going to rescue him from Dante because the sly fox would know what I was doing and ignore any effort. Instead, I left him to fight on his own, but secretly I think Wes liked the teasing game the two of them had going on.

"Dante," Wes nodded in greeting. "Did you get dinner?"

"Child," Dante drawled, stretching out the single word. "You know I don't eat carbs like that. How else would I be able to fit into these suits I get custom made? No, I'll simply drink my calories and be quite satisfied." he shared as he accepted the glass I handed him. "Tell me one thing, who made the move first?"

His knowing eyes moved back and forth between us as Wes pulled me to sit on his lap. I grinned and took a sip of my drink, aware Dante wanted to hear all the salacious details from Wes.

"That would be me," Wes said proudly. "After I thought I lost her at that party when the Saints took her, I knew the moment I got her back, I would tell her everything."

"I take it you were well received then?" Dante inquired.

Cognac let out a bark of laughter. "You could say that. The bastard fucked her on the counter right in front of me."

Dante's eyes went wide. "Goodness, they do say absence makes the heart grow fonder. Seems to have been true in this situation." Then he turned to Cognac. "Tell me, sugar, was he as good as I think he'd be in my head?"

The poor man's jaw dropped, stunned at the question.

"Dante, leave them be. They don't know you well enough to ask them things like that," I cut in. "Besides, the one you should be asking is me since I'm the one who got fucked."

Dante pouted at me. "You're no fun. I just wanted to make sure that this beautiful bronze statue of a man didn't play both sides."

The warm feeling in my stomach from the brandy was squashed at his words. I pulled out of Wes's hold and stared down the man. "Dante, let me be clear. They. Are. Mine. Have I made myself clear?"

"As crystal," Dante answered sincerely. "My apologies, sweet girl. I didn't mean anything by it, but it seems my joke has gone too far."

"Dad, didn't I warn you about pushing her?" Cam admonished, coming to stand behind me, resting his hands on my shoulders. "Times are different now. We are hers in every way, and none of us will take kindly to you messing around like that."

"You're right, son. I did push that too far," Dante agreed, which had me far more surprised.

"Why?" I demanded. "You never give in and back off this easily."

"Before, Weston wasn't yours. Of course, I knew he would be one day, but during the time I was flirting shamelessly, he was unattached. Dax, my sweet girl, you are family to me, and I would never purposely do something to upset or hurt you. All the teasing was meant in jest, but as my son has pointed out, things are incredibly different now than they were when I last saw you."

While it was hard to believe a con artist, I'd known him long enough to see the sincerity in his eyes. He was truly remorseful and that spoke volumes to me. "I shouldn't have snapped at you like that either. This day has been nothing but one crisis after another, and I'm not handling anything that pushes my buttons well."

"Regardless of that, I will do better by watching my words. You are the daughter I always wanted and the woman my son loves more than his own life." Dante gave me a warm smile, then reached out and took my hand. "I'd hoped to offer you my help as you take down the De León Cartel, but if you don't think that would be wise, I will be on my way in the morning, no harm no foul."

I squeezed his hand in return. "Only an idiot would refuse your offer, Dante. I would love your help to bring these bastards down."

"Good, good," Dante muttered, releasing my hand and looking at the others. "My apologies to you all as well. You know what they say about in-laws and all that."

"Don't sweat it, man," Cognac said, slapping Dante on the shoulder, making the man wince. "We've said worse stuff to each other and still managed to be family, so I think you're in the clear. Maybe let's leave our sex lives off the table. It's just weird to talk about with any parent."

That had me snapping my gaze to my Latin lover. "Or anyone else... right?" I asked, the warning clear in my tone.

"*Loba*, if we make it obvious like we did earlier in the pool, then we can't avoid the subject coming up entirely," Cognac pointed out. "You saw that already with the agents."

"Then you just end the conversation like I did," I reasoned. "Let them wonder what you did to get those kinds of sounds out of me. I'm sure it will be just as fulfilling for them as they rub one out."

Cognac chuckled. "Yeah, I'm pretty sure if I found out someone was thinking about you while they jacked off, I'd remove it."

"Then we stick with the plan not to allow any talk of our sex life," Picasso decided. "If we hear them talking, we squash it. As the leadership of the Phantom Saints, they can just deal with it and find their own woman to think about."

Everyone agreed, and that awkward conversation was brought to a close.

"How about we watch a movie?" I asked, feeling how tired my body was but knowing my brain wasn't going to let me sleep."

"First, we clean up the kitchen. Just because Eagle isn't here to kick our asses doesn't mean we don't do business as usual," Sprocket interjected. "Then we can watch a movie."

Chapter Four

Dax

At some point during the movie, I drifted off to sleep, and when I woke, I found myself curled around Picasso in a room I hadn't seen before. There were skylights to let in tons of natural light on one half of the space where a whole art studio we set up. An easel stood with a canvas on it that had the beginnings of a painting splashed over its stark white color. Next to it was a table full of paints, brushes, and other art supplies.

Where we were sleeping was up on a loft platform, allowing there to be more room for the studio portion of the space. Picasso was still passed out on his stomach. His was turned toward me with an arm flung across my waist, so I reached out and brushed the hair out of his face, noticing it had gotten pretty long on top, the sunlight showing the hits on red in the deep brown color.

The black and gray tattoos that ran down the length of the arm over my stomach stood out against the black shirt I was wearing. Slowly, I let my finger trace the designs, taking in all the details of his artwork he had placed there. Eventually, I was gonna need him to draw me something and have Wes tattoo it on me. Picasso's talent deserved to be forever on my body, always keeping a piece of him close. When I reached his hand, I lifted it to my mouth and kissed the back of it.

"Someone's rather adorable for so early in the morning," Picasso mumbled as he pulled out of my hold and used his hand to tug me against his chest. "Did you sleep well, spitfire?"

"I must have because I didn't wake up until just now," I answered. "When my body decides it's time to get up, I'm not quite so grumpy. It's when others do it that the bitchy side of Dax comes out."

Picasso huffed. "Right, that's the only thing that does it."

"Hey now, don't ruin the moment," I scolded as I snuggled into him, tucking my head under his chin. "Do you think there will ever be a day that's normal for us when this is all over?" I asked.

"Guess it depends on what you think is normal," he countered. "Personally, I think normal is boring. Could I go for less danger to those around us, yeah, but I don't think life with you around is ever going to be what others consider *normal*," he added.

I took a deep breath and let it out again. "Damn, I knew you were going to stay something like that."

"Do you really want things to be mundane, get a dog, settle down, and do the typical American dream?" Picasso asked, his voice full of curiosity.

Rolling onto my back, I looked at the sky with the puffy white clouds going by. "Some days I wonder what that would be like... then I remembered my childhood up until college. None of that was great either. Lots of heartache, loss, and experiences I never what to go through again. Now I have far more control over my life, making my own rules to live by no matter what anyone else thinks."

"They why ask the question if you like your life?"

Turning my head, I looked in his hazel eyes and cupped his cheek. "Because it's not just my life anymore. It's our life together, the seven of us. What worked for me alone isn't going to fly with you guys. It's the reason you're all so upset with me about yesterday. Or at least that's what I think all of you were trying to pound into my skull all night."

Picasso leaned his forehead against mine, not saying anything for a moment, simply letting us be. Then his hand gripped the back of my head and pulled my lips to his. Our kiss was languid, full of reassurance, and enjoying the moment of being close to each other. I rolled and hitched my leg over his, just wanting to feel more of him. His other hand grabbed my ass and pulled me flush, no space left between us.

He rolled us over so I was on my back, and he straddled me, looking into my eyes, searching. "You really mean that, don't you... that we're a family?"

A grin tugged at my lips. "Did those words finally make it past the morning wood?"

"Don't," he pleaded, shaking his head. "Don't pull back and use humor to shield yourself right now. You were so vulnerable a moment ago. Each time you show me a glimpse of you before Two Tricks, it vanishes in a second. Why won't you let me know that part of Dax too?"

"Having you, all of you in my life makes me more vulnerable than I've ever been since I lost my twin. Devin was the other half of my soul, the part you still see a glimpse of. When the darkness of the world stole him from me, they also robbed me of my innocence. There are parts of you that remind me of him, and that's when you see the old me appear, but just like my brother, there's no getting back what's been taken from you." I reached up and molded my hands around his face, letting the scruff of his beard he'd let fill in prickle my palms. "The fact you even catch a flash of that part of me should tell you how much you mean to me, Picasso."

His lips captured mine once more, only this time it was more urgent, filled with the need. The two of us had been feeling the pull toward each other, but each time we'd get close, one of us would do something to piss the other off. We've shared intimate moments here and there, but something had been holding us back from taking the plunge.

For me, he reminded me of my twin, and I never wanted to face the feelings that came with that. Picasso was who my brother could have been and become with the right people behind him.

Now all I saw was one of the men who had fought their way into my heart, never letting me push them away. Fighting to be with me for God knows what reason, but it worked, and I was finally ready to give in. I would surrender to this man who saw into the depths of my soul, deep enough to find a sliver of that girl even I didn't know remained.

Pulling back from his kiss, I met his gaze and spoke from the heart just like he pleaded I would. "I love you, Picasso. We might fight and disagree on the ways of the world, but you also challenge me to see more than what's in front of me."

"God, I fucking love your crazy stubborn ass too," Picasso answered as his hands slipped up my ribs, bunching my shirt up until he yanked it over my head. He looked down at my bare upper body and smiled as love and lust swirled in his eyes. "Looks like I got you in my bed just how I wanted you. What did you say back at the ranch?" He paused to kiss up my stomach until he got to my breasts.

"Try," he said, swirling his tongue around my nipple, holding my gaze, then moved to the other side.

"Try." His lips latched onto the other nipple, still tender from Cognac's attention to it last night, as his hand slipped into my boxers and flicked my clit.

"Try, again," he finished as he slid a finger inside me.

The groan that burst from my mouth echoed off the ceiling, reverberating through the converted garage. My back arched, begging for him to touch me more.

"Just so you know what's coming, I plan to take my time with you. This isn't going to be a quick, meaningless fuck, spitfire. I'm going to make love to you until your body never forgets the reward for letting down your walls," Picasso murmured along my skin, making me shiver.

His words made my body burn with desire, knowing that he would make good on his words. Each of my men pleasured my body in different ways. Some wanted to rule it, torture it drawing out to the finish, while others knew I could take a pounding. It would only make sense that my rose-colored-glasses-wearing Picasso would need to make my heart surrender to him as he explored every inch of my body.

Sitting back, he pulled off the boxers and tossed them over the railing to the garage floor. Now I was stripped, body and soul, for the taking. His hands started at my ankles, letting them skim up my legs, then back down again in a rhythmic motion kneading my muscles. Closing my eyes, I let him do as he pleased, trusting he would do right by me. Picasso's hand moved up to my knees and pushed outward, spreading me open to him. Then the touch of his lips as he kissed my inner thigh right to where my leg joined my torso had me moaning until he stopped.

A whimper escaped me when he started up the next leg, stopping once more at the crease. This time, he brought his lips to the top of my mound, hands brushing along the sides of my pussy, but not touching where I wanted most. His kisses moved up my stomach, between my breasts to the base of my throat. The feel of his palms skimming over my ribs until they grasped my breasts made me suck in a sharp breath.

"Tell me what you feel, spitfire," Picasso instructed. "I want to know all the thoughts that are running through your head."

I gulped and tried to find the words for what I was feeling. "My body is hot. It feels like my skin is on fire, begging for you to touch me more. I can feel how wet I'm getting and the desperate need for you to touch my clit, to fuck me." I opened my eyes and looked at him, watching my lips. "Goddammit, I want you inside me so badly it's hard not to take control."

Picasso hummed in enjoyment as he kissed up my neck to my ear. "You try to take over, you're not going to get any of those things. This is your punishment for making plans behind our back, treating your life with disregard, and making me worry more about you as I sat in that hospital than my own brother."

This was the side of Picasso I knew lived just under the surface. The part of himself that he was afraid of but came out when his brother was threatened, disrespected, or in danger. I, myself, had been on the receiving end of it a few times in the early days. Picasso had his own monster lurking in the depths, but he'd spend his whole life trying to hide it.

"I will accept my punishment," I whispered as he sucked on my earlobe, then moved back down my neck rolling my nipples between his fingers.

"Look who can be a good girl," he teased as he retreated back down between my legs. "Let's see if you taste as good as I remember."

He spread me open and laid his tongue flat, licking me from ass to clit, making me scream at the overwhelming sensations that roared through my body. I'd been so primed and ready to go from his touches that with a simple lick, I was blessed with my first orgasm of many, I hoped. "Holy fuck, you better not stop at just that."

"What did I say about this being quick? I might love you, but I'm not *that* selfless to pass on getting my own release. Filling you up with my cum, marking my territory, because I'm the one in charge this morning," Picasso reminded, his hot breath teasing my needy cunt.

My hips undulated as if begging him to touch me once more. That one single lick wasn't enough to satisfy the fire he'd built up in me. His beard tickled my flesh, driving me crazy as I knew how close he was but kept from doing more than teasing me. Then a finger slowly glided through my wetness and circled my opening but hardly applied any pressure. Picasso was truly planning on making this a punishment of the best kind I wouldn't forget anytime soon.

He slid a single finger inside me, and he curled it up and down right where my G-spot was. My back arched as I felt another orgasm being teased out of me slowly then when my walls started to clamp down on him, he pulled his finger out. Instead, he trailed it down to my asshole and started to massage his slick finger around the entrance.

"You enjoy your tight little hole being fucked, don't you? Which do you like more, pussy or ass?" Picasso mused as he pushed the finger in just enough to get past the tight ring, working it and encouraging it to relax for him. "I think from what I've heard, you might like anal better than normal fucking. What do you think? Should I take you in the ass this morning?"

"Are you really giving me the choice?" I rebutted, knowing he was enjoying being in control for once.

Picasso flashed me a smile that told me all I needed to know. "I suppose not, but I guess I was curious as to what your answer would be."

"My answer is take me however you want me. I will enjoy every second of it either way," I said, running my hand through his hair and out of his face. "Do with me what you want. I'll be able to handle it, don't you worry."

Picasso caught my hand and kissed the palm of it, then let it go, scooped up my legs and bent me in half so my ass was up in the air, feet over my head. His tongue ran over my asshole, making sure it was good and wet as he ate my ass out. It was as if he was determined to get me to loosen up for him as fast as possible with talent and technique I'd never experienced before. Never did I think feeling the rough sensation of a beard swirling over my hole would feel so good.

Then he made sure to get me nice and wet with his spit before he reintroduced his finger, pushing it in further. Picasso took his time working it in and out, swirling and stretching until he could add a second finger. I loved the way my body felt when people fucked my ass. There was this innate urge to push it out, but when you relaxed into it, there were sensations that would blow your mind. Never did I think my ass could have so much feeling to it, but hot damn, people were missing out when they ignored this forbidden pleasure.

"I think you're ready," Picasso announced as he rolled off the bed and pulled open a drawer, grabbing a bottle of lube. "While spit might work, it can only get you so far, and I plan on owning that ass of yours for a good long while. Now flip over and stick that ass up in the air."

Without hesitation, I did as he directed, wiggling my ass in excitement as I felt the shock of cold lube hitting my skin. He used those two fingers again to make sure I was as wet as a slip n' slide before the blunt head of his cock pressed at the entrance. Letting my mind go blank, I relaxed my whole body, leaning into the pressure welcoming him inside me.

God, I wanted to be fucked so bad, for him to just slam into me, but he was the one running the show.

Inch by inch, he filled me until his thighs met my body, having taken everything from tip to root. His hands landed on my hips as he pulled out just as slowly, making me quiver and moan as the feel of him stroked the parts of me that few took the time to find. A few more rounds of achingly unhurried movements,

Picasso felt I was ready for the show to begin. His hips moved faster as he kept each thrust as deep as he could make it. I turned my face to the side, needing to suck in as much air as possible with how he was driving me mad.

"Please, Picasso, please just let go and ruin me," I begged.

He leaned over, draping his body over my back so he could speak into my ear. "Is that what you really want, to be ruined by us? Something tells me you don't know what it feels like for someone to make love to you, always pushing for it to be rough and raw. That's not going to happen this morning, spitfire. I'm going to teach you it doesn't always have to be frenzied."

Fucking hell, this man was going to kill me. Other than Cognac's version of lovemaking which involved heavy amounts of denial, I'd always encouraged things to be rough. That's how life was unless you could hold your own. It chewed you up and spat you out. What Picasso wanted was something I didn't know if I could do.

Brushing my hair from my neck, Picasso started to kiss his way down it to my shoulder. His arm curled around my waist until his fingers found my clit, which he started to rub in a circular motion. Hearing his labored breaths in my ear as the feel of his body covering mine made me feel protected in a strange way. The other had found my breast and started to knead it as his lips kissed any skin he could find.

"That's it, spitfire, surrender to me, let me love your body, worship it as it was meant to be worshiped," Picasso murmured, his pace speeding up a little more with shorter strokes.

With the uptake in speed, he used more pressure on my clit, driving me over the edge into a climax. "Picasso." I moaned as I felt him join me in finishing.

Picasso grunted as he thrust into my ass, ensuring he was as deep as he could get while he came. "You. Are. Mine, spitfire," he growled into my ear with one last pounding thrust.

Both of us breathing heavily, he rolled us to our sides but didn't remove his cock from me. Instead, he pulled my top leg over his and speared two fingers into my pussy. Before I could even comprehend what was happening, he was stroking my sweet spot with single-minded determination. Another orgasm slammed into me, making my body go rigid, clamping down on his cock still inside me. We groaned in pleasure, but he wasn't done with me yet, finger fucking me through the moment.

Everything was feeling too sensitive, and when I turned to tell him to let me have a break, his lips descended upon mine, cutting off my words. He started to move his hips slowly in time with his fingers double fucking me in a way I'd never experienced. My body started to shiver and convulse as another wave of euphoria washed over me, making me babble senseless words and completely at his mercy. This man single-handedly turned my brain into mush by just making love to me as he promised.

"Picasso, please, I don't think I can take any more," I begged as he stilled his fingers and cock, just holding me in suspended pleasure as my pussy twitched around the digits.

Picasso nuzzled into my neck. "Just let me hold you like this for a bit. I love the feeling of being this intimate with you, knowing I'm one of the lucky bastards you claimed."

"You just like that it means you can fuck me whenever you want," I teased.

He snorted, nipping at my ear. "We both know that's not true. How long has it taken me to get you in my bed?"

"I kept telling you all you had to do was stake your claim before one of the others did. You just can't say no to them if they challenge you," I pointed out. "You might be the vice president of the club, but that doesn't mean you are second place in everything."

"Are you gonna sew that for me on a pillow so I don't forget?" he asked, the humor clear in his voice.

Wriggling out of his hold and letting his dick slip out of me, I turned to face him, tossing my leg over his hip, still wanting to feel all of him against me. "Nah, that shit would look awful. Instead, I'll just make a rule that I won't sleep with you unless you make the first move. If you know you want some of this, then take it. I won't turn you away."

"I mean, you and Void had sex in the middle of a battlefield, so I guess that's true, isn't it," he commented with a smile, moving in to kiss me in such an unhurried fashion I was learning to love.

There was a loud bang on the door, followed up by Cognac's morning greeting. "You two done fucking yet? We got shit to do, and Dani called saying Eagle will be back around one-ish."

Picasso growled but sat up. "I love that man like my brother, but fuck do I want to beat his ass sometimes."

"Pretty sure that goes along with you feeling like he's your brother," I said, poking him in the gut. "I'm gonna go shower since someone needed to get me all sticky."

He just grinned at me, far too pleased with himself, as I headed down the steps and out into the house. For a place with so many people to only have two bathrooms, well, one really, since I'm the only person Eagle begrudgingly let's use his. Now with the addition of Cam and Wes into the mix, I was thinking we might need to add on or pick a different setup altogether.

"Fucking hell, shortcake, don't just wander around naked," Wes blurted after he spat out his coffee. "You have no idea who might be in or around the house right now."

I gave him a cheeky smile and wink, continuing on my way to Eagle's room.

Chapter Five

Dax

It was just as I left it last night, which was good because I did not want to deal with a pissy, bossy man if things were out of order. Our dear president had a small case of OCD and needed things to be exactly as he had them in his own space or he couldn't relax. I knew it was more than just a personal preference. It pained him if things were not just so. Did I use that to my advantage on occasion? Hell yeah, I did. But only when it served a higher purpose, not just to be a dick.

Hopping into the shower, I cleaned up, toweled off, and got dressed, then headed out to find coffee. When I appeared in the kitchen, Wes was still glowering at me but handed over a fresh mug with, *The Blood Of My Enemies* written on it. Popping up on my tiptoes, I kissed his cheek before sitting at the counter.

"How are you this morning? Seem a little grumpy if you ask me," I commented, then took a sip of the lifeblood of the world. All would be well as long as coffee was still in existence.

Wes just gave me a flat look and flipped me the bird before placing a bowl of cereal in front of me.

"Okay, so clearly I did something else wrong if this is what you're feeding me this morning," I mused, taking in the bowl of bran flakes with wrinkled raisins. "Did I miss your birthday? No, that's not for another month... I didn't take your bike without asking. Hell, I can't really remember what happened last night after I fell asleep during the movie. You're gonna need to give me a hint."

Weston crossed his arms and looked me dead in the eyes as if searching for something in my expression. "You don't remember, do you?"

"Ah... that's what I've been trying to say. What the hell happened?" I demanded.

Not giving me an answer, he snatched away the bowl and opened the oven to pull out a large dish full of fluffy egg casserole.

I gaped at him in horror. "You were going to make me eat a disgusting bowl of gravel when you made *that?*" I screeched.

"Whoa, what is happening in here?" Sprocket questioned as he walked over to the coffee maker.

"Weston was trying to kill me," I blurted.

Sprocket turned to Wes, who just rolled his eyes. "She's being dramatic. I gave her a bowl of fiber cereal, thinking she remembered last night, but she didn't."

"Ah, I see," Sprocket answered, nodding his head, then glancing at me. "You really don't remember?"

Irritated, I growled and stabbed the knife that was lying on the counter into the wood. "No, but someone better explain before I stab something else. What am I getting punished for now?"

"Easy, little demon, Weston is taking this more to heart than he should, and Sprocket isn't helping by teasing you," Void said, coming up behind me, wrapping me in his arms. "When the movie was over, we were asking you where you wanted to sleep, or should I say with whom. Since you didn't give us an answer, Wes scooped you up, but you told him that he snores too loud and farts in his sleep after eating Italian because he's allergic to parmesan cheese."

My jaw dropped, and I looked at Wes in full understanding. "Okay, wow, yeah. I would give me something to make me fart all day long too. Damn, I can't believe I said that."

"It would seem that Wes is sensitive about his bodily functions," Cognac added as he sauntered into the kitchen. "Smelled the food and figured it was grub time, but I didn't know we were having a morning recap of your most embarrassing moments there, Westly."

"Fuck off, or you won't get any of the food I make for the next week," Wes threatened.

Cognac threw up his hands in surrender. "My bad, I'll keep my lips sealed."

Cam and Picasso were the last to join us and that had me looking around the space. "Where's Dante?"

"Dad is staying with Tilly and her husbands. There isn't any more room here, and he thought it might be best to give us our space," Cam answered as he cupped my chin and placed a kiss on my lips. "So did the vice president do right by you, or do I need to finish things off under the breakfast table?"

Picasso made a move to slug Cam, but Void grabbed his arm. "If you don't react, then he'd stop teasing you. The black knight likes getting a rise out of you."

Cam winked at me, then turned to face Picasso. "Guilty as charged," he said with a shrug. "You turn this interesting shade of red when you get pissed but try to hold it back. It's fascinating."

Wes slid a plate over to me and slapped the back of Cam's head. "Keep it up and you're cut off from the food too, Cammy."

The two men glared at each other, but much to my amazement, Cam backed down first. "You're right. I need to be better about my teasing. Pushing things too far seems to be a family trait."

Quickly, food was passed out and some found space around the kitchen while others went to the living room. The counter with its four seats would only get us so far.

"So, since this is now *our* home, what do you think about maybe moving the pool table to another place and getting something all of us can sit at together?" I ventured. "Another thing I've noticed is that we're running out of bedrooms."

"What do you mean running out of bedrooms?" Cognac asked. "Wes has the guest room. You float around to whoever which I love. What problem is there?"

I pointed my fork at Cam, who had the audacity to steal the bite of egg off of it. "What about him? Can he cuddle up with one of you guys too?"

"Ah..." Cognac answered.

"That's what I thought," I quipped, then looked at Cam. "Steal my food again and I'll stab you with this fork."

Cam leaned in and kissed me once again. "Don't threaten me with a good time, beautiful. I love it when the crazy comes out to play."

Rolling my eyes, I shoved him away and stuffed a bite into my mouth before someone could snatch it from me. The others seemed to ponder over my suggestions as they ate, which I was fine with. What I was asking was a lot, and they'd been living here just fine, but if we wanted to make this work long-term, a space that was all of ours needed to happen.

"Cognac, you said Dani called," I asked, changing the topic. That wasn't one any of us would have an answer for.

"It's an hour ahead there, and she said they were leaving as soon as he got discharged. Everything looked good. No issues from the surgery, but he'd need to take it easy for at least a week. They didn't want him to ride his bike for two weeks until the stitches came out," he relayed.

"Was he raging in the background while she was sharing this?" I asked, just picturing how pissed he would be.

Cognac just laughed as he finished his breakfast. "I feel like we need to send a donation for all the people who took care of him to get counseling for his bad attitude."

"Lucky for him, we need at least two weeks to make a plan and figure out what we know. Speaking of, where is Demitri?" I questioned.

"Since we didn't want to raise suspicion or the FBI to get wind of anything, we sent him home. He understands not to do anything without talking to us first. After the events of yesterday, he's fully aware that with you involved, there's a chance to save his sister," Picasso answered.

While I didn't love the idea of the kid not being within arm's reach, I saw their point too. "He said he works in the garage full-time or part-time? Didn't sound like he was going to college."

"He's not... tried a few classes at community college, but that was more his sister's thing. She's just like her mother. Demitri took after his deadbeat dad, who left them high and dry when Elena was born. Thought he could handle a wife who was the breadwinner and high-powered lawyer but turns out he couldn't," Picasso said, his tone telling me he had no love loss for his brother-in-law.

"Maybe he should meet Kimber. It sounds like they would be a perfect match," I suggested. "But then again, if she's shacking up with one of Marco's top men, then who knows how long she'll be alive. She has a knack for pissing people off in just the right way to make you want to slit her throat."

Cognac let out a whistle. "Sounds like if she's not dead, she will be soon."

"Yeah, lots of sisterly love going around for her," I muttered, jumping off the stool and raising my plate before putting it away. The last thing Eagle needed was to have a fit about his kitchen when he came home.

Feeling the itch to be doing something, I started to gather everyone else's dishes and cleaned up Wes's mess from making breakfast.

"You alright there, little rebel?" Sprocket asked as he came to lean on the counter next to the sink.

I glanced at him and shrugged. "All things considered, yeah, I'm fine."

"That's a load of bullshit," Sprocket stated with a snort. "Let's try not to lie through your teeth this time, shall we?"

"The Mad Dogs were easy, but the De León Cartel is another story. We will be going into a place where we have no support or connections, the center of enemy territory," I explained. "Think about how much planning we did for this last job and how fucked up it got."

Sprocket watched me for a moment, then took hold of my arm and pulled me to stand in front of him. "Clearly, we took our punishment too far if now you're standing here telling me that all hope is lost. While I don't support you throwing yourself into danger unnecessarily, I'm not looking to change you into someone you're not. Dax, we need your brand of crazy to make this work because only someone with a screw loose would ever attempt to take down the people we are going after."

"You realize that is the opposite of what you've all been telling me the past twenty-four hours, right?" I grumbled.

Sprocket smiled and shook his head. "No, it's not, but I'm glad that something has broken through that stubbornness. What we want more than anything else is to be a team. Tell us the plan, the *whole* plan, not just the parts you think we need to know. Be honest with us. We can take it, I promise. I won't say there might not be disagreements but at least give us the chance to talk it out. It's not you against the world, Dax. It's us against the world. What attacks you, attacks us, and we don't back down for anyone who hurts what's ours. There are eight of us all coming from different backgrounds and expertise, don't count us out because we're a bunch of bikers."

"I would never," I countered with a scowl. "You've all proven that you're smarter than the average biker thug."

"At least we have that going for us," Sprocket mumbled before continuing. "You say we don't have connections in New York City, well I hate to break it to you, little rebel, but we do. The FBI is there, and Cam can work whatever magic he has in that work, and don't forget about Void. He's our ace for this job, having spent a fair amount of time in the underbelly of New York as a cage fighter."

"I might have been banned from official fighting, but the underground doesn't mind when you leave bodies behind. Who knows, maybe we could get you in on a fight or two for fun. I know a guy who'd kill to have someone like you in the ring," Void interjected from behind me, making me jump.

For a big guy, he was a silent motherfucker. Glad I trusted him at my back and with my life. Peering over my shoulder, I met his icy-blue eyes. "It won't draw too much attention for you to make a return?"

"Little demon, are you thinking we are gonna show up in New York and no one will notice?" Void asked with a chuckle. "You might not rule the East Coast, but that doesn't mean people don't know who you are. The reputation of Two Tricks is far and wide. There will be no sneaking around."

"Then how the fuck are we going to pull this off? If everyone knows who I am, and I draw a crowd, then there's no way Diego won't know I'm gunning for him after the mess I made of the Mad Dogs," I spluttered.

Void's eyebrows shot up, and he looked over my shoulder at Spencer. "Has she had coffee yet?"

"Pretty sure, but she was just washing dishes, so I feel like this might be a case of the body snatchers," Sprocket teased.

I pulled away from Sprocket so I could face them both, arms crossed, chin up. "What is that supposed to mean? I clean up after myself, and so what if I'm wanting to be more prepared for this next hit?"

"Little rebel, you only put away your dishes after one of us has asked. It's not something you do naturally. Which is fine but to consciously make the effort is out of character, wouldn't you say?" he pointed out. "As for what Void's worried about is that you sound like you're scared, and our Dax isn't scared of anyone."

I scoffed at them, dropping my hands to square my shoulders. "I'm not scared of those bastards."

"Then I suggest you act like it because right now it sounds like you are terrified to attack these guys," Void challenged. "Little demon, they framed you for the murder of a son Diego killed himself. You just need to get mad. Then this problem will go away. The Mad Dogs threatened you, Harper, and us by making a mover against the Saints. Right now, you have nothing invested in taking them down other than it will hurt Marco, who you're absolutely pissed at."

Sprocket nodded his head as he scratched his jaw deep in thought. "I think that will be solved once we tell Eagle about Elena. Dax doesn't know anything about her, so there's no connection. They can pull out the pictures and home movies and share how hard she worked to get into that school. If that doesn't work, I'm sure Wes has a list of shitty things they do. We can start running through them to see what hits home." My jaw fell open as I watched them talk about this like I wasn't standing right here.

Did they really feel like I wasn't invested in this part of the plan? Fuck, I'm the one who made the plan. But did they have a point about me being so reluctant to make this happen? When it came to the Mad Dogs, I was willing to put myself in danger to get the end result I wanted. *Did this mean Harper was safe? Or would Marco keep gunning for her until I brought him down?*

The call from Harper last night told me they'd made contact with Prim, so she must be alright. Didn't sound like it was a great experience, but what teenager is fun to be around? Would they be back in time to help? Maybe we did have more people at our backs than I originally thought.

"I think we lost her," Cognac fake-whispered as he waved a hand in front of my face. "*Loba*, are you in there? Earth to *loba*."

I batted his hand away and scowled. "What the fuck, man?"

"Ah, there she is," he cheered, grinning at me like a fool. "Did these two take away your coffee or something?"

"Why does everyone think I haven't had my coffee?" I snarled.

Cognac booped me on the nose and answered, "Reaction like that, and the fact your mug is barely touched and sitting on the counter cold as ice."

"What?" I blurted as I pushed past him to find that he'd been correct. "How did that happen?"

Another mug appeared before me, steam rolling out, signaling it was fresh. I glanced up to see it was Cam offering up the beverage. "It's better for all our sakes to ensure you drink all of it," he stated, his face blank of expression.

Rolling my eyes, I took the happy bean juice and made a show of taking a big gulp even though it scorched down my throat. "Ah, good as new," I announced. "Now, is there anything we need to deal with before Eagle gets back?"

Before anyone could answer, there was a knock on the door, then seconds later, Gabriella Rossi walked in with her son. I hadn't seen her since the party the guys kidnapped me at but seeing as she's the older sibling to Eagle and Picasso, it was inevitable.

"Oh, do come in, don't mind the fact I'm not wearing any pants," I greeted, then hid my smirk at her glare by taking another sip of coffee.

"Mom, I told you to wait for them to answer the door. It's not just the guys anymore," Demitri muttered, rubbing the back of his neck.

She turned on him, pointing a finger in his face, making him flinch back. "Not a damn word out of you, boy. You've done quite enough to this family by flapping your lips."

The cool, calm, and collected woman I met back at the tattoo shop I owned with Wes and then again at the party was gone. She might be wearing the business suit of a high-powered lawyer, but the energy that was coming off her was erratic and ready to snap at whoever got in her way.

"Gabby, what are you doing here?" Picasso demanded. "We told Demitri to stick to the normal routine because he's probably being watched."

"Don't you talk to me like that, Teo, you might be the vice president of this club, but when it comes to *my* children, I will do what I see fit," she shot right back. "Where is Eagle?"

"He's not here right now, which is why you should have called or let us know you were coming," Picasso pointed out, not backing down. "If anyone finds out that we know about Demitri and Elena, then it only puts Ellie in more danger."

"You don't think I know my baby girl is in danger," she screamed. "They sent me her motherfucking finger, Teo, a *finger*. They wanted to know who Tricks was, and if I'd known it was that bitch all along, I would have never let you get involved with her. Now hell is coming down around our ears, and there's nothing I can do about it. They have me by the balls, Teo, do you get that?"

Picasso didn't even flinch under the attack. Instead, he just took it, knowing his sister was a mess. "Gabby, we're working on a plan to get Ellie back. You need to trust us. This is far bigger than any of us realized." He ran a hand through his hair in frustration, turning away from her. "How could you not tell us what the fuck was going on? There might have been something we could have done to prevent this."

"You have a child kidnapped and a finger cut off for not giving them what they want, then you can talk to me about not telling you what was going on," Gabriella snarled. "I did what I thought was best. It worked out for you in the end, didn't it?" She added, waving her hand in my direction.

"Don't make this her fault. She's a victim of this as much as we are," Sprocket cut in.

Setting the coffee down, I hoisted myself up on the counter so I could get a better view of the family feud going on.

"Really, and what has that bastard done to her?" Gabriella demanded.

"Oh, I can answer that," I interjected, waving my hand like a kid in school. "Let's see, he tried to kidnap my best friend, sent assassins after me multiple times, blew up my house, and wants my head on a spike in his front lawn," I shared, counting off each event on my fingers.

This seemed to shake dearest Gabby out of her self-pity. "What?"

"Oh yeah, this asshole is trying to take me out so I stop ruining his business. So he's going after anything or anyone I care about. Seems like a good thing you're on my shit list for setting Harper and me up at that party," I reminded her. "It wasn't very nice. She really believed you might become her client and spread the word about her business."

"If you'd just given me the information I wanted to know, then none of it would have needed to happen. I would have my daughter back, and you wouldn't be dragging my brothers down with you," Gabriella countered. "You are one cold-hearted bitch to let them take the fall for you."

My brows shot up so far that I thought they would be lost in my hair. "Wow, okay, you're going to need to explain that to me. How the hell have I become the cold-hearted bitch when they fucking kidnapped me, put a shock collar on my ankle, and tried to use me as bait for Two Tricks?"

"Ladies," Cam cut in. "This isn't going to help the situation or get your daughter back. What would help is if you walk us through what you do know. When was Elena get taken? Where was she? What information have you gotten and how do they communicate with you?"

Gabriella let out a sharp laugh. "What are you, the FBI or something, asking questions like that as if it will do a goddamn thing."

"Actually, I am the FBI," Cam answered, pulling his badge out of his back pocket. "I've been assigned to work with Dax and her crew to help bring down criminal terrorists just like the man who has your daughter. We've found it's better to work alongside the underbelly that knows how to interact without getting caught instead of infiltrating."

Fuck me sideways. I forgot how good Cam was at manipulating people. Seems there's far more of his dad in him than I ever realized.

Gabriella just looked at him skeptically, but it was Demitri who stepped up to do the right thing. "Mom, he's right. It's time for us to stop thinking we can handle this on our own and ask for help. He's with the FBI. He'll have connections we could never get doing this alone."

"Fine," she said with a sigh. "Where do you want to start?"

"Let's take a seat on the sofa, get comfortable," Cam suggested. "Can we get you coffee? Something to eat?"

"I'll take a glass of Jack with some ice," Gabriella answered.

Okay, maybe I might actually like my inevitable sister-in-law after all. If the woman wanted a glass of whisky at ten in the morning, having a bad day, then she'd damn well get one. Hopping off the counter, I grabbed a glass, put ice in it, and poured her a healthy dose of the liquor. I brought it over to her, where she'd taken a seat on the couch, but when I handed it over, she looked suspiciously at it.

"For fuck's sake," I muttered and took a swig of the burning liquid, then handed it over. "If I wanted to kill you, I'd do it to your face. I'm not a poison girl. Far too impersonal if you ask me. I like them to know who ended their life."

"I suppose I can respect that," Gabriella begrudgingly admitted, then drained the glass.

Wes grabbed my hand and tugged me to sit next to him a little farther down on the couch. He had his laptop open and ready to go on the coffee table. If there was information out there to be found, Wes was like a bloodhound. He'd find it.

"Are we sure we shouldn't wait for Eagle?" Demitri asked, fidgeting nervously.

Ah, so this story wasn't going to paint him in a good light at all. Why would he want Eagle around then? He'd be the first to beat his ass. Unless when it came to family, he was a big softy?

Picasso shook his head. "We don't know exactly when he's coming back, and Eagle isn't in the best condition to handle news like this."

"That, and do you really want him tanning your ass until you can't sit for a week?" Void asked.

Demitri deflated in on himself as he shook his head furiously. "No. God, I'd hoped none of you would have had to find out about this."

"Yeah, sorry, but that ship has sailed, Demitri. You just need to be honest with us about *everything* from this point forward," Picasso warned. "Let's start at the beginning when they first contacted you?"

Chapter Six

Dax

Demitri took a deep, steadying breath and then began to tell his story. "It started when I went to see Elena during spring break. She wanted to show me around New York City to prove to me that she could handle herself. While I was there, she still had lots of work to do on an end-of-the-year project. Some big article she was writing about the slums and how mental health and homelessness were a big problem. Which meant as we toured the city, we also visited some really shady parts to interview people.

"For the four days we stayed in the city, she wanted to check out a few shelters, a local drug house, and some spots that were common for the homeless to panhandle for the day. Ellie is as stubborn as anyone in our family, so I knew she was going to do this with or without me. It was gonna be safer if I went along and kept an eye on her. Problem was, Ellie picked the wrong day and the wrong time to visit the drug house. Seems there was a turf war over the spot between the De León's and another smaller gang getting too big for themselves." Demitri paused, picking at the skin around his thumbnail, trying to collect himself.

He raised his gaze to meet Picasso's. "I should have never let her go there, it was a dumb idea, and I was too cocky for my own good."

His uncle reached out and squeezed his shoulder. "We all make mistakes, D. You know my story and the hell we went through with our uncles. While I can't promise I won't be disappointed, you're coming clean now, and we're going to fix this, but I need to know what I'm up against first."

Demitri nodded and continued, "It was some time after five when we went to the spot. It was abandoned and falling apart with cracked-out people lying around all over the floor. She was taking pictures with her phone and that's what did us in. One of the dealers thought we were with the gang, trying to sneak intel so they could take the house back from the cartel. He grabbed Ellie and snatched her phone, demanding answers from me. I didn't know what to do, so I used the only leverage I could think of and said that I worked for Tricks, and if they messed with us, he'd come down on them."

"Fuck," Cognac groaned, knowing exactly how wrong of an answer that was.

Hell, it would have been better for him to be honest and say he was related to the leaders of the Phantom Saints. They were a known name out here and would have added some backlash if they got hurt. Instead, he chose to use my name, and Diego and I had been enemies since I stopped his import of drugs from Mexico the easy way. Now he had to go through Texas or take the long route by boat to the East Coast.

Everyone knew that Texas wasn't a state to fuck with. They didn't like it when people broke the law, and everyone had a gun to do something about it.

"Yeah, that's a pretty accurate response to that situation," Demitri agreed. "Using Ellie as motivation, he got me to zip-tie myself, then her, and took us back to one of their warehouses. That's when I met Anthony, Diego's oldest son. He was the one to question us, and he figured out pretty fast that I'd lied and that made him furious. Anthony gave me two choices, take a bullet to the head or find a way to get myself in with the Hidden Empire. If I managed to do that, then the next part was to find out who Tricks really was and tell them."

I leaned forward, watching Demitri, and something told me he'd managed to do the first part. "How?" I asked, knowing he would understand.

Shifting, he looked at me with regret and sadness in his eyes. "Jeff, he got me a job helping fix things a few days a week when I wasn't here with Sprocket. He thought I was some down-on-my-luck guy who just needed a break. Jeff paid me cash under the table whenever he had things for me to work on at first, then brought me into the shop. He vouched for me with Ivan, and I was in."

My heart squeezed at the mention of the man who'd been Brian's partner in crime and someone I worked closely with for a long time. Jeff had gotten married a year before, and his wife had just had their first child. Since Jeff had been like family to me and died because he was one of my people, I was making sure that little baby girl and her mother had the life they deserved and would worry about nothing. It killed me that the funeral had happened, and I couldn't be there, but from what Brian told me, Brenda understood. That woman was a saint to put up with me and what I put those men through as my enforcer squad.

"Tell me one thing," I managed to choke out. "Did you kill him?"

Demitri's eye widened in horror. "*No*, there's no way I could ever have done that. He died trying to save me, thinking I'd gotten mixed up in the wrong crowd. It was actually what got Ellie's finger cut off. They wanted me to get him somewhere Anthony's men could grab him and torture the information out of him. Instead, he was shot, saving my life, but they used it to send a message. When they found out you'd been taken by the Saints, they decided to pull me from infiltrating the Empire to gathering information from you, Dax."

"That's good because I would really hate to ruin my chances with these men, but I would have killed you," I answered bluntly. "Jeff was family to me, and I will never let that kind of act against my people go, no matter who they are that did it. Let that be a warning to you and anyone else who needs to hear it," I added, meeting Gabriella's gaze.

She met mine unflinchingly, rage simmering just under the surface. "So if Enzo and Teo are your family now, what does that make my kids and me? Are we valued enough for you to put that same emotion behind getting my daughter back? Or is she a lost cause because my son sold you all out?"

God, this is why I wasn't friends with many women. They always had to come at you with their claws out. I mean, seriously, what the hell?

"Just to be clear, your son isn't the only one who sold me out. You did too," I rebutted. "As for the question about your daughter, she's innocent in all of this. How you've managed to keep her alive this whole time is beyond me with how sloppy you've both been. If anyone deserves to be rescued and given a fresh start, it would be Elena."

Wes groaned with irritation behind me, letting me know I'd done something I shouldn't have.

"The answer is yes, Gabriella. We will get your daughter back to you. While I can't speak for the ramifications for Demitri like Dax said, Elena hasn't done anything to deserve this," Wes translated for me.

"I'll take whatever punishment you and Eagle choose to give me," Demitri said to Picasso. "If there is anything more I can do to help with getting Ellie back, just say the word."

Picasso looked over at Wes. "What information do we need for you to start breaking down the network? I'm sure you already have a filing cabinet of information on them, but I'm sure Demitri will have some sort of new nugget of information."

"I'll sit down with him and go over everyone he's met, talked to, or been contacted by. Also, nailing down how they relayed information can be helpful. I'll also need the location of that drug house you got pulled from in the beginning," Wes explained, grabbing his computer.

Since those two would be lost for the next few hours, it looked like I should find something useful to do. Getting up from the couch, I slipped on my shoes and headed for the door.

"Ah, ah, ah, beautiful," Cam whispered in my ear. "You don't get to leave the house without one of us as your shadow, or did you forget you're grounded."

"I was gonna go check in on Tilly before Eagle gets back," I answered. "You up for some girl talk?"

"That sounds like more of a job for Cognac. Tilly's husbands didn't seem to like me much," Cam said, making me snicker.

"Riiight," I said, drawing out the word to punctuate my absolute disbelief in that statement.

Void ambled over, waving Cam off. "Those two are good friends. I'm sure we can find a way to entertain ourselves while the women chat."

"Better you than me," Cam answered with a shrug and headed out the door.

I dashed out after him. "Hey, where are you off to?"

"What kind of agent would I be if I didn't check in on my fellow man?" Cam shared cryptically.

"He's going out to the battle site," I muttered to myself. "Damn, the asshole played me."

"Come on, little demon, let's go. I believe Mutt got the new Grand Theft Auto game, and we haven't had a chance to play in a while," Void commented as he headed off in their home's direction.

I took in the scattering of homes that orbited outside the center of the compound and clubhouse. Eagle's house was directly across from the clubhouse, which I'm sure was purposeful as president to keep near the center of things. The houses were all of different styles and sizes but were basic in appearance. Trees were scattered throughout, giving us shade as we walked down the gravel path that intertwined from house to house.

"Do you think Eagle would ever be open to the idea of adding on to the house or maybe building a new one?" I asked, kicking at a rock and sending it off into the trimmed grass.

Void didn't answer right away, but I knew he heard me. "Eagle is an interesting man when it comes to his home and personal space. Until you crashed into our lives, creating chaos wherever you go, he never allowed someone into his room. Now he emptied a drawer and got you a toothbrush to use that he keeps in his bathroom. I don't think he ever thought he'd find a person to settle down with."

"Really?" I questioned. "That doesn't seem right to me."

"He was never willing to risk letting someone be more important than the Saints," Void explained. "That's one reason he created the rule we would all be with the same woman and everyone had to agree on it. If one person wasn't interested, it was a no for us all."

"Damn, that seems kind of crazy, doesn't it?" I muttered to myself. "Like how many women are out there and would be fine with having five men to deal with all the time?"

"Which is why I said he didn't want to make it easy for us to find love and have us led around by our balls," Void reasoned.

Since we'd reached Tilly's house, I decided to put a pause on that conversation until we were alone. Right now, I wanted to check on my friend. I didn't have many of them, and they seemed to be in varying levels of danger at the moment. Without ringing the doorbell, I turned the handle, and when I found out it was unlocked, I cracked it open.

"Void and I are coming in, so hurry up and finish or carry on as you please. We don't care," I yelled.

"Fucking hell," I heard one of her husbands swear. "You better have a goddamn good reason for just barging in."

That had to be Gator. He was the grumpier out of the two. If it had been Mutt, he probably would have teased about paying for the show or something.

"Oh, calm the hell down," Tilly snapped. "Come on in, Dax. We're decent."

"The fuck I am," Gator challenged.

I followed the voices into the kitchen, where Tilly was kneeling in front of Gator, who had his pants around his ankles. The death glare we got from him told us it would be wise if we didn't say a damn word. Tilly was stitching up a wound on his hip. Her slow, steady movements as she worked had me at a whole new level of appreciation for this woman.

"Damn, you do that so much better than I do," I said as I leaned in to get a better look. "How do you make them so neat?"

Tilly chuckled and gave me a sideways glance. "Not doing it to yourself is the biggest factor. Otherwise, slowing down enough to make sure you get them done right, I've always found helpful."

"Spiteful bitch," I teased. "Here I am giving you a compliment, and you're calling me out. I see how it is."

"Ever heard of personal space, Dax?" Gator asked through his teeth.

My gaze flicked up to him. "I'm good, but thanks for asking."

"Little demon, I think he was saying he wanted some personal space while he's getting stitched up," Void pointed out.

I flashed him a smile and winked. "Oh, I know. I just didn't care."

"Dax," Tilly chided. "Go find Mutt. He's in the other room playing video games. I'll grab you when I'm done here."

Letting out a heavy sigh, I begrudgingly left with Void to see what Mutt was playing. Sure enough, there he was on the couch, sitting cross-legged with a bag of Doritos and a giant can of Monster next to him on a tray.

Spotting us, he paused the game and grinned. "She gonna let you hang out and play? I've got two extra controllers if that interests you at all, Dax."

"Nah, I'll watch. I prefer the real thing. I'm not so good at video games. Somehow I always end up getting stuck somewhere completely lost. That or I'm killed every five seconds because of pussy-ass snipers hiding out in tall buildings. To me, that feels like cheating, just come out and face me like a real man," I explained.

Mutt looked at me, confused. "Uh, all you had to say was no thanks. I'm not one of those assholes who would make you play."

"Don't mind her. She's in a mood because Eagle isn't here, and she can't keep an eye on all of us," Void explained.

"That makes total sense. Tilly definitely gets that way when Gator's gone on long trips and he hasn't checked in for the day with her," Mutt said in understanding as he tossed Void a controller. "Now that they have each other, maybe it won't be so bad for us men folk who never know how to say the right thing."

"I'd be careful how loud you say that," Void warned, glancing at me with humor in his eyes. "Never know how they might react when they learn that kind of stuff about us men."

I laughed and shoved him to take a seat on the couch next to Mutt. "Play your damn game. You've been excited about it since you knew we were coming over."

Soon, the two men were on a team together, taking out people on a battlefield, yelling warnings to each other, and giving the worst shit-talking I've ever heard. Thankfully, it didn't take long for Tilly to come and grab me with a knowing smile.

"We'll be on the back patio, boys, if you need us," Tilly announced.

Void looked at me, holding my gaze. "Don't leave without telling me."

"Promise," I said, wanting to make sure he knew, without a doubt, I wasn't going to pull any stunts.

He grunted his response and went back to his game, leaving me to spend time with my friend. When we got out to the back patio, she handed me a mug and curled up on a swinging bench leaving room for me to sit beside her. I took a sip of the coffee and nearly choked on it.

"Shit, how much whisky did you put in this?" I asked, coughing. "Damn, that shit will put some hair on your chest."

"After yesterday, I figured we could all use a stiff drink or two," she admitted. "Gator hates to get stitched up, so we tried to bandage it last time, but I knew it was too deep of a cut. When it didn't stop oozing blood this morning, he finally relented."

"I guess I can't blame him. Stitches suck ass," I said, taking another more controlled sip of coffee. "Is that the only injury out of the three of you?"

"Yeah, they had me in the back the whole time reloading for those who needed ammo. Gator didn't get hurt until the end when they realized how badly they were losing. A Mad Dog went down swinging and caught him in the thigh with a knife. Mutt was helping to coordinate everyone's movements, so he was all over the place. That man has more lives than a cat the way he can narrowly miss being in trouble," Tilly shared as she stared off into the distance toward the direction the fight took place. "If you hadn't called when you did, we wouldn't have made it. Then the backup came at the right moment, just when we got hit with all the cars trying to ram the fence."

"I'm glad we figured out their plan in time. The whole mission was chaos. Nothing turned out the way that it should have. Everyone got blown up. Eagle almost died, I got kidnapped, nearly blew up again, then arrived here to find a machine gun strapped to a pickup truck. Who the fuck had one of those laying around their house and thought it was a good idea to use?" I blurted.

"Seems Marco wanted to make sure they could take everyone out for picking sides with you," she mused. "Not that I would have it any other way, but damn. You hear stories like this happening all over the world, and you think it would never happen to us. That's just crazy. Not so crazy it seems."

I took a big gulp of my drink, letting the whisky burn until it hit my stomach. "Now we have to go to New York and do it all over again."

"Does that mean we get stuck babysitting the Saints again, or do we get to come play?" Tilly asked with a raised brow.

"Who else would look after things here?" I challenged. "If there is someone you can get everyone to agree on babysitting, then, by all means, come join the chaos. If not, there's no way that Eagle will let that happen."

Tilly groaned. "No, there isn't anyone they would all agree on, not for this type of shit. Why do I always have to miss out on all the fun?"

"If there is a way that we can include you guys, you bet your ass it's gonna happen. Right now, it's all the boring planning and figuring out how the hell we are going to show up in New York and not get shot on sight," I grumbled. "Here, I was thinking I could just sneak in and sneak out. Then Void laughed at me."

"Babe, I would have laughed at you too. You could change your hair color and dress a different way, but there isn't anything you can do to disguise that mouth of yours. The second you start talking or spouting off about something, they'll figure out who you are," Tilly tossed back her head and laughed. "Fuck, woman, you are like the Grimm Reaper's sexy assistant the way you leave bodies behind."

I shrugged. "What can I say? I like to make an impression."

"So do that, find something you can do that's legit business and has nothing to do with the Hidden Empire and will give you the excuse you need. They can't take you out as easily if you're expected to be at something that will draw in all the big'n'bad from all across the globe," Tilly reasoned.

Cocking my head to the side as I stared down into my coffee, I thought over what she'd just said and what Void had mentioned earlier. "Do you think an underground cage fight might be able to draw enough attention?" I asked, looking up to meet her gaze.

"That depends who's going to be at the fight... Dax, the enforcer, or Two Tricks, the newly discovered Queen of the Hidden Empire?" Tilly inquired. "Because I'll tell you what, the Tricks name holds more weight to it than you probably ever wanted it to."

"What kind of opponent would add to the draw?" I pressed, the wrigglings of an idea playing in my head.

She took another pull on her coffee, thinking, then set down the mug. "That's what you need to find out. You and Void need to scour the internet for the baddest motherfucker out there right now, and you need to own his ass. I'm talking about the scum of the earth that people love to hate and won't give two shits when you kill them."

"Damn, maybe we do need you on this trip. Any way your men would let you come with us?" I asked with a chuckle.

"You let me see to that if I feel the plan needs me. Having an entourage would be helpful, keeps you in the limelight so others can do the work around you," Tilly said, then pointed at me with a knowing look. "Unless you can't handle not being the one who does the behind-the-scenes work. I know you tend to be as much of a control freak as Eagle is."

"Wow," I said with mock hurt, clutching my chest. "Shot fired. I've been hit right in the feels, man."

She just laughed and shoved me with her hand. "I'm sure you'll survive. Now was there another reason you came by other than my brilliance, of course?"

"Nah, just wanted to make sure you and the guys were good," I admitted. "When you don't make friends easily, and you lose them as fast as I do, it makes you more attentive, I suppose."

"Then put your mind at ease because we are all just fine here. I also don't plan on ditching you as a friend anytime soon, so toss that thought out in the garbage where it belongs. We women who live our lives on our own terms have to stick together in this world. Just be prepared to get a lot of shit for having as many men as you do," Tilly reminded me. "I only have two, and the looks I get are rather entertaining, to be honest, but can be frustrating after a while. Yeah, I know you don't give a flying fuck what people think, but it wears on you."

Tilly made a good point making me remember Agent Eggers' reaction and the nurse at the hospital. People could be so closed-minded to anything that wasn't deemed *normal*. Even if I say fuck the status quo, others won't be as quick to let it go. New York would be an interesting experience if the plan I had brewing worked.

The sound of someone opening the back door of the house pulled me from my thoughts, and I spotted Void. "Eagle's five minutes away. Figured you'd want to be at the house when he gets there."

That wasn't really a question. I was more than ready to have Eagle back home. There was something about not having all my men in one stop that was driving me crazy. We'd all agreed that us splitting up never seemed to be a great option. So once

Eagle was back, I'm sure there would be a conversation about that along with many other things.

Kissing Tilly quickly on the cheek, I gave her a wink. "Thanks for the brilliant idea, T, but I've got to go greet my man. You know how whiny they can be when they're hurt."

"Good luck, babe. Let me know if you need any more help," she called as we walked around the back of the house.

I knocked my shoulder into Void's arm and looked up at him. "Did you talk to him or Dani?"

"It was a call from the car phone, so they were both there, and for your next question, he sounded fine. Pissy, but that's to be expected since they wouldn't let him walk out of the hospital. He had to be wheeled out," Void answered.

Snickering, I grabbed his hand and swung it between us. "Let's see who's the worst patient, him or me."

"Oh, it will be him. You could be reasoned with," Void said, giving my hand a squeeze. "Just remember not to take anything he says personally when he's like this. Sometimes his temper gets the better of him."

Well, this was going to be interesting. Let's hope he still loved me after experiencing my bedside manner.

Chapter Seven

Eagle

Shifting in my seat, I tried to find a position that wouldn't hurt so damn much. Why the hell did I tell them I didn't need any painkillers before leaving? Who was I trying to impress? Dani? Nah, she knew exactly how much pain I was in, but we couldn't fill the prescription until we got into town. Something about narcotics and state line, who the fuck knows?

"How much longer until we get to the pharmacy?" I asked, trying to keep my voice even.

Dani looked at me with a knowing expression. I wasn't fooling her in the slightest.

"Do you want something over the counter to help at least take the edge off?" she asked. "I told you it would help if you laid down in the back, so you're not putting so much pressure on it."

"I've been lying about for almost a day. I can't take it anymore." I growled as I yanked the seat belt looser so it wasn't pressing on the wound.

Dani let out a sigh as we pulled off the highway and onto the road that would lead us to the pain meds. "Once you take one of these, it's going to put you on your ass. You'll be sleeping whether you want to or not, so be a stubborn ass. The meds will win."

While Dani had been around for a few weeks when Dax was shot, I hadn't really spent much time with her one on one. Having had the pleasure over the past day, it made sense why Dax brought her into the fold. Dani was smart, didn't take shit from anyone but had a real heart for taking care of people. We needed someone like her who could handle what most people would consider too intimidating to tell them to shut the hell up.

Before I was released, she made one more round to the other hospitals, looking after the guys, making sure they would all have rides home and people to look after them. It put me at ease to know she cared for everyone with the same protectiveness that she did Dax and me.

"You're staying here," she ordered. "I will be right back, don't do anything stupid."

"What the hell could I possibly get into like this?" I demanded, gesturing to my side. "I've got a five-inch incision that got rooted through and stitched up. Did you know they just glued and stitched to make sure it would heal right?" Dani gave me a withering look, and I tossed up my hands. "Don't beat up the wounded guy."

"God, Dax is nuts to have seven of you in her life," she muttered as she got out of the car and slammed the door.

I looked around the little strip mall where the pharmacy was and noticed someone I recognized heading into the smoke shop. The problem was, I couldn't place how I knew the guy in the first place. Then it dawned on me. It was Dax's right-hand man. *What the hell was he doing all the way out here?*

Shoving open the door, I slowly eased myself out of the car, grabbing my gun from the glove box. I shoved it down the front of my pants because there was no fucking way I could twist to get in behind me, let alone grab it to shoot someone. We'd met right after Dax got shot and he was working with Wes to run the Empire while Dax was out for those two weeks. For her to put that much trust in the guy, he must be someone she vetted and earned her trust.

As I opened the door, it hurt like a motherfucking bitch. One would never know how many muscles were working all at the same time until you damaged them, and they screamed at you that they existed. Gritting my teeth, I looked around the small shop and found him looking through vape juice flavors. He seemed relaxed, unhurried, not at all concerned with getting noticed or acting like he shouldn't be here. *Had Dax called him in? He'd been part of the second wave of her team in Vegas, but it doesn't explain why he's* here.

I moved through the aisles, looking at the various products and paraphernalia they had for grinding, dabbing, and other things I hadn't the faintest idea how to use. Sure, I'd smoked weed a bunch of times, but I didn't use a bong or anything like that. I just smoked it like a cigarette. I'm sure the others wished I smoked more often, but I couldn't allow myself to let anything impair me while being the leader of a group as big as the Phantom Saints. We grew way faster than I thought with Tricks's no biker gangs policy. Funny how things change in such a short amount of time.

That was something we were going to need to talk about. How did we move forward? Dax was ours, and she'd made it clear that our people were hers along with the five of us. We'd need to find a way to blend the two into something that benefited both.

"Eagle?" Brian's voice called out.

My head snapped up, and I realized I'd almost completely forgotten why I'd come here in the first place. "Yeah?" I answered, trying to act like I didn't remember him, so it wasn't awkward.

"Right, sorry, I'm probably more of a voice on the other end of the line to you," he chuckled and held out his hand. "Brian, I'm one of Dax's men."

I raised a brow at the phrase.

"Fuck. Sorry, I didn't mean 'man' in that way. We're good friends but nothing more than that. I've never been interested in her like that. She's my boss," he rambled utterly flustered at the slip.

Clearly, this guy wasn't wandering around looking for trouble. "It's alright. I knew what you meant. You're the one who's been keeping the Empire still running while Dax deals with the current issues."

"Yeah, that's the short and sweet of it," he admitted, rubbing the back of his neck.

"What brings you out here? Weren't you with the second wave in Vegas?" I asked, curious to see if he would tell me.

Brian's eyes went wide with shock. "Do you not know that your compound was attacked?"

"Yes, I'm aware of that. What does that have to do with you?" I challenged, not understanding the connection.

"Dax sent us out right away as reinforcements to the compound. We got there just in time to turn the tide until Dax and the rest of the guys got there to finish them off," Brian informed me. "The FBI has been running all over the place dealing with the dead bodies and such. Interviewing random people, so I thought I should get out of there for a while. Dax has immunity, but I'm not so sure that applies to the rest of us, and a fair amount of those people have a bullet in them from my gun."

That certainly made sense and sounded like what my little hellcat would do. She liked to make sure she had all angles covered. I held out a hand, and he took it, shaking it gently, clearly knowing I'd been hurt.

"Eagle," Dani snapped as she walked into the store. "What did I tell you about leaving the car?"

Ignoring her for a moment, I met Brian's gaze, but he was already lost eyes only for the fiery woman behind me. That was a look I knew well, and it took everything not to smirk. "Thanks for taking care of my people, but it seems my jailer has found me. Stop by the house, have a drink, and stay for dinner. I know Dax considers you family."

Brian shook his head and tried to cover up that he hadn't heard half of what I said. "Yeah... sounds great. Are you heading back to the compound now?"

"If she has anything to say about it. Dax put her in charge of me for the next two weeks until I get these damn stitches out," I answered as I headed for the door.

Dani looked like she was about to cuss my ass out until she noticed Brian. "You better not be talking him into smoking anything. With the meds he's on, that would be a disaster."

Okay, clearly the infatuation didn't go both ways.

"No, no, I came in here looking for more juice for my vape," Brian blurted out.

Dani's nose wrinkled in distaste. "You know, just because it's not a cigarette doesn't mean that's any better for you. We don't even know the damage those things can do, not to mention how much nicotine you'd be ingesting without even realizing it."

Poor Brian just looked at her, gaping like a fish, not having a clue how to handle this situation.

"Leave the man alone. You're nagging at him like you're an old married couple," I interjected. "Did you get my meds? I really want to get home, eat something that tastes like food, and put my feet up."

Now Dani looked taken aback at my observation and chose to focus on me instead.

"Alright then, let's go," she said, holding the door open and gesturing for me to exit.

Not wanting to make a big scene in the store, I headed out and over to the car. I paused when I got to the door, wondering if I could manage to pull the damn thing open.

"I got it, boss man," Brian offered as he reached past me and opened the door. "I get the feeling you and Dax are pretty similar. She wouldn't have admitted she couldn't open the door either."

Part of me wanted to be pissed he'd called me out, but it wasn't like he was wrong. Nodding to him, I slid into the car, then looked around the lot. "Did you need a ride?"

"No, I'm good. I got my bike. It's hidden by that big-ass truck. Think I'm gonna stay out of their way for a bit just to be safe," Brian shared, giving us a wave before shutting the door.

Dani had us back on the highway heading home, and I couldn't be more thankful. I wanted to be back in my own space with people I trusted and a world I could control because there wasn't much of that happening right now.

"You were with Brian's group in Vegas, weren't you?" I inquired.

"Yeah, when the explosion happened and everyone was getting shipped off to hospitals, I had one of the guys take me while everyone else stayed at the ranch waiting for orders," she explained. "I didn't know they all left to help until well after the fact, but it makes sense. Not like I could've done much since you were made my top priority."

"Sorry about that. I'll try not to get shot next time, so you can go with Brian," I teased.

Dani snapped her head in my direction. "What are you talking about?"

"You mean to tell me you didn't notice that man has a total hard-on for you?" I asked. "He would have been sending smoke signals if he knew how."

She just shook her head and focused on the road. "I'm not looking for anything right now. My last relationship was a shitshow, and I don't need that in my life. For the first time, I'm doing things how I want to, playing by my own rules. To add someone into the mix would ruin that, so I'm keeping things loose and easy."

I could absolutely understand where she was coming from. Before Dax, we'd had other women who claimed they could be with all of us, but it never worked. They'd pick favorites or exclude one of the others, not really having any interest in them. So we took a break and just had flings, just sex, no attachments, but damn, did that sometimes make things harder. It was worth it, though, to wait for Dax, the little hellcat I now called my own. When I told them that she was my wife at the hospital, it wasn't just for convenience. I one hundred and ten percent planned on wifing her ass up. She would be mine, well ours, legally with a contract and everything. No way was she going to get away from us because there would never be someone who could take her place.

The sound of a phone ringing pulled me out of my musings, and I realized Dani was calling someone. "Dani," Void answered. "Everything okay?"

"Yeah, I just wanted to give you a heads up. We're about five-ish minutes away. I'm sure things there are kind of crazy, but I figured you'd all want to be around," Dani explained.

"I'm warning you, if anyone thinks they're going to treat me like an invalid, I'm gonna shoot them in the leg. Then they'll be the ones people need to look after," I growled out, feeling the need to set expectations.

Void just chuckled. "I'm well aware of how you feel about being wounded, Eagle. Can't speak for the others, but I'm not gonna get in your way. Little demon might have other thoughts, but you can take that up with her."

"Oh, like she was a treat when she was shot," I muttered. "Shooting her again might get me buried six feet under."

Dani burst into laughter. "God, she really has you men whipped, doesn't she? To be fair, she was one of the most difficult people I've had to work with."

"You just keep remembering that for the next two weeks, or I might do something drastic. Like make her your next patient," I warned.

"Alright, you two, I'll see you when you get back," Void said, ending the call.

He was never a man who talked on the phone. I should be grateful he even picked up the phone to begin with.

When we got to the entrance of the compound, Dani stopped the car, put it in park, and turned to me. "Look, while I know you are the big man on top here, I won't allow you to disrespect me in front of others to make yourself feel better. I'm looking after you because it's my job and I respect Dax, who is my boss. She signs my paychecks, and she is the one who calls the shots on where I spend my time, not you."

Shocked, I blinked at her for a moment. "Have I given you the impression that I'm that disrespectful to women or would be to you?"

"We weren't on your turf. Now we are," she challenged. "I know bikers. My ex was part of the Wild Aces in Arizona. The biggest part of why we split is because he viewed women, how many in the MC world do... as less than. I wouldn't stand for it, that wasn't my world, and I didn't want to be a part of it. I realize the Phantom Saints are different, but I'm laying down the law now, so if you pull some shit, I will bring it up to Dax."

Well, fuck, whoever her ex was certainly did a number on her.

"I hear you, Dani," I said, holding her gaze so she knew I meant it. "While we're clearing the air about things, I hate how MCs run their crews, but we are a bunch of insecure dipshits who can't handle a woman being better at things than we are," I announced, making her crack a smile. "I might be an ass when I'm in pain, but you have my permission to bitch my ass out if I cross the line. You're here helping me out and what kind of man would I be if I treated you like shit for it?"

Dani searched my face for a moment, then nodded, throwing the car in gear and peeling down the gravel drive. I regarded her out of the corner of my eye and wondered if she might actually be related to Dax in some way. While they were incredibly different women, they held many of the same values. All I knew was I was glad she was on our side, making sure my people were looked after.

Seeing the house and everyone hanging out on the porch chatting made me feel an immediate sense of relief. The compound didn't look worse for wear or show any signs of there ever having been a fight. Granted, I remember Dax saying something about keeping them outside the fence so it wouldn't have been near here. Damn pain was making my brain fuzzy.

Picasso was at my door, pulling it open before I even realized he'd left the steps where he'd been sitting. "I could have gotten the damn door myself," I muttered.

"Yeah, yeah, we know you're not a gimp and can do everything yourself. Let's get you in the house before you piss everyone off," my brother commented sarcastically as he waited for me to get out of the car.

Dax met me standing on the second to last step, so we were at eye level. Her silver-blue eyes scanned me over as if to make sure I was just as she left me. Reaching out, I grabbed her chin and pulled her to me so I could kiss the shit out of her. I might be out of commission for a bit, but I was gonna take what I could when I could. She responded instantly, wrapping her arms around my neck and deepening the kiss. When I pulled back, I gave her one more quick peck and smiled.

"It's almost like you missed me or something," I said with a chuckle.

"Ignore whatever is about to come out of her mouth," Sprocket interjected. "Our woman has been a wreck all day waiting for you to come back home."

Dax glared at my road captain, but he didn't seem bothered in the slightest. "Come on, little hellcat, let's get in the house so I can take my pain meds and get more comfortable."

That had her moving and dashing up the stairs to open the door for me as I slowly made it up the steps. Fuck, why did my body have to hurt so fucking much? I aimed right for the couch and laid down on the short end with my head on the armrest. Before I could even ask, Dani was handing me a glass of milk and the pain pill.

"Milk?" I questioned.

"These might upset your stomach if it's empty, but the milk will help fill it some," she explained.

Shrugging, I took a few sips, then swallowed the pill, finishing off the glass and handing it over. With a groan, I sprawled out, relieved to finally be home and not having to worry about being without backup. Yeah, the FBI made sure to have someone in my room to make sure no retaliation from the Mad Dogs happened, but I didn't like being on my own.

"So, anything important happen that I haven't been told about yet?" I asked, letting my eyes fall shut.

There was a shuffle of feet as the others came to join me in the living room. I knew Dax sat down by my feet because she was the only one small enough to fit in the space left.

"I filled him in on the basics when I talked to him last night," Dax shared. "The FBI is still wandering around the compound, taking statements, cleaning up the crime scene, and being a bother."

"Ah, *loba* just doesn't like them because they were spouting off, and she had to teach them a lesson," Cognac said with a chuckle.

The asshole loved it when she got all stabby. Something tells me he would have done something just so she'd get wild.

"There is one other thing we need to fill you in on, but you're not going to like it," Picasso offered hesitantly.

That had me cracking an eye to look at him. "What the fuck does that mean?"

"How many different ways can you take that statement?" Dax sassed.

I scowled at her. "You keeping something from me, little hellcat?"

"Nope, we always planned to tell you but thought some things should be talked about in person. Too risky over the phone, never know who could be listening in, right, Wes?" Dax countered, trying to get back up which told me even she was worried about how I'd take it.

Struggling to sit up, I waved to my brother, who moved to help me, but I got into a sitting position eventually, looking at all the men who'd been my family for over ten years. "You better tell me what's going on right now."

Picasso fidgeted and took a deep breath before he looked me in the eye. "The De León Cartel has Elena and they've been using Demitri and Gabby to get information on Two Tricks. They are the moles in their organization and in our own. Pinky was ratting us out too, but that was more recent since Dax came into the picture."

It took my brain a moment to sort through everything that I'd just been told. I couldn't tell if the meds were working faster than expected or what, but my mind was in a complete and utter fog. My body began to sway and that's when I knew what had happened. Looking over my shoulder, I found Dani by the kitchen, perched on one of the stools giving me a knowing look.

"You drugged me," I slurred.

She nodded. "You're in too much pain and traveling so soon wasn't a great idea. If you want to heal faster, you need to rest."

It was now a struggle to keep my eyes open, and the world started to swirl around me.

"Oh shit, he's going down," Void warned and someone grabbed my arm. "Let's get you to bed and we'll talk about all this after you've woken up."

"Traitor," I muttered.

"Just looking out for my president," Void countered as he hoisted me up with an arm over his shoulders.

"You better not carry me like a fucking princess." I growled.

Void just shook his head and all but dragged me to my room, then laid me on my bed. "Sleep. You'll feel better for it, I promise."

Chapter Eight

Dax

Eagle slept for six hours before he started to wake. I'd taken up watch in his armchair, looking over the files that Wes already had on the De León Cartel. Objectively, they had a pretty amazing operation, dividing out the work into different sections that never connected, so if one part crashed and burned, it didn't take the rest down with it.

"That was mean," Eagle grumbled as he shifted to look at me. Then he reached out a hand and wiggled his fingers. "Come here, hellcat. I've missed you."

A grin tugged at my lips as I set the computer down and crawled into bed. I snuggled into his unwounded side as he wrapped his arm around my shoulders and kissed my forehead. "You know it hasn't been that long."

"Funny, you keep saying that like it matters," Eagle rumbled, his lips brushing my skin. "Does it have to be forever for me to miss you?"

"Damn, you are drugged if you're talking like that," I teased.

While I'd accepted that I loved these men, and they loved me, it still had me looking for the nearest exit when it came to the mushy stuff like this.

"Hmm, maybe, but it's the truth."

I peered up at him to see his eyes warm with affection. "I missed you too. Sprocket wasn't joking when he told you I was a mess. It was so bad I washed all the dishes from breakfast and didn't finish one cup of coffee."

Eagle's eyes widened at this. "Wait, you did *all* the dishes? As in like other people's, not just your own?"

"Don't look so shocked," I said, lightly smacking him on the chest.

He groaned and faked that I hurt him far worse than was possible, clutching his heart. "You would hit a wounded man?"

"Hmm, I seem to remember someone going on and on about how he didn't want to be treated like an invalid. Any idea who that could be?" I mused, tapping my chin.

Eagle growled and pulled me in for a kiss. Unlike most of our sexual interactions, this kiss was gentle, caring, and full of the love we felt for each other. Both of us had thought we'd lost the other, and now it was sinking in that we were home safe and sound. Never did I think I could feel like my soul was split into seven pieces, but when one of them wasn't with me, I felt it. Not one to be all lovey-dovey, this was a new and slightly terrifying place to be.

There was a knock on the door, and I could tell by the sound that it wasn't the guys—which left Dani. Pulling away from Eagle, I sat up but didn't move away as he cupped my ass with his hand. I shot him a look, but he just smiled and nodded toward the door.

"Come on in, Dani," I called.

The door opened a crack and she peered in before fully entering. "Hope I'm not intruding, but I want to make sure he gets his next dose of pain meds, and I need to change his bandage."

"Wes was supposed to be close to finishing dinner," I told Eagle. "I'll make up a plate for each of us, and I'll be back, okay?"

"Sounds great. The food at the hospital was absolute shit," he grumbled, then turned to Dani. "You couldn't have changed them when I was passed out? Haven't you done enough to torture me?"

Dani laughed. "Oh, I haven't even begun if I wanted to really torture you."

Leaving him in capable hands, I wandered back into the kitchen. Wes was standing at the stove stirring a large pot of something that smelled amazing. Peering over his shoulder, I discovered it was beef stew.

"Dude, it's the middle of the summer and you're making stew?" I asked, leaning against the counter to the side. "I'm just saying, aren't we hot enough out here?"

"If you don't want to eat it, then you can make something yourself," Wes quipped.

"Well, glad to see some things never change even when you're in love with someone," I said, heaving myself up on the countertop. "So I promised Eagle I would get him food. Would you say you're close to being done?"

Wes set the wooden spoon he'd been using to the side, then turned to me. "Oh, so you're using caring for the sick and injured to get the answers you want?" He stepped closer, pushing my legs wide so he fit between them. "That's low even for you, Two Tricks."

"What can I say? I've been feeling off my game and needed to even out the score," I shared with a shrug. "Didn't get to the top without stepping on a few toes... hands... heads... dicks. Well, you know how it goes."

He chuckled as he leaned in, setting his arms on either side, boxing me in with his body. "Do I? See, what I remember is the broken nose, bloody lip, stitching up knife wounds, and a bullet wound or two. Someone had to look out for that fine ass of yours, yet you keep taking all the credit."

"Hmm?" I mused. "Let's see who's the one who decided I needed to be the big bad working my way up through the ranks so no one would know that I own it all?"

"Fuck," Cam swore. "How did it take you two so long to start fucking? The sexual tension between you two is insane. I feel like I could just come from your verbal sparring."

I glanced over at my first love and how he stroked himself over his jeans. Cam had never been one who cared where we were or who was there. If he wanted something, he was gonna take it. Oddly enough, I felt the same way, but I quickly learned that it was more rare than I assumed it would be.

"You pull that thing out in the kitchen, and I'll chop it off," Wes warned as he leaned in and kissed my neck, trying to prove he wasn't feeling threatened.

"So what you're saying is if I stand behind the breakfast counter, I'm safe?" Cam inquired.

Wes glanced over at Cam, an evil smirk on his face. "Guess it would be cruel to say no since it's the only action you're gonna get until you win us all over."

Cam made a shocked face covering his mouth with his hand. "Wes, I never knew you played both sides, wait until I tell my father."

A snarl from Wes was the only warning as a knife went flying through the air. Cam ducked, and the knife embedded itself in the wall of the dining room. As Cam rose, he let out an impressed whistle. "I see Dax taught you well. Not many people could make a throw that well with an unbalanced kitchen knife."

"Cam," I warned. "He's right, you know, I might have decided to keep you, but more than that won't happen until you make peace with the guys. We won't be able to win this fight without the eight of us being a team, trusting that we have each other's backs. Marco likes to play people against each other, and I need to know that won't happen with us."

My dark knight rested his elbows on the counter and looked me square in the eye. "I'm more than willing to bury the hatchet as it were, but I can't be the only one who does it. Without a mutual ceasefire, there won't be peace. Someone will always be waiting to stab me in the back. I'll own up to the fact I didn't start things off well, but I'm not the only one who needs to make some changes."

The bastard had a point. If each of them didn't make the effort, none of this would work. It had to work, there was no way I was giving any of them up, and I knew they wouldn't walk away from me either. Somehow there needed to be a middle ground. I just didn't know what that was.

"Start at the beginning, like we did," I suggested. "Learn everyone's boundaries and limitations, hard no's and negotiables. Hell, you and I need to go over those again anyway. Neither of us are the same as we were when our current guidelines were set up."

Wes frowned at me. "Why do you make it sound like some contract?"

"Because between him and I, it was," I answered. "Wes, the games we used to play were not your average slap and tickle. Not all couples need a real contract, but I wanted to make sure he knew the limitations. We negotiated consent for knife play, minimal blood play, and a few other situations."

"Oh, don't be shy, beautiful. You forgot our game, hunt and fuck," Cam added. "Sometimes it would be in a park, at school, or even at a party. She would hide, and I would find her, then we'd fuck like animals."

While I'd expected Wes not to be a fan of what I'd just described, I hadn't been expecting to see a glint of curiosity. "Can *we* make our own contract?"

My brows shot up. "I mean, it's something we can talk about for sure, but I didn't think you were into those kinds of kinks."

"I don't want to do those," Wes said with exasperation. "No, my idea of a good time would involve ropes, toys, and a blindfold."

Just hearing him say that had my mouth going dry and my pussy dripping wet. "Fucking hell, you don't need a contract for that. I'll let you do that whenever you like."

"Oh, so you like the idea of that, hmm... shortcake?" Wes murmured as his lips brushed up my neck. "We had so much fun that night I tied you to the bed and fucked you into the mattress. I'd never heard you scream my name so loud. It was as addicting as a drug."

I moaned, letting my head fall back against the cabinet as I remembered that night. I'd been fucking pissed at the guys, and Wes was right there to keep my mind off them. *Fuck, this means I'm gonna need to install a bed like that in one of these rooms. Maybe we could have a playroom if we built a new place?*

"Weston," Cam interjected. "Do I have your permission to masturbate as you tease our woman?"

Wes faltered, looking at me questioningly as if unsure how to respond. "It's your call. Cam already knows I don't mind being watched. It's your permission he needs, but you can say no. He'll leave and finish himself off in the bathroom without argument."

The two men stared at each other for a moment then Wes gave his answer. "Watch and learn, Cameron. I'll show you what makes our woman purr."

Wes slid both hands up my shirt, groping my tits. "I'm not even going to have to touch her pussy since that wouldn't be hygienic in the kitchen, but I'll have her coming in no time."

Fucking, fuck, fuck. Thank God I had a high sex drive, or these men would be using me up like a dirty old sock with how often they found a way to play games like this.

His fingers found my nipples and rolled them, making me arch into the sensation. Teeth nipped at my earlobe before he sucked it into his mouth and gave it a slight tug, mixing a bit of pain with pleasure. A groan was pulled out of my mouth when he released my ear but pinched my nipples and pulled just enough that there was tension on them.

"Fuck yes," I whimpered.

"See that, Cameron? I bet she's about ready to beg me for more, but I'm not gonna give it to her. She needs to work for it," Wes shared as he shoved up my shirt so he could see my breasts. "What should I do? Suck on one, or maybe you're craving something a little rougher?"

I met his gaze and felt he might be into it if I played my cards right. "I want you to choke me as you suck on my tit."

The smirk that grew on his face told me he was more than fine with my idea. A hand trailed down my leg then back up, but this time, ran it over my clothing-covered pussy with just enough presser to make my hips thrust, but nowhere close enough to get any relief. Up and up the hand slowly moved, swirling around my nipple, then making the final journey to my neck just under my jaw.

"Is this what you want?" Wes asked, his lips brushing mine as he talked. "You want me to take control of whether you get to breathe or not?"

Just hearing him say the words had my breath quickening with excitement. "Yes, that's exactly what I want."

Having gotten the answer he wanted, he devoured my lips, nipping, sucking, and licking them as I opened to him. Wes's tongue fucked my mouth as his fingers slowly tightened around the edges of my neck. When it got to the point I struggled to get in the air, I stilled for a moment letting the natural panic subside. Weston would never hurt me. This man had protected me my entire life. There was no way he'd purposely harm me with his own hand. My eyes fell shut as I trusted in his hold, letting the lightheadedness fill me, knowing when he released me, the euphoric sensation would be amazing.

I gasped, letting air fill my lungs as he released the pressure only to reapply it two breaths later. He moved his mouth down to my breast and his tongue flicked furiously over my erect nipple. At the same time, he released me, then sucked my nipple into his mouth hard. My body convulsed, hips thrusting forward, trying to find any source of friction to ease the pain building. As he kept up the suction, his tongue swirled and flicked, making my eyes roll back, and I moaned.

"God, please, Wes, let me come. Please, please, please, just touch my pussy," I begged. "Hell, just slap my pussy. I'm so close and so wet... fuck. I just need to come."

Clearly ignoring my pleading, he cut off my air once more, released that breast, and moved to the other. Applying the same torture as he had on the other, my body was screaming for the ability to come. I was so close to the edge. I just needed that last push, the overwhelming sensation that would send me plummeting into an orgasm.

Like one would expect from a man you've known most of your life, he pulled back, dropped his hand from my neck, took a nipple in each hand, and pulled sharply with a slight twist. I screamed as I came, my body shaking with the force of it as I slumped forward, clinging to Weston. He nibbled on my neck like I wasn't drawing out one of the most intense climaxes, flicking my nipples with his fingers just to ensure I lost my goddamn mind.

The sound of more than one male grunting in completion made its way into my blissed-out brain. Turning my head, I found Cognac and Cam slack-faced in bliss as they finished in their hand. *Why the fuck is it so sexy to know I'd made them so turned on they couldn't do anything just jack off while watching?*

"Umm, is it safe to come out yet?" Dani called from the back of the house.

Fuck. The whole point I'd come out here was to get dinner for Eagle and me, but here I was getting titty twisted into oblivion.

Wes grabbed the roll of paper towels and chucked them at the guys. "Make sure you clean up real good. More than just you will sit over there, and I, for one, don't want to worry about finding dried spunk on the wall."

"Give us a minute to zip things up, then you're safe," Cognac replied to Dani.

Poor woman was gonna be dodging sexy time left and right if these guys had any say about it. I slid off the counter, but Wes grabbed my shoulders to make sure I didn't fall over when my feet hit the ground.

My knees threatened to buckle, but they held strong, and I grinned up at Wes. "Is dinner ready now? I've worked up quite the appetite."

Wes snorted a laugh and grabbed bowls out of the cabinet. "Yeah, it's ready, has been for about fifteen minutes."

"What?" I gasped as my fist slammed into his arm. "Not cool, man. I could have grabbed some and left instead of giving everyone in this house blue balls."

"Guess you shouldn't have complained about what I made then, huh?" Wes countered with a raised brow. He then handed me two full bows and placed a hunk of bread on the rim of each. "Enjoy."

"Thank you, I will," I muttered as I marched back to Eagle's room.

Chapter Nine

Dax

When I charged into Eagle's room, I realized that Dani was still waiting for the all-clear. The one the guys had forgotten to give her.

"Sorry, girl, seven men, someone's always horny. I promise nothing gross happened. Wes is incredibly particular about kitchens and being sanitary," I said with a shrug. "Anything I need to make sure he does or doesn't do while he isn't under your watchful eye?"

"No, he will probably want to sleep or at least doze after the pain pill kicks in. After he eats, if he wants to come out and lay on the couch, it should be fine. I just want to make sure the meds are working before he starts to piss off the wound," Dani shared.

Nodding, I stepped aside so she could leave and headed over to Eagle. Then setting the bowls down on the nightstand, I set up the tray that went over Eagle's lap. "Hope you like beef stew."

"It's the middle of the fucking summer," Eagle blurted. "What the hell is he doing making fucking stew?"

Grinning, I handed him his meal and sat at the foot of the bed to eat my own. "That's what I said, but then I pissed him off, and he got all feisty."

"Oh, is that what happened?" Eagle asked with a knowing look. "How does complaining about dinner end up with you coming? That doesn't seem very Westly like."

I didn't answer right away and took a few bites of my stew. "I blame Cam for giving Wes ideas."

Eagle's brows shot up. "Excuse me?"

"Cam wanted to know if he could masturbate while watching Wes tease me as punishment for complaining about dinner. Then it turned into a whole thing, and I got choked, and my nipples yanked until I came right there on the kitchen counter."

"Fuck, and I missed it?" Eagle groaned, leaning his head back. "Damn, I bet it was a sight to see."

"You can ask Cam or Cognac. He showed up at some point to take part in the fun," I shared while shoving another spoonful of stew in my mouth. *Damn, this stuff was good.*

"How am I going to survive two weeks of not playing with you? I can't even jerk myself off because it hurts too much to bend like that," Eagle muttered.

I paused and cocked my head. "Um, have you already tried?"

"What the fuck else was I gonna do left alone while you guys saved the crew?"

He had a point there. I'm not sure what I would have done in his situation. "Well, maybe if you ask nicely, I could take care of it for you. Not today or tomorrow. You need a few more days to let your wound settle before we start skirting the rules."

A hungry look grew in Eagle's expression. "I think I can hold out for that."

There was a rap on the door before the group filed into his bedroom all with bowls of stew. They found places to sit, making themselves comfortable.

"What the fuck do you all think you're doing?" Eagle demanded. "Who the hell told you bastards you could be in here, let alone with food?"

Picasso, who was sitting on the other side of the bed next to his brother, shrugged. "How else are we gonna talk to you?"

"Dani said I could move out to the couch, now get the fuck out." Eagle snarled.

Cognac shook his head. "Sorry, pres, but not today, we need to go over stuff, and it would be better to have you where we need you. Just in case we need to knock your ass out again. Stress isn't good for a healing patient, you know."

A vein on Eagle's forehead started to pulse, but he was trying his best not to explode on them. "Does this really need to happen now?" he bit out.

"The longer we leave Elena in the hands of the De León, the worse it is for everyone," Picasso reminded. "You think you can put aside your neurotic behavior for just one night?"

That had the president shutting right up, but he still glowered at the others. I took that as acceptance and turned to Wes. "Did Demitri have anything useful to tell us?"

Wes shrugged. "Yes and no. There was a lot that we already knew but a few names I hadn't heard before. When I looked them up, I found they were tied more to Marco than to Diego. It could be that they were sent to help with the big-picture goal or that Marco doesn't trust Diego to get the job done the way he should."

"What do you think it is?" Picasso asked.

Wes chewed on his bite for a moment before swallowing. "I think it's both. This is a big deal to Marco. The detailed plot he'd been putting up to draw Dax out is insane and took lots of planning. We've been playing defense or catching up on every move. Even with the Mad Dogs, they were still a step ahead."

"Yeah, but if Demitri was telling the truth, taking Elena and using him as a mole wasn't the plan. Not to mention they somehow got Gabriella sucked in too," I pointed out. "While I don't think he is lying, it seems a little suspect they just happened to end up at the one drug house that's been under attack. Who gave her the tip about the house in the first place?"

"You make a good point, beautiful," Cam interjected. "If we can track down that person, it might shed some light on if this was an *accident* or the careful planning of a man with way too much time on his hands."

Eagle was nodding as Cam spoke. "Gabby isn't a fool, and she taught her kids to be smart. Elena might be strong-willed and a risk-taker when it comes to a story, but she's got good street smarts. There's more to that part of the story than we're getting."

"It wouldn't surprise me if she knew about the drug war and picked to go there on purpose," Picasso commented. "That boy has never been able to tell his sister no, especially after their dad left. He felt the need to take that role and watch over her."

That got me thinking. "Would she lie to her brother to get him to go with her there?"

"Absolutely, she would do something like that," Eagle shared, seeming to follow my train of thought. "Might be worth looking up her classes and talking to the teachers in case she was writing a whole different story than she let on."

"That's what I would do if Devyn wouldn't take me someplace he thought was dangerous," I added.

Wes laughed. "You mean that's exactly what you did on many occasions."

"What? I had you looking out for me too. The three of us survived, didn't we?" I challenged, tilting my head to the side as I waited for his answer.

"By sheer luck," he muttered. "I can hack into the school and see what she was up to. Who knows, maybe she wasn't taking any of the classes they thought she was. If she's related to these two, there's no telling what she might have gotten mixed up in."

"Hey," Picasso shot back. "What the hell does that mean?"

"Dude, you're the VP of a biker gang. What more evidence do you need?" I asked.

That seemed to have him retracting his outrage. "Fine, fair point. So we do the work and find out what Elena was really up to, then what?"

"We can't plan beyond that for that particular angle, but we can work on dealing with another problem," Cam said, then pointed his spoon at me. "How the fuck are we going to be in New York City without everyone trying to kill her?"

"I actually have an idea," I answered, raising my hand like a kid in school. "Well, Sprocket and Void helped give me the seed of the idea."

"Care to share with the class, *loba*," Cognac teased.

Rolling my eyes at him, I set my empty bowl aside. "Before you freak out at the idea, let me finish explaining it first, cool?"

The guys looked at me dubiously but nodded their agreement.

"Void mentioned that he had some connections to the underground fighting ring, and they would kill to have me do one." I could see some of the men holding back their comments, but just barely. "You know how when there's a huge fight in Vegas and people come from all over to see it? What if we did that for me? Find the biggest baddest guy they won't mind if I kill in the end and make it a show no one can miss."

I could see I was losing them, so I soldiered on. "Think of it... a fight only advertised to those in our circle. The worst of the worst coming to see Two Tricks either get her ass handed to her or slaughter the motherfucker. With that much press from deadly people, it would be more dangerous for Diego to take me out. Meanwhile, we have you guys doing recon, working with the FBI on some sting operation, I don't know, but the attention will be on me."

No one spoke right away, which I took as a positive sign. I wasn't being grounded or threatened with another shock collar to train the crazy out of me. Hell, they were the ones who told me I was being a pussy about how we approached this situation. Couldn't say that now since I wanted to paint a big-ass target on my back. My gaze fell on Spencer. He'd been the one who told me all they wanted was to be in on the plan.

Welp, here it is, boys. Plan on a platter, hope you enjoy it.

"That wasn't the craziest option," Cognac pointed out. "I thought she was going to say skydive out of a plane and land on top of the Chrysler Building or something."

I perked up at that. "Ah, was that an option?"

"*No,*" they all yelled at the same time, and it had me leaning back.

"Well, shit, no need to blow out my eardrums," I grumbled. "Be honest, though. How else can I waltz right into De León territory and not get slaughtered? Fuck, you guys could go ahead of time and scope things out with Cam and the FBI while I hide out elsewhere in the state."

"Hold up," Sprocket interjected, raising both hands to add to his words. "Am I hearing this right? Is Dax the ruler of the

Hidden Empire, the ruthless tyrant known as Two Tricks, telling us we can take the lead on this?"

"Don't go saying that too loud, or she might change her mind," Picasso said, then laughed when I flipped him the bird. "It's really not the worst idea. Problem is, can it even be done?"

Void scratched his jaw as he mulled that question over. "Let me make a few calls tomorrow, gauge what kind of fighters they have going on, get a pulse for that world again. If it would help, I'd be willing to sign up for a fight myself."

"Alright, so we test out this plan, see if it fits while we gather more intel on Elena. Who knows, that might lead to something that gives us an in," Eagle commented, his voice sounding tired. "Cam, do you have any gauge on what the FBI might be looking for? Maybe something we can help them get to make a move on Diego or any of his men?"

"I'll make some inquiries and look in the database to see what active investigations we have going on. With this task force, I've been given more leeway to look into cases that aren't mine if I think we can help," he informed us, making him even more valuable to this team than I would have guessed.

"Good, then at least we have a place to start," Eagle said as his eyes started to droop shut. "We can't fuck up on this one. An innocent life hangs in the balance."

"Damn straight," Picasso added. "Now everyone gets the hell out of here so Eagle can rest. The faster he can heal, the better it is for all our sanity."

"Fuck you," Eagle mumbled as Wes folded up the tray and set it next to the bed.

Picasso just shoved his brother's leg in response before slipping off the bed and heading out of the room. I stood and walked to the head of the bed, kissing Eagle's lips. "Sleep well, boss man, we got lots of work to do, and you need to get better."

He muttered something under his breath and grabbed my arm. "Stay."

"Let me do one more thing, and I will come curl up next to you, okay?" Eagle grunted and let me go as he settled deeper under the covers.

Back out in the living room, I looked at the guys and crossed my arms. "Look, even if we don't end up going the fighting route, I feel like we need to still train. I know I'm out of practice from being shot and we've been so busy surviving there hasn't been time. This fight can't end with one or more of you wounded and laid up in bed, or heaven forbid one of you gets killed."

"You make a good point, little demon," Void agreed. "We need to be stronger than our enemy, and I know I'm not anywhere close to that. So far, the battles have been won with strategy and bullets, but we need to be prepared for it all."

"Something also tells me they will jump at the chance to have a fight night where Void makes a comeback and Two Tricks make an entrance," Sprocket pointed out. "In the mornings, we train. After that, we plan."

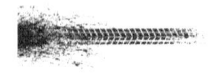

The next morning we got down to business. Dani was in charge of Eagle duty for half the day while we trained and worked on other things outside the house. Then he'd join us for the afternoon planning session. We didn't want him to overdo it, but there was no way we could keep him out of the middle of it even if we wanted to.

"Damn, you guys have a decent setup," I complimented as I took in the part of the clubhouse they turned into a gym of sorts.

Unlike mine at the warehouse, there wasn't a boxing ring per se but more like a padded area meant for fighting. Along one wall were a few heavy bags, a speed bag, and a weight bench. They didn't have the fancy weight machines like I did, but what they lacked in that area, they made up in free weights. You could do all the same stuff, it was just old school.

"Do you guys have a routine?" Wes asked as he took in the space. "Just asking since Dax and I have a basic plan that we follow for keeping in shape, then tweak it if we need to work on a certain area."

Cognac shrugged. "It's been a long time since we did more than work out to keep fit, so whatever you have to share, I'd be interested in trying."

"I've got a few different routines depending on what I need to accomplish," Void added. "How about we see what you two do, then maybe I can add in what will be helpful for fighting a little more dirty. Underground cage fights aren't about following the rules. It's about who comes out alive."

I nodded, knowing exactly what he meant. Most of my fights turned out that way, and I knew I'd been lucky so far after getting shot. A month of downtime and taking it easy, my muscles and endurance were nowhere near where I needed them to be.

"Today, I think I'm going to pace myself, gauge what needs more attention and what hasn't suffered so much," I shared, walking over to the treadmill. "I know for sure I need to beef up my endurance after sitting on my ass for so long recovering."

The rest of the guys scattered, warming up their own way. I'd gone to visit Tilly this morning, asking if I could borrow something to listen to music on. I really needed to get my shit together and start replacing things I'd lost. Wes was making a running list of things we needed to pull from some of our safehouses and other locations we stashed stuff to build a new command center at the compound. So I would just have to add to it when I thought of something.

Placing the headphones over my ears, I scrolled through the options on her MP3 player, amazed they still made things like this. Then I spotted a playlist called *Bad Bitches Do It Better*. That sounded like it would be perfect. When the beat to "Get Ur Freak On" by Missy Elliott started, I bobbed my head and started up the treadmill. Keeping it a brisk walk to start as I warmed up, then I upped the speed every few minutes when I felt comfortable. Soon, I was jogging and lost in the feel of my body burning after being abused in the battle and lack of exercise. Sweat started to drip down my back and forehead as I ran.

When I reached the point I wasn't sure I could keep going, I challenged myself for another two minutes. Then I started to bring the speed down, cooling off enough I wouldn't cramp but not enough that I couldn't continue my workout.

When I was finished, I hopped off. As I wiped my face with a towel, I noticed Cognac and Picasso on the mats sparring with each other. Watching those two men shirtless, sweat glistening on their bodies, made my pussy weep. Fucking hell, these guys were turning me into a sex addict, and I was totally fine with it. I'd always had an engine that revved higher than others. Now I had enough men to keep up with it.

"Damn, girl, how do you handle that much man all the time," Tilly asked as she came to stand next to me. "I've got two and sometimes a girl just needs a night off."

"Well, we haven't been together as long as you have with your guys. Right now, I can't seem to keep my hands off them any more than they can do the same for me." I glanced at her. "Seems kinky fuckers are just drawn to each other."

Tilly burst out laughing. "Damn, girl, just telling it like it is, huh?"

I shrugged. "Why fight it? I do feel a little bad for Dani, who has to share the house with us right now."

"Where is the poor woman even sleeping?" Tilly asked.

"Last night, she wanted to be on the couch, so if there was any trouble, she would be there to help. But I think the guys decided they are going to double up and get some air mattresses. Void and Cam seem to get along the best and Wes will either join Cognac or in the garage with Picasso," I shared. "My suggestion was getting a new house, but none of them were willing to commit to that right now. They're the ones on blow-up beds so..."

Tilly shook her head. "Men can be so stubborn sometimes, seriously."

We stood there a moment in silence, watching the two men grappling each other on the ground. It didn't look like either one of them was trying anymore, goofing off, but I wasn't gonna call them on it.

What we needed more than physical training was a way for us all to grow as a unit. The Saints knew how to work well together, but now, with Wes and Cam, their groove was thrown off.

"Wanna spar?" Tilly asked. "I'm pretty proficient in kickboxing if you want to do some work with pads."

"Think you can aim low enough if I'm the one holding the pads?" I challenged.

She just looked down at me. "Think you can jump high enough to reach the ones I'm using?"

"Guess there's only one way to find out," I said, heading over to the large metal storage cabinet that held all the supplies.

Tilly and I switched off until we were both dripping in sweat and barely able to hold up the pads. While it took me a bit to get back in the rhythm, once my body was on board, I was full steam ahead. Tilly was a great partner, and it was nice not to worry about her holding back for fear of hurting me like the guys would have done. Nah, the two of us had an understanding, no one else in the real world was gonna be pulling their punches.

"Alright, everyone, I think we should call it," Picasso announced to the room. "Let's head back, shower, eat something, and work on the tasks we planned last night."

Seeing Picasso stepping up and taking a more leadership role was sexy as fuck. I'd known he had it in him, but he was so worried about stepping on Eagle's toes he held back too much. Now having no choice but to lead, it was good to see him own it. I fell in step beside him as we walked through the main clubhouse area. Guys were sitting along the bar drinking, others played darts or pool, and some had their hands full with a sweet butt in their lap.

Most nodded respectfully to us as we made our way through until one man stepped into our path. This dude was big like a mountain that had legs and arms. His head was shaved and shined in the overhead lights. His cut was weathered, telling me he'd been part of the crew for a long time. The patch on his chest told me his name BigFoot, which made perfect sense to me.

"Sup?" I asked, leaning my head back to look up at him.

"You're Two Tricks, right?" BigFoot asked, his deep voice booming out of his chest.

I nodded. "Something I can do for you?"

He reached out his hand as if he wanted to shake mine. Knowing if I didn't extend my hand, it'd be a major insult, and I had a whole room of bikers looking at me. I decided it was best to play nice since I knew I hadn't done anything to upset someone—that I knew of. Placing my hand in his, he gently closed his fingers, then jerked my hand up and down in a way that had my body getting pulled forward at the strength of it.

"Whoa, easy there, BigFoot," Picasso warned, grabbing my shoulders to steady me. "She might be a badass, but she is still tiny."

"Just wanted to thank her for saving our asses the other day. Not many people I know would jump out of a helicopter and take out a machine gun for people that aren't their own," he explained as he released my hand. "Pinky had you all wrong, Little Queen."

I flashed him a smile. "Is that my road name now? Have I earned my cut here among you Phantom Saints?"

BigFoot stood to his full height, shoulders, back, and bellowed, "*Quiet.*"

The whole clubhouse fell silent instantly, and I was impressed. He'd even managed to get the background music to stop that had been thumping in the speakers.

"I know I'm not part of the leadership, but I was chosen to petition them so we make you an official member of the Phantom Saints. You've spilled blood protecting us, sent your own men to our aid, and took down the enemy without hesitation," BigFoot said to Picasso. "We know some of the old timers have their thoughts about women in the crew, but we know this one is more than capable of living our lifestyle. Fuck, she rules the goddamn West Coast from what I can tell."

Picasso's face was expressionless as he listened to what BigFoot had to say. "Your petition has been heard, and we will vote on it during Church. Give Eagle a few more days to recover, and we will send out the call."

BigFoot nodded and looked back at me. "Little Queen, I know you already have the leadership behind you, but no matter if you get sworn in or not, you have our respect."

His words warmed my dark little heart in a way even I didn't understand. I'd never wanted to be part of an MC. Hell, I fucking hated them for a long time. However, this group of men and women were quickly becoming as important to me as my own Empire. Goddamn, these men are slowly turning me into a big softy.

"Thanks, BigFoot. I really appreciate it," I said and patted the man's arm as I headed out, standing tall in front of all these men.

Chapter Ten

Dax

A week passed, and we all fell into a routine of sorts, managing things for both the crew and the Empire while getting ourselves prepared for what was coming next. During that time, I coordinated with Harper, the triplets, and Levin to get his granddaughter set up in a small private school in New York. Prim needed to be hidden away for a bit until things died down for their escape from Russia.

Levin sent the tank he'd promised me with them, so it was now hidden away in a cargo airport in New York. Soon he would be sending the guns I'd also gotten as part of the deal. While we wouldn't need them to deal with the De Leóns being in the city, going after Marco would be a whole different story.

Eagle was now up and moving about the compound. He still had to take it easy and couldn't lift anything too heavy. Thankfully, he was more focused on healing faster, and he was fine with the limitations. Weston was kicked out of the kitchen since that was one thing he could absolutely do without a problem.

Dani didn't need to stay with us in the house, so she used one of the dorm rooms they had for new recruits to the crew. Eventually, we would need to figure out where having her located would be best, but for now, this plan worked.

Wes got his command center set up in a spare room just outside the security room they had. He's been working on helping them upgrade that as well since they already had to replace a bunch of things from the attack. The FBI was long gone and didn't really reach out to contact us about anything, which allowed that whole event to come to a close. The Mad Dogs were done for, and there was no fear of them coming back. Did that mean there wasn't still a threat to the compound? No, but for now, we were doing all we could to beef things up.

"Hey," Void said as he sat down on the coffee table in front of me.

I glanced up at him from the report I was reading from Brian about a situation going on within the Empire. "What's up, hot stuff," I greeted with a wink.

We'd been working ourselves hard in training and dealing with everything else. While I slept in someone's bed each night, we'd been too worn out to do more than cuddle or make out. I wasn't worried our relationship wasn't built on sex, no matter how much we all enjoyed it.

"Ruban got back to me about our idea. He took it to a few others in the game, and they had a meeting. He was all fired up about it, but if this is going to be as big of a deal as we need it to be, all four of them need to be in on it," Void explained.

The four men he was talking about ruled the underground fighting rings. Each had a different area they were in charge of but all worked together to make the money flow and keep the secrets hidden.

"So, what's the answer?" I asked, sliding the computer off my lap so he knew he had my full attention.

"Good and bad... full of strings and promises we might not want to agree to," Void admitted, running both hands over his face.

"You're gonna need to give me more than that, big guy," I murmured, reaching out to rest my hand on his leg.

"One of them is they want us to each fight a person of their choosing, which we expected." I nodded as he paused to look at me. "Then, if we both win those fights, they want us to fight each other."

Now I could see why he was upset. Void might be as ruthless and bloodthirsty as I was, but when it came to me, I was his Achilles heel. There was no way he would be able to fight me the way they would want him to.

"Is there another workaround?" I asked. "There has to be something they would find way more interesting than the two of us going head to head."

"That's what I've been trying to wrack my brain for," Void muttered.

I didn't like seeing Void like this. He was the cold, detached enforcer of the Saints. "Call him back."

"What?"

"Call the dickwad back. I want to speak to him," I said slower this time.

Void pulled out his phone, and soon, I could hear it ringing. I reached over and hit the speaker so I could hear everything being said.

"Void? That was fast. Do you have an answer for me already?" the man who I assumed to be Ruban answered.

"Not quite," I answered, letting the man know it wasn't who he thought it would be. "Ruban, right?"

"Ah yeah..." he answered hesitantly. "Who is this?"

"That depends. My friends call me Dax. Everyone else refers to me as Two Tricks," I quipped, trying to make sure this idiot knew exactly who he was dealing with.

There was silence for a moment, then the sound of a door being shut, and the background noise faded. "How do I know I'm talking to the real deal?"

"I'm sorry. Do you think someone else could claim to be me and still be breathing?" I shot back. "Don't waste my fucking time, Ruby. I want to make a business deal with you and that won't happen if you're being a dick."

"Holy fucking shit," Ruban blurted. "Void isn't one to lie or make promises he can't keep, but I have to admit, when he said he was shacking up with Two Tricks, I was skeptical."

My gaze flicked up to Void. "Shacking up? Really? Is that what you told him?"

"No," he bit out. "I said no such thing. Never would I degrade what we have, little demon, to such terms."

Ah, there he is. Seems like the big guy just lost his footing there a bit.

"Hey now, I didn't mean any offense. I'm a simple guy with simple logic," Ruban explained hurriedly.

"You got a woman, Ruby?" I inquired.

"N-no, why does that matter?" he stuttered.

I hit the mute button and glared at Void. "Who the fuck is this idiot? He can't be one of the four. There is no way he came up with the terms for this whole thing."

"He's not. Ruban is the go-between. You don't talk to the four. They only speak through their people. It's how they make sure who they are isn't discovered," Void informed me.

Groaning, I dropped my head to his knees. My men were amazing, and they got shit done their own way, building up the Phantom Saints into what they were now, but damn, did they have a lot to learn about the criminal underbelly.

"Ah, hello?" Ruben called.

Lifting my head, I smacked the mute button and took the phone from Void's hand. "Listen up, Ruby Slippers, because this is vitally important."

"Yeah, okay, I'm listening," he answered.

"Good, now, put this phone into the hands of one of the four, or I'm going to hunt you down and skin you for the information with a dull knife," I added for encouragement.

The sound of Ruban sputtering filled the air as he tried to come to terms with what I'd just told him. "Wha... how... you don't understand. You might be fucking scary, but you're not just behind the next door, ready to fuck up my shit if I even think about doing that."

"No, I might not be right behind the next door, but you'll never know when I'm going to strike," I warned, letting my voice purr with danger. "Ruban, would you like to live to see your next birthday? You know the one that is in two weeks."

"How do you know that?" He gasped.

"I also know where you live, eat, sleep, take a shit, and stick your dick," I informed him. "So I would think real hard about my request before telling me no."

"Can you give me time to think this over?" Ruban asked.

Okay, well, that told me these four weren't someone to be trifled with. The threat I just laid down for Ruban was one not many wouldn't buckle under.

"You have a half hour. If I don't hear back from you, then I'll assume you've chosen to keep your secrets, and I'll need to carve them out of you," I said, then hung up the phone before he could utter any reasons.

I looked up and found Eagle, Wes, and Cam standing behind the couch, watching me with a mix of expressions. Some were impressed, while others seemed to be incredibly disapproving.

Giving them a small wave, I smiled. "Hey, guys."

"How the fuck did you know all that?" Eagle blurted. "I didn't think we had anything on those guys."

"Ah, well, it seems that the one thing Wes found other than Ruban's full name was his birthday because it was listed on his Snapchat. Then when I added him as my friend, I was able to see his location on a whole bunch of places that he goes to all the time. No clue if they are any of the locations that I referred to, but it seemed to freak him out enough," I shared.

Wes just shook his head, smirking. "Damn kids and their apps."

"Little demon, doing what you just did could ruin the whole thing," Void scolded. "If Ruban decides he isn't going to make the deal and let us talk to one of the four, they'll just pass on the whole thing all together."

"Yeah, I know, but it's a risk we have to take. I'm a big player in this world, and if they won't take my phone call, then I've fallen to a point we might as well give up the fight and let Marco take over. This will tell us who is against or for us. While the actual battle might be between Marco and me, whoever wins will change the game entirely," I explained. "If Marco wins and I'm kicked out, the whole West Coast is going to change. Power will shift, creating a vacuum, and since no one actually knows how much I control, they don't realize how big that vacuum will be."

Cognac jogged down the stairs and plopped on the couch, looking confused. "That doesn't make sense. If he takes you out, then doesn't he get the Empire?"

"If they'll let him take it," I answered with a grin. "See, the thing is, the people who aren't in California that I oversee personally run their business like a store manager. They report to me, but they drive the ship and send me my dues. While I'm one person and the head of the snake, the body could still survive without me. I don't keep records of everything all in one spot. It's scattered in many different locations on backup servers and such. Everything is renamed with numbers, so you can't tell who it is or where they are."

"So that's how you did it," Cam mused. "I always wondered why no matter how hard we dug and who we got to turn on, you didn't have anything useful to tell us. It helped me from having to cover up stuff all the time. It's quite brilliant."

I yelped as the phone in my hands started to vibrate, scaring the piss out of me. Looking down at the number, it wasn't saved, but it had a New York area code. Glancing up at Void, he nodded, so I answered it.

"Tell me you have good news for me, Ruby," I said once the call connected.

There was a moment of silence before a voice cleared, then spoke, "This isn't Ruban. You can call me Mr. Three."

A smile bloomed on my face as I looked at the others and pointed to the phone as if proving my point. "It's a pleasure to speak with you, Mr. Three."

"Ruban said you had something you wished to chat with us about?" Three inquired.

I took half a beat before I answered just because, as far as I was concerned, we were equals in this world of ours. "Yeah, see, the thing is that I wanted to do this whole fight thing as a whole coming-out party. The world knew me as Dax, the enforcer, but what I need now is for people to see me as Two Tricks, the ruler of the Hidden Empire. The terms you laid out just aren't matching with the respect I'm owed and why I'm even considering doing this."

"Respect... I see," Three mused. "What exactly did you have in mind? We are always interested if it can be made into a profit for us. What do they call it?"

"Mutually beneficial," I offered, knowing full well he knew the term.

"Hmm, yes, that's the one," Three agreed. "Now tell me how you can help us and help yourself at the same time. Don't think we aren't aware of your feud with Diego. If you're going to bring hell down around us, that isn't going to benefit us in the slightest."

"Diego and I have never liked each other, but for him to blame me for the son he killed is taking things a little too far. All I want to do is prove I can show up on his turf if I wanted to and leave still alive," I explained. "As for what I can offer you, that depends on how many bodies you want to clean up after. The bloodier the fight, the more the crowd loves it. They drink, gamble, and fuck their way through the night. So that being said, the only thing I'm not willing to do is fight my own people."

"You understand how things work here perfectly," Three complimented. "I wasn't in favor of you fighting Void as it was. One of you would die, and in my eyes, that would be a lose-lose situation. He is one of the most ruthless and blood-thirsty fighters I've ever witnessed, but word on the street is you two are matched in that."

"My little demon and I are soul mates. We are perfect for each other in every way," Void stated.

Part of me cringed at him saying that, knowing it would tell them we are also each other's weaknesses. Men like Three would glean any information they could about people to use against them when the time was right. While it was clear I was with all these men, I wasn't sure advertising just how far I would go to protect them or avenge their deaths would be wise.

"Delightful," Three crooned through the phone. "Then let me propose a few different ideas. We still want fights with you two, individually. That will be expected. What I want to change is weapons will be allowed, not guns obviously but knives perhaps?"

I glanced at Void and he shrugged, not caring one way or the other. "Knives would be fine. Is there any other weapon just so we make sure to prepare to give you the best show? You wouldn't want it to be over too quickly, now would you?"

"Oh, you are as sharp as everyone says," Three said with a chuckle. "The other crowd favorite is bare hands with brass knuckles. People still bleed but don't die quite as quickly."

"Either of those options is fine with us. Just know if it ends up being something else, or you try to surprise us with a weapon out of left field, it won't end well for you," I warned. "What is the other idea?"

"Instead of you fighting against each other, we want you to fight as a team against an unknown number of attackers," Three answered.

Hell, that was a piece of cake. We proved that when we fought the other day. I wanted to agree outright, but something told me to question it.

"Weapons as well?" I asked.

I could hear Three laughing on the other end as if I'd just said the most hilarious thing to him. "Why can't more people be like you? It's far more fun to plan these things with criminals who know the game. To answer your question, yes, with weapons."

"No guns," I ordered.

"Absolutely, as I said before, to die too quickly means we lose out on money," Three agreed. "Now, I just want to make sure I got this information correct, but you are giving us free choice in who you fight as well as who we invite to the event?"

Glancing at the others, double-checking they didn't have any last-minute changes of heart, I answered, "Had to make it worth your while."

"Indeed, this is going to be the biggest event we've ever hosted," Three commented. "We might even need to find a different venue that will hold everyone. While you two will be the main course, the others have fighters they want to put in the ring as well. They will be the warm-up, getting the crowd going for you to make your appearance."

"Works for me," Void said, and I echoed his agreement.

"It was lovely to speak with you, Tricks. I do hope that however this feud ends, we might see more of you in the future," Three stated cryptically before he hung up.

Setting the phone down on the couch next to me, I waited for the others to share their thoughts. None of them seemed eager to speak, so silence hung in the air.

"It's what we hoped for," Void said, breaking the quiet. "It could have been much worse for us if our little demon hadn't been so wise to his game."

"Cockroaches like him always have a game. It's just figuring out what motivates them," I explained. "Really, that's the secret to getting most people to do what you want if we're being honest."

Eagle nodded and ran a hand through his hair before letting out a heavy sigh. "Okay, so this is our main plan, but I still think we need to have alternatives if this doesn't play out the way we want. There's no guarantee they won't back out or flip on us."

"Let's call a meeting of the minds," Wes suggested. "I finally got word back from her teachers and hacked into the school's database to pull her submitted work for the school year. It's not at all what everyone was led to believe."

Eagle pulled out his cell and sent out a text, calling the others back to the house. They left earlier that day to deal with an issue at one of the garages. It'd been broken into and vandalized. It seemed one or two Mad Dogs still lived and weren't at all happy with how things turned out.

"When are you calling Church?" Void asked. "The Saints are getting restless and want to be informed of what's really going on. The rest of us have been telling them to shut up and wait, but that's not gonna last much longer."

"Tonight, we'll have our meeting. Then we'll have everyone gather in the clubhouse at eight o'clock sharp. I want *everyone* at this meeting, Void, women included. Cam and Wes can watch the kids at the daycare while we chat," Eagle instructed.

Cam's head snapped up from where he'd been reading something on his phone. "Hey, why the fuck are we watching the kids? Aren't we part of this?"

Eagle just looked at him almost as if he was waiting for him to figure out the answer on his own.

"What?" Cam asked, exasperated.

"Why do you need to be part of the meeting when you know everything that's going on? You're not a member of the Phantom Saints, and I'm not sure I want them knowing you're an FBI agent," Eagle explained. "We are a group of one-percenters. We do illegal things all the time and having a Fed wandering around freely might freak them out."

Cam seemed to take a second to consider that and nodded. "Fine, but Dax has to be with us too. She isn't part of the Saints either."

Getting up from the couch, I walked over to Cam as he turned to face me. "Funny thing about that... part of the meeting is to see if I'm voted in, so I have to be there. Guess you're gonna have to deal with the rug rats all on your own."

"Wait, what?" Wes demanded. "You're a woman?"

"Glad you remembered. I wasn't sure since no one's checked in the last few days," I quipped. "Look, I didn't put them up to this. BigFoot approached Picasso, had enough of the crew backing him up. It had to be put to a vote by the leadership."

"What if they say no?" Cam asked, cocking his head. "Does that mean you can't live here?"

I let out a bark of laughter. "You're only asking that because you're tired of sleeping on an air mattress in the same room as Wes."

He shrugged. "Can't blame a guy for trying to better his situation."

"If they wanted to get rid of me that easily, they lost their chance a long time ago. Now these assholes are stuck with me," I informed them all.

Eagle and Void both had big dopy smiles on their faces.

"Forever, you forgot the forever on the end of that statement," Void pointed out. "Because there isn't a chance in hell we would let you leave."

Cam caught my arm and spun me around so my back was to his chest with his arms wrapped around me. "As long as you're fine with the baggage she brings along with her."

The guys chuckled at that, but the conversation was derailed as the others arrived. Cognac looked pissed, which was highly unusual for him always being my happy-go-lucky-glass-half-full man.

"What's wrong?" I asked, pulling out from Cam's hold.

Cognac just shook his head and went right for the refrigerator, where he grabbed a beer. I turned to Sprocket, who took a seat at the breakfast counter, looking subdued. When my gaze shifted to Picasso, my brows rose at seeing the look of rage on his face.

"Okay, someone needs to talk and tell me who I'm stabbing," I ordered. "What the fuck happened?"

Picasso met my gaze as he spoke through clenched teeth. "They left us a present at the scene."

"What? I thought this was the Mad Dogs retaliating?" Eagle questioned.

His brother let out a huff. "Yeah, that's what we thought too until we found this." Picasso pulled an envelope out of his pocket and handed it to Eagle.

Quickly he opened it and pulled the letter out and scanned it quickly. "Show me." Eagle snapped.

"I won't show it to you, no one needs to see that, but I'll tell you what reminder they left for Demitri," Picasso said before taking a shaky breath. "It was her ears."

"Who's ears? Elena?" I asked, snatching the letter out of Eagle's hand.

It seems you are no longer useful to me, Demitri, with how little information we've gotten from you as of late. I think you've forgotten what it is that I still hold in my possession, or do you not care anymore? Possibly you need a reminder, so I've sent one along.

How many more pieces of her can I keep cutting off before it becomes something she can't afford to lose? If you want this to end, then keep up your part of the deal. Two Tricks is planning something. Rumor is she's coming to me. Get me information on the plan, and your sister will keep what is still attached to her body.

P.S. I couldn't decide which one to take, so I sent them both.

Diego De León

Chapter Eleven

Dax

We knew word of us coming to New York wasn't going to stay quiet for long, but I didn't plan on Diego retaliating this fast. Demitri had sent word that Pinky had been found out and killed, so he was laying low until the dust settled. It would seem he felt it'd been too long and wanted answers. Well, the bastard just upped the ante by pulling this kind of stunt. If the Phantom Saints weren't out for blood before, they were now.

"That man's a sick fuck," Cognac muttered, slamming his beer on the counter. "We never would have known about the letter if Demitri hadn't shown it to us. They placed it in his locker along with the present wrapped in a pretty wooden box."

"How do we know they are her ears?" I asked.

Picasso gripped his stomach like he was trying not to gag before he could answer me. "Demitri said the earrings were the same she wore the day she was taken. Opal studs Gabby got her for her birthday just two weeks earlier."

"Do you have the ears?" I pressed.

"Why the fuck are you asking that?" he challenged. "We're talking about my niece here, not some two-bit criminal you can gawk at the remains. Have some respect."

While I knew he was coming from a place of anger and fear, I didn't appreciate his attitude or the fact he assumed I was asking out of morbid curiosity. "Listen, jackass. I'm asking this because it's really fucking simple to cut off someone else's ears, put in the damn earrings, and claim they're your loved one. Fuck, have a little faith in me, would you? I'm not a complete monster."

Picasso looked appropriately scolded but didn't say anything as he walked out of the house. My assumption was he went to get the ears, but I wasn't sure, so I followed after him. He headed right for his bike parked right at the bottom of the stairs and lifted the flap to one of the saddle bags.

Seeing him pull out the wooden box, I jogged down the steps and placed my hand over his. "You already had to look at this once. Just let me handle it from here. I know family means everything to you, and I want to do my best to bring her back home safe and sound."

Without speaking, he nodded and let me take the box from him. I didn't return to the house. Instead, I headed for Wes's command center, where no one but my guys would bother me. Weston made sure everyone knew they weren't welcome in the new space, and if he found anyone messing with things, he would break their hands. And they call me the crazy one. *Ha!*

I flipped on the lights in the snug little room, setting the box on the desk. Opening one of the side drawers, I pulled out the magnifier Wes used when putting tiny computer parts together. This wouldn't be the first time I've been skeptical about body parts being sent to me. Hostages were valuable and you didn't do anything that might kill them off while they were still of use to you.

Slowly, I opened the lid and used tweezers to lift the edge of the cloth wrapped around them. To me, it looked like a fancy handkerchief with the initials DDL sewn into one corner. The man was good with theatrics if you asked me, but it was the same reason I like to leave an ace card with my flaming skull on it, so they knew who did the deed. It's how you trained people to fear you, which was half the battle of gaining power.

While I obviously had no medical training to be able to tell if these ears came off a woman or if they matched the right age, I could tell if the earrings were shoved through the ear once they were cut off. At first glance, they looked fine, but with how gruesome something like this was to the loved one, they don't look that close at the details, just like now. One earring was far too off-center and angled funny. Even with a piercing gun, it wouldn't be at this angle, plus I would bet money that there was no way a woman like Gabby would let her kid have a jacked-up piercing. She was far too detailed and liked to make a show of being a well-off lawyer to draw in clients. It made me wonder if she owned that house or rented it for the part to make us think she owned it.

Feeling confident that there was a high chance of these not being her ears, I went to hunt down Demitri. He might be a guy and clueless about earrings, but he might remember a disapproving conversation between mother and daughter. As I walked through the clubhouse, I spotted him knocking back a shot. Can't say I blamed the guy after what he just found. Hopping up on a stool next to him, I caught the eye of the new bartender, Tops.

"I'll have one of what he's having," I said.

Tops scowled. "You sure? He's got horrible taste in liquor."

"What is it?" I questioned, curious what could be so bad that a bartender would warn you off it.

Grabbing a bottle, he slammed it on the counter and just raised a brow as I read the label. "Oh, that shit can fuck all the way off," I blurted. "Damn, son, why the hell are you drinking El Toro? Do you want to feel like a shit stain tomorrow?"

"What does it matter? I'm the reason my sister doesn't have ears anymore," Demitri slurred.

My gaze snapped up to Tops. "How many of those has he had?"

"Oh, this is his bottle. It was full when he set it on the counter. I told him he couldn't drink it like that. I don't want people thinking I actually use this swill," Tops explained.

The bottle in question was about half full and that just made me feel nauseous. "How long has he been sitting here?"

"Twenty minutes or so ago, he stumbled in," Tops answered. "Figured it was better to keep an eye on him instead of kicking him out for being a drunken mess. Damn, you should hear the things he's been babbling on about. Guy needs to stop playing so many video games or something."

Great. So much for keeping this on the down low.

"I'm gonna take him back to the house. You hide that bottle or dump it out for all I care," I instructed, feeling it was best to get him the hell out of the public eye.

"Good call. Someone might actually believe what he's saying about being a rat," Tops commented, giving me a look that told me he was one of them.

I held his gaze a moment, but I didn't see any trouble coming from him, just being a true brother to his fellow crew member. "Thanks, Tops, you're good people."

Sliding off the stool, I shoved the box in my back pocket where it barely fit, but I needed both hands to deal with the drunken mess. "Alright, here we go." Grabbing an arm, I pulled it over my shoulders and dragged him with me.

Thankfully, he could still stumble about and wasn't dead weight. At this point, I would have taken him by the ankles and hauled his ass back to the house like the moron he was. *What the hell was he thinking, getting lit and flapping his gums about being a rat?* Fuck, I had so many other things to worry about, and taking care of this kid wasn't one of them.

Sprocket was on the porch steps, probably waiting for me to come back when he spotted what I was dealing with. He set his own beer down and made his way over to us. "What the hell happened?"

"What always happens when you drink bad tequila, poor life choices," I answered. "Damn fool is sharing all the secrets as he tried to smother his sorrows in a bottle of paint thinner."

Sprocket took the other side, but our height difference made this awkward in another way. Finally, I gave up and just let Sprocket handle the problem as I got to the top of the stairs first to open the door for them.

"The fuck is going on?" Eagle demanded from his nephew. "God, why does your breath smell like it could be lit on fire?"

I chuckled to myself. "That's about all that shit is good for. Found him in the clubhouse knocking back shots like it was water. Kind of impressive for it being El Toro if you ask me."

"Sprocket put him on the couch, and someone find a bucket that boy can puke in," Eagle instructed, then he turned to me. "So?"

"There is a chance it might not be her," I answered in a low voice. "I stopped to talk to him because I wanted to know if he remembered her fighting with Gabby about getting her ears pierced without permission. One piercing seems too far off the mark for it to have been done professionally."

"No, Gabby took her on her tenth birthday to get her ears pierced. It was all she wanted for her birthday," Eagle shared. "I remember Gabby telling me how still Elena sat for the lady doing it, saying she wanted them to be perfect. Elena is just as particular as Gabby is about details. It would have bothered her to have it off-center."

"Then these aren't her ears," I stated, pulling the box out of my back pocket. "My money is on that wasn't her finger either. They've kept her too long, and I doubt they would waste a hospital trip to keep her healthy. If you don't treat a missing finger, you could bleed out."

Eagle's shoulders sagged in relief as he guided me toward Picasso's room. "Tell him. He won't listen to me, but I bet he'll listen to you."

"That is if he doesn't cuss me out again," I muttered, entering into the space.

There he stood before his easel, a new canvas set up that he was sketching something out. Keeping silent, I approached and tried to figure out what he was trying to process. It was a tree, but not one I would think of depicting life. Instead, it looked like it was sick, dying, gnarled, and knotted. The branches seemed to be trying to reach out and grab the viewer if only they could make it off the canvas. What I was more curious about was to know who exactly this was depicting. Himself? Me? Our enemies? Maybe even the world as a whole.

"I'm almost positive they aren't hers," I whispered.

His hand faltered for just a moment before he continued. I understood this state of mind. It had been building and building up inside him until he was ready to burst. Now he was using that emotion and spilling it onto this canvas. So I watched and waited, picked up a pad of drawing paper, and started to sketch him. I was trying to capture everything I could feel flowing out of him, curious to see if that could translate into an image when there were no words to explain it.

Having no idea how long we stayed like this until Eagle opened the door to call us for dinner. That seemed to be enough for Picasso to break out of his trance and jump in surprise when he saw me sitting on a stool next to him.

"When did you get here, spitfire?" he asked.

Flipping the pad around, I showed him my drawing, knowing that would give him a better answer.

"Why didn't you say anything?" he questioned as he slid his hands up my thighs until his fingertips slipped under the hem of my shorts.

I narrowed my gaze at him. "You really don't remember me coming in here and telling you that I'm pretty sure those aren't Elena's ears?"

His whole body snapped back at my words. "What?"

"When I looked at them more closely, I noticed that the earrings had been shoved through the lobes and were super off-center. Eagle and I talked about it, and there's no way they could be her ears," I explained.

Picasso dropped his head on my shoulder, letting out a heavy sigh. "God, I can't believe I said those things to you before. I'm so sorry, spitfire. I was so mad I couldn't help but take it out on everyone. That's why I knew I needed to come in here and draw, paint, something to get my feelings under control."

I gripped the back of his neck and gave him an awkward neck hug. "If anyone understands that, I do. Art is what helps us process, and you haven't been able to do that while Eagle's been out of commission. Now that he is healing, the weight of responsibility has been lifted from you. Thank you all the same for apologizing and admitting you were an ass."

"Hey now," Picasso warned, nipping at my neck. "Don't push your luck."

"Ha," I laughed, pushing him off me. "That's what I do every damn day, and I don't see it changing anytime soon."

His hand snapped out, grabbing me by the throat as he pulled me in for a kiss, slow and wanting. I could feel my body perk up at the idea of maybe getting some action, but we both groaned when there was a sharp rap on the door.

"Let's go, I want to eat," Cognac hollered.

Hopping off the stool, I tossed open the door. "I've got something you can eat, lover," I teased Cognac, who was leaning near the door making sure we came out.

A slow, sultry grin crossed his face. "Damn, who could pass up an offer like that."

"Hey," Eagle barked. "Sit the fuck down for dinner."

While many of my ideas had fallen on deaf ears, moving the pool table and putting in a real dining room table where we could all sit had stuck. Now, for almost every meal, we all gathered and ate together. It had become something I looked forward to. We made a rule that at breakfast, we couldn't talk about anything to do with this job. It had to be about us. Dinner was the opposite. It was our chance to compare notes of events that happened during the day.

I'd spotted Demitri passed the hell out on the couch and hadn't even flinched at Eagle yelling. That's what made me feel like it would be safe enough to talk about things while he was here.

Today I was sitting between Sprocket and Cognac. They'd come up with this silly rule that every dinner, I had to rotate around the table so I wasn't sitting next to the same person all the time. If it's what made them feel better, then so be it. Things around the house had been relatively friendly, for which I was thanking whatever being was looking down on us.

"Dax, why don't you start us off with what you found out," Eagle suggested. "I feel like that will ease quite a few minds."

Shrugging, I shared my discovery. "I would bet just about anything that those ears aren't Elena's, and if I'm being honest, I don't think the finger was either. She is far too valuable as a hostage and cutting her up that bad doesn't serve the greater purpose. What they hope for is exactly what happened. The loved one is far too shocked and doesn't even look twice."

It was almost as if a hidden tension in the room broke at my words. Everyone around the table seemed to relax ever so slightly.

"Fuck, I'm glad to hear you say that," Cognac blurted. "I know the little girl, and she doesn't deserve that kind of torture. She's a good kid."

"About that," Wes interjected. That had everyone's attention. "I talked to a bunch of her teachers, and while she was still at school, she wasn't attending classes, not the ones she signed up for, at least. They remember her being there for the first few months, then she dropped off. One or two of them commented that they saw her on campus, but she wasn't in those classes for months."

I could feel my brow knitting as I considered this information. "Is there any way to find out if she switched classes? Or started sitting in on a different lecture or something?"

"I'm pulling security footage for around the time they remember her no longer showing up. There's also some cameras around her dorm room, so I'll see what I can find there too.

Whatever was happening, it wasn't an article for her class that had her in the city during that break," Wes reasoned.

Looking at Eagle and Picasso, I could tell they were heartbroken to hear about this. What made it even harder for me was that I knew the signs, and something in my gut told me that Diego had got his claws into her. He knew damn well who the Phantom Saints were and how he could use someone like them to get to me. I'd hated MCs forever because they turned their backs on each other but not this group of men. They were just the opposite. What had my stomach churning was if Demitri had given them far more information than he realized.

Just how much could Diego De León really know about me? If they wanted the power to manipulate Two Tricks, then all Diego had to do was use the guys. No. I couldn't think like that. There had to be a different reason as to what caused Elena to drop out of her classes.

Chapter Twelve

Sprocket

While having the information that Elena wasn't missing her ears, finding out she wasn't taking her classes seemed to dim that revelation. Dax seemed to vibrate with hidden anxiety as I'm sure she was trying to process what that meant as much as we were. My little rebel was skilled at covering her emotions but not from me. She'd never been able to. Since the day I met this woman, I'd been able to read her like a book because we were so much alike.

"What else do we know?" I asked, hoping someone would have another piece of this puzzle.

"Dax and I solidified the terms for the fight," Void shared. "They will have us doing cage fights with knives or brass knuckles against whoever they choose to pin against us. Then, after we win those, we'll be paired together against however many people they want to put against us."

Carefully, I glanced at the others around the table, gauging how they were taking the news. While this was a smart plan that met the needs to keep us alive in the city, part of me wondered if we needed to go to such great lengths. *What if Elena chose them?* One of their men could have gotten to her and now they were using her as leverage against her brother and us to get information. Every step of the way since Marco made Dax his mission to destroy, we'd been one step behind.

"Are we sure this is the best move?" I questioned. "I know none of us want to think this, but what if Elena isn't a hostage? We need to consider that she might have given her loyalty to them and they've been using her to get what they want. Marco's whole purpose is to destroy Dax, and she's survived everything he's thrown at her, but he is a man who plays the long game."

She shifted in her seat to look at me with an expression that told me she'd been thinking the same thing.

Eagle nodded. "You're right."

"What?" Picasso demanded.

If there was anyone blind to the reality that family could turn on you, it was Picasso. His brother complex didn't just apply to Eagle, but anyone in his family, even though he knows they've both been betrayed by that very same family before.

"Let's face it, Picasso. Elena isn't a little girl anymore, and she's been in New York almost a year. We haven't seen her since her high school graduation. Lots can change. I'm not going to sit here and pretend I know Elena or what choices she would make in life," Eagle stated as he scooped food onto his plate and passed it around. "If we want to survive going to New York, we need to have our eyes wide the fuck open."

The table fell into silence as we dished up food and started eating. Dax was the one to break the quiet first.

"It could be as simple as love," she said. "When a woman believes she is in love with someone, it can be all-consuming. Let's say someone from the cartel ran into her at school, they hit it off, started to go out, and she shares her upbringing. They find out about the Phantom Saints, they know you're trying to make a deal with me, and they see the perfect in. When you're that young, love makes you stupid," Dax added, her tone harsh as if she was talking more to herself than to us.

My gaze flicked to Cam, who looked at her with a flash of sorrow and regret. It was clear something deeper than we know happened between them, but I was a firm believer people will tell you their story when they're ready or they won't.

"Son of a bitch," Wes swore as he pushed away from the table and grabbed his computer.

Taking his seat, we waited as he searched for whatever he was looking for, and when he found it, he stabbed his knife into the table. "How the fuck did I miss that? Goddamn son of a bitch, I'm an idiot."

Cam leaned forward on one arm and grinned. "Tell us something we don't know."

The knife that had been in the table went flying across the table and left a nick on Cam's cheek when he didn't move out of the way. "Shut the fuck up, or next time, I won't just scratch you." Wes threatened.

The idiot mimed locking his lips and throwing away the key, then perched his chin in both hands, waiting for Wes to continue.

"Diego has a son who is two years older than Elena, who goes to school there. He's going for his MBA and has an excellent GPA for never attending any of his classes. Yet, somehow, the work always gets done and submitted right on time," Wes shared as he scanned whatever information he was looking at.

"How many kids does this guy have?" Cognac asked, rubbing his hand over his buzzed head.

Wes looked up from the laptop and twisted the thing around to show us a list of names. "Just a few."

"Jesus," I blurted, looking at the long list that appeared on the screen. "Most of them have different last names, bastards?" I guessed.

"From what I can tell, he supports them all but only gave his last name to the children they bore with his legal wife Mariana," Wes explained. "I'm sure there are reasons for that, but what it tells me is that he has a relationship of sorts with these kids. What if one found out about Elena's connection to us and manipulated her into thinking she was helping or that he was in love with her, like Dax said? This at least gives us a starting point."

Everyone nodded their agreement as we turned to our own thoughts on the matter. It was one of the quietest meals we'd had in a long time, but under the circumstances, what more did we have to say? When we were done eating, we left the clean-up for later since we needed to get to the clubhouse for the meeting Eagle called.

Cam and Wes headed off to deal with the ten kids who would be left in their care. I had faith in them, even if they both looked clueless about what to do. Most of the kids were toddlers, the rest under the age of six. Plus, if they needed help that badly, we were one building over.

Eagle had the five of us standing on the stage as everyone else gathered around. Dax was off to the side, leaning against a wall keeping a lower profile than I expected. Not once had she asked us what our answer would be when it came time to vote if she was added to the crew or not. Granted, she knew regardless, we were never going to let her go, but her faith in us to make the best choice hadn't gone unnoticed.

The room was full of people talking amongst themselves, moods ranging from curious to nervous. We hadn't called a meeting of this magnitude in years, and that had been at the beginning of our time as leaders. The room fell silent when Eagle stepped forward and raised his hand to get everyone's attention.

"Thank you, everyone, for making it here tonight. I know we don't do these types of meetings often, but I feel like it's only fair for everyone to know what's going on," Eagle started trying to settle nerves. "I wanted to start with the announcement that there is an alliance between the Hidden Empire and the Phantom Saints. When you mess with one of us, you have to deal with us both. I'm sure you noticed when we were attacked by the Mad Dogs, we had the Empire stepping up to assist."

Everyone nodded and whispered to each other in a positive manner about the situation.

"That being said, the Empire, more directly Tricks herself, is being targeted by a rival drug lord from Mexico. His one and only mission is to take her out and absorb her network into his own, making him the ruler of the West Coast. The Mad Dogs were part of that, but we crushed them under our boots like the cockroaches they are," Eagle roared at the end, sending the room into a flurry of cheers and whistles.

He let it go on for a few moments, then gestured for them to settle down. "Soon, we will have another enemy to crush that has gone after Dax and one of our own. The De León Cartel has taken my niece hostage and is trying to leverage her for information that will help bring the Empire down. This will not be tolerated, and we will not stand by as they go after our families because we look after our own."

Cries of agreement and more whistles echoed his words. I couldn't help but grin as our president stood tall and strong, glowing in his element. This is what made him the leader they all respected. He valued the same things they did, fought beside them, and knew how to rally his people to the call.

"The other day, one of you approached Picasso requesting that we vote on allowing Dax to become a member of the Phantom Saints. We took our time considering what would be best for our crew and the future of the Saints." Eagle looked at me, and I turned to grab the two items he was looking for just as the clubhouse door opened, showing Wes and Cam joining us as we planned.

Casting a glance at Dax, I saw her push off the wall clearly aware that we were planning something she wasn't aware of.

"Most of you know Dax isn't just another member to us but our lover as well. She is with the five of us along with Weston and Cameron," Eagle explained as the two men joined us on the stage. "This is an arrangement we've all agreed on and hold it with the same sanctity you do with your partner. That being said, Dax, will you come up here to hear our verdict on the request to induct you into the Phantom Saints."

The cagy look that she gave us had me holding back laughter. If there was one thing Dax hated more than anything, it was surprises, public ones being an even worse transgression. Stepping up on the stage, she looked ready for anything, her hands loose at her side but ready to pull her gun from her low-back holster. This woman loved us but living in the darkness of the world trained you to always question situations you couldn't see the outcome of.

As if we'd rehearsed it, we all dropped to one knee as Eagle lifted the ring box, lid pulled back so she could see what we offered her. It was a ring with an ace of spades with a skull on top of it, the eye sockets filled with two diamonds. It was a combination of our logo, her personal calling card, and what engagement ring would be complete without a diamond or two.

"Dax Rose Blackmore, will you marry us?" Eagle asked.

I once believed that nothing could shock this woman, but from what I was seeing at this moment, we'd made her speechless.

"We've all talked, and there is no one else for us but you. Please make us the happiest men forever by being ours as much as we are yours," Picasso added, trying to give her time to wrap her head around what was going on.

Dax shook her head slowly as a smile tugged at her lips. "The fact that you all want to tie yourselves to my crazy ass means you've lost your ever-loving minds."

"So, is that a yes?" Cognac asked, his voice hopeful.

"Fuck my life in the best way possible, yes," she answered, tossing her hands up in the air like she had no other choice.

The room erupted in cheers so loud I thought the building would come down. We'd all known if we did this with just the eight of us, she would have found a way to avoid the answer. Doing it in front of everyone was risky but also forced her to give us her true and honest choice. Eagle stood, passing the ring box to Void, who pulled it out and slid it on her finger. Now she was smiling like an idiot, fully accepting what we were offering.

Void pulled her in and kissed the shit out of her. Next was Cognac, then Wes snuck in there, whispering something in her ear that made her laugh before he stole his own kiss. Picasso pulled her out of his hold, but instead of kissing her, he guided her to the front of the stage.

"Now that we've gotten that part settled, I feel confident in giving you our answer on membership," Eagle said with a chuckle as he displayed the cut he'd had draped over one arm. "I present to you, Little Queen, our co-president and wife. This is unorthodox for an MC to even consider adding a woman to the crew, let alone making her leadership. I think you would all agree she has more than earned her place in our midst as well as shown her value as a leader. As queen of the Empire, it would have been wrong for her to be anything less than our partner in crew as well as in life."

Eagle shifted, holding the cut open for her to slide on easily. Dax's eyes were wide as she took in the eager faces of the crew, then back to us. Ever so slowly, she slipped her arms into the cut and grinned down at the patches sewn on it.

"That's not all," Picasso interjected. "We would also like to welcome Weston Price to the Phantom Saints as our new Sergeant at Arms. He is now fully in charge of security and defense of the compound. It's what he's already been doing. We're just officially giving him the title. Next, we welcome Cameron Black into the crew as our Secretary. He will be in charge of all meetings, records, and coordination between outside law enforcement."

"As your leaders, we know this is a big change, but if you think about it, these men have already been doing these roles, having zero expectation of being brought into the crew. What we want the Phantom Saints to represent is how important loyalty is to each and every one of us. Every person earns the right to wear these cuts and no choice is made lightly," Eagle explained, noticing the uncertain looks flitting about the crowd.

Dax stepped up in between the two newly patched men and gave everyone a wide grin. "Don't worry. If they fuck up, I'll see that they're punished to the full extent of my abilities."

That simple teasing set everyone at ease, making them chuckle. They might not trust the guys, but Dax had them eating out of the palm of her hand. The bold, brash woman said it like it was and didn't hold back. This is what made people trust her. She said what she meant and meant what she said.

"Alright, everyone, settle down. We have one more important matter we need to discuss," Eagle announced, waving his hands to hush everyone. "In another week or so, the eight of us will be leaving for New York. In our place, Mutt and Gator will be proxy president and vice president. They will still be in contact with us about how things are going, but if there is an immediate need, they will be who you're going to. These men are like brothers to me and have been loyal since the beginning. They play vital roles but for us, every day, recruiting business as well as members along with managing our other shops off property. Give them the respect they deserve, and I know everything will go smoothly."

My brows rose as Dax stepped up next to Eagle, resting her hand on his arm, letting him know she had something to say. The choice to make Dax a co-president was one that all seven of us argued about for days. It wasn't until yesterday when the patch had to be placed that we agreed it was the best call. I'd been team co-president all the way, but Wes and Picasso worried adding more to her plate might not be wise. What they didn't understand is she was going to take that role whether we gave her the title or not. She didn't know how to be anything other than a leader of people.

"Eagle might be one for the diplomatic approach, but I'm sure you've seen that isn't really my thing. That being said, Gator and Mutt bleed Phantom Saints, so does Tilly for that matter," Dax stated. "If word gets back to us that you've been disrespecting those we've decided to put in charge, then you'll be having a chat with me about it when we get back."

That was threat enough for most people to take seriously. They'd all seen how her *talks* went. Most ended with something bleeding or broken if they didn't catch onto the problem fast enough.

"Any questions?" she asked, leaning her head against Eagle's arm, acting all sweet. Murmurs of no and shaking of heads were the unanimous responses to her question. "Delightful. Was there anything else we needed to go over?" Dax questioned, looking back at all of us.

Void chuckled and came up behind her, settling his hand on her hips. "I think that's enough for one night, don't you think, little demon?"

Her answer was to pull him down into a quick kiss. "Works for me, big guy."

"You heard the lady," Cognac called out to the members. "Enough of the heavy, let's party, turn on the music, and bust out the champagne. The queen of the Hidden Empire said yes to our sorry asses."

The room cheered, and Tops slid over the wooden bar to start pulling out the plastic glasses and bottles of champagne. After all the fighting and surviving we've been doing for the past month, now it was time to celebrate the life we still had, and there were no better people I wanted to party with than right here.

Chapter Thirteen

Dax

The bass reverberated through the air as we danced and partied the night away. Currently, I was sandwiched between Cam and Void, a combination I had no idea would be so explosive. Hands and mouths were everywhere on my body. I couldn't tell who belonged to what. Never once did I ever think I would be engaged or even find a man who would be my partner in life. Now seven of them had a piece of the puzzle that made up my heart. I'd locked it away, believing it was better to keep things shallow and meaningless. Each and every one of these men decided to show me differently, chipping through the ice wall I'd made to take their prize.

Every so often, another glass of champagne would be placed in my hand that I threw back, desperately thirsty from all the dancing. Ha, who was I kidding? We were practically having sex with our clothes on. If one of them were to even touch my clit, I'd come so fast, and I wouldn't even be ashamed of it. These men were working me up into a frenzy, and all I knew was they better damn well deal with the aftermath.

"What do you say we slip out of this party, beautiful? I think there's some celebrating that should be done all on our own without the public eye," Cam suggested as if he'd read my mind.

Not needing any more encouragement, I slipped out from between them and grabbed their hands. "Let's blow this joint."

As we weaved through the crowd of bikers, their women enjoying the night as much as we were made me smile. This was what they needed, a reason to let loose and forget the hardship that was going on around us. There was still life to live and those around us to live it with.

Tilly and her men were so intertwined I couldn't tell where either one of them started or ended. It was the first time I'd seen them all throw caution to the wind and revel in their choice of love. Another part of me questioned if her men didn't seem far more comfortable than I'd ever seen mine when playing together. Guess some secrets were for them and them alone.

I spotted Eagle and Sprocket chatting at the bar with someone I didn't recognize, but they'd called everyone in for this meeting. Some people chose to live off the compound, especially if their partner had a job in or near the city. While a majority decided to make this their entire life, others were loyal, coming whenever called but had other obligations as well.

The two of them spotted me dragging the others, and I just cocked a brow at them before continuing on. Cognac was playing pool, bent over aiming up his shot when I released my grip on Void to slap his ass.

"Fuck," Cognac swore totally botching the shot. "Do you have a death wish, asshole?" he snapped as he turned around, stopping short when he saw it was me.

"Sorry, just saw that juicy peach of yours and had to know if it would jiggle or not," I teased, grinning from ear to ear.

"Well? Did it?" Cognac asked, a cheeky smirk on his lips.

I tilted my head to the side, trying to see it again. "You know what? I couldn't really tell, mind bending over for me again to check?"

Cognac's head fell back as he laughed, then he grabbed me around the waist, tossing me over his shoulder. "Here, feel free to check all you want, but I must warn you, it's far more fun with less clothing on."

I heard Void say something, but it was drowned out by the music. When Cognac started to walk off with me, I figured they filled him in on the plan to have some *alone* time. Setting my hands on his tight ass, I pushed up so I could see what was going on. Laughter bubbled out of me as a trail of men followed after us like I was the Pied Piper of hot-ass bikers. I wasn't sure where Wes or Picasso appeared from, but they'd clearly caught wind of what was going on.

"You sure you can handle all that, girly?" one of the older Saints hollered after me.

I grinned and yelled back, "The real question is can they handle *me*."

He guffawed and clapped his hands, clearly enjoying my comeback. If I were being honest, all night, I'd been waiting for the older crew to have an issue with what happened here tonight, but not a peep was heard.

Soon I was carried up the steps and into the house, where I was finally set on my feet. All of my men looked at me apprehensively as if waiting for me to lose my shit. "What?"

Eagle rubbed the back of his neck as he looked at the others. "We were expecting some kind of fallout from pulling that kind of stunt on you."

"Do you want me to be mad?" I asked, crossing my arms as they all shook their heads no. "Do I appreciate being blindsided like that? Fuck no. Was that how I pictured my night going, ending up engaged to seven men and having *wife* labeled on my chest? Hell no, but who in their right mind would?" Dropping my hand to my hips, I looked at them all. "How long did it take you to plan this and actually agree?"

"About five days, give or take," Sprocket answered. "The final decision wasn't made until yesterday afternoon when we had to know what the patch was going to say."

I nodded absently as I tried to picture what kind of shitshow that might have been. "Look, did I ever want to get married? No, really. I didn't think it was in the cards for me, and it was easier to forget the whole idea. What I do know is that I don't want to lose any of you or spend the rest of my life without you. If saying yes to being your wife is what got you all to work together for a common goal without me chewing your asses out, then fuck yeah, I'll be your wife."

Taking a deep breath, I braced myself to be honest and vulnerable like I'd been trying to be better about. "Like you guys said to me on that stage, you seven are it for me. You are who I want to grow old with, but the reality is we might never see that end. With all we have going against us, I'm all about taking risks at this point."

Wes snorted. "Shortcake, when have you ever been against taking risks?"

"Real answer... my heart," I said with a shrug. "Now that's all the sappy bullshit you're going to get from me tonight. I was under the impression that you hauled me out of the party so we could celebrate as one does with their husbands."

That had Wes moving in a flash, scooping me up and heading for the stairs. The rest were hot on his heels with no argument, as if they had a plan for how this part of our night was going to go as well. Cognac cut ahead of us and threw open his door, where black rose petals littered the floor.

"See, I have the biggest bed that comes with all the added fun," Cognac explained, wagging his eyebrows as Wes tossed me on the bed.

I yelped as I bounced on the mattress, sending the petals flying into the air around me. Smirking at the guys who all stood at the end of the bed with matching looks of hunger written all over their faces, I was about to be eaten alive, and goddamn was I here for it.

Cam stepped forward and pulled something out of his pocket. I watched as the fabric slid through one hand, showing me what it was—a blindfold. "Do you remember this game, beautiful?"

Licking my lips as my mouth went dry with anticipation. "Yeah, I remember this game. It was one of your favorites if I remember, but I don't think there's room for me to run."

He flashed me a smile that was all teeth. "That only works when it's you and me. This time I thought it would be fun with this being the first time we'll all be together, that you don't know who's doing what, where, or when."

A shiver of anticipation ran through my body at his suggestion. "Fuck yes, that's exactly what I want for tonight. To me, all of you are equal. None of you mean more to me than another, so I think this is the perfect way to prove how each and every one of you is perfect for me in your own way."

Cam sat next to me on the bed, bringing the blindfold up to my face. "Any rules?"

"All of you have to come in or on me at least once, and if one of you becomes uncomfortable with whatever is going on, you speak up. This is about all of us finding pleasure together. That won't happen if something freaks you out." I met each of their gazes, making them acknowledge that rule before I turned to my black knight. "No blades, no blood. That is only for you and me."

He nodded as he leaned in, kissing me gently on the lips. "I agree completely. You're the only one who can control the darkness when I let go. That would freak them out instantly anyway."

I ran a hand along his jaw, pulling him in for another deeper kiss. "Thank you for understanding. Now, let the games begin."

The black silk was secured around my head snuggly, ensuring that I couldn't see anything. I could feel a slight breeze making me think Cam was waving his hand in front of me, checking his work.

"Alright, she's good to go," he announced. "But I think you've been ready for one of us to ravage that pussy of yours for days now. What would you say if I told you it was my idea to deprive you, so when tonight happened, you would be begging for our cocks?"

"I'd say you're the same sadistic bastard that you've always been," I shot back, grinning. "On top of that, I'm pretty sure tonight is going to be well worth the wait."

Cam chuckled as his hands slipped under my shirt, lifting it off my body. Then he removed the bralette I'd been wearing, leaving my upper body bare to them all. While I'd slept with all these men, it had been years since Cam and I were together. Even still, that man knew my body as well as any of these men, made evident when he brushed his hand down my back and dug his thumbs into the curve right above my ass.

Arching into the pressure, I felt someone moving in their mouth, closing around one of my nipples. "Oh God, you're all going to fucking ruin me, aren't you?" I gasped.

"Only in the best way possible, little rebel," Sprocket whispered into my ear before guiding my mouth to his cock. "Open wide and take it all. I know you can," he ordered, fisting my hair as he slid into my mouth.

Fuck, I loved when Sprocket, my quiet level-headed man, got bossy in the bedroom. This man knew just what he liked and wasn't afraid to say it, but he was as much a giver as a taker. I let my jaw relax as I took him deep down my throat, letting my tongue swirl around him as he pulled out. When I tried to chase after him, his grip on my hair kept me still. He was the one in charge, and I was going to listen whether I liked it or not. Lucky for me, I had no problem being the submissive if it got me off the right way. With these men, I had no worries in that department.

The mouth on my chest moved from one breast to the other, using his hand to flick the one he'd just left. Gasping at the bite of pain from how sensitive it was, I shimmied my chest, begging for more. Cam moved from behind me and guided me back as Sprocket pulled out to shove pillows behind my back so I was propped up. Then he climbed over my face and put me back to work. This move left the rest of my body open for them to descend upon and did they.

Someone spread my legs wide, letting their fingers glide up my inner thigh using their thumbs to massage around my pussy. These men clearly were in no hurry to get down to business. Instead, enjoying the fact I had no control over the situation. Fingers trailed through my pussy, parting it, swirling in the wetness I'm sure was pouring out of me at this point. A thumb worked around my clit as a finger teased the entrance to my pussy. My money was on that being Wes. Ever since he got me to fucking squirt all over him, he'd been begging for the chance to do it again. Hands grabbed mine, squirting lube into them before they were wrapped around a cock and urged to move.

Getting fucked in the mouth while having your pussy teased and trying to manage working two cocks was a hell of a lot harder than I thought it would be. Certainly gave me a fuck ton of respect for all those porn stars that make this look simple as shit. Eventually, I got into a rhythm, but it all fell apart once the person who was teasing my pussy finally sank two fingers deep inside me. Almost instantly, they found my G-spot, then their mouth sealed around my clit, sucking in time with their finger curls.

The overload of sensation I was getting slammed with right now had me unable to keep up with my hand jobs. Lucky for me, they understood my dilemma and weren't easily deterred. They just gripped my hand and fucked into it. Sprocket's hips were starting to get erratic with all the moaning and groaning I was making, causing crazy vibrations in my mouth.

"Ah, shit," he swore, the grip on my hair getting tighter as he fought to keep from coming.

Now that I knew how close he was and slightly distracted, I started sucking harder and using my tongue more.

"Hell, Dax, you're gonna make me come already," Sprocket grunted as I swallowed while he was deep down my throat. "Shit, shit, shit, I'm gonna come."

Seconds later, he slammed into my mouth as his load shot inside. His hand left my head as he must have put them on the wall, supporting himself as he gave short thrusts, emptying himself into me.

"Fuck, Dax, your mouth is simply the best," Sprocket praised as he moved off me only to claim my mouth with his.

If fucking me with his cock wasn't enough, he followed it up with his tongue, not at all bothered I probably tasted like him. Now that I didn't have a dick in my mouth, the fingers between my legs started to move faster, thrusting in and out. My hips bucked as I whimpered, feeling the pressure building deep in my core. I was going to come and come so fucking hard with how the sensation was barreling down on me.

Sprocket pulled back from my mouth and twisted one of my nipples, giving that jolt of pain, making me scream as my whole body exploded. The fingers and mouth didn't stop. If anything, it sped up to warp speed, causing me to thrash as I tried to get away from the sensation that was overwhelming me.

"Come on, Dax, give it to me," Wes encouraged, telling me I'd been right all along. "You can do it, fucking come all over me like a good little slut."

Oh, fuck, it seemed Cam spilled the beans on the dirty talk that I enjoyed when the mood called for it. Now was absolutely the right time, and it worked just like it always did, throwing me into another climax, my pussy gripping Weston's fingers like a vise as he teased me into giving him what he wanted. The sensation was unlike anything I'd experienced, and even though I now knew what it meant, I still felt like I was pissing myself, but God, it felt unbelievable to give in to that pressure and let it all out.

"Yes, just like that, keep it coming. I want you to drench this bed so badly, Cognac will never get your scent out of it," Wes ordered as I begged him to stop.

"Too much," I whimpered. "It's too much."

"Not a chance, *loba*, we're just getting started," Cognac said to my right. "I want to feel your pussy squeeze me as tight as Wes's fingers right now. That way, when I come deep inside you, that perfect pussy doesn't miss a drop."

Another cry was torn from my lips as fingers pinched my clit, causing a third orgasm. This one didn't bring about the waterworks, but it had my chest heaving, trying to suck in as much air as I could as my eyes rolled back in my head. The two who had been using my hands pulled them off their dicks and gave me a moment to just lay there a second, wondering if my soul had left my body.

Chapter Fourteen

Dax

"That was the sexiest foreplay I've ever seen," Eagle commented, his voice rough with need. "Now I think it's time for the real fun."

The bed shifted, and the others helped me to straddle who I assumed was Eagle. He hadn't gotten his stitches out yet and this was probably the best way for this to work. I was more than happy to have him lay there as I took full advantage of his cock. My hands ran up and down his chest, feeling the ripples of his muscles. Then I tweaked his nipple just for the fun of it as I slid down his length.

"Dammit, little hellcat," Eagle bit out as his hand gripped my hips tightly. "Play nice with the wounded man, would you."

"Ha," I laughed. "If you think that's gonna fly, then you don't know me at all."

Even though I was sensitive as fuck on the outside of my pussy, the inside was another story. Rolling my hips, I took him deep, then swirled to the right, then to the left, just to drive him crazy. They wanted to play rough then I was happy to oblige. Knowing he still couldn't take a beating, I settled my hands on his pec muscle and used that as my leverage. Keeping the thrusts deep and only raising my hips enough to get the friction I needed, I rode him like a jockey in the Kentucky Derby.

A hand cupped my cheek and another dick was fed into my mouth. This time I had more control over the game and tasted every inch of that cock. Another hand drifted down my back, stopping at my ass, parting my cheeks as the cool sensation of lube was dripping on my skin. These boys were going to stuff me full in whatever spot I had available, and it sounded like heaven to me. The finger massaged the tight entrance working me, but I knew it wouldn't take much effort. I loved the idea of each of my men stuffing my holes full of their cocks, owning me in every way possible. This is what I'd been dreaming of since I knew these men were utterly and completely mine. I just wasn't sure they'd enjoy the idea. Clearly, they'd worked out their differences enough to make this night happen, so I was going to stop worrying and just enjoy what they had for me.

My hips faltered as they used two fingers in my ass, making me moan around the cock in my mouth. *God, why did this feel so amazing? Who knew so many cocks all at once would be a kink for me?*

A hand settled on my low back, stopping me for a moment as they crawled up behind me. The blunt head of their cock rubbed against my ass as they made sure to lube it up before entering. Feeling I needed a better angle for this, I laid down on Eagle's chest, making sure my weight was even across his body and my knees didn't hit his sides. Last thing we needed was to rush to the hospital because I had broken his wound open, but it had been a little over a week, and I was optimistic everything would be fine.

With this new position, it gave whoever was taking my ass a straight shot which he took. In one steady motion, he pushed in until his body came to a stop at my ass cheeks. Panting, I reached out for whoever had been in my mouth, knowing this made it harder for that to happen. It didn't take me long to find it as they adjusted so I could grip it easily. Dealing with one in the hand and two inside me was easier than two but still took more thought than I'd imagined.

Eagle started to thrust up into me slow and steady while whoever was in my ass moved faster, creating the friction of fast and slow. I could feel them gliding in and out of me, hitting every single nerve with how full and stretched I was. As I relaxed even more, someone added additional lube and started to probe with a finger at the edges of my asshole, almost as if he wanted to add it to the mix.

Holy fuck were they thinking of trying to get two dick in my ass like Cognac had suggested? This new level of teamwork was either going to be epic or I was going to run out of here with a broken asshole. Guess there was only one way to find out and that was to let them try.

"Oh, did you figure out what we want to try?" Cognac asked, a sultry purr in his voice. "Look at you pushing back against my finger, so eager for more to be stuffed inside you. I think I'm going to let these brothers have their fun with you, stretching that pretty asshole out, warming it up for what we have in mind. Who knows, maybe we'll try it out with your pussy too. I know how hungry it can be for cock."

Yep, I wasn't going to survive tonight. They were going to kill me with their dirty words and even dirtier ideas of what to do with my body.

"What you aren't going to know, *loba*, is who the two are that are comfortable enough with each other to let their dicks share the same hole. You keep saying you want us to work better as a team. Well, I think this is a great start, don't you?" Cognac asked as the tip of his finger slipped inside my ass.

I groaned, burying my face in Eagle's neck. "Fucking, fuck, fuck. God, that is too much. How can a finger feel like *so* much more?"

Eagle chuckled and slapped my ass cheek. "Take it like the badass we all know you are."

In retaliation for that comment, I bit his neck, sucking the skin into my mouth, giving him a hickey that would last for weeks. He growled, and I could feel the vibration of it in my mouth, making me smile. He slapped my ass even harder and thrust deeper and faster clearly disregarding the fact he was still wounded. Right now, he was on his own. There was no way I could possibly be the responsible party at this moment.

Releasing him, I arched my back, lifting my head as I moaned, but it was soon cut off by a cock getting shoved down my throat. I gagged, but when they pulled back, I felt something that I knew for a fact none of my men had. A fucking Jacobs ladder was pierced on the underside of this dick, and I let my tongue play along the rungs to discover the tip was also adorned with a ring fitting snuggly to the flesh. *Fuck my life. Cam certainly surprised me on that one.*

Letting go of the dick I'd been stroking, I grabbed Cam's cock and let my hand wander down the shaft feeling all that adorned it. Really, I shouldn't be surprised. If any of my men were going to do this, it would be Cam. He had a love for being unexpected and not minding pain in the pursuit of pleasure. Bastard had been holding out on me this whole time. I could hear him chuckle as I used my thumb to swirl over the tip, making sure that it was only the ring he'd added.

"I see you found my surprise for you," Cam teased. "Didn't you always tell me you wondered if dick piercings were worth it?"

"What did the other women say?" I asked, having no delusions even if he kept telling me I was the only one for him.

A hand gripped my jaw tightly and his breath fell on my face in hot bursts. "How many times do I need to tell you, Dax? There had never been anyone for me but you. No other second-rate pussy could ever lure me away from what I knew I'd already had. You, my beautiful devil, are perfection incarnate."

His mouth latched on to mine as he kissed me hard, full of teeth and tongue. It grounded me as the two inside me groaned as I clenched tighter when Cam tugged on my nipple. The spark of pain helped me to clear my head enough to realize Cognac had told me Picasso was in my ass while his brother fucked my pussy. Now Cam was making out with me and no one argued or tried to push him aside. They truly had settled their differences enough for the time being.

After having had four orgasms back to back, I wasn't surprised that this next one was slow to arrive. Even if those two finished before me, it wouldn't matter. There were still five of them to go. Picasso's movements sped up, and he leaned over me, kissing my shoulders and neck as he pummeled my ass. My whole body tightened as the change caused Picasso to swear, shooting his load in my ass. Eagle was still thrusting away, keeping his movements steady, refusing to let himself go before I'd come.

Picasso gave his last few grunting thrusts into me before resting on my back for a moment, whispering in my ear, "He's right, you know, you are perfect in every way for us. No one would be able to match up." With a gentle kiss on my cheek, ignoring that Cam still had my lips, he pulled out.

Now it was my turn to have some fun with the president. Shoving Cam back, I sat up tall on Eagle and grinned, looking down to where I guessed his face would be. "You ready to get fucked, pres?"

"What?" Eagle asked, clearly confused. "You're not shoving anything up my ass if that's what you mean."

I laughed and shook my head. "No, that's not what I had in mind, but it's good to know. I've pegged a man once or twice in my life. It can be fun with the right partner. What I had in mind was a little more simple."

Swinging off his body, I grabbed his leg and pushed up. Then I grabbed his hand and made him hold his leg up while I gestured for him to do the same with the other side.

"Dax…" Eagle warned.

Obviously, I couldn't see what he looked like, but I'd done this a few times before to know he looked like he was asking to take it up the ass. "Calm your tits, alright? Trust your wife."

Stumbling a bit, I got myself in the position I needed, crouched in a squat of sorts grabbing his dick and lifting it straight up. Then I sat down on it, but the way he was positioned gave him no choice but to let me have control of the situation. When I started to move, it was as if I was fucking him just with my pussy instead of another dick.

We, women, did this all the time when we stuck that suction cup on the floor and fuck it like it was our job. The way it hits up inside you was so different and gave me more control for it to hit that deep pleasure point most men didn't know existed.

I was glad the others were willing to let me do this without needing to get in on the action since it would throw off my groove. We had all night and the rest of our lives to fuck around but being able to own the president and fuck him into the mattress was priceless. Now to see if he enjoyed the dirty talk he dished out.

"How do you like that, hmm? I can feel how hard you are for me inside my pussy," I taunted. "You like the way I fuck you? Want me to drain your dick dry as you come deep in my snatch?"

Eagle just groaned and his hips bucked slightly as if he were unable to give up total control. Letting go of one leg I'd been using to keep steady, I slapped his ass. "Relax, boss man, and enjoy the ride. It's not every day the queen of the Hidden Empire owns your cock."

"Fuck, why is that so hot?" Cognac whispered.

"Because you hope we all want to be Eagle right now," Wes answered.

"Makes me think I might let her try pegging my ass at least once if it's anything like that," Cognac admitted. "What?" he blurted. "Like you wouldn't try it at least once if she asked."

I laughed to myself at their commentary as I found the right rhythm that was gonna get us both to the finish line. Holding his legs, I leaned back just slightly to tilt my pelvis and that was when the head of his cock hit right, just right. My breathing became more labored, and I tossed back my head, letting my moans fill the room as Eagle grunted in time with my movements. We were both so close that I sped up, slamming down on him even harder, then the slowly building orgasm exploded within me just as Eagle's release happened. The feel of his cum filling me only amplified my pleasure as my pussy walls gripped him tightly.

"Ah, fuck, Dax, you're fucking killing me," Eagle bit out as I refused to release him, still slowly pumping my hips, drawing out his orgasm like they had mine.

I slowed down, then came to a stop, leaning all the way forward until I reached his mouth with my own. "All is fair in love and war, right?"

Shrieking, I was yanked off Eagle and cradled against someone's chest. I could tell it was Void. With all the training we'd been doing, I knew that chest well. It took every ounce of my discipline not to fuck him on the mats as we sparred. Not saying I let him take me down to the mats so we could grapple, but it might be a thing.

"Don't torture the wounded, little demon," Void murmured into my ear before nipping at it. "Besides, the rest of us want to play with you too."

"What did you have in mind, big guy?" I asked, nuzzling into his neck.

His chest rumbled with his chuckle. "That's for us to know and you to find out, now isn't it?"

"I suppose it has been rather fun so far," I agreed. "Do with me as you will."

"Don't you worry, we were going to anyway," he answered as he sat down on the bed. "Now I'm going to spread your legs and stuff you with my cock using Eagle's cum as lube, little demon."

A shuddering sigh escaped my lips as he leaned back, propped up against something, keeping us at a slight angle. He pulled apart my legs until I fell over his hips, so I was on full display to whoever was at the end of the bed. Then his fingers slid over my stomach and down to my pussy, shoving two fingers inside, and swirling them around.

"Just wanted to see how wet you were for us, little demon," Void rumbled in my ear, his beard rough against my face.

Then true to his word, he slid his cock inside me and thrust up in a long, deep stroke that had my body sliding up his chest with the impact.

"Hey now, there's no running away, beautiful," Cam scolded as he grabbed my thighs and pulled me back down, impaling me on his pierced dick.

I screamed and writhed as just the tip made its way inside me. The stretch was so intense I couldn't tell if I liked it or not. Void slowed down his movements, not making them quite so deep as they worked to help me adjust to the added cock. Cam just rocked back and forth, not trying to add more, letting my body take what it could manage. My breathing came so fast and loud in my own head. Just when I felt like it might be too overwhelming, gentle hands smoothed over my stomach and up to my chest. Their fingers danced over my nipples, teasing them into tighter peaks than they'd already been.

This helped to get my brain to relax, not so zeroed in on what was happening with my pussy, and allowed my body to understand it wasn't in danger. A tongue flicked over a bud, making me hiss as I reached out and slid my fingers into Sprocket's hair. Besides Void, who only had long hair on one half of his head, all the others had short hairstyles. Yet I think I already knew it had to be him, the man who knew how I was feeling about things before I did. I'm sure he saw the panic I was fighting down. In no way were these men taking more than I was willing to give, and damn, I wanted this, but one's body also instinctively protects you.

Slowly my body accepted what was happening, and I was able to take deeper breaths soothing my anxiety. Starting at my toes, I tried to get my body to relax inch by inch until I felt Cam's cock slide all the way in. "*Yes*." I whimpered. "Fuck yes, you're both filling me up with your cocks. Now fuck me, dammit. I want to see sound by the time you're done with me."

Their movements increased, but it still wasn't as fast as I wanted it, so I rolled my hips, encouraging them deeper. Soon they were moving at a pace they would if there'd only been one of them inside me. The sound of their growls, grunts, and groans drove me even higher, knowing I was the reason they were making those noises. It was my body they craved so badly they couldn't wait for a turn. They wanted to push me to my limits and surpass them.

"Tell me, little rebel, what does it feel like to have two cocks fucking your pussy?" Sprocket whispered in my ear as he flicked my nipples with his fingers in rapid succession.

"Full, so fucking full it's almost too much to take," I rambled, not sure if I was even speaking the right words. "Feeling their cocks pulsing as they get close to coming is one of the most amazing things ever."

My words seemed to affect them as much as they did me. Their strokes became more erratic as my core squeezed tighter if that was possible. All of us cried out when it happened, and Void let out a roar as I felt him coming, quickly followed by Cam. They both thrust in at the same time, hitting deep inside, making my whole body convulse as I came. Sprocket had to hold onto my shoulders so I wouldn't slide off Void's chest.

"That's what I'm talking about," I screamed, hands clawing into the sheets under me. Then Cam took his hand and slapped my clit as he pulled out, sending a rocket of sensation through my already electrified body. Overwhelmed, my brain decided it was time for a break, and the world started to go dark as I passed out from pleasure.

Chapter Fifteen

Weston

Watching Dax with all her men was better than any porn I could have imagined. When the woman you loved more than anything was getting hit with orgasms left and right to the point she passed the fuck out, it was pure magic. I came just from watching that last round, my cum coating my hand as I worked my cock to the point of pain.

In a way, it was good that she passed out because I felt like she needed a breather after something like that. When Cam went for it, Cognac had to hold me back from yanking him off her. It was too much, too fast. Yeah, I'd warmed her up, and the brothers fucked her, but that wasn't nearly enough to prepare for a double-vag to happen.

"Easy, bro," Cognac said, gripping my arm. "Just give her a minute. If she didn't want this, she would have happily kicked Cam right in the face."

He'd been right. Dax had zero problem telling any of us to kick rocks if she wasn't interested. Sprocket joined in soothing her, and it seemed to do the trick. While I'd always assumed I knew Dax better than anyone, it didn't take me long to figure out that each of them understood a part of her. Shortcake and I were a team. We'd always been that way, able to predict what the other was going to do. Now we were out of our carefully constructed empire, and the rules had changed.

When Eagle pulled us all together and told us the plan he'd been cooking up while left alone in the hospital, I thought he was nuts. Then Picasso told us about the crew wanting to bring her into the fold, so I decided to reconsider my stance. Working through this choice and putting her at the center of it was what finally got us all to see eye to eye on a few things.

I glanced over at Cameron, who was combing his fingers through her sweat-soaked hair as she rested. That man loved her more than life, but he was shit at working with others that were on equal footing, which was why he kept trying to prove he was above us. As we talked the first two days, it was spent mostly on getting him to pull his head out of his ass. Unbeknownst to Dax, there'd been a fist fight or two that we'd brushed the bruises off on training because she never missed a detail about us all.

For the most part, we settled the big issues, but the one thing Cam refused to discuss was what really happened between them.

His gaze would turn hard, and he'd give the same response. "That's more Dax's story to tell, not mine, and I won't share it if she hasn't. All I will say is we were young, dumb, and woefully un-prepared to deal with the disappointment that came to everyone. Some just stick with you longer than others."

Part of me wanted to rage at him because I'd had to clean up his mess. She'd lost two people she loved back to back, and I wasn't going to be the next person who walked away from the self-destructive woman she turned into. Instead, I did everything in my power to support her, even giving up the whole life I'd had planned, devoting it to Dax. It was a choice I would never regret for as long as I lived. She was worth it. So if learning to find a balance between the seven of us was the price to be paid, so be it.

I stepped out to clean up in the bathroom down the hall. For how many people lived in this house, only having a single bathroom upstairs was tricky. Thankfully, none of us guys were that shy and could manage, but damn, I didn't want this to be forever. Dax had been dropping hints left and right that we needed to add on or find a new place to live. I wholeheartedly agreed with her on that. This place had been great for the five guys, but now with eight of us, it was too small.

As I was heading back to the room, I heard a knock on the front door. Frowning, I grabbed a towel from the bathroom and headed down. Something in my gut told me this wasn't just someone telling us to keep it down, so I grabbed the gun I knew was stashed in the side table near the couch. Sideling up beside the front door, I moved the blinds to see who it was. From this angle, I couldn't see anyone, so I waited and listened for any sound. If a person really needed us, it would have been urgent, and they'd bang on the door again.

Outside there was just the low thudding beat of music coming from the clubhouse. No creaking of wood from someone standing outside on the porch or breathing that I could make out. Dropping down, so I was squatting next to the door, my back to the wall, I turned the doorknob and cracked it. Holding my breath, I waited, but nothing happened. If someone had been looking to kill one of us, they most likely would have shot through the door, or a friendly would have spoken up. Gripping the knob, I yanked the door open, still keeping off to the side as I whirled on the balls of my feet, pointing the gun out the door.

There was nothing but night and the soft glow of the porch lights illuminating the entrance. I glanced down and spotted a manilla envelope with *Queen of the Hidden Empire* written on the front. Searching the area once more, I picked it up slowly, making sure some booby trap wasn't attached to it. Breathing out a sigh of relief, I stood, and closed the door, moving to the breakfast counter, and flipped on the light.

"What is it?" Sprocket asked from behind me.

Whirling around, gun raised before my brain caught up to who spoke. "Jesus fucking Christ, Sprocket. I could have shot you," I snapped, lowering the gun and flicking the safety on so I didn't make a horrible mistake.

"Sorry, I thought you saw me coming down the stairs before you opened the door," he answered, setting his own gun on the counter. "Came down to get her some water and saw you at the door. What happened?"

"Heard someone knocking and with all that's gone on tonight, I figured it was either something fucking important or someone trying to kill us," I answered. "Seems they just had a package to deliver."

Sprocket picked up the envelope and examined it in the light, but it was too thick to see through it. The top wasn't sealed all the way, just secured with the silver tabs through the single hole. "We need to open it before she sees it," I decided. "Who the fuck knows what that could be, but my gut is telling me it's not good."

"Have we heard anything from Harper lately?" Sprocket asked, reading my mind.

I shook my head. "They talked right after they got out of Russia to figure out where they were going to place Prim once they got to New York. I assumed it would take them about two days, if not three of driving to get where they needed to meet for the flight out. Everyone agreed it was best to keep silent until they were stateside once more."

"Alright, we look at this first, but no matter what is in here, we tell her about it," Sprocket ordered, pinning me with his fierce gaze.

"I agree," I answered.

Slowly, he opened the envelope and slid out two documents and a picture. There was also a handwritten note that was stuck to the inside of the envelope that I grabbed. Scanning the documents, I frowned, none of this making any sense. It was adoption papers with some guy's name on them that I'd never heard of before. The photo turned out to be two, one of Diego De León holding a baby in his arms with a woman smiling down at the baby. Diego actually looked happy as he smiled broadly at the camera as any proud father would be. The second image was of a man in his thirties who was the spitting image of Diego.

"What is all this?" I murmured, flipping the family picture over.

Written on the back was a note that looked like the same handwriting as the letter I'd yet to read.

The true heir to the cartel is still out there.

"The fuck?" I blurted. "What does any of this have to do with us?"

When Sprocket didn't answer, I looked over to see him reading the letter, utterly absorbed in it. Setting the picture down, I waited, glancing over the adoption papers again. The boy had been given up at what they guessed was around six months. He'd been found on the steps of a fire station in Boston. All he'd been left with was a note that said his name pinned to his blanket, *Tommaso.* The boy had been adopted shortly after into an affluent family who I knew had ties to the Italian mafia. They were no friend to the De León Cartel, but something had always held them back from making a move to take over. Now it had me wondering if it was because of Marco being the true puppet master.

"Whoever this is, really doesn't want Diego in power. They just handed everything needed to make an official coup d'état happen over who rules the East Coast," Sprocket explained. "This boy is Diego's oldest son from his first wife he married, who I might add was the daughter to an incredibly important person in the Italian mafia. It was a way to broker peace, but when his wife suddenly showed up dead and the child gone missing, war broke out. This letter says that's when he sold his soul to Marco so he could keep his hold over the East Coast. Now it has me thinking his second wife has a connection to Marco in some way. Which is why only those kids take his last name and can inherit."

I sat heavily on one of the stools looking over the picture of the man who might just have solved all our problems. Yeah, there was still going to be a war, but even after we removed Diego, we'd need to come up with a plan to fill that void. If we had control over who that could be and built a strong alliance, it could change everything. Just imagining the biggest powers in the US who ruled the coastlines working together was mind-blowing.

"We present this to everyone, but I don't want us making any moves until I look into things more. This paperwork and photos give us a place to start, but I'm not going to take some mystery person's word as law. That and I plan to watch the security footage to see how the fuck they got to the house without anyone noticing," I grumbled, tossing the photo on the counter. "Why the hell does this all need to be so complicated?"

Sprocket grinned at me. "With great power..."

"Oh, shut the fuck up," I laughed, shoving him. "Get the damn water and we'll tell the others what happened."

"You know doing that might cut your chances of getting your dick wet tonight," Sprocket warned.

Shrugging, I gathered up the papers. "I waited thirty-some-odd years for her. Missing out on a night isn't that big of a deal. Besides, now that she is mine, I have the freedom to wake her ass up later and fuck the shit out of her. Morning sex is a fantastic way to start the day."

Sprocket smiled and laughed as he grabbed a bunch of water bottles out of the refrigerator. "You make a valid point, man. One that I will have to keep in mind for another time."

"Yeah, well, you might want to clean up that shithole you call a room," I suggested. "No woman wants to sleep on a twin mattress on the floor with engine parts scattered all over the place."

"Guess I've never had to worry about it until now. I'd always go back to their place since Eagle didn't allow fucking sweet butts in the house. He always said when we found the person we wanted for real, we'd appreciate not having mucked the palace up with other women," he sighed, pausing at the top step. "Fucker was right, but you never heard me say that."

Miming, I zipped my lips, tossed away the key, and grinned. "I told her the same thing, no fuck buddies at our house. There's no way I would've been able to hold my shit together knowing someone was fucking the woman I'd always considered as mine in *our* house."

"Ah, so that's why she had the apartment," Sprocket commented as we entered Cognac's room.

The guys had their boxers on and were lounging on the bed watching something on the television while Dax sat in the middle of them all buck ass naked, glaring at us. "Where the fuck have you two been?"

"Calm down, shortcake," I said, waving the envelope. "We got a surprise delivered. Sprocket and I were just making sure it was all clear. Last thing we need is another bomb making us homeless."

Dax crawled forward and snatched the envelope right out of my hand. "Too soon, Westly, too soon."

Sprocket flipped on the lights, making everyone mutter and swear at the sudden brightness.

"Shit, man, a little warning next time would be nice," Eagle snapped.

It took them a moment, but they seemed to realize something had happened. Apparently, they'd all lost their brain power after sex. Dax read over everything, then read it again before looking up at us. "Is this true?"

"That's what I plan to look into tomorrow. If it is, then this job got a whole lot easier but far more complicated," I answered.

"We knew this wasn't going to be easy, but if what these papers say are true, then it solves one part of this we hadn't figured out," she mused, handing over the papers to Cognac. "Does this mean we need to change the whole approach? Is the fight still necessary?"

"It will be even more important," Cam interjected. "If the plan is to put the Italians in power, we need a reason for them all to be in New York without building suspicion. Everyone who's anyone is getting an invite. We just need to make sure those who can be trusted are informed."

Glancing at the clock, I flinched, seeing it was two hours away from sunrise. "Let's get some sleep, and we'll deal with this after I've had a chance to do some fact-checking."

Everyone nodded and while Cognac's bed was big enough for us all to fuck on, it wasn't to sleep on. Plus, we kind of made a mess out of it. I'm not sure anyone would want to sleep on it.

"Where're you sleeping, little demon?" Void asked, brushing a hand down her arm.

She looked at me, then Cognac. "Wherever those two land, they were the only ones who didn't get their happy ending."

The guys snickered, but Picasso slapped Cognac on the back. "You three take my room in the loft, it's big enough for the three of you, and I'll take Weston's bed."

Cam leaned forward, invading Picasso's personal bubble. "Does that mean I get to cuddle with you like I do dearest Westly?"

Picasso rolled his eyes and shoved the man off the bed. "You could try, but I can't guarantee you'll have all your body parts if you do."

"So cruel," Cam gasped with mock hurt. "Seems I will be once more relegated to the air mattress."

"You could sleep here if you don't mind rolling around in everyone's cum," Dax pointed out with a smirk. "I find it to be rather enjoyable."

Cam gave her a droll look. "If you were still going to be in this bed, then I might consider it. Otherwise, I feel like we might as well just get a whole new bed at this point. Not sure it can be saved. Silk is horrid material to get stains out of."

We all laughed, hearing a bit of Dante in those words. "Come on, shortcake, let's try and get some sleep. Seems we have a coup to organize."

Sleep came quickly as the three of us flopped onto Picasso's bed. Once I rolled onto my back with Dax using my chest as a pillow and Cognac's head on her ass, we conked out. When I opened my eyes, the sun was well up into the sky, flooding the room with light.

It was the perfect spot for an artist, so it made sense why Picasso converted it.

Dax was sprawled over my chest, drool seeping out of the side of her mouth, but she was too cute to be mad at. I combed my fingers through her hair, surprised she'd gone so long without cutting or coloring it. It fell just past her shoulders and normally, it was shorter with lots of choppy layers that gave her that grungy look. Personally, I had no feelings about how she wore it. Whatever made her happy was fine by me.

Maybe it would be a good idea for her, Tilly, and Dani to go have a girls' day or something. I knew she'd be doing the fight when we got to New York, so getting her nails done wouldn't be that big of a deal. I just knew she cut it short so people didn't have much to grab on to when they attacked her. Not that it happened much these days, most people knew better than to piss her off.

She stirred under my touch, humming as her hand pulled me closer to her. Smiling, I just enjoyed the moment of her being so vulnerable and not weighed down by all that was happening. This had to come to an end. Once we dealt with Diego, it would be time to hunt down Marco. Cam and I talked a bit about that part of this, knowing he had far more information with his connection to the FBI. Hell, I didn't even know if I should have been looking out for the guy in the first place. Marco was like the monster under your bed you heard people talk about but didn't really believe would be there. Then one night, he reaches out and grabs your ankle, making his presence known.

"Hey," Dax whispered, followed by soft kisses pressed to my skin. "What has you making that face?"

Frowning, I looked down at her. "What face?"

"That one," she said, poking my forehead. "It's the one you make when you realize you might have missed something that could put me in danger."

"Oh really," I murmured, cocking an eyebrow as I stroked my hand over her hair again. "I have a face just for that situation?"

"Yu*p*," she commented, popping the P. "It's been happening a lot more lately, but it's one I've seen over the years. Took me a bit to figure out, but when I put the situations together, it made sense."

"Hmph," I grunted, not at all surprised she could read me so well. After how long we'd been around each other, you learned their tells. "So, when are you going to tell them you're not really going to marry them?"

Dax shifted so now her arms were folded over my chest, and she could rest her head on them. "I don't know what you're talking about."

"The government won't let you marry them all," I reminded her.

"Well, duh," she said with a snort. "There are other things you can do that mean the same thing."

"True, but you, missy, aren't going to do the white dress, walk down the aisle, toss the bouquet type *thing*," I teased, booping her nose. "You said yes to being our wife in name and commitment, but there won't be paperwork stating that fact in a legal government database."

"Does that really matter?" she countered. "If you are my husbands, and I'm your wife, we combine all our resources, have legal documents giving power in each other's lives, then what does it matter there isn't paperwork that specifically states I married you all?"

"So you're keeping your last name?" I asked.

She shrugged. "Yeah, if it means that much to you all, then take my last name. It's way easier to just do things that way than to argue whose last time I would take."

Cognac stirred next to Dax, popping his head up, bleary eyes trying to focus on our woman. "Fuck, I didn't think about the last name thing." He cocked his head, then grinned. "Juan Blackmore would sound pretty cool if you ask me. I dig it."

Dax shifted to give him a quick deep kiss. "You would." She giggled. "You think the others will put up a fuss?"

"Most of us, besides the brothers, don't have family that's living or we give a shit about," Cognac pointed out. "It might take those two a bit to wrap their heads around the idea, but I don't see them saying a hard no. Eagle might have more of an issue with the fact you don't want a wedding."

"What are you talking about? We had one last night," Dax announced. "To me, that was perfect. Get a ring, get the guys, get fucked. What more could a woman ask for?"

This logic had me snorting as I tried to hold back my laughter. If that wasn't the most Dax thing I'd ever heard out of her mouth, I don't know what it would be. "Oh fuck, I love you," I murmured before kissing her cheek, then slapping her ass. "Come on, let's get up and get shit done. I have no doubt everyone else in this whole compound is hung over as fuck from last night. Good thing it's Sunday, so no one has to go to work."

The other two groaned and threw pillows at me as I crawled out of bed to the stairs. When I turned around, I noticed that Cognac got distracted and was sucking on one of Dax's nipples as his hand drifted between her legs. When the hiss burst out of her mouth, it had us both snapping to attention.

"Okay, so I might be a bit sore," she admitted. "That was a lot last night."

Cognac kissed up her neck, then caught her lips, making her moan before pulling back. "Then we will just have to give your kitty a rest for today. She worked very hard last night taking all those cocks one after the other," he said in an incredibly serious tone. I had to leave before I made an idiot of myself.

Fuck, this family I found myself in was weird as shit, but I was glad to have stumbled into it.

Chapter Sixteen

Dax

Three days after the envelope was dropped off on our doorstep, I was on a plane flying out to Massachusetts. Wes had buried himself in his office and dug up every scrap of information on Tommaso that he could. It seemed he took after his adopted father's footsteps and became a lawyer who worked heavily for the Italian mafia. Not that he advertised that publicly on a business card, but if you knew what to look for, it was clear.

Wes found he'd been looking for information on his birth parents at one point back in his high school years. Nothing was found, but it gave Wes the idea he needed to set up a meeting with the man so we could explain ourselves.

We had five days to get this man on board or finalize the plan B we'd been working on initially. I looked over the information we had on him and all the indications he was someone I wanted to work with.

On the outside, he might look like a lackey to the Italians, but I paid close attention to what deals and situations they put him in charge of. He did both criminal cases as well as business ones, depending on how big of a deal it was. Tommaso was a shark who found his opponents' weakness and went for it, but there were some situations he could have taken advantage of that he didn't. When it came to wife and kids, he left them the hell alone. The thing about family was everyone has someone who can be used as leverage.

The other thing I noticed was he was the first choice if there was a case that wasn't an easy one to win. A money house had been raided, and they got a few of their higher-up on the food chain people, but he managed to get them out, no time served on technicalities. No matter how hard Wes searched, he couldn't find bribe money being exchanged either. This guy was criminal-minded to the core but had rules he played by as well. Just how I liked to run my operation. Follow the law when you could, then when you had to break it—be smart.

"Do you think he'll kick us out once he realizes we aren't really there to talk about his family?" Cognac asked from the seat next to mine.

Somehow, Cam managed to talk the FBI into letting us use their jet to fly privately for the weekend. He'd explained to them that we needed to keep my arrival and the conversations we were having on the down low. Since this plane was owned and run by the FBI, no one would ever think it had anything to do with me. While the jet was nice, it certainly wasn't overly luxurious. More practical to get work done as you traveled.

Turning away from the view of the early morning sky, I mulled over Cognac's question. "That depends on how we lay it out for him. My hope is he won't be the only one in that meeting. If he has his father or anyone else tied to the Italian mafia, then Tommaso might be overruled if he tried to give us the boot."

Cognac rubbed his chin before turning to Wes. "Remind me again who his mom was?"

"She was the daughter to the consigliere to one of the previous mob bosses whose since passed away. The family was still held in high regard, which is why there was so much backlash when she was found dead in their summer home in upstate New York. The baby had gone missing, but Diego wasn't focused on finding him with how 'grief stricken' he was," Wes answered, adding finger quotes to show how little he believed that bullshit.

"Do we know how he got in touch with Marco?" Sprocket asked. "Even with all the information we have from the FBI, he's a fucking ghost. No one seems to know where it is he hides out, always moving from place to place."

I glanced down at the picture of Diego and his first family. The happiness in this photo was legit, but how could he turn his back on his son? Was he really that affected by her death? They'd only been married two years... unless they knew each other from before.

"What do we know about his mother, Felicia? Like how in the world did the man who was trying to take control of the East Coast find himself with the daughter of someone who was once the advisor to the Italian mafia?" I questioned.

Wes shifted in his seat, frustration written all over his face. "That's what I'm having the hardest time figuring out. They must have had someone wipe all that from every database they could manage because I only could find random mentions of her. Even at the hospital, there is no record of her giving birth to Tommaso, and I know that's where she went. Diego's finances match up to paying for it."

"So either they were protecting Tommaso from knowing, or whoever adopted him knew exactly who Tommaso was. Like it was a planned situation to get him out from Diego after his mother died," I mused. "Fuck, this is like a mafia thriller movie that affects my life, and I don't like it one bit."

"Look," Eagle said, grabbing our attention. "No matter what happens, we gave it a shot. Hell, if we can get the Italians on our side just by telling them we're taking Marco out of power, then to hell with all this other shit. Tommaso is just our in for the situation, not the solution."

Cognac let out an impressed-sounding whistle, then grinned. "Look at Eagle laying down the facts. Impressive, pres." Eagle flipped Cognac the bird, sending the man into a fit of laughter.

"Do we have any other connection to the Italians?" Cam asked.

Then it hit me. "Yeah, we most certainly do," I shared with a wide grin. "Harper made nice with none other than François Barilla, one of the top mafia mobster families in Italy. We didn't get a chance to talk for long, but in the speed version of what happened while she was out of the country, I did pick up that tidbit of information."

"It's almost as if it was meant to be," Void interjected, resting his hands behind his head. "Now we need to stop worrying and let the cards fall, so we know how to move forward."

Each of us looked at the man like he'd lost his mind. Ever since I said yes to being their wife and wearing the ring they had made for me, Void had been on cloud nine. Nothing could take the pep out of his step and that shit needed to end before the fight this weekend. We had two more days before we needed to fly into New York, the fight being Saturday night. It was crunch time, and I couldn't have Void off his game. With all the training we'd been doing, I was back in shape, not top-tier shape but the best we could do in the time we had, which meant I needed Void to be on his A-game to keep me alive.

"Wow, look at the city," Picasso commented as we broke through the clouds.

I'd never been to the upper East Coast, so I was excited to check out a new city. Each one had a life of its own, a heartbeat that pulsed with life and crime, good and evil. The trick was figuring it out fast so you survived. Now we were about to go knock on the front door and see if anyone was home.

We landed, grabbed our bags, and headed for the hotel. While I wasn't one to dress up much, I knew this meeting needed to go well. Part of that was looking like we weren't bikers and gangsters. So I went out with Dani and Tilly to go shopping, get my hair done, and pick out things for the guys as well. Now each of them had two business casual outfits that looked sexy as fuck. I might have gone overboard on mine, but who would I be if I didn't take things to the extreme?

The hotel was downtown, nothing special with adjoining rooms but all of us would have to share rooms. This was becoming a theme in my life. Never enough space for all eight of us to be together and I was starting to get sick of it. I'd pushed to rent out the fucking penthouse, but everyone shot that down, saying we needed to keep a low profile.

"Dax, we have forty-five minutes for you to get ready. We're heading down to the restaurant to get something to eat," Wes called.

Yeah, well, when they were already dragging me out of bed at four in the morning to make our flight, I wasn't getting up to take no damn shower. Looking at myself in the fluorescent bathroom light, I grinned at the fresh, bright hair and much shorter shaggy style I preferred. Not needing a full shower, I quickly washed my body and face so I could put on my makeup.

It was different doing this without Harper around, and I realized how much I missed my best friend, having been apart for almost two months now. Good news was, she was back in the States, and I could see her when I got to New York. We had so much to catch up on and hardly any time to do it before we needed to get down to business. Her triplets were going to come in handy for this job since we needed stealth to get Elena out of their clutches. We'd decided as a group no matter if she was blinded by love or something else, we were going to get her back. Once this was all over, we'd deal with the fallout.

Seeing as it was still late morning, I kept the makeup light and professional. Then when I looked at my clothes, I grinned, knowing they were going to get some looks. The leather pants were soft and buttery on the skin with spikes on the knees in little rows. They also lined the pockets and waistband. My shirt was a black and white distressed band tee that was cut into a crop top. Then to finish it all off was a fitted black blazer that, when buttoned, showed off some of my stomach. Was this the most professional option? No, probably not. Was this the best Dax-style option? Fuck yeah, it was.

The final touch that topped the whole outfit was my pink Doc Martens, and I was ready to kick this day's ass. Stepping out of the room to join the guys down at the lobby where the restaurant was, my stomach grumbled, unhappy I hadn't fed it yet, but I hoped my men would know well enough to get something for me. If not, then I might have to question if they truly loved me or not.

It wasn't hard to spot them gathered together at a table dressed in nice jeans, button-downs, or polos. Really, I couldn't blame the front desk ladies for gawking at them or the bartender, who I might have to wipe the drool off his face. They were absolutely pretty to look at, just don't fucking touch, or I'd have to do something about it, and no one wanted that.

"Please tell me you love me," I whined as I got closer, my stomach raging at the smell of food.

Eagle looked up first, and his smile widened as he looked me up and down. "Fuck, if I didn't before, that outfit would have me on my knees for you all over again."

I blew him a kiss but aimed right for Cam who was sitting at the end of the table with two plates in front of him. Peering down, I spotted a breakfast sandwich that hadn't been touched and a cup of coffee to go with it. "That wouldn't happen to be for me, now would it?"

Cam shifted his chair back and to the side so he could look at me. "That depends..."

"On what?" I asked, my eyes narrowing.

"Can you eat it in ten minutes before our ride gets here?" he challenged.

I let out a huff of laughter and plopped myself on his lap, snatching up the sandwich. This, of course, had been his plan all along, giving him the opportunity to wrap his arms around me while he kissed up my neck.

"If we have time, I want to take you on a date in New York," he murmured in my ear. "Just the two of us."

Pausing a moment, I looked at him over my shoulder, then shoved the last two bites of the sandwich in my mouth. Now that he'd asked for the chance, I was surprised none of the others had before now. Swallowing, I licked my fingers and answered. "The others okay with it?"

"Yes, I've brought it up. We all agreed that none of us should have any issues with you having one-on-one time with us. As long as it's kept fair," he explained. "It's something that we should have been doing long before this."

"I agree. A date sounds wonderful," I said. "Problem is we have the fight Saturday night and who the fuck knows what will happen after that."

Cam nodded mischief in his gaze. "Then sounds like we might need to get there Friday instead. Trust me when I say you're not going to want to miss this chance. After we make our move, I'm not sure if this place will still be around."

"Okay, now you've piqued my curiosity," I admitted. "Who knows, maybe things will go so well here and we don't make it back to California before the fight. New York is just around the corner, and no one is expecting us."

Leaning in, Cam caught my lips, humming with delight as I opened up for him to kiss me more deeply. "I love the way you think, beautiful," he whispered against my lips.

"Time to go, you two," Picasso called.

Sighing, I grabbed the to-go coffee cup and quickly chugged half of it. "Alright, let's make a deal with the enemy of my enemy so we can be friends."

The guys chuckled as we headed out, and I made sure to wave at the front desk ladies. They didn't seem to appreciate my greeting—like I fucking cared.

"Little demon," Void said with a chuckle as he wrapped an arm around my shoulders. "I wouldn't worry about them. The only woman we will ever have eyes for is you."

A black SUV pulled up with the rideshare sticker on the windshield. The driver rolled down the window and looked at us. "Enzo?"

"Yeah, that's us," Eagle said, waving his phone at the guy.

When he tried to get in the front seat, Cognac grabbed his shoulder and shook his head. "You know I get car sick. I'll ride up front."

While Eagle might have gotten his stitches out and been given the all-clear from a local doctor, we knew he wasn't a hundred percent. If this stranger turned out to be someone we needed to deal with, I didn't want Eagle being right up front in the thick of it. Bastard was lucky enough to be alive after the last ordeal.

I reached out and took his hand in mine. "Come sit with me." Tugging him into the front row of the SUV kept him from arguing with Cognac.

We'd agreed to meet Tommaso at his office, hoping that meant we would have a higher chance of meeting with others of the mafia. The driver pulled up in front of a tall cylinder building near the Boston Harbor, which made sense to me since the mafia controlled what went in and out of here. It was the only part of the East Coast that Diego couldn't steal from them, not for lack of trying.

When we entered, there was a large plaque with the names of all the companies that were located in the building. Tommaso's law group had the whole fifteenth floor, it seemed, which made it easy to find once we exited the elevator.

A woman dressed in a bright yellow dress that showed far too much cleavage and made me wonder how she kept from spilling out greeted us.

"Hello, welcome to Civello, Dolfi, and Riggo. How can I help you?" she asked, rising from her seat.

Wes stepped forward and gave her a smile in return. "Yes, we have a meeting With Tommaso Civello at eleven thirty."

"Oh yes, if you'll follow me, I'll get you settled in the conference room just down this hall. Can I get you gentlemen anything?" she inquired, clearly making a point to ignore me.

Everyone mumbled no as they took their seat at the table. While I was all for women having each other's backs, what I couldn't stand was when we saw each other as threats. I'd done nothing to this woman in the five seconds we'd interacted, yet she was treating me like dirt.

"I would love a cup of coffee, black, please," I requested as I passed by her.

She gave me a tight-lipped smile. "Certainly." Spinning on her ridiculously high heels, she left the room.

Swiveling in my chair, I looked at the guys, confused as shit. "What the fuck is it that I do to make women hate me instantly?"

"It's not what you do, little rebel," Sprocket expressed. "What they dislike about you is the confidence you have in yourself and your place in the world. Knowing your worth isn't something you can teach because it's something you have to take for yourself."

Crossing my arms, I leaned back in the chair, thinking that over. I had to fight, bleed, and claw my way to get where I am. After doing that much work, the knowledge that you fucking deserved to be treated better was just innate.

The sound of hard-sole shoes clacked on the marble floor, alerting me that someone was entering the conference room and had me sitting up. While I might have earned respect in my life, it didn't apply to all people everywhere, and right now, we were in someone else's territory. Tommaso and another gentleman I recognized from articles walked in with him—Sergio Civello, Tommaso's adoptive father and number one ringer to the Italian mafia when it came to legal disputes.

"Hello all, and thank you, Weston, for traveling all the way from California to speak with me," Tommaso said, reaching out to shake Weston's hand, then gesturing for us to take a seat.

"It's our pleasure. We felt like this conversation was best had in person," Wes explained. "Allow me to introduce who I've brought with me. My wife, Dax, and her other husbands, Enzo, Lachlan, Connor, Teo, Juan, and Cameron."

This information had both men looking at us with shocked expressions. "I'm sorry, I don't mean to be rude, but did you say she's married to you as well as these other men?" Sergio questioned.

Wes gave him an understanding smile. "Yes, I guess you could say we are a family unit since we all live and work together as well. We understand it's not a normal situation, but for us, it's what made the most sense. Now the purpose for our visit, at one point, you'd been looking for information on your birth parents, and we know who they are."

"It's true I was incredibly eager when I was younger to understand where I came from, but even private investigators came up empty. How is it you managed to find something? Pardon my skepticism. It comes with the job," Tommaso challenged.

"No, that is smart of you not to trust right away, but I'll be upfront with you if you offer to do the same with us," Wes counted.

Sergio tensed at this, narrowing his eyes on Wes. "What exactly does that mean? If you're coming to us looking for a favor or a payout of any kind, I'll tell you right now that's never going to happen."

"What about the chance to overthrow Diego De León and get back what was stolen from you?" I asked, cocking my head slightly to get a better look at the older man. "We know who you really work for, and if you want us to come clean about *everything* we know, it comes with the price of honesty in return."

"Wait here. We need to make a call," Sergio ordered as they both got up and walked to the door.

Before they could leave, I let out a quick shrill whistle getting them to look at me. "Tell Valter, Two Tricks is in your office looking to deal." Sergio's eyes went wide for a fraction of a second before he nodded sharply and left.

Chapter Seventeen

Dax

A moment later, miss perky tits showed up with a small Styrofoam cup with coffee in it. "Here you go, coffee, black."

Why the fuck do they always make me be the asshole?

"Yeah, sorry, princess, but I know an insult when I see one," I said with a tired sigh. "Let me guess, did you spit in it? Dip the cup in toilet water or something before filling it?"

"What?" She gasped. "No, of course not. Why on earth would I do such a thing?"

"Only you can answer that, but I'm for damn sure not going to drink out of that." Shoving out of my seat, I left the conference room and headed for the front desk.

"Wait, what are you doing?" tits for brains called after me.

Looking around the space, I ignored her as I spotted a man with an empty coffee cup heading down the hall to the left. "Since you clearly didn't want to serve me, I'm just going to do it my-damn-self," I muttered as I followed after the guy.

He turned into a room marked *Employees Only*, but I charged in all the same. In the break room was a fancy state-of-the-art espresso machine, coffee maker, snack bar, and even a refrigerator with champagne chilling. I spotted a stash of mugs with the firm's logo on it and assumed that's what my beverage should have been in.

"Umm, ma'am are you lost?" the gentleman asked me when he realized I wasn't supposed to be there.

"Nope, just getting my own coffee since the daffodil over here wasn't willing to do her job," I shared, taking the pot from his hand. "You were done with this, right?"

"Yeah..." Then he seemed to snap out of it, turning to the woman still making irritated noises at me. "Beverly, what's going on?"

"She asked for coffee, and I got her some, but she decided to get it herself," Beverly grumbled. "Something about toilet water, I don't know. She's crazy."

"Beverly," the man hissed. "That is no way to talk about one of our clients, let alone to their face."

"You asked me what happened. I'm explaining it," she said with a pout on her lips as she talked. "Don't be mad, Carl."

I leaned back against the break room counter and snorted. "Wow, is that how you still have a job? Are you gonna drop to your knees and beg for forgiveness with his dick in your mouth?"

Carl looked stricken like I'd figured out some big secret or something while Beverly looked horrified at the suggestion. "I would never. He's a married man."

"Save it for someone who believes your shit," I sighed. "What or who you do isn't any of my concern. What I took offense to is your obvious dislike of me when I'd done nothing to you. There was no reason for it."

"Why should I give you the same respect when you're just like me, cuddling up to whoever can give you the lifestyle you want." She sneered.

I tossed back my head and laughed so hard I almost had to set my coffee cup down for fear of spilling it. "Oh, you really read that situation so wrong. You might want to consider toning down on the hairspray. I feel like it's killing what precious brain cells you have left." I wiped my eye with a finger trying not to smear my makeup. "Those men are my husbands, and as for the lifestyle part, I'm the one who has all the money and power, babe."

Beverly's face scrunched up as she looked at me completely confused. "I don't get it."

"It's okay. Everyone has to stick with what they're good at," I shared, walking over to her and patting her on the shoulder as I passed by. "You must be skilled in other areas besides serving coffee, I'm sure of it."

Enraged at my words, Beverly let out a shriek before she grabbed for me. I sidestepped out of the way, set my mug on a table, then grabbed her arm, twisting it up behind her as I pulled my travel switchblade out of my back pocket.

The blade snapped open and rested against her throat. "I can handle the looks, the comments, and whatever you tried to pull with that first cup of coffee. What I will never allow is for someone to lay a hand on me. This would be the moment I would use whatever brain power you have to make a smart choice right now, Beverly."

"Make sure you're listening to her words, Bev," Tommaso commented from where he was leaning against the door frame. "That is one of the most dangerous women in the criminal world who's also known for never calling a bluff."

"You're going to let her do this to me, Tommy?" Beverly cried, fear making her words shaky.

Tommaso looked at her with sympathy. "Some lessons you need to learn the hard way, even if you are my sister."

Well fuck, why the hell did she have to be his sister? How could he let her act this way in the first place? Damn, let's hope Sergio doesn't witness this. Then there he was. So much for that wishful thinking.

"What the hell is going on here?" Sergio roared. "Unhand my daughter right this moment."

"No, Dad," Tommaso cut in, resting a hand on his father's arm. "She got herself into this mess, and Dax has every right to correct her. We've warned her the world we live in doesn't suffer fools lightly. She didn't listen."

Hmm, maybe this guy is who we need to fill the spot when Diego is gone. First things first, I had to deal with Beverly dearest.

"Listen to your brother, Bev, because next time, you might do something that's going to actually get you killed," I commented. "Having more respect for yourself and others might be a good place to start. All of this could have been avoided if you'd just treated me the same. Not to mention, you might want to change your viewpoint on other women. It's the twenty-first century, and we're more than able to be badasses in the world. Stop selling yourself short."

Giving her a shove toward her father, I released her. "If I were you, I'd stop letting her look like a hooker at work and sleeping with everyone in the office. Not that I have anything against a woman with a high sex drive, I take issue when it's used as manipulation. Fuck whoever you want as long as it's your idea and because you want it, Beverly. I know how the old-school mafia men like to keep their women in a certain role. If you ever need an out, call me. I'll find a place for you in the Hidden Empire."

Grabbing my mug, I headed out of the break room and back to the conference room, where my guys looked a little peeved. I gave them a sheepish smile and pointed to the mug. "Really needed coffee."

"Sit down," Wes ordered, pointing to the chair I'd been seated in before. "Something tells me that's not all that happened."

"Fun fact, Beverly, the chick with the boobs is Tommaso's sister," I shared while taking a sip of my coffee. "Damn, this is good. I'm gonna need to ask what it is so we can get some."

"For the love of God," Picasso groaned. "Spitfire, I realize you believe you can fix any situation with enough sass and a sharp blade, but please tell me you didn't fuck this up for us."

Before I could answer, Tommaso walked in with two new men in addition to his father. Valter, I knew instantly. He'd been a man we'd watched for a long time. The older Italian man was dapper as ever in his nice suit, dyed black hair fooling no one, and cane to help with his limp. It's always wise to keep tabs on threats to your business or others in case a coup ever did happen.

The other man wasn't someone I recognized and that had me slightly worried. Wes had made sure to keep track of all the big players in Valter's top crew.

He was about the same age as Valter, tanned skin, a head of neatly maintained white hair along with a matching full beard, and intelligent brown eyes. He looked at me as if he knew exactly who I was, putting me even more on alert.

"Thank you for waiting. I felt it was in all our best interests for those in power to be here for this conversation. Dax, I assume you already know Valter Lombardo, Don of the Italian mafia based here in Boston," Sergio introduced, then gestured to the other addition. "This is François Amato, a close and valued friend visiting from Italy to attend your fight this weekend."

My jaw dropped when I heard the name. "Wait," I blurted. "Are you the same François that knows Harper?"

"Si, such a lovely friend you have in Miss Peirson," François answered with a genuine smile. "Those boys are incredibly lucky they put a ring on her before I had a chance to make a move."

I tried to keep the surprise off my face at this news, but I hadn't exactly told her about my change in status either. "I can see she made quite the impression, must mean she really liked you. Otherwise, you wouldn't think so fondly of her and her sharp tongue."

"Ah, that is where you are mistaken, Mrs. Blackmore. I quite liked how bold she was. While she might be new to the game, she's got an instinct for it that you can't teach," he shared with a chuckle. "But we are not here to discuss these matters, and I do not wish to take up Valter's time with idle chatter."

"My apologies," I said, turning to Valter. "I realize what it means that you've come to speak with us directly, and I promise this will be worth your time."

We all took our seats once more and Wes pulled out the paperwork that had been given to us, explaining what else was found while doing our own research. The men listened and looked over everything, allowing us time to speak before asking their questions. While this was what we'd hoped would happen, my stomach churned with the knowledge they could take all this information and cut us out of the deal completely. Or just kill us. That was always an option when it came to the mafia.

"What of Marco?" Valter asked, his voice deep and raspy.

"Once we cut off any connections he has to getting goods in and out of the US, sending him running to wherever he's hiding, then I'll kill him. The hardest part of trapping a rat is anticipating where they'll show up. With all other avenues taken from him, he'll be so fucking pissed at me he's bound to make a mistake," I offered. "Marco's one and only goal is to take me down because I've been the biggest thorn in his side. He blames me for the Tesoro Cartel almost being destroyed while his father still ran things."

Valter watched me with a calculating gaze. "What is it you want from us? I'm sure you're not doing this out of the kindness of your heart."

"My goal is to get Diego out of power. Being able to fill the void he would leave is a bonus. Something I would like to see happen and feel would benefit us both is a friendship. I don't want anything to do with your business or to build an alliance that has to be drawn up in contracts. That being said, I feel like a healthy respect for each other would go a long way for both groups. Just think about the benefits of having the ability to call up the person who controls the whole West Coast if you're having a problem," I said, leaning forward on the table, looking both at Tommaso and Valter. "Friends like us are very good to have in our world, wouldn't you say?"

That finally got the old man to crack a smile. "Yes, I would agree with you on that." His expression sobered slightly as he also leaned forward. "Yet it is hard for me to believe that you don't want a more vested stance in this power play."

"You want to know what I'm really getting out of this? Fine, I get the satisfaction that finally I get to stomp out Diego, who's been trying to undermine me the moment I got any real power. He tried to blame his son's death on me when he's the one who had him killed. Between him and Marco, they've blown up my house, gone after my best friend, and tried to kill me on numerous occasions. Being able to help place the person who will take over so the De León Cartel can never rise…" I leaned back with a smirk. "Well, that's just the icing on the cake. Just imagine when his flesh and blood is his demise."

Tommaso snorted, returning my grin. "It's clear how you've managed to get where you are today. Your mind sees everything from all angles and will pull from any direction to get the piece that will solve the problem. If we are to consider friendship, you and I, then allow me to ask a few questions."

"Go right ahead. I'll answer them if I feel like they're valid," I agreed.

He looked at my men in the room, then met my gaze. "Are you sure you wouldn't want to add one more to your group? I know you haven't legally married any of these men, but you and I could. As you said, think of the combined power we'll both share doing that."

"Wow, clearly I misjudged you, Tommy," I said with a disapproving click of my tongue. "Tell Valter to take his hand out of your ass and let you speak for yourself. If you ask another asinine question, we'll go with plan B and pretend we never had this meeting."

Tommaso burst out laughing and a genuine smile shone on his face. "I can see why you need seven men to keep up with you, Dax. You're too much for any one person to handle." He took a moment to compose himself, then seemed ready to ask his real questions. "You said you wanted a friendship between us. I see the benefits it will bring to me, but I'm not sure what you feel you'll get out of me?"

"Ah, now we're talking," I responded, clapping my hands together and rubbing them before I answered. "I looked into you, Tommy. Sorry, we aren't friends yet. Can I call you that?" I asked. He nodded and encouraged me to go on. "While we were digging up information to make sure the claims were true, I was looking for other aspects of who you are as a person. You play by the rules but aren't afraid to break them when it really matters, good or bad. I knew you had siblings that were born after your father adopted you, and from what I could tell, you looked after them. Just like you did with Bev back in the break room. What I appreciate most from you is that, like me, we don't hide who we are from those around us when we can, yet we shelter those who can't handle the truth of who and what we are."

I paused a moment to look at my guys, then back at Tommaso. "You aren't married or have a steady woman in your life because it's too hard to handle both, so it's easier to do without. I used to think the same way until these assholes decided they had a different plan for me. To do this, you'll eventually need a partner in life. To be clear, I'm not talking about myself. Seven is more than enough for me to keep track of," I teased. "You'll be good for business, plus I think you and I could work well together having similar moral compasses. We aren't pitch black on the scale of things, but we're nowhere near white or even light gray. You and I, we live that dark gray life, my friend."

Tommaso seemed to ponder over my long-winded answer, a finger tapping on his chin. "What would you say if you found out that I sent you those papers?" he asked, seeming to have come to a conclusion about something.

"I would say it makes a whole lot more sense," I answered. "The more we looked into your adoption, I just had this gut feeling that Sergio knew exactly who you were. Did they have a plant in the house to know something happened to your mom and steal you away?"

"Just like that, you roll with it, and all you want to know is how they got the boy out of the house?" Valter demanded, his face a mask of confusion. "Tommaso basically told you we set you up."

Now it was my turn to look at Don of the mafia, confused. "Valter, just as you said before, people don't do things out of the goodness of their hearts. There had to be a calculated reason for someone to leave behind that kind of information. Add to it that someone close to Tommy's mother had to supply the photo since I'm sure Diego destroyed them. Why would he want anyone to know there could be a mysterious firstborn child out there? So no, I'm not shocked it was any of you that put that on our doorstep. My real question is, did we pass your test?"

Valter seemed satisfied with my answer and yelled something in Italian. Seconds later, in walked Beverly, her face washed clean of makeup and wearing a much more appropriate dress for working in the office.

This was the part that shocked me.

This bitch had been a plant.

"What the fuck is going on?" Cam demanded. "If you wanted us to come here and offer you an alliance, why all the games?"

Beverly, if that was really her name, sat next to Sergio. Her father smiled as he patted her leg affectionately. "Allow me to formally introduce you to my daughter, Betta. She does work here, but she's in charge of finances for the whole production, as it were."

"Ciao," Betta greeted with a little wave before turning to me. "I'm sorry about all that earlier, but they told me I had to push you until you snapped to see how you would handle it."

I pointed at her as I glared at the men. "Now that kind of shit I don't like," I snapped. "Do you realize what kind of danger you put her in? Thank God she didn't make a move on any of my men, or I would have slaughtered her in a heartbeat."

Sergio blanched at this, but Valter didn't even blink an eye. "If you did that, then it would have told us you aren't the person we want as our ally."

"You were willing to put her life on the line to make that call?" I demanded, as my anger started to boil inside me. "It's men like you who live in the old world, thinking that women are disposable, and that make me sick. So because I didn't kill her, I'm better than Diego or Marco? That is one of the most asinine things I've ever heard."

"Little demon," Void warned, placing his hand on mine.

I knew I was overreacting, but it was shit like this that got my twin killed. If he had a crew that really stuck by him and saw his value as a brother in their family, things could have been so different.

"She has a point," Tommaso interjected. "They didn't tell me about this exercise either until this morning because they knew I wasn't going to like it. If I'd come into that break room and found you truly ready to slit her throat, I would have intervened. Instead, you were using your blade to get her attention and make a point, then you offered her a way out if she wanted it. That interaction told me everything I personally needed to know about who you are as a person, Dax."

My gaze drifted over to Betta, needing her to tell me the truth. "Why? Why were you willing to do as these men asked, knowing who and what I was."

"As you said, we women are allowed to be badasses in the world. While I might work here in an office, I have a position of respect as the treasurer of the whole organization. Yeah, I don't rule an empire or know how to fight like you. I still demanded my respect from these men," she answered, her tone cool and confident, nothing like the woman she was pretending to be moments ago. "Who knows, one day, I might be hitting you up for a job if we become as good of friends as these men want."

I sighed, slouching in my chair. "They sure have a fucked-up way of showing their intentions. God, I feel like I'm back in grade school where the kid who pulls your pigtails is in love with you."

Betta and Tommaso chuckled at that, along with my guys, but the older men didn't at all seem amused.

"So what now? Do you need me to bleed on something? Offer up my firstborn child?" I asked, feeling the energy drain out of me at all these games they insisted on playing.

"That would do us no good since you lost your firstborn, then ensured it couldn't happen again," Sergio muttered.

Cold shock slammed into me at his words. "What—"

My words were cut short as Cam vaulted out of his seat, grabbed Sergio by the back of his collar, and slammed him to the floor.

"How *dare* you." Cam snarled, shoving his gun into the man's chest. "Do not speak of things you don't understand, or you'll never live long enough to meet any future grandchildren."

My body shook with rage and panic. No one knew about that. With Wes's help, I made sure we wiped all my records when I started building the Hidden Empire. Dax Blackmore needed to be a ghost. There shouldn't have been a spec of evidence regarding that left in the world. Reaching down to my boot, I pulled the gun I had tucked there, stood, and aimed it at Valter.

"How does he know," I demanded. "No one should have been able to find that information."

Void was right behind me, the warmth of his body telling me he was protecting my back as I focused on this. If they wanted to see what would make me snap, give up caring about my morals—well, good for them, they'd done it. Now they were going to suffer the consequences because I wouldn't let anyone use that information against me.

"I don't know how that information was discovered, but I do know it was one of my moles in the De León Cartel," Valter informed me. "If you'd tried to make a move to take over by proposing a marriage where no heir could have been produced, it was useful information to know." Valter glanced at the man Cam was currently choking out, watching Sergio's face turn purple, fighting to free himself. "Truly, I don't know why he even brought it up. You've made it clear that was the last thing you wanted from us."

Not believing a word that came out of his mouth, I shook my head slowly. "It's obvious to me you wanted to push me to the brink. Your stunt with Betta didn't work, nor did lying and manipulating me, then throwing it in my face. So here we are. How does it look to stare into the eyes of the person who will be your death?" I asked. Even to my ears, my voice sounded emotionless, empty of any humanity that I'd had.

"This isn't what I had planned, Dax," Valter said, his tone urging me to understand. "Tommaso and I are on the same page with him taking over the De León Cartel, some not so much. You have to understand, he acted on his own. Take his life if that's what you feel will make us even for the mess he's made."

I let out a bitter laugh, dropping the gun to my side. "Whatever deal you wanted to make with me is over. I won't work with a bastard who feels the need to drudge up the past that has nothing to fucking do with anything. As you said, I wanted nothing to do with merging our empires together. It was a low malicious blow, and if I ever see your face or Serio's again, I will kill you instantly. Cam, let the man go. I won't be the one to give them a reason to start a war when we're already in the middle of another one."

Shoving the gun down the front of my pants so I could get to it easily, I charged out of the conference room. I threw the glass door open so hard it shattered into a million pieces on the floor. Fucking bastard was lucky that's all he had to suffer. The only reason any of them were still alive was that it would create more complications that I didn't need before taking down Diego. Let's hope they know I keep my promise no matter the fallout it could cause.

Chapter Eighteen

Dax

No one spoke as we descended in the elevator, which I was grateful for because I wasn't sure I could keep from lashing out even at them right now. Rage, unlike anything I'd experienced before, put me in a fog to the point I wasn't sure I knew what my body was doing. All I knew was I needed to get out of this building, or I was going to burn it down with everyone inside. There had been many moments where I thought I'd seen the worst of myself, but the way I was feeling right now was darker than any pit I'd been in before.

"Void," I said through clenched teeth.

"Little demon," he answered, concern clear in his voice. "What do you need?"

"Find me a fight, one where they won't miss the body after I'm done with it," I stated as I pushed through the front doors and headed right down to the pier.

What I needed right now was space, not to be trapped by my past or the pain I'd endured through that. When I reached the end of one of the docks, I sat staring into the water, my own reflection staring back at me. I didn't want images of that time flashing through my mind. It was too much. They'd been locked away deep in my soul in a metal box wrapped up in chains, tossing away the key to never be found. Those memories didn't exist. I'd buried them away in a small hole that I never once visited.

"Dax," Cam rasped as he came up behind me, shaking me out of my thoughts with no concept of how long I'd been sitting here.

I shook my head. "No. Don't you fucking dare say one more goddamn word."

"You're right. I have no right to say anything. I wasn't there," he agreed, his own pain clear in his voice. "Void found what you're looking for, and we have a ride waiting."

Standing, then spinning on my heel, I headed back up the hill and found the ride in question was a Hummer limo. "What the fuck is that?"

"Mr. Three says he's looking forward to seeing a sample," Void answered.

Glancing at him out of the corner of my eye, I saw he wasn't thrilled with this gesture. "Did you warn him there will be clean-up needed?"

"Yeah, he said, not a problem. They had trash to take out as it was."

Not needing to hear anything else, I climbed into the limo and took a seat. I spotted a row of liquor bottles, but I didn't need what that would offer me. What I wanted right now wasn't to be numb and lost in a drunken haze. The clarity I had about my life and how this was going to end was all I needed to keep me in control. If the criminal world thought they could fuck me over and use the one moment in my life I was weakest, I would show them the hurt that came after it.

"Dax, I think it just needs to be said, we will never ask you about what was mentioned," Sprocket said once we'd gotten underway. "If you choose to share that part of your life, so be it, but we won't be asking for it. The woman we love is you here and now. Whatever happened in the past won't affect that, so it doesn't matter if we know or not."

My rage had reduced enough for me to absorb what was happening around me. I looked at all of them, the men who loved me and all my sharp edges. They didn't question or fight me on this. They wanted to be there for me, however I needed them. Right now, they were doing everything right, just letting me process from this blindside and affirming we were alright. How I ended up this lucky when so many others don't was simply a miracle.

"Thank you," I whispered and turned to look back out the window.

We drove for what seemed like a half hour, heading more inland. The contrast to the nice polished Hummer we were riding in to the area the driver brought us to was quite drastic. Most of the houses were boarded up, covered in spray paint with gang tags and other randomness. The cars were older models, dented, paint peeling, and rust chewing away at the sides. The driver turned off the main road and brought us to what seemed like an old factory area that had been shut down when work was sent overseas.

When we came to a stop in front of one of them, the overhead door rolled back, and two thugs stood in the entrance. Shoving open the door I was closest to, I hopped out of the Hummer, landing with a thud on the broken asphalt. My guys poured out using both doors and came to flank me as I approached the two lackeys.

"Mr. Three sent us," I stated.

One of the guy's brows rose as he looked me up and down. "You're the badass he told us was coming to blow off some steam?"

I blew a strand of hair out of my face, grabbed my gun, and shot the asshole in the thigh. He dropped to the ground screaming and clutching his leg. "Fucking bitch, you shot me."

"That badass enough for you?" I asked as I walked past him into the warehouse.

The space was huge and wide open with the late afternoon sun streaming in from the high windows. Dust motes drifted about as a breeze kicked up from the door being open. In the center of the space was a circular fighting ring with chain-link fencing around it, making it into a cage.

I spotted a bench near the ring that I headed for, pulling off my jacket. Then taking a seat, I unlaced my boots and removed my socks. Before I handed over my gun to Void, I dropped out the mag and handed that to Eagle. Sick and tired of being shot, I wasn't taking any chances.

Standing, I debated if I was going to keep my pants on or take them off. While the leather was soft and pliable, I felt like it would still hold me back. The guys started to grumble at this until they noticed I had on black boy shorts for underwear. It would cover as much as what I would wear for fight night, so they let it go. I'd worn a lace bralette under the crop top since if I lifted my arms, you'd see under boob, so I left the shirt as is.

"Who's got a knife? I might need a backup?" I asked.

Cam pulled one out. It was a butterfly knife he favored using. I took a closer look and found it was the one I'd given him for Christmas when we were still dating. The bastard really hadn't ever given up on us, had he?

"You gonna tape up or use gloves?" Void asked.

"Nah, I'm not expecting these to take that long," I answered, shaking out my arms and legs. "All I'm going to ask is that no matter what happens in the ring, you let me handle it until it truly looks like I might be in danger."

"You're gonna need to narrow that down just a tad, *loba*," Cognac requested.

I looked them all in the face for a moment before I answered. "Where I'm about to go in my head for me to release this, I won't feel pain. I'll take hits left and right, brushing them off until I'm so worn out, I can't fight anymore. That's where you all come in. I need you to protect me from me."

That had the guys looking a little worried, well, all but Void. He stepped forward and gripped my chin, searching my face before he kissed me ruthlessly, biting my lip hard enough I thought it might bleed. "If your demons become too much, we will save you like we promised."

Nodding once, I turned to the cage and entered, picking a corner to start in away from the door. Since we had arrived, I hadn't seen anyone here but the two thugs, but I knew somewhere people were watching. My money was the Four were either up in some hidden box or watching through cameras a safe distance away. It was a smart plan, and I was giving them a sample of what was to come. This might be the stupidest idea I'd ever had, but this was the only way I could process what I was going through. I'd tried therapy before, but talking about something you couldn't change didn't do a damn thing.

Right here, right now, I was in control of my fate. How this fight turned out was all on me and my abilities. My body had betrayed me before, and since then, I'd made a point to ensure it could never do it again. Getting shot started this spiral, and I'd managed to hold it back. Now I knew it was time. After everything I had gone through since that fateful day Kimber, my ex-sister-in-law, came to pay me a visit, shit had gone south.

Hearing someone step onto the mats, I opened my eyes and found a man standing there at the entrance. His eyes were dead, holding no hope in them. It wasn't the same as him deciding to give up, knowing his death was inevitable. No, this was the look of a man who'd killed so many people his soul had become blackened from the hit. He would kill anyone he was told to, no longer caring about the repercussions of it.

"Knives or no knives?" I asked him.

He shrugged. "You can have a knife. It might mean you last a little longer in the ring."

I cocked a brow at this. "Did they tell you who you were fighting?"

"Doesn't matter, you'll end up dead, or I will in the end. What good is knowing who you are or who I am?" he answered as he started to approach me.

Well, isn't this guy a bundle of joy and roses. Guess this explains why they don't care if I take him out.

Setting my blade on the edge of the ring, wanting to use Cam's for this, I faced my opponent, feeling it was better just to use one. There hadn't been any established rules, but I didn't really want any either. Crouching into a low fighting stance, I took a deep breath and yanked open the door on my banked rage. It exploded out, but instead of causing it to make me once more fall into that haze of furry, I used it to hone in on my target. This man in front of me was where I placed all the pain, anger, and emotions I hadn't dealt with over the years.

This man was the person who killed my twin, betrayed me one too many times, the faceless Marco who was hunting me down, and the first man I killed who tried to rob me and caused me to lose my baby four months along.

With that last addition, I felt the switch flip, and the darkness reared its head. That night was the first time I'd met the part of myself that created Two Tricks. It was then I knew I could do whatever it took to survive, and I wouldn't ever be assaulted like that again. Charging forward, I dropped to the ground and slid past the guy using my knife to slice up the back of his jean-clad leg. My knife was sharp as hell, but it didn't get as deep as I wanted it to with the fabric in the way.

Rolling away, I popped up to my feet, knife at the ready, as he turned to face me. "You're good. I might actually die today."

"No question about it. You won't be getting out of this ring alive," I stated. "They sent you in here to die."

"It will be a good death then, one I will have to work for," he commented before making his first move.

The bastard was damn fast and didn't give a shit about the fact I'd sliced up his calf. Blood made the mats slick, but that made things equal footing for us. The guy had to be an expert in taekwondo or muay Thai with how much he used his legs and tried to grab me in close. I was more of a kung fu, karate gal who used speed and quick movements to keep out of my enemies' arms. With how big he was compared to me, I knew if he got me on the mats, then I was in more trouble than I wanted to be.

Flashes of that night I was attacked bubbled up in my mind. I'd had a craving for ice cream, and I knew this 7-Eleven had it down the street. Cam wasn't around that night. He had a final coming up he needed to study for. Harper was in and out, going to this or that party, always trying to get me to go with her. I'd never told her I was pregnant, and thankfully, I'd always turned her down for those things, not being much of a party girl. Her fashion friends were too superficial, and I didn't know how to play nice.

I hadn't told anyone but Cam that I'd gotten pregnant, still unsure if I was even willing to have the baby. It was my last year of college, and I didn't have a stable job, and neither did he. Hell, I was only twenty-one, almost twenty-two, but I wasn't planning on getting married and having a family. Neither Cam nor I were remotely ready for that kind of thing to happen to us. I'd had the world's shittiest upbringing. *Who was I to parent a child?*

The thoughts went round and round in my head until I reached four months and past the chance to get it taken care of. During that time, I'd started to get attached to the little alien in my belly that made me have to pee all the time and crave weird things like dipping beef jerky in chocolate ice cream.

Our college town was safe enough, and I'd never once felt like I couldn't handle my own. So when a dude jumped out of an alley with a knife in his hand that was shaking more than my vibrator—I ran. The problem was, I ran back toward the school, not to the shop which was closer. The tweaker pounced on me, screaming for me to give him all my money. I fought, kicking, screaming, clawing, anything I could do to get this bastard off and stop him from beating on me.

"Just give me the damn money, you bitch," he screeched, spit flying in my face.

He landed a blow on my head, stunning me, allowing him to get to his feet and start kicking the ever-loving fuck out of me. I curled up, trying to do everything I could to protect myself and the little alien inside me. It was then I noticed he had dropped the knife, so I reached out and grabbed it, slicing out at his ankle. I must have cut just the right way to sever tendons or something since his leg gave out and he fell to one knee.

With a roar, I shoved myself up and launched at him, knife tip first. It impaled his chest, slicing through right between the lower ribs. He froze, stunned at the pain, but I was lost to the need to survive and protect what's mine. Yanking the knife out, I slammed it in again. Missing, I'd ended up hitting his sternum, but it was a hard enough blow it knocked him to the ground. Crawling on top of him, I stabbed until he stopped moving under me. Tears streamed out of my eyes, and I could taste blood on my tongue, making me retch all over him.

Stumbling my way off his body, I leaned against the brick wall of a building and tried to pull myself together. Then a horrible shooting pain started in my stomach, and I noticed my sweatpants were soaked in blood. I have no idea who called the ambulance or what they even said to me as they got me on a gurney and took me to the hospital. By the end of it, I'd lost the baby, and the internal damage was so bad they needed to ensure I couldn't have kids anymore, so they removed what they needed to.

A week later, I found out that Devin had been killed and two weeks after that, I left Cam to start my journey to become Two Tricks. I would become something this world feared and respected, allowing me to protect my loved ones. It's probably why I always put myself at risk over others. If I could save them, then it would make up for not being able to save those I had already lost.

That's why Valter and his goons digging up *that* fact about me hit so hard. Once more, everyone I loved and cherished in my life was in danger. Too bad for them, they dared to hit on the moment in my life I failed the one most important thing I had to keep safe, reminding me of the promise I made in that hospital while I was all alone.

I would never be a victim, and the world would fear the day they touched those who belonged to me.

"Enough," Cameron snapped, grabbing me by the throat, and forcing me to look at him. "That's enough, Dax."

"Why weren't you there? I needed you to be there that night, Cam," I choked out, fighting back tears. "They made me deliver her because my body was already too far along in the process. I had to do it *alone*."

Cam reached up and took my hand, removing from the knife that was protruding out of his bicep. "There isn't an answer I can give you that will fix what you went through. Nor can I make up for not having my phone on at least vibrate while I was studying. I failed *you*, the woman I love more than anything in this whole world who was carrying my child. You're one hundred percent right. I left you to go through that all on your own. I had no idea how to even start to atone for that sin. Truthfully, I still don't. Is there even a way to do that?"

Tears ran down my cheeks, and I looked down to find the man under me, just like that night. Blood seeped out from under him and Cam kneeled right in the worst of it to get to me. This time he was here, right by my side, not letting the demons take me.

"You can make it up to me every day of your life. You'll never leave my side in life or death. You will be right here," I ordered, my voice cracking with the emotions I was struggling through.

Cam nodded, shifting his hold on my neck so his thumb ran up and down my pulse lovingly. "I made that vow to you when you carved your name over my heart, but I'd already planned to do it with or without your permission."

"Asshole," I muttered and yanked out the knife, making him grunt and rest his head on my shoulder for a moment. "Sorry I stabbed you."

"You're lucky I don't mind pain when it's inflicted by you," Cam reminded me as he scooped me up in his arms. "There's nothing for you to continue to fight in here, so let's get you out of this mess."

When Cam stepped out of the ring, I found Tommaso and Betta standing there with my guys. My whole body froze at the sight, then, just as quickly, I twisted the knife still in my hand so I could throw it at one of them if needed. "What the fuck are you doing here?"

Chapter Nineteen

Dax

Tommaso raised his hands in a sign of surrender. "Trying to find a way that we can still be friends," he admitted. "No games, no tests, no old men who don't know how to play by the new rules. Just you and me... well... and them." He gestured to my guys, then to his sister. "Betta is my right hand, so I brought her to prove we're both invested in making amends. So what do you think? Is there a chance my father didn't fuck this up as royally as I think he did?"

"Give me one good reason I shouldn't kill you right here right now and save myself the trouble? At this point, I could just take you all down and rule over both East and West coasts?" I challenged, tapping on Cam's arm to set me down.

He slid me down his body rather suggestively and kept one arm wrapped around my shoulders, keeping me close. To them, I'm sure it looked as if he was trying to protect me, but really, he was protecting them *from* me.

"That man you just obliterated with more vengeance than I've ever witnessed before in a person is who gave us the information," Tommaso explained. "We found out from him that Diego learned about the event from a woman named Kimber. Seems she's some woman one of Marco's lieutenants is fucking."

A growl seeped out of my lips as I once again wished I'd killed her the moment I had the chance. That woman had been nothing but a fucking thorn in my side since the day I met her. I loved my twin but choosing her was what killed him when it came down to it.

"So you think that since I got vengeance on a person who spilled my story to your boss makes us even?" I asked cocking my head slightly as I gauged how hard it would be to land this blade in this eye socket.

Tommaso shook his head. "No, but it's a start and something you would have asked for at some point. Since we already had him at the ready and you wanted a fight, it just seemed to make sense. I want to propose a different plan to you than was presented at the office." Reaching into his inner suit pocket, he pulled out folded documents, then handed them over to me. "Written here is my personal offer that no one but Betta knows about."

Reaching out, I took the papers, blood from my hand, smearing over the white surface. I unfolded it and scanned over the first page, trying to read through the legal jargon to figure out what he was really saying. Lawyers love to put in all kinds of different backhanded loopholes hidden in words you couldn't understand. When I finally got into the meat of the matter, my brows shot up in surprise.

"Wow, I have to say I didn't see that coming," I commented as I flipped to the next page that broke down a diagram of names, roles, and their place in Diego's cartel. "You came to bat with all the right things to get my attention, but how are you going to pull this off?"

"That's where you come in," Tommaso said, gesturing for me to flip to the next page. "I wrote it all down, but if you think there is a better way, then I'm open to suggestions."

Laughter burst out of me as I looked over Tommaso's plan to oust the current Italian leadership as well as take over the De León Cartel at the same time, combining the two. He'd used the research they'd done on me to incorporate where it would fit best into this hostile takeover. It was a brilliant plan and one I would have come up with myself if I had all the pieces to pull it off. Turning to the last page was his plan for the future, including our friendship and siding with me when the showdown with Marco happened.

That had me pausing, reading over the wording again before I asked my question. "Is this what he's really doing?" I asked. "Does he really think he can become the king of the criminal world if he takes me out? While I'd like to think I'm that much of a badass, I don't think I have that much pull outside the US."

Betta looked at Tommaso in complete shock. "Does she really believe that? She can't be that blind to the truth, can she, Tommy?"

"Do you think now is the time to be talking about me like I'm not standing right fucking here?" I asked as I handed the papers over to Wes. "I mean, I'm already dirty. What's a little more blood?"

"Whoa, there, girlfriend," Betta said with a chuckle. "I'm definitely not looking to pick a fight with you after seeing how you handled that guy. The way that guy got himself in good with Diego and his men is by becoming their pet fighter and killer of those who pissed them off. He wasn't just some chump, and you demolished him like the devil himself lived in you. Really, I consider myself lucky you decided to spare me during the whole break room stunt."

A wave of exhaustion hit me as the events of the day settled and the last of my adrenaline drained to normal levels. "I wouldn't have killed you for being a bitch unless you did something I couldn't look past. Now in the efforts of you making nice, explain to me what the fuck you meant a moment ago?"

"I was just simply shocked that you have no clue just how big of a player you are in this world. When the fight was announced, it caught everyone's attention across the globe. People are declaring whose side they're on in how they bet," Betta explained. "Marco is supplying some of his own men for the challenge along with many of the others who are backing him."

Rubbing my forehead, I felt like I was missing a key point in all this. "How can you possibly know all that?"

"Well, because I'm Madam Two," she answered with a grin. "I run any and all betting that happens in our fights. Remember when I told you that I earned myself a position of respect? I wasn't just being cheeky when I said that."

"Please don't tell me Mr. Three is one of the men who pissed me off today. I'd really like to not have my fate in the hands of a man I will kill on sight," I asked with a sigh.

"No, the only person who knows about my involvement in all this is Tommaso," she answered, waving off my concern. "My father would be incredibly disappointed in using my skills this way, but there are many times it comes in handy dealing with situations behind the scenes. The other three men I work with are neutral enough, but if they had to choose a future that would be more advantageous, it would be putting their lot in with you."

"Okay, say that's all true, then this fight night is turning into the beginning of a world war of crime lords," I pointed out. "Are we sure that's the best plan?"

"It was going to happen whether you did this fight or not, Dax," Tommaso reasoned. "Marco is the one driving it, and when push comes to shove, they will choose one way or the other. You respect those who give it. Anyone who doesn't, well, they get put in their place to learn from their mistakes. What everyone knows and is choosing to side with is that you aren't looking to rule the world. You just want to run your own empire and do business. Marco wants to have his fingers in all the pies and reap the benefits."

He paused, seeing he was losing me in his long-winded explanation. "Fine, here's the cut and dry of it. You're the person who's willing to stand up to Marco, so you automatically became team captain of the opposing side. They respect you and want to rally behind you, so they don't have to be the one to do it if everything goes to hell."

"Well, fuck," I grumbled. "This is making my brain hurt, and all this blood is drying, making me incredibly itchy. Is there a place I can rinse off, even if it's a hose? Not sure walking around Boston looking like Carrie is my best choice."

"Yeah, there are showers in the back. I'll show you," Betta offered.

"Great," I looked over my shoulder. "Who's coming with me?"

The guys looked at each other, a little surprised at the offer but quickly pulled it together as Cognac and Sprocket stepped up. Since Cam was still acting like my shadow, I assumed he was coming too. I really should look at his arm to make sure the damage wasn't too bad. It was almost to the point I felt like we needed to bring Dani with us everywhere we went. Good thing Sprocket was way better at stitches than I was.

"Lead the way. The others will keep your brother company," I said, gesturing for her to move along.

She cocked a brow at me. "You think little old me deserves three of your men watching your back?"

"No," Cam stated. "It's to make sure you make it back to your brother alive."

The color in her face started to bleed out of her face as she realized who the dynamic at play was. "You're gonna need to work on that if you're going to be his right hand in this coup. We women need to be fearless in the face of all danger, aka, fake it till you believe it. Soon enough, you'll believe it since you've said it so often to yourself." Betta nodded as we headed deeper into the warehouse.

"Is this what the place in New York will be like?" Cognac asked, trying to ease the tension.

It took her a moment to catch up to the change in topic and smiled at him. "No, it will be much nicer. This is more for people trying to earn their stripes in the whole game. Where we are going to host in New York is far nicer. It's an actual fighting ring that's built underground and has many entrances, so it's not easy for law enforcement to find it. Not that we haven't paid them off, but there's always a few young bucks looking to get that one case that will get them promoted to chief."

"You mentioned betting. What kind of stakes are we talking about?" Sprocket inquired.

I had to admit I was curious about that as well. If they were making it known whose side they were on, it had to be substantial.

"While we might be working on becoming friends, if I told you that kind of information, I'd be setting myself up for trouble. If the other three found out I gave you insider knowledge like that, I'd be lucky to keep my hand, let alone my head," Betta shared, rubbing her left hand like she was worried she might lose it.

"Damn, they play by those rules," I muttered. "Can't blame you for not sharing."

"Yes," she agreed. "They are progressive enough to allow a woman into the mix, but they won't go easy on me if I fuck up. I told them I was going to tell you who I really was and my connection, but to give you more than that wasn't agreed upon." She paused at a door that swung slightly off its hinges. "This is the locker room with the showers. I figured you'd want to go in on your own. There should be a towel or two left. We had some fights over the weekend, and it's not restocked."

I gave her a two-finger salute and headed in, the guys following after. Sprocket stayed by the door as the rest of us ventured through the rows of lockers until we found the open shower area. I tugged off my shirt, chucking it in the trash can I spotted. Not like I was going to be able to save it. The showers were those lame kinds where you had to hit the nozzle and it only ran for a few minutes before turning off. It wasn't like I was planning on indulging in a long shower, but it just pissed me off to keep whacking it.

The soap was in a dispenser on the wall, which I was grateful to have since dried blood was a bitch to scrub off without it. Feeling like I was as clean as I was gonna get, I gestured to Cam. "Come here. I want to take a look at your arm. I feel like we need to at least wash it and wrap it before we head back to the hotel."

Cam unbuttoned his shirt and peeled out of it, flinching as it pulled on the wound. Thankfully, he'd been wearing black on black, so you couldn't spot it was blood making his shirt damp. Grabbing his forearm, I moved and twisted him around until I could see the damage I'd done. Fortunately, it didn't seem too deep, but it would absolutely need stitches. The blade was two inches wide, and I'd gotten him deep enough it cut the widest part. Blood slowly oozed out of it from my poking, but I was pretty confident I hadn't hit any major blood vessels or arteries.

"Sprocket, you feel like playing doctor tonight and stitching him up?" I called.

A moment later, he appeared, and Cognac went to take his place by the door. My guys weren't fucking around when it came to my safety. We might be talking about friendship, but that didn't mean trust came guaranteed. Sprocket took my spot to see in the best light this dinghy locker room could provide.

"That should be easy enough. It's a clean cut with no rough edges, so that's good. The only thing I'd be worried about is whatever that other guy might have since it still had his blood on it," Sprocket pointed out. "Might be worth stopping by the hospital so he can get a shot of antibiotics or something. Is it worth seeing if our new friends have any suggestions?"

"I think I might rather call Magnus to see if they have a safe option for us to go to. Hospitals get all weird about unexplained knife wounds," I grumbled. "If only I hadn't lost my shit like that, this never would have happened."

Cam reached out and caught my chin with his hand. "Beautiful, I knew the risks going in to stop you. That's actually why I volunteered. Void couldn't have anything happen to him and Eagle has just recovered. The last thing we need is one of the major players getting wounded."

"You're a major player," I countered, not liking he didn't see his value in all this.

He smiled and pulled me in for a quick kiss. "Thank you, but you know what I mean. Coordinating with the FBI doesn't require me to be in peak condition. Besides, it needed to be me in there. I had to be there for you this time no matter what."

My eyes burned with tears I refused to shed right now. "Yeah, I get it." Stepping back and clearing my throat, I looked around. "Did we find any towels?"

Sprocket grabbed one off a bench that Cognac must have found. I dried off the best I could and headed back out to the main area. The bralette was black, so if I didn't get all the blood off it, no one would see, not to mention the jacket over it. Leather pants on damp skin with wet undies were a bitch, but we all had to suffer in our own way.

"Wes, can I borrow your cell?" I asked. "Gonna call Magnus and see if we can't find an option for Cam's arm to get looked at."

"You don't have to do that. We've got a guy on call," Tommaso offered. "We can even send him to your hotel if you prefer."

I eyed him suspiciously but looked to the guys for their thoughts. Eagle rubbed at his chin, thinking for a moment, then nodded. "Yeah, it would be better to get it taken care of quickly. I assume we don't need to tell you where we're staying?"

Tommaso had the courtesy to look apologetic as he rubbed the back of his neck. "No, I've got that information. He should meet you there or arrive shortly after our driver gets you back there."

Eagle grunted and turned to head out the door. Once more, we all climbed into the limo, only this time, Eagle snagged me and plopped me right between him and Void. Both of them cuddled up against me offering their support physically and emotionally without a word. The drive back to the hotel was much faster, making me think the driver had been stalling for time on the way to the warehouse.

"What do you think?" Eagle asked in a low voice. "Is it worth taking the risk to trust them?"

Void grumbled something under his breath only to settle my legs over his lap, so I leaned more on Eagle. "If he's willing to betray his own father and their Don, what makes you think he won't do the same to us? A traitor is always a traitor."

"Not that I don't feel the same way, but would you say the same thing about Demitri? He's betrayed us countless times, but yet you still seem to trust him?" I countered.

Void seemed to chew on that for a moment. "I think I trust him because the motivation was to protect someone else, not for his own gain, if that makes sense."

I nodded. "That makes sense, but you have to admit the fact that he gave us this whole plan in writing means he's putting trust in us that we won't turn on him and sell him out to Valter."

"She makes a good point," Eagle agreed. "If we took that and gave it to Valter, he would know exactly what was going down and how to stop it."

"What if it's another game? They could be testing us to see if we would support a coup," Picasso interjected. "Yeah, he said no games, but who the fuck is willing to believe that? He also said that guy was the one who got the information from Diego and his men. There's no way to check that out since he was already dead."

"Wes," I called over to where he was absorbed in reading over the contract again. "You mind calling our best buddy, Magnus, for me when we get back? I'd really like to check in and see how things are going for them."

It had been a while since I had to speak in the code we'd made up for texting so no one would pick up on what we were really saying. He gave me a thumbs up and went back to his reading like it wasn't all that important. What I'd really asked him to do is see if Magnus had the four-one-one on our new friends. If they could tell us that this fighter was one of Diego's pet fighters, that would help further the proof they were being honest. Right now, going back to California wasn't an option for us. So instead, I felt like it was time to pay a visit to my bestie and her new boos.

When we got to the hotel, the doctor was already waiting for us in the lobby. He made quick work of stitching Cam up, giving him some meds I made him inject into himself first. If it was antibiotics and a slight pain killer, it shouldn't cause any harm, right? Wes reached out to Magnus and was told he'd get a call back when they had information to share. I took a much longer shower in scalding hot water scrubbing from head to toe, making sure all the blood was gone. If I was going to try and get some sleep, I needed to know I was clean before curling up with Cognac and Picasso. My sins couldn't taint them. That was the last thing I wanted.

I'd been afraid nightmares might start to plague me after reliving that moment again, but thankfully, I slept the sleep of the dead. When I got up the following morning, I was informed we were going to New York to stay with Harper and the Wright brothers. My men decided it was best to hash out this offer not being in their territory.

This ought to be fun. It was the first time all my guys would meet them. I knew I should've brought Dani along on this trip.

Chapter Twenty

Void

The FBI needed the jet back, and we decided it was better to stay in the area than to go back to California only to come back a few days later. While Dax slept, the rest of us talked, trying to figure out the best plan going forward.

"Doesn't it seem like things are falling into place too easily?" Picasso asked, joining us once he knew Dax was fast asleep. "I mean, come on, they just happened to send us the documents hoping we would think of the same plan they were about combining forces? They had to be working on this for far longer than we even knew about Marco."

Wes leaned back against the bed's headboard in the room we'd gathered in next to Dax's. I hated the setup of this. It was hard to keep an eye on things with us all spread out over four rooms, even if they did connect. Next time we would just take the penthouse and not worry about drawing attention. I'd rather know we could control the setting than keep a low profile.

"You make a good point, Picasso, but the only part I want to push back on is that everyone seemed to know Marco was gunning for Dax except us. He'd been building allies around the world and making his moves in such a way it didn't draw her attention. Like Betta was saying, our woman has more pull in this criminal world than she understands," Wes pointed out. "Hell, even the Wright brothers knew, but they aren't ones to get drawn into what's going on in the world since they work for the highest bidder. Well, they did. I feel like since they are now apparently engaged to Dax's best friend and soul sister, their team Dax all the way."

"Fair, I will admit, as we've been dealing with this, it's clear we were late to the party," Picasso agreed. "So maybe this is all legit, and I'm just the one being overly guarded."

Cam shook his head as he waved his glass of whisky at the same time. "No, it's wise to be that skeptical. Nothing in a deal like this should be taken at face value. There is something in the contract they're trying to hide. Now I'm not saying it's something we'll have an issue with, whatever it might be, but everyone is always looking out for themselves."

Eagle shifted through the pages that Tommaso gave us, looking over the contract portion. "This shit is so full of legal bullshit I don't know how anyone knows what it says. Dax has to have a lawyer on hand we can send it to and will give us an opinion."

"Yeah, I already emailed it to him," Wes answered. "He should have an answer for us tomorrow at some point. This guy has helped us on tons of business deals and caught small changes that could have a big impact later on down the line, so I trust if it's there, he'll find it."

Sprocket ran his hands through his hair, scrubbing at his scalp, telling me he was fighting off one of the migraines he got when stressed. It's one of the only times he can't stand to have his hair up in his typical messy bun.

"We can't stay in Boston," he muttered. "It would be stupid for us to be here like sitting ducks as we try and figure out what to do. Besides, as far as the big bosses know, the deal is off, and Dax isn't interested in trying to fix it. If we leave for New York City and hang out with Harper, then it shows we aren't waiting for them to make an offer. From what I understand about those guys, no one is going to fuck with us while we are there."

"I was going to say even if we wanted to stay, we can't in this situation," I voiced. "It's too hard to monitor."

"Got to agree with you on that, man," Wes added. "Alright, it's settled, I'll tell the triplets we're coming, and we'll leave whenever Dax wakes up. I don't think we should wake her up. After that kind of blow and the emotional upheaval that happened today, I say let her sleep till her body is ready."

Everyone mumbled their agreement, and Picasso went back to join Cognac, who'd stayed with her. Out of all of us, he was more than happy to go with whatever we decided, not one to feel the need to be involved in all the choices as long as we told him what the plan was.

"I think we need to keep it to two rooms," I stated. "As well as one of us staying awake to keep an eye on things. I just don't trust that the big bosses won't try to pull some crap with how things ended. Not to mention if they get wind of what went down at the fighting ring."

"Smart call, Void," Eagle approved. "Who wants the first watch?"

Cam raised a hand. "I didn't let the doc give me anything too strong for the pain, and I don't think I'll get much sleep with the dull throb going on right now. She didn't need to know that the tip of the blade almost came out the other side. It would have only made her feel worse."

Having been shot and stabbed a few times in my life, I would take getting stabbed any day, but I knew exactly what he was talking about. Even though the wounds were clean cuts, the way they sliced through the muscle just made your bones hurt with every flex or movement.

I walked over to Sprocket and tapped him on the shoulder. "You want me to do that thing?" He looked up at me with pain clear in his eyes and gave a slight nod. "Sit in the chair so I can get a better angle."

Cam and Wes watched, expressions curious. The other guys were used to this weird fix we'd found that helped lessen the pain for Sprocket. He hadn't gotten a bad one of these in at least two years, but with everything going on, I'm not surprised one got triggered. Sprocket had a bad habit of letting things get worse, not wanting to go to the hospital or take pain meds of any kind. After what I learned about his mom, I couldn't say I was surprised.

I felt down his neck and shoulders, feeling how tight it all was. I set my forearm on his shoulder and started to stretch out his neck muscles. He hissed at the burn I knew this caused, but I had to get him more movement to do the second half of what was needed after working both sides, getting more to give by the time I was done. Then as soon as I felt Sprocket relax into my hands, I twisted, and a loud crack filled the room.

"Ah fuck," Sprocket muttered. "It's one of those things that feels so much better but also hurts like a bitch when it happens."

Shifting, I got him to relax in the other direction and felt him take a deep breath, then let it out, which was when I made my move. Another crack, and I started to work the muscle with my forearm, trying to get the muscles to move better. After the adjustment, it made a huge difference, and I could already tell the pain had lessened some. "That should do it."

"Thanks, man. I can never trust anyone else to do it," he admitted. "I'm always afraid they're going to break my neck or something."

I patted his shoulder and urged him to the bed. "Get some rest. I'm gonna check Dax's room real quick. Then I'll take the floor."

Sprocket didn't argue. He knew with my back that sometimes the harder surface of the floor was better than a bed that was too soft. Being a fighter was what I loved, but the way I did it back when I was younger sure was stupid and fucked me up. I'd let them get their hits in for a while, so the fights weren't over as fast, but that meant I took a lot more damage than I needed to.

Slipping into the other room, I spotted my little demon curled up in a ball, face hidden in Cognac's chest, while Picasso guarded her back with his body. If I hadn't known to look for the shock of pink hair, I wouldn't have seen her right away with how nestled in she was. My little demon had truly gone through hell today, faced her demons, and made it out the other side. She wasn't anywhere close to being over whatever had happened to her, but I felt like she might have acknowledged for the first time she wasn't okay.

The door in her room was locked along with the safety latch, but when I tested the lock, it didn't hold as snugly as I would have liked. There was too much give, so it would be easier to just bust in on us. That made up my mind. I wasn't going to sleep in the other room, I'd sleep right here in this little hall by the bathroom. If anyone tried, I would hear it right away. There was no way they'd be getting past me. Our woman fought her battles today. It was our turn to keep her safe and protected.

I grabbed a pillow one of them had kicked off the king bed and settled in for the night. My gun was on my chest, a bullet ready to go in the chamber. One simple pull of the trigger and they'd be dead before they knew I was there. As I tried to sleep, my mind raced with all the things that could go wrong in this fight coming up, knowing that all the people who hated us were trying to get their fighters in the mix. Dax was a fucking animal when she honed in on a fight, and if I let myself get to that point, we would be perfectly matched. Thing was, if we dove that deep, would we be able to pull ourselves out of it?

When Eagle found me all those years ago, I wasn't sure I'd ever be able to come back to the surface. It's one of the reasons I picked Void for my name. That's all I was at that point. A void full of rage, and I allowed people to use that against me. The drinking and drugs didn't help matters. While I could drink some these days, I couldn't touch another drug, or I'd fall right back into the pit. Instead, I found other ways to use my skills and ground myself in healthier alternatives.

Now I had my little demon to look after, a woman who shared the same dark soul I did. If I could keep her from getting lost in the bleakness of rage, then maybe there was hope for myself as well. I could never be a good man, but thankfully, she didn't want me to be one, happy to take me as I was—black soul and all.

"Who's fucking idea was it to try and fit everyone in this goddamn car," Picasso grumbled as we hit the halfway point of our drive.

We'd stopped for food since we decided to get out of Boston as quickly as we could. Dax surprised us by being up by ten, so we decided to just grab coffee and hit the road.

"You're not the only one who doesn't get a seat. I have to be on someone's lap for the whole four hours," Dax snapped.

There seemed to be a miscommunication with the rental car company, and we ended up in an SUV that fit only seven people. They didn't have anything bigger, so we decided to just roll with it instead of trying to find another company to work with.

"Don't you even," Eagle cut in, pointing a disapproving finger at her. "You were offered the chance to take the front seat, but you gave it to Cam, so I don't want to hear it."

Her silver-blue eyes flashed at the challenge. "Right, so I was just supposed to sit on his lap and squash his arm? You have to drive since you're still not a hundred percent yet, so that leaves me."

"Little hellcat," Eagle growled.

Cognac cut in between them, seeing just as I did that those two would either start fighting in earnest or fuck each other in the back seat if we didn't end this fast. "Hey, now I have an idea that will fix this whole problem."

Both of them glared at him, waiting for his answer.

"It's simple. I'll just sit on Dax's lap. See, problem solved, and everyone's happy," he suggested, a shit-eating grin on his face.

Dax rolled her eyes and playfully punched him in the gut as she climbed back into the car. Wes and Sprocket were already there, so my guess was she went to hang with them in the jump seat. I side-eyed Eagle grinning at my best friend. "You know she gets like this when she needs a good fucking. It's like she doesn't know what to do with her pent-up feelings, so she picks a fight."

"Yeah, well, I would have been more than happy to bend her over the front seat and give her what she needed, but we're in public, and no one but us gets to see that shit," Eagle said as he pulled the keys out of his pocket. "It's only two more hours, then I'm sure we can deal with our woman's issues."

I chuckled as we walked back to the car and climbed in. Dax was in the back like I suspected. Wes was showing her what information he'd gotten back from the lawyer. For the most part, the contract was legit and the only loopholes were more to ensure neither party had control over the other's businesses or money. She'd been sleeping in my arms when Wes first gave us the rundown. This was better, though. Those two were best friends before they ended up lovers. Even though there were eight of us involved in this relationship, we needed our one-on-one connection with her as well.

Everyone seemed to keep it together for the last leg of the trip arriving at the high-rise that Magnus had sent us to. I was interested in meeting these men. We'd spoken to them on the phone a few times, but Wes was the only one who'd actually met them in person.

As we pulled up, a man stepped out of a little hut opening the door for Eagle. "Welcome to the Garden Heights Condominiums. Will you be staying overnight?"

Eagle looked over at Cam, who nodded. "Yes, we are guests of the Wrights. We'll be here for a few days."

"Excellent. If you leave the keys on the dash and you take this ticket, I'll get it all settled. In case you need the car, just give that number a call," the man instructed, tearing off a claim ticket and stepping aside.

Cognac leaned closer to me, whispering, "This place is fucking fancy. Are we sure we're at the right place?"

"Oh yeah, we're at the right place," Dax announced. "Those boys have a flair for the dramatic. I bet you money they have a whole floor for themselves just so they don't have to worry about sharing space with anyone."

Tumbling out of the vehicle, we stood looking up at the building, not even really being able to see the top of it because of how high it went. The sliding doors opened, and a shriek sounded as a woman came bolting out, aiming right for Dax.

My first instinct was to intervene, going for my gun, but a hand grabbed my shoulder. "I wouldn't suggest doing that, my friend," a voice said. "One thing you never want to get in the middle of is two best friends who haven't seen each other in a long time."

Shifting, I found a man with a carefree smile and brown eyes and gave off every signal he wasn't as deadly as he was. Clearly, this was one of Harper's men, and I was impressed he could move so fast without me noticing him. "I don't know about your woman, but I'm pretty sure mine would consider taking my balls if I hurt Harper."

"Yeah, Dax is efficient like that, isn't she," the assassin agreed. "Harper would make our torture something less bloody but equally horrifying, like making us be her mannequins for her latest design idea. Do you have any idea how much it hurts to get stabbed by those little pins? Fuck, I'd take most kinds of torture over that."

My attention drifted back to the two women gushing affection all over the place as they talked over each other and hugged again. "I feel like I'm learning a whole new side of Harper right now."

He laughed and stuck out his hand. "You must be Void. Ghost, good to finally meet you."

"Feeling's mutual," I answered, shaking it and purposely trying not to make a pissing match out of it.

Two more men who looked identical to Ghost exited the building, talking heatedly to each other. Then the one with hazel eyes cut off the other and turned his attention to the two women. "Doll," he commanded.

Harper rolled her eyes and sighed, looking over her shoulder. "Yes, Maggie?"

"What did I say about running out here without one of us? The only safe place is—"

"In our four walls," Harper sassed as if she'd heard this a few times. "Ghost was right behind me. Besides, like Dax's guys would ever let anything happen to me? They're practically like my big brothers now they made an honest woman out of my girl," Harper announced, grabbing Dax's hand to show off the ring. "She's engaged too."

By the nickname, I gathered that *Maggie* was Magnus leaving the other to be Jaxson.

"She makes a good point," Jaxson interjected. "Now, let's play nice as we meet the *whole* family for the first time. Think you can pull that off?"

"Can we at least take this up to the house? I don't see why we need to make it easier for them to make a move standing out here in the open," Magnus reasoned.

Stepping up to Dax, I rested a hand on her shoulder, causing her to look up at me. "He has a point. While we might not be able to keep our arrival quiet, it's best if we don't cause chaos the moment we get here."

"That's absolutely no fun," Dax said with a pout.

I gripped her jaw and leaned down to whisper in her ear. "If you're a good little demon for us, I'll make sure it's worth the effort. Maybe we should play the game of how quiet can you be as I take you over the sink in the bathroom while they talk?"

Her whole body shivered at my words, telling me that I'd been right about what was making her so feisty. "Or are we to the point where you can't wait? Should we take the elevator up by ourselves and give the security guy a show?"

"*Fuck*," Dax whimpered. "How about all the above?"

"Hmm, I think we should see if you can even pretend to be good for at least an hour before you get your reward, little demon," I decided, knowing I'd gotten her in hook, line, and sinker as I kissed her roughly before releasing her.

Dax's expression was a little glazed over, then she shook herself out of it and clapped her hands together. "Right, so we were going up to the apartment?"

Harper hooked our girl's arm through hers and led the way with Ghost and Cognac hot on their heels while the rest of us grabbed bags from the car. Magnus grabbed one from me and knocked my shoulder with his. "You'll have to tell me what you just did to get Dax of all women to comply."

I grinned wide enough that it showed my teeth. "Some secrets you have to figure out on your own, and it absolutely wouldn't work for you."

Understanding flashed in Magnus's eyes and he let out a bark of laughter. "Well played, Void, well played."

Chapter Twenty-One

Dax

When the elevator doors opened, and the apartment was revealed, my jaw dropped. "Holy shit." I gasped.

"Yeah, we were in another one that you'll be staying in one floor down, but when this became available, I made them snatch it up," Harper shared. "I mean, look at that view, and it has direct access to the roof. The guy who owned it before clearly was an idiot to give up something this amazing."

I gave her a sideways glance, then I turned to look at the brothers, who were doing everything possible to avoid making eye contact. "Totally, real stumper on why something like that would happen."

"Come on, let me give you a tour," Harper urged, dragging me up the stairs. "We have our room and two others for guests or whatever the future might bring for the four of us."

That had me digging in my heels, looking at her strangely. "Are you?"

"Oh goodness no." Harper laughed, waving off my question. "Is that what you think? They got me pregnant and now I'm marrying them? No, this is the real deal for us, I know it seems so fast and most people will judge us, but when you know, you know." She grinned at me with a shrug. "What am I even explaining this to you for, Miss I Have Seven Husbands?"

Chuckling, I followed her into the master bedroom, finding it had pretty much just a giant bed in it. Dressers were built into the window seat along one whole wall giving them storage. It was an interesting concept and for New York, where every square foot counted, it was smart. The bathroom had me jealous, but we didn't spend long in there before she was whisking me away to the next room.

This was clearly her sewing room with fabric lying all over the place with sketches pinned up on the wall. A large table with a sewing machine took center stage, and I could tell just by looking at it that it was no Walmart purchase.

"Damn, girl, do these men have any money left in the bank?" I teased since the whole room smelled new. "You've only been back for like what, a week and a half?"

"What can I say? I was inspired by all the traveling we did. Have you ever been to Bali? It's amazing, and I hope we get to go back sooner than later after all this. There is just so much life, color, and sights to see there," Harper gushed. "The guys took me cliff jumping in the most beautiful place."

I grabbed Harper's arm and looked at her from head to toe. "Who are you and what have you done with my best friend?"

Harper rolled her eyes at me. "Yeah, yeah, yeah, very funny. I know I wasn't all that into adventures, but the guys have made it their personal mission to make sure to try new things. Well, before we got back and I was once again hiding from Marco. Did you know he sent someone after us in Bali? Thanks to your mission, we got out of there just in time."

That bastard is tying the noose tighter and tighter each day.

"Whoa, no need to go all dark and broody, Dax. I'm fine, we got Prim out of Russia, smuggled in your tank, and now we're back together. To be honest, I'm glad we had to come back and face things head-on. There's no way I can be on the run my whole life, and he's going after my family too. You, Wes, and your other guys are my family besides the triplets. It's been killing me not being able to fight. Always running and hiding is going to get us nowhere."

I pulled Harper into a hug, realizing how much I needed my best friend right now. My guys had been right to make this call. Being here with her and the brothers was best. "God, I missed you, Harper."

She hugged me back just as tightly. "Not as much as I missed you. Now, let's head back down and make sure the guys haven't come up with some crazy idea in the name of bonding."

"Oh shit, if Ghost and Cognac take charge, this is going to be so bad," I muttered, running down the stairs to see Ghost with lighter fluid in one hand and a lighter in the other. "Stop right there," I ordered.

All the guys looked at us with surprise written on their faces.

"Did you not want to grill out tonight?" Ghost asked, cocking his head in question.

"*Loba*, the man went out and bought a grill just for us to use tonight. It's even a charcoal one that will make everything taste like it should, unlike those gas ones," Cognac explained, coming to stand next to the man he was defending.

Harper was behind me, trying to cover her giggles, but she was failing epically. "No, I don't have a problem with grilling out tonight. That actually sounds amazing. What I was worried about is that you two had cooked up some plan to burn your arm hair off of each other or something equally asinine." The two of them looked at each other with excited expressions. "Hey now, that was not a suggestion or encouragement to do it," I barked.

"Oh, I get it," Jaxson interjected. "Madam Two Tricks here is worried if we join forces and gang up against her, she'll lose."

That had Cam smirking. "I do know Harper would be on her side. Do you think the ten of us could handle the two of them?"

"Depends," Magnus said, rubbing his chin. "I think if we keep our fun to something that shouldn't get us killed, they might give in."

Void scoffed. "Then what's the point in doing it? If the threat isn't there, then it takes all the thrill out of it, don't you think?"

"Hmm, I'm thinking if our goal is to not end up in the hospital, that leaves enough wiggle room," Eagle added his two cents. "Two of us are already on the mend, so it might be better to keep this gathering on the tamer side than come up with something really epic later."

Ghost clapped his hands together, then shot two finger guns at Eagle. "I like the way this man thinks. Get him a beer."

Harper tugged on my shirt sleeve and leaned in. "Is it just me, or did they all just become best friends?"

"Wes is keeping his distance, so we might not have lost them all, Sprocket's also been pretty quiet, but he could go either way," I murmured out of the side of my mouth, trying not to draw attention to our conversation.

Jaxson, Cognac, Ghost, and Cam left to deal with starting the grill. "Take a fire extinguisher out with you," I hollered after them.

"Such a mother hen, today, spitfire," Picasso said, pulling me to his side. "What happened to the woman who was more than happy to bust our balls at any given chance on the ride up here?"

I glared up at him. "Look, each of you spread the crazy around between all seven of you. Some have more. Some have less. Those three, yeah, they got my level of cray jam-packed into each of them."

"She's not wrong," Harper announced. "They are batshit crazy for sure, but in some strange way, I find it incredibly sexy."

Magnus moved over to wrap her up in his arms, kissing her forehead. "Is that so, doll?"

"I might be screaming and swearing at you while it's all happening, but you always have a plan," Harper answered with a shrug as she entwined her arms around him. "Can we just make sure we don't burn the house down? I just got it how I wanted it."

Magnus tipped her chin up and kissed her deeply before letting her go. "I'll go keep an eye on them."

"Might as well come with you, not that Cam will listen to anyone but Dax," Eagle muttered. "Like a damn dog, that one, but he's ours, so I'll try and keep him alive."

Grinning, I leaned more into Picasso, loving how everyone was interacting, even if I feared something idiotic would happen. With Harper practically being my sister, I really wanted the guys to get along because I'd hoped we'd be spending a lot of time together once this was all behind us.

"Why don't we take drinks and hang out on the patio? It's lovely out, and that way, we can talk about what's going on while they cook?" Harper suggested.

Wes walked over to her and pulled her into a hug. "Damn, it's good to have you back, Harper, but it's really strange to have you involved in this part of things. We've spent so long keeping you in the dark it's hard to remember we can just be open and honest about it all. You've got as much skin in this game as we do now."

"I hope you mean that figuratively and not literally because having someone's ick all over me once is more than enough," Harper explained, shivering in disgust.

"What?" Wes asked, looking at me in confusion.

"Oh, ah yeah," I started with a little laugh. "Remember that guy we met who knew Harper? So his son tried to make a move on Harper and Magnus shot him point blank in the head while he was still holding onto her."

"Damn," Sprocket commented. "That absolutely would have been messy. I don't blame you for not wanting to go through that again."

"Anyways, let's grab drinks and bring out a cooler for the others, and we'll make a party out of this night yet," Harper decided, putting us all to work.

The night seemed to take on this surreal quality that made me almost believe there was nothing wrong in the world. I had my men, my best friend, and the guys who were clearly over the moon about her. Everyone laughed, ate, drank, and just enjoyed hearing stories about our adventures apart.

"You really asked him to pee on your leg?" I laughed. "Girl, don't you know that's just some made-up bullshit?"

"Now I do," Harper said with a pout. "How was I supposed to know that *Friends* would do me dirty?"

I laughed so hard my face hurt, and I was about to cry. "Damn, that is the best story I've ever heard."

As our laughter died, Magnus pulled out his phone and frowned. "Looks like we have visitors, but they won't get far unless I let them."

He flipped the screen around so I could see what he was talking about. There was Tommaso and François talking as they stood in the elevator. "How the fuck do they know where we went or where you live?"

"François is a tricky bastard. He always seems to appear in the oddest places," Ghost muttered. "Why would he be with Tommaso? I thought the only one who was in on this was his sister?"

"That's what we were led to believe," Eagle grumbled. "Seems he didn't like that we left without giving our answer."

"What are our options here?" I asked. "Can you make them arrive on any floor?"

Magnus nodded. "Yeah, I can send their asses right back to the main floor too if I wanted."

"You said there was another apartment that we'd be using? I want to see what they have to say, but I don't want them in your home," I explained. "Something tells me I really want to hear what they have to say. Tommaso looks just as upset as I feel. Not the face of a man who's come along on this trip willingly."

"We can do one better," Jaxson said. "We own both apartments on the lower floor, the second one is empty and we just use it for storage. That way, they have no idea where any of us are staying. Mag can also change the number on the display, so they don't have the right floor if they try to come back."

"Smart," Cam agreed.

Wes leaned over and looked at the phone. "You're gonna need to tell me how you did that and connected it to an app on your phone."

"Oh, the great Weston needs me to teach him something?" Magnus teased. "Yeah, I can show you what we did."

"We should probably head down unless you want to leave them waiting in there," Harper pointed out.

Magnus glared over his phone at her. "You're sure as hell not coming with us. I don't want you in the same room as François if I can help it. He looks at you like he's trying to steal you from us."

Standing, she walked over and draped her arms around his neck, kissing his cheek. "Lucky for you, I'd never let that happen. He's far too old for me, and besides, you already proposed twice. If I were going to cut and run, I wouldn't have said yes twice."

"When the lady is right, she's right," Ghost commented, smiling at them.

With large amounts of grumbling and reluctance, we all took the stairs down a level. Jaxson let us into the space and it was just full of random boxes here and there. When I opened a lid, I found grenades just chilling in packing peanuts.

"What the actual fuck, you guys? This is what you store in the spare apartment?" I asked, raising one to show everyone. "Someone could just break in here and blow the whole building up."

"That's where I left those," Jaxson blurted. "I've been looking for those at each house we stop at. I knew we had more somewhere."

"Well, if you look on the bright side, if they have an army of Italians downstairs, we can totally take them," Cognac reasoned.

Yup, it's official. All of us were batshit crazy. I actually felt like that was a totally logical point to make.

Magnus smacked Void in the chest with his hand, motioning for him to follow. "Let's go get the fuckers and see what the hell they want."

Void followed as I placed the grenade back and glanced at the other boxes just to see if there were any more explosives we should keep an eye on. Everything else looked like it was gear they needed for various jobs but weren't commonly used so they were stored here. Really with the things in this room, we could get out of this building seventeen different ways, from repelling to paragliding.

We all went for our weapons when the door opened again as Harper moved behind Ghost. Void entered first, then held the door open for Tommaso and François, who were being prodded along by Magnus.

"This wasn't quite the reception I assumed I would be getting, but I understand. No one likes people to drop in unannounced when they shouldn't even know where you live," François said, his hand up showing he had no weapons. "Oh, Miss Peirson, it's so good to see you again. Are you happy to be back in the States?"

"Enough," Magnus snapped. "Tell us why you're here, François."

"Yes, yes, we shall get right down to business if you so choose." He sighed. "Tommaso, why don't you fill them in since this is your doing?"

When I looked at him, I noticed the black eye he was sporting. I hadn't been able to see it from the way he was standing in the elevator. "What the hell happened to you?"

"I don't know how but my father figured out we met with you after the meeting. He was furious, saying we didn't need you to pull this off, but he's wrong. There's no way for us to pull this off if you're not part of it. We might have the numbers but not the influence needed to hold a position like that for long." He sighed, rubbing the back of his neck. "I told him as much, and he got pissed, which is how I ended up with the black eye."

"While that sucks, I'm not sure how that tells us why you're here, in New York, looking for me?" I pushed.

"My father called Valter and told him that Betta and I went rogue. They got to Betta before I could warn her, so I pretended I wanted to talk, make amends, then killed them all," Tommaso explained. "The coup is in motion, and I'm here to beg you for your assistance."

I waved my hands to get him to stop talking. "Whoa, back the fucking train right up. You killed Valter?"

"Yes, and my father. He refused to side with me, and I couldn't risk him going to Diego," Tommaso answered.

Cognac whistled his shock as he crossed his arms. "Damn, man, that's cold, but you had to do what you had to do. Nothing about a hostile takeover is easy or black n' white. You make split-second choices and hope to God it was the right one."

"Did you get to Betta?" I asked, understanding how protecting family could make you do drastic things.

"Yeah, she's at the hotel. They beat her up pretty good, trying to get information out of her, but she didn't talk," Tommaso answered, pride in his voice. "I know I said you could have time to look over the agreement, but we don't have that now. Things are set in motion, and there's nothing I can do to stop it."

Wes came to stand at my shoulder as he addressed Tommaso. "Then what's he doing here with you? The plan didn't include outsiders."

"François is the representative from the head of the Italian mafia. He's here because it's proof that they support my claim over Boston's branch and will also back me in taking over the De León Cartel," Tommaso explained. "Now, all I need is the Queen of the West Coast to add her endorsement, stating that she will aid in my fights if it comes to it, knowing that it will give me enough time to establish my own base and loyal followers."

Eagle frowned at that. "Wait, are you telling me you're taking over all of this, and you have no one but outsiders backing you? None of your own people are waiting for the signal to help make this happen?"

"No, that's not what I'm saying. Think about it, though. The Italians have been a small fish in this game, and I'm about to take a massive slice of the pie. People will be pouring out of the woodwork to try and take this from me," Tommaso argued. "I've got men at the ready to make this happen. I just need to know if you're in this or not?"

"I can't give you that answer right here right now," I stated. "This is not just my choice to make or whose life I will be putting on the line, so I need tonight to discuss things, and I'll give you my answer in the morning."

Reaching for his back pocket, he pulled out a folded manila envelope. "This is just to show you what value I bring to the table. Giving this to you means you don't need me as much as I need you. I hope it proves that I want this to work. The criminal world needs to be brought into the twenty-first century, and only having fresh blood is going to do that."

Taking the papers, Void and Magnus escorted them back to the elevator, leaving the rest of us to look at what he'd given me. Opening the envelope, I pulled out papers but also pictures of a woman in her twenties and a guy who seemed around her age. There were pictures of them in the city, leaving a building and getting in and out of cars together. My guess was since she looked so much like Gabby, it was her daughter.

"Look at that, she's got both ears and all her fingers," I pointed out, handing one over to Picasso. "Now we know for a fact those belonged to someone else."

Shuffling through the papers, I found one for the son where Elena was living with him. I was glad she wasn't going to be in the main building. It would make taking it down easier. Out of all the planning we'd done, trying to balance firepower and ensuring we could get her out alive was tough. You can't take over a whole office building and not risk shooting someone you don't mean to.

"He gave us everything we needed to get Elena out of here tonight if we wanted to," Eagle commented. "Is this what he meant when he made it so we didn't need him?"

When I looked over the next page of information, my brows shot up. "Ah no, pretty sure it's the detailed schedule they have of Diego's habits, mistresses, and restaurants he frequents. If we didn't want to hit the office building, we don't have to at this point. Fuck, he even has the locations to his two homes, one in the city, one over in the Hamptons."

That had everyone converging upon me, looking at the information. Thankfully, no one tried to snatch it out of my hands. Then I might have stabbed someone.

"Let's get back upstairs, and we can really map this out and talk logistics," Jaxson suggested. "We have an office with all the things we need."

Once more, we climbed back up the stairs, grabbed a beer, and got to work.

Chapter Twenty-Two

Dax

It was hard to fight against the adrenaline rush you got from making a plan that was falling into place so perfectly. I'm not sure any of us got much sleep last night because of it. The information Tommaso gave us helped to fit the pieces we couldn't figure out perfectly. We had all the names of the biggest players in his cartel, where they liked to hang out, and who was important to them. Not many of them had families, which was smart. This was no life for kids to grow up in.

"Holy fuck, if this works, it's going to be one of the most epic takeovers ever witnessed," Ghost said, flopping onto the couch in the living room. "They're never going to see it coming."

"Now the trick is to get Tommaso to convince everyone to do their part," I countered. "He might have taken out his immediate competition, but I'm pretty sure he knew all along he'd have to do that. This is going to be that on a massive scale."

Wes looked up at me from where he was lying in my lap, poking my side. "If he doesn't have the balls for it, then just do what everyone assumed and take over both coasts."

"Yeah, I'm not sure I want that much work," I said as I absently brushed my fingers through his hair. "Think of how much work it is to run the Hidden Empire, then double it. There would never be a chance for us to do anything but put out fires flying all over the place. It just sounds awful."

"Fine, then we put Harper in charge," Sprocket suggested. "The two queens ruling the US criminal world together."

"Not a fucking chance," Magnus grumbled.

Jaxson looked down at the sleeping Harper in his lap, lovingly brushing hair off her face. "I don't know. I think she'd be an amazing queen. It's not like she would be doing it on her own. We would be there to back her up."

"You want to give up being our own bosses and traveling the world?" Ghost asked, his face showing his surprise.

"We would still be our own bosses, but let's be real, we know Harper runs the show. She just lets us think we call the shots for his ego," Jaxson said, gesturing to Magnus with his thumb.

"Once things settle down, why wouldn't we be able to travel? Besides, you're telling me that being assassins isn't getting old? The last dozen jobs have been so boring. This would be new, and we wouldn't have to leave our gorgeous girl."

Void grunted at that from where he'd been lying on the floor. I thought for sure he was asleep but clearly not. "I get that feeling. Not sure I'd be able to handle Dax flying all over the place if we couldn't all go with her. Makes me twitchy when she's not in the house with us... not sure I could handle her being in another state."

"This is all assuming the kid doesn't have the stones to pull this off, but I have a feeling we're cutting him short," Cam interjected. "This plan is based on eighty percent of the work he's put into the takeover."

"It's always good to have a backup plan," Picasso argued. "If things were to fall apart, we'd need to know how to move forward."

"Did anyone bother to ask me if I wanted to be queen?" Harper asked with a yawn as she rolled on her back. "Why the hell would I want to run a criminal empire like Dax? I'm not the kind of gal to handle being shot, hunted, and constantly looking over my shoulder for danger. One day, I think I'd like to have kids, but that for sure isn't gonna happen if they can't be safe."

Jaxon traced her face with a finger, then booped her on the nose. "Then that settles it, no ruling empires for you."

"Really? Just like that, you're fine with it?" Harper questioned.

"Yup, I want kids with you someday, and if that's going to get in the way of my filling that belly up with my child, I don't want it, gorgeous," Jaxson answered honestly.

Watching those two stare at each other with so much love had me looking down at Wes. He must have known how this conversation was going to rattle me a little as he pulled me down for a sweet kiss. "I love you, Dax, no matter what. As long as I have you in my life, nothing else matters."

I kissed him again and playfully rubbed our noses together before sitting up, smiling. The rest of my guys were all looking at me now, making me freeze like I'd missed something important during our tender moment.

"That goes for all of us, Dax," Eagle stated. "You're the woman we all fell in love with, not for any other reason that you crashed into our lives and made it impossible to let you go after that." He then glanced at Harper, who was watching me as well. "I have a feeling those kids are going to need some kick-ass uncles and one badass aunt in their lives."

Harper sat up and clapped her hands excitedly. "Just think how much fun this will be. You can do all the things I'd never allow them to do or their fathers, for that matter. I'm pretty sure they will turn into the biggest worry-warts as the kids start getting into things. They're going to need people to turn to when we drive them crazy. Who better than you guys?"

"Now, why would you go and say that?" Ghost demanded. "I'm going to be the coolest dad ever."

Harper just looked at him and patted his leg. "Yeah, we'll see. I've seen how you act with me. When it's our children, I only see your smothering getting ten times worse."

Ghost pouted at this but didn't really argue either, making me think it might be true. "Now that we've got that all settled, I think it's time we call Tommaso and find out if he's willing to play our game," I suggested.

Wes handed over a cell, and I dialed the number Tommy had left on the sheets for us. It rang twice before I realized it was six thirty in the morning and he might not be up.

"When you said you'd call in the morning, I didn't think you meant the ass crack of dawn," Tommaso answered.

"Yeah, sorry not sorry. I haven't gotten to bed yet, and I'm taking it out on those who got to sleep," I shot back. "Do you want my answer or not?"

"Okay, shoot," Tommaso said as I heard the rustling of sheets and assumed he realized he wasn't going back to bed at this point.

"You've got the Hidden Empire backing you if and only if you agree to the plan that we've made. It will put you in power, take out Diego, but give me what I need out of this whole situation," I warned. "Still interested?"

"One hundred percent, but I feel like this conversation shouldn't happen over the phone. I'm going to send you an address to my operations headquarters in New York. This way, as you lay out your plan, you can sell it right to the men who are going to help us pull it off," Tommaso offered. "Unless you don't trust me enough to do that?"

I pinched the bridge of my nose, trying not to bitch this guy's ass out for getting sassy before I had any sleep or coffee. "That's fine. It makes the most sense if you're confident that you'll stick by what we came up with."

"Trust goes both ways, and if it gets me in power and meets your needs, then who am I to argue?" he reasoned.

Grunting, I leaned back against the couch. "Send me the address but give us a few hours to pull ourselves together before we head over there. I'm sure you need to get your ducks in a row as well." I paused, thinking of something I should have asked last night. "Hey, does everyone know you killed the big boss man?"

"No, François has helped me keep that under wraps. Valter is known for going off to see one of his mistresses in Pennsylvania, so we are just playing that story up for now," Tommaso answered. "Take the time you need. If we're going to pull this off tonight, then you need some sleep."

"I'll text you back at this number when we're heading over," I shared, then hung up, tossing the phone on the couch next to me. "Seems he's all in, wants us to go to his base of operations to settle up the plan and put it into action tonight."

"Little Demon, what about the fight? It's tomorrow?" Void asked.

I rolled my head to look at him. "Oh, don't you worry about that. I have a perfect plan for that situation. It's going to be so much more fun and ensures that neither of us will get hurt."

He narrowed his eyes. "What did we say about sharing the plan, little demon?"

"Can I just ask you guys to trust me on this, and once we get the important part settled, I'll tell you the rest?" I requested. "This can only happen if the whole plan goes as it should, but we've seen how well that goes."

"Does it put you in more danger, *loba*?" Cognac asked.

"Nope, it actually takes me out of danger," I shared.

Cognac shrugged and looked at the others. "That's all I needed to know. You guys good?" Everyone nodded and mumbled in agreement. "Great, now I think we need to get some sleep so we aren't dead on our feet."

Magnus grabbed keys out of his pocket and chucked them at Sprocket. "These will get you into the apartment downstairs. It's set up for you guys, even food in the fridge."

Heaving ourselves up, we managed to stumble into the apartment downstairs, and I flopped face-first on the bed. I felt the others come joining me, but I didn't know who managed to fit, but I didn't care. I just needed sleep.

Looking out the car window, I chewed on my thumbnail as we headed for Staten Island. Now that I'd gotten four hours of sleep and ran through the conversation I had with Tommaso over again in my brain, I realized I should have questioned why he had a base of operations in New York. If he'd been based out of Boston this whole time, when did he have the chance to make a place here that Diego didn't know about? It was smart as shit to have people already planted where you wanted to take over. I just didn't get the feeling he'd been that prepared.

All of this was setting me on edge. So much of this came down to relying on others that weren't my people. It had me second-guessing everything. A hand reached up and grabbed mine, tugging it away from my teeth.

"Don't be so mean to yourself, little rebel. We'll handle whatever comes our way. The eight of us are a strong unit, and with the triplets added in, I don't see much getting in our way,"

Sprocket murmured, kissing the back of the hand he held. "I know giving up this much control is hard, but you're not in this alone. The victory or the failure will be ours to share. Just keep your eye on the prize. We're almost done with this whole thing."

Letting out a heavy sigh, I leaned into him, allowing him to hold me, giving me his confidence in this that I was lacking. This wasn't who I was. Dax Blackmore was a woman who stabbed first and asked questions later. Now here I was asking all the questions, afraid to make the wrong move. Then again, it had just been Wes and me. Now, I was suddenly the quote-unquote *mockingjay* heralding in the change of the criminal world as we know it.

As Eagle turned into a subdivision, I sat up again, looking around utterly confused. *What the hell was he doing making a base here?* Children rode bikes up the street, and there was even a playground with kids and mothers chatting as they played.

"Is he mad?" I demanded no one in particular. "Who the fuck thinks having a base of operations in the middle of happy hometown suburbia was a good plan?"

Cam looked at me from the front seat. "If he wanted to make sure that if someone figured out where he was, they'd think twice before doing massive damage. It's rather brilliant. I'm not saying I agree with him, but in a way, it's incredibly cunning. Who would even consider him being here?"

I grunted as Eagle pulled into the driveway of a house at the end of a cul-de-sac that had a large field behind it and a baseball mound set up. At least he didn't have innocent people all the way around him. Magnus parked beside us, his face telling me he felt the same way I did about all this.

Tommaso might be smart, but he played on the edge of being someone I might need to take out. If he couldn't see the lives he was putting in danger, I might have to reconsider my plan altogether.

"Don't pass judgment yet," Wes warned me as he settled his hands on my shoulders. "Let's see what's going on first. Then we can make a judgment call."

If anyone understood how much I hated bringing innocents into our fight, it was Wes. Criminals could kill, maim, and blow each other up all they wanted. Bringing it into a situation like this where people who had no place in our fight were casualties, I couldn't stand for that. Wes pushed me forward, guiding us to the front door, where he reached past me and rang the doorbell.

Betta was the one who opened it, looking like hell. She had a massive black eye, split lip, and even more bruising around her neck like someone had been choking her. Her eyes were hard and full of rage when she met my gaze.

"Keep that," I told her. "You're going to need it until this is over. The first taste of the reality of this world is a bitch and a half, but chances are you'll never let it happen again."

She didn't answer, only nodded and stepped out of the way, letting us in. In the front sitting room, I found François sipping coffee, reading a book like it was just a normal Friday afternoon. He glanced up and smiled, gesturing for us to come in and join him.

"Please sit. I'm sure Tommaso will join us in a moment," François said as he set aside his book. "We are quite eager to hear what sort of plan you've cooked up for us, Miss Blackmore."

"We'll see if you're still excited after I've told you what it is," I answered, flopping down only to stand right back up. "Wait, is there more coffee somewhere?"

"I believe you should be able to find some in the kitchen," François offered.

Waving everyone else to stay seated, I headed deeper into the house. If it was like any other typical American home, where they would keep the kitchen as the *center* of the house. Sure enough, I was right, but what I also found was it connected to the living room, and there were four men watching some trash soap opera. They looked up at me but didn't seem at all worried, turning back to the show.

It didn't take me long to find the mugs and pour some coffee into one. Just when I was about to head back, a woman holding a toddler came out of a room off to the side. She spotted me and came to a halt, eyes wide with fear. Glancing at the guys watching television, she noticed they didn't seem bothered and approached.

"Hello there, can I help you find something?" she asked.

"I'm sorry, I didn't realize this house was actually someone's home. I assumed Tommaso was just using it as a front," I said as I reached out a hand. "Dax Blackmore, and there is a group of us in the front room with François, just so you're not surprised... again."

She shook my hand tentatively, giving me an odd look. "Cynthia, Tommaso's wife. It seems it slipped his mind to tell me we were having guests."

Even though I tried to keep the absolute shock off my face, it was impossible. "I'm sorry, did you say wife?"

"Yes, we've been married a year now," she answered. "In order to keep me safe, we live apart during the week, and he comes to spend the weekend with little Michele and me. He told me about you, said that you were what he needed to pull this off so we can be a family for real."

Holy fucking shit, how many other surprises was I going to get with this guy?

Tommaso came down the stairs looking at something on his phone but came to a halt when he saw the two of us talking. "Oh, ah..."

"Don't worry, we've already introduced ourselves to each other," I said, giving him a disapproving look.

"Good, that's good," he stammered, unsure of what to do next. "The others here with you?"

"They're in the front room with François," I answered. "Was there a better place you wanted to talk?"

"Yes, I'll grab them, and we can head downstairs. Leonardo, gather the others and meet down in the prep room," Tommaso ordered before he went to get my guys.

Taking a sip of my coffee, I glanced at Cynthia. "So you know everything?"

"There are no secrets between us, Two Tricks," she answered sharply.

"Hey now, no need to get territorial. I have seven of my own men to deal with. There's no way I want to add another. Besides, I'm not the other-woman type," I reassured her. "I know his father was talking about some bullshit marriage, but trust me, I don't want any of it. What I'm interested in is helping your husband get into power and being someone I can have to watch my back while I deal with the asshole gunning for us all."

Cynthia took a deep breath and hugged her son tightly. "Sorry, I've been a secret for so long, I forget that not everyone is trying to steal what's mine. People see him as unattached, and to protect us, he can't let anyone know. All that's going to change, though, with your help. I'll finally be able to come out of the shadows and be by his side as a wife should."

Tommaso returned with my crew following after him down into the basement. With one more glance at Cynthia, I sighed. "Be careful what you wish for. This is a hard life for anyone to survive in. Keep those you trust with your life close and those you don't closer."

Leaving her with those parting words, I joined the others.

Chapter Twenty-Three

Dax

The *prep* room was clearly the code word for war room because everything he'd given us was in its raw form all over the space. It was behind a fingerprint-locked door that must have been constructed to be a panic room of sorts. It was under the garage, leaving the rest of the space open to be used as a child's play area.

"When you said base of operations, you meant your own home?" I asked once the door was shut, keeping what we said to just his room. "Your wife didn't seem to know that we'd be coming over today."

"Look, I get why you feel this is a slap in the face, but it's the best way to keep her safe. My men are always around to look after her and Diego is too prideful to even consider that I might be right under his nose without him knowing. I wasn't planning on falling in love or her getting pregnant, but I loved her too much to let her go. So, instead, I'll do whatever it takes to keep her and my son safe, like being the new ruler of the East Coast criminal empire," Tommaso explained as he leaned against the massive wooden conference table.

"Any other tidbits of information you haven't shared with us we might want to know about?" Eagle asked, crossing his arms and giving him a look that a lesser man would have crumbled under.

"No, that was the last thing I've been holding to myself for good reason," Tommaso snapped back. "None of us really trust each other, and I get that, but you can't take every slight as a sign I'm going to fuck you over. That being said, are you still willing to share your plans?"

Everyone looked at me, even Tommaso's five guys who were seated at the table. "Let's get started. We have a lot to do and not a lot of time to do it in. First off, how many men do you have on hand to help us with this takeover?"

"Trusted men, a thousand, men who will help pull this off so they don't die... altogether fifteen hundred," Tommaso announced.

My jaw hit the floor. I knew he said he had guys at the ready, but for him to have pulled that many and know where they stood on the matter was fucking crazy. "So we have fifteen hundred men, including us, here to pull this off?"

"Dax, I don't think you're understanding that I've been planning this for two years," Tommaso pointed out. "The moment I found out Cynthia was pregnant, I knew I had to find a way to be top dog. Nothing would be safe if I was at the whim of others. Family is collateral to everyone in our world, and I *won't* ever let that happen to my wife and child."

Pulling back a chair, I took a seat. "Now that's some shit I can get behind, and with that many, we can count on this being a cakewalk compared to me thinking we only had a few hundred max." I pointed at one of the lackeys. "Let me see what maps you have of the city, the areas surrounding Diego's New York house, and his son's. I'll also need to know what kind of firepower we have at our disposal. I've got a few ways to get some but the less we have to tip off our hand, the better. Wait, where's Betta?" I asked, looking around the room.

Tommaso looked at me curiously. "Why would she be part of this?"

"Isn't she your right hand?" I asked. "If that's changed, then fine, leave her be. Otherwise, she better get her ass in here. She's got her own part to play in all this."

He left the room without another word, and the rest of us got to planning. The five guys were leaders of different areas where his men were integrated. Some were just in the city, keeping an eye on activity, while others were inside the De León Cartel. They'd been able to manage so many people by having them report to one contact person. Any real-time information we needed, they were the ones to give it.

Our biggest part of this plan was hitting multiple locations all at the same time, causing so much chaos they couldn't react to it all at the same time. We knew the location of money houses, drug storage, and cartel hangouts. They were going to have so much blow up in their face, they wouldn't know what hit them.

"I don't get it. Why take out perfectly good operations? Then we'll need to start all over," one of Tommaso's men questioned.

"It was like when you wanted to make a hit but didn't want anyone to figure out it was pinpointed, so you took out a bunch of random others to mask your intended target," Jaxson explained, shocking the others.

Leave it to the assassin to come up with an example that made perfect sense but was completely fucked up at the same time.

Harper just punched him in the arm with a glare. "What was that for? It's a perfectly good explanation and totally works."

"I know you kill people for a living, but can we try not to make it sound like you don't give a shit about human life as you kill off those *random* people to cover up your work?" Harper muttered.

"Gorgeous," Jaxon's tone was kind but had a hint of a warning. "We've talked about this."

She opened her mouth to argue, then noticed all of us watching and shut it. Crossing her arms, Harper grunted and leaned back in her chair, clearly not happy about being told to keep her thoughts to herself. The door opened, and Tommaso returned with Betta right behind him, neither of them looked happy, and it had taken far longer than it should have to get back down here.

"I'm here," Betta announced as she flopped into a seat.

Magnus took a breath like he was going to start his explanation again, but I held up a hand to stop him. Pinning Betta with a look, I cocked my head, trying to figure out what exactly it was that pissed her the fuck off.

"Hey, *you*," I snapped.

Her gaze flicked up to meet mine.

"You in or out?" I demanded. "If you're in, then you better fucking act like it because this isn't some game. People are going to die no matter how well we plan this, but a shitty attitude like that is gonna get even more people dead."

I knew I was being an asshole, but she needed to understand the stakes. "You don't want to be his right hand anymore, fine, get the fuck out. Just to be clear, when I say get out, I don't mean this room. I mean, pack a bag, pick a location, and get the hell out of dodge because having you around is only going to fuck us over."

Betta looked at me like I just punched her right in the tit by how shocked she was. I was betting no one had talked to her like that in a long time, but I wasn't going to go soft on her. Women in this world needed to be tougher than the men, and right now, it was time to nut up or get out.

"How dare you sit there and speak to me like that," she finally spat out through clenched teeth. "You have no idea what I've just been through."

"That's where you're wrong, but I'm not going to compare beatdown stories with you because it doesn't fucking matter. What's your answer, Betta? You gonna brush off the wounded puppy act and get to work making these fuckers pay, or should I help you pack a bag? This won't be the last time shit like this happens to you if you stay in this role," I reminded her.

Betta just let out a scoff and looked at her brother. "You're not going to tell her off?"

"No, because she's right," he answered. "Dad's gone, and I'm not going to shelter you from the storm that's coming. I'll help you get out if you want but speak up now, or it's going to be too late later."

I had to respect Tommaso for that. He understood what I was saying and knew it was crunch time. If we were going to pull this off, we needed everyone in or all the way out.

"So that's it? Right here, right now, I have to commit to this?" Betta demanded from the room.

Sprocket frowned at her. "The fact that you are even asking that means you've never been behind this choice. You don't step up to being a leader's right hand if you're not willing to give your life for the job. If they can't get to him, they'll come for you. It's part of the job."

"Then if I say I'm out, I have to leave right now and never come back?" Betta asked, looking hurt and confused.

I shot out of my chair and walked over to her, planting my hands on the armrest, boxing her in. She reared back from me, terror written on her face. "Suck it up, buttercup. You got the shit end of the sick last night, and it's rough to deal with when the darkness you've been flirting with bites back. Here's the thing, though, unless you bite right back even harder, you will be marked weak, vulnerable, and a victim for the rest of your goddamn life. Where the fuck is the woman who fought for her place among the four? That's the bitch we need right now. She'd know how to get the job done and stop sniveling over a split lip and a black eye."

Rage flashed in her eyes, the most emotion I'd seen all day from her. "That's right, get mad, build that fire up inside you. Trust me when I say it will keep you warm and motivated far better than any drug or alcohol." Pushing away from her chair, I took my own and looked at the rest of the table. "She's good now. We can proceed."

Tommaso looked at his sister, then back at me, not at all understanding what just happened, but that was fine. He didn't need to. I'd been where she was, and more than anything, I wish I had someone who would have given me that talk. Wes was like her brother, though, but wasn't going to push me the way I needed to be pushed.

"As I was saying before," Magnus started after an awkward pause filled the room. "Our goal is to get Diego and his son at the same time even though they are in totally different locations. Adding in the hits to some of the other places before we go for the real targets will cause so much chaos they won't notice till it's too late. Doing this also ensures they will put both of them under house arrest, thinking it will keep them safe. This is the protocol most people have, knowing if they're bold enough to go after their money, why not the boss?"

Cam picked up where Magnus finished. "We will have five teams hitting various locations as well as another team going after the house in the Hamptons. Diego is staying in the city because of the fight tomorrow night, so he knows he won't be there. It just adds to the urgency of the attack if they have to send more men all the way out there to deal with it. That group we are sending isn't going to really have to attack the place. More like throwing a few grenades or Molotov cocktails to make it a good show, draw out the neighbors and cops."

"That's what you guys call not really attacking a place?" Charles, one of Tommaso's men, commented. "What does really taking one down look like?"

"Simple," Void answered. "There's nothing left of it, no chance of it ever coming back, just rubble and blood."

Charles whistled, nodding his head as if he was impressed by our tactics. Each of us took turns breaking down the plan making sure everyone knew what was going on. Once they understood the basics, we moved on to planning out how many men would be going where and what we had to work with as far as weapons went. Tommy boy certainly had a pretty tight operation for someone who had been keeping this all a secret from not one but two criminal organizations.

"This is all well and good, but I don't see where I come into play," Betta cut in.

Grinning, I leaned forward on the table. "Oh, girlfriend, do I have a special job for you. How much pull do you have with the other three of your fight club?"

"Enough where it counts, but I would only be able to use those cards once," she answered, her tone curious. "Tell me what needs to happen, and I'll let you know just how many of those cards I have to play."

"Two parts," I announced, holding up just as many fingers. "One, I need to know how big this fight is going to be. Are we talking like the room is going to be packed with all the big bads of the world, or are we talking more live streaming to keep the world from ending?"

Pulling out her phone, she searched for something, then scanned over the information. "Looks like we are going to have a thirty-seventy situation. The lesser influential players in our world will be there at the event, but eighty percent will be online since they are the real deal. Too many people have grudges or just plain hate each other, so they won't be in the same room with each other. The other three felt it was best to encourage many of the biggest names in the game to remain home, and they would get an official TV crew to film the fight."

Nodding, I chewed on my thumbnail as I thought about the next part of my plan. This could only work if everything else went perfectly. Before, I wasn't sure it could be done, but now, with how much help we had, it was looking up.

"Before everyone freaks out at what I'm about to say, just know it's part of a far bigger plan. My end game is to back Marco into a corner he can't get out of, and I need something that is going to push him over the edge. Taking over the cartel, then handing it off to the new player with my blessing is going to do most of the work. Yet it still needs just one more thing to put the icing on the cake," I explained.

My guys watched me with wary expressions knowing this was typically when I suggested something out of left field and put myself in danger. Funny thing, this time, it was all about the show, playing the game that Marco started with all these crazy stunts. Now it was my turn to make a move on the chess board, putting his ass in checkmate.

"I need Diego and the bastard son who tricked Elena into turning against us to remain alive until Saturday night," I announced. The stunned looks on everyone's faces told me they hadn't been expecting that. "There is an incredibly valuable reason that I need them alive, and it also means neither Void or I will be fighting. They're going to get the bloodshed they want, but I need them alive to make it all come together."

Betta's face turned into a scowl. "There's no way they will allow that. All the money we stand to make is off the fights you two are going to be in."

"Don't worry. I'll make sure they know anyone who bet against me is donating their winnings to the cause and if they don't want to lose more than that, they'll make sure to stay out of my way. That's the other part... I need is a list of who bet for and against me so I can make sure to act accordingly if I were to run into them again," I shared with a smile. "Wouldn't want them to think they can side with the man who wants to be king over us all, now can we?"

Betta looked unsure, but she gave a groan of agreement. "While it's not nearly what we would have made if the fights happened, it will more than cover the cost put into it."

"Don't forget, just because Void and I aren't fighting, they can't do what they planned for the rest of the night. Let everyone think things are going according to plan until it comes to my turn, and I'll deal with the rest. The biggest thing I need is to make sure no one steps into the ring unless they are escorted, bound, gagged, and bleeding by one of my men. Oh, and the list of names," I added.

She sighed and rubbed her forehead like I was giving her a headache. Seemed I had that effect on more people than I would care to admit. "Every bit helps to make them see reason without this burning me for good and cutting me out of the deal altogether."

"Ah, you don't want to be mixed up in that once Tommy here gets to be in power," Cognac interjected. "Too many loyalties means one of them will be tested. When it comes down to it, my money is that you'll pick your brother. Follow this through, then say your goodbyes. They'll only want to keep you around so they can squeeze you for favors."

"Man's right," Charles agreed. "You needed to prove you could play in the deep end getting in with that group. No need to slum when you'll be sitting pretty next to your brother."

Shoving out of her chair, she stood, brushing off her pants like it was a nervous habit. "Welp, I better get to work. This isn't going to be easy, so I might as well get started on it now. As soon as I have the information you need, I'll send it through to Tommy. We have secure communication already established. This isn't information anyone else needs to know."

Impressed with her turn around, I saluted her and gave her a wink before she left the room. The rest of us got to work on the last bit of the plan before we had to split up and rally our teams. Since my men would be splitting between dealing with Diego and getting Elena, we needed to make a plan to reconnect afterward. As much as we wanted to stick together, it didn't make sense when both pieces of this plan were so important. I *needed* men I could trust on the job. This was our future and family on the line.

Chapter Twenty-Four

Picasso

Looking out over the city as dusk started to fall, knowing that in a matter of hours, we would be declaring war on the second biggest criminal boss in the States was an odd feeling. Of course, it helped I was on the side that was going to win, but it had me thinking back to when I first met Dax. The night I'd learned just how far she was willing to go for the people who were important to her.

We'd argued about the sanctity of life, and she'd been right to tell me to grow the fuck up. The Phantom Saints didn't back down from a fight. Typically, we weren't the ones to start them, but we finished them. As a leadership, we found there were better ways, but it hadn't really been true. If Eagle had taken out all the Mad Dogs like every other MC had before us did, then half this mess wouldn't have had to be dealt with.

Dax had stepped up and held her end of the deal, putting the Mad Dogs down. Now, it was our turn to return the favor and settle things with Diego De León once and for all. The bastard had gone too far, bringing in my family. They'd never been part of this.

My parents, of course, knew what we were and pulled away from us. Gabby had been the only one to stick by us, helping where she could, but we'd worked hard to keep her out of the thick of things. Legal help and advice didn't warrant them going after her kids.

Demitri was a good egg, but he wasn't cut out for being a Phantom Saint, which is why we had him helping in the garage outside the compound. Yet somehow, all of them were being used against us.

The rage I'd seen Dax deal with since they went after Harper, I now understood. You don't fuck with family unless you're willing to die at the hands of those who love them. I'd told Dax this before, but emotions don't make you weak. They can be more powerful when turned into proper motivation, which I had plenty of right now, thanks to the fucking prick who lied and manipulated my niece.

"Hey, you get everything you needed?" Eagle asked, grabbing my shoulder and giving it a squeeze.

I glanced at him and nodded. "I'm no Void or Cognac who likes to take all the fancy toys. Give me a well-oiled gun and enough bullets to do the job, and I'm happy."

Eagle grunted his agreement. "You have to admit, though, some of those toys are pretty epic."

"In what situation would we need to use a rocket launcher?" I asked with a laugh. "We're trying to save Elena and keep the dipshit alive until tomorrow night. I don't see that helping us in that department."

"True, but damn wouldn't it be fucking cool to shoot one off?" Eagle added with a grin.

I shook my head. "You've been spending way too much time with Void and Cam. That's absolutely something they would say."

"Probably," Eagle answered with a shrug. "Come on. Everyone is meeting upstairs for the final debrief before we split."

"We sure this is the right plan? I don't like the idea of us splitting," I questioned, sharing my biggest fear in all this with my big brother. "I feel like every time we split, there's a chance not all of us will make it back to each other. You might be my blood brother, but the rest of them are family too. We always say that if one of them died, Dax would lose her shit and never come back to us, but I'm not sure any of us would be any better."

Eagle didn't answer right away, just looked out the window at the cars and people moving to and fro, clueless as to what was about to go down. "That risk is something we make every day in the world we operate in. I agree with you completely, we've all become a family, and no matter what happens, we'll deal with it like a family does... together. Shit happens and life is fucked up, but if we have each other's backs first and foremost, we'll come out of this even stronger."

"While that load of bullshit was pretty, it didn't actually answer my question," I pointed out to Eagle. "Fuck, let's just get this over with to get one step closer to ending this whole goddamn thing."

With a slap on the back, Eagle turned on his heel and headed for the front door, then stopped to look at me over his shoulder. "You ever tell Cam I said that shit about him being family, I'll ruin every paintbrush you own."

I mimed zipping my lips and just grinned at him as we headed out. Dax was wrong to think I was the only one who wore rose-colored glasses in life. If Eagle hadn't ended up in this life, he would have been some great philosopher mulling over life's toughest questions as he smoked a shit ton of weed. Too bad the bastard was too uptight to ever allow himself to smoke the stuff. He was one of those, my-whole-body-is-a-temple bullshit, taking after Mom and her need for order way too much for my liking sometimes. Thank God one of us took after Dad and his more relaxed personality.

Entering the triplets' place, it was chaos with weapons, ammo, and other supplies we would need for this whole mission. Everyone was dressed in black tactical gear placing the last items they needed into the many pockets on their clothing.

Dax looked up, hearing us enter, and smiled, sauntering over to us. "Where have you two been hiding out?"

"I was talking to Gabby, filling her in on the basics of what's happening. She's flying into New Jersey tonight, so when we have Elena, she'll take her back home. The last thing we need is to save the girl and then have her land back in their clutches," Eagle shared.

When her eyes shifted to me, I just shrugged. "Just needed a minute to myself to get my head on right for this. Gotta take off the rose-colored glasses and all for this job."

She reached out and took my hand, giving it a squeeze. "Don't lose them completely. We need someone with a different point of view to make sure we don't end up like the bastards we're going after."

I pulled her against me and smirked down at her. "Are you telling me that you might have been wrong?"

"Ha." She laughed. "I wouldn't go that far, mister. Let's just say I can appreciate an alternative viewpoint."

Cupping her face, I kissed her deeply, letting my tongue sweep the inside of her mouth, tasting her like I might never get the chance to do it again. If we were going to split up, I needed her to know how much I fucking loved her so there was nothing left unsaid between us.

When I released her mouth, I kissed her nose, then her forehead. "I love you, spitfire. Don't you ever forget it."

"I love you too, Bob Ross," she teased but pushed up to give me another quick kiss. "Don't worry about tonight. You won't get rid of me that easily."

"What about if something happens to me?" I questioned, unable to have her blind optimism.

She shrugged. "Then I guess I just have to make a trip to Hell and tell the devil he can't have you because you're mine."

"That so? Well, for the sake of the devil and humankind, I better stay alive. No telling what kind of trouble you'd cause in Hell," I murmured, releasing her so we could join the others as Magnus called us over.

It was easy to see why the other two brothers had no problem with Magnus taking the lead in planning their missions. He was almost at the same level as Dax with how his mind worked. Putting the two of them together while throwing Wes and Cam into the mix was just terrifying. If the four of them wanted to take over the world, I believed they could. The rest of us had our moments, but most of the heavy lifting had been done by that crew. What surprised me even more was Harper catching some important holes in the whole situation that could have left us scrambling.

"Alright, team Take Down Diego is Dax, Cam, Cognac, and Weston, along with the three of us. Team Rescue Elena is Eagle, Picasso, Void, Sprocket, and the men from Tommaso. The attacks at the other locations will start at seven on the dot, which means we need to wait until seven forty-five to make our hits. We need the police to be so overwhelmed with everything else going on that even if our marks get calls out, they can't respond as quickly." Magnus paused, then turned to Eagle. "You good on your plan?"

Eagle nodded. "Ours is going to be a much easier hit since he lives in an apartment building. Thanks to Dante and his connection getting us these SWAT bulletproof vests, it will make it all that much simpler."

"The thing we don't know, though, is who else is in that building," Jaxson warned. "There could be more of Diego's men there to keep an eye on his son, so keep your eyes open and don't get tunnel vision."

He made a good point. While we'd looked up everyone in the building, that didn't mean whoever was living there was who they said they were. The shit stain of a son—Axel—didn't even pay for that apartment. His daddy dearest did under a shell company name. Diego had proven he was a smart man, but I had a feeling on his home turf, where he thought he held all the strings, he'd made mistakes.

"Any last thoughts, comments, suggestions?" Ghost asked as he nuzzled into Harper's neck.

It had been a unanimous vote that she remain here at the house as our contact person. If we needed help, then she was who we reached out to. Her and Betta would then coordinate between the two groups to send backup wherever needed. All of us would be eyeballs deep in bullets, so we couldn't handle something like that. Harper had been less than thrilled, but when we explained it could be the difference between life and death, she realized this wasn't a ploy just to keep her out of the fight.

When no one spoke up, we gave our goodbyes—meaning we all kissed the fucking hell out of our woman and bro-hugged it out between the guys. None of us wanted to be sappy shits, but on the other hand, we were too aware of what was about to go down. Our lives were lived on the edge of a knife and you never knew when the wrong step would land you on the blade.

The four of us climbed into our blacked-out SUV and headed off to the meet point where we would connect with Tommaso's men. One of his lieutenants we'd met at his house, David, was going to be there ensuring the men followed orders. We would be heading up this operation since it was our family we were going after but having David there to make sure shit got done eased some of the worries.

Void leaned his head back and looked as if he was just going to nap for the twenty minutes it would take us to get where we needed to go. There were times I thought the man was unhinged, but right now, I envied that he wasn't worried at all about tonight. If he had a gun and a body to shoot, he was a happy camper. My biggest worry was if Elena had truly turned against us and we couldn't save her.

Had they done too much damage for us to fix? Would we ever get the sweet, brilliant woman back who wanted to write the stories of those who never got a voice? Fuck, I hope we weren't too late.

Glancing at my watch as we pulled into the parking garage, it was 6:50 p.m. This location was five blocks away from their apartment building, so we'd be close when we needed to roll out. Dante had worked his magic and gotten us far more than just the vests, his connection even had lights for us to put in the vehicle so when we came speeding down the road, we wouldn't be stopped or yelled at for parking in the street. People stayed out of SWAT's way, knowing if they got called in, it was a big deal.

"Any updates?" Daniel asked when we got out of the SUV.

Eagle shook his head. "Nope, we've got the vests for everyone in the back of the car and everything else for that part of it. Your men strapped and ready to go?"

"Fuck yeah, we've been waiting for the day we finally get to make our move against Diego," Daniel said, then gestured for us to follow. "I've got twenty men who are going to infiltrate with us and another fifteen or so who can be waiting as backup if we need them. If we had everyone swarming the building, it would draw too much attention. This way, when they arrive, people will assume we called for backup."

"Wise approach," Sprocket commented as he looked over at the men standing and chatting with each other. "They understand the plan is to keep everyone alive, right? Bodyguards, if they have any, can be taken out, but we need Axel and Elena alive. Especially Elena. She's our family and none of us will take kindly to her being roughed up."

"I'll make sure to remind them, but does the same care need to be applied to the boy?" Daniel asked. "That might be hard to enforce. Axel is known for being an entitled little shit who will do just about anything to get Daddy's approval."

"Nah," I answered. "As long as he's still breathing and you can tell it's him, we're fine. Just let them know if he dies, it's Two Tricks they're going to have to answer to."

Daniel's eyes went wide at that. "Pretty sure that threat alone is all they're going to need to keep the bastard alive."

Tommaso's men snapped to attention when they saw us approaching. Eagle went over the plan again with them, Daniel adding in his two cents here and there to back him up. He seemed like a good guy and determined to make sure this went without a hitch. I think it helped that this was the first time any of Tommaso's men were going to prove how loyal they were to their new leader. Once that was all settled, we passed out gear and got the lights hooked up to the SUV and truck we'd be taking.

By the time we'd arranged all that, we were minutes away from putting this all into action. Trying to take a page out of Void's book, I leaned against the SUV and closed my eyes, taking deep breaths. My adrenaline was already coursing through my body, but I needed to use it in the right way, helping me zero in on what was important.

"You good, Picasso?" Sprocket asked.

Cracking open an eye, I found him standing in front of me arms crossed with a smirk on his face. "Peachy."

"Looking a little pale, need me to get you a paper bag to breathe into?" he asked, knowing it would piss me off.

"Fuck off, Sprocket," I shot back. "I'll be just fine once we get this show on the road. It's all this waiting that's got me all wound up."

He slapped me on the arm. "Hell, man, let's do this like our little rebel would. Hit them hard and fast, kicking them right where it's gonna fucking hurt. The powers that be need to know not to fuck with our family. If they do, we'll hit back ten times harder, and it wouldn't be worth it in the long run."

I grinned back at him and shoved off the car. "Wait till she hears you said that after the shit fit you had over her stunts with the Mad Dogs."

"This is different," he grumbled. "We all know the plan and can work together."

"Sure it is," I commented as I pulled open the passenger side door. "Because she's the type to see the difference and be reasonable."

Sprocket flipped me the bird and climbed into the SUV, making me laugh. I shoved up so I was standing on the doorsill and looked over the top of the vehicle. Raising my fingers to my lips, I let out a loud shrill whistle. "Load up. Let's get this show on the road."

Everything was set in motion with that announcement. Men grabbed their rifles and helmets and finished strapping on their vests before climbing into vehicles. Our SUV was the lead, and we would signal when to turn on the lights. Eagle slid behind the wheel and banged a hand on the side of the SUV, then whirled a finger, signaling for us to head out.

Tires squealed as we flew out of the parking garage, shooting out onto the street. Once all of us were out in the open, Eagle flipped the switch, blaring the siren and lights as we roared down the road.

Traffic darted out of our way as we moved just as we hoped they would, believing we were indeed law enforcement. Arriving at the apartment building, we drove up onto the sidewalk, stopping right at the entrance, and flung open the doors. The building was six floors and had a buzzer system to let you inside but not much else security-wise. One of Daniel's men had an auto lock picker and jammed it into the keyhole, then twisted, allowing us entrance. The sound of boots storming up the stairs to the sixth floor echoed in the open center space of the building.

A woman on the third floor opened her door carrying a trash bag, saw us, gasped, and slammed the door closed. It would make our lives easier if everyone reacted the same way. As we rounded the stairs to the sixth floor, I drew my gun and flattened to the side of the wall next to the door. Void charged up to the door marked *6-C* and slammed his boot into it, busting it open. Screams could be heard inside that were definitely more than two people.

Diving in after Void, we found ourselves in the living room where it seemed Axel and friends were watching a movie and eating pizza. "NYPD, everyone, put your hands up," I bellowed, keeping my voice low so Elena wouldn't recognize it right away.

"Oh my God, oh my God, my parents are going to kill me for getting arrested again," a girl wailed as she dropped to her knees on the floor, hands behind her head. Clearly, she'd been arrested more than once.

I grabbed her, zip-tied her hands behind her back, and passed her off to one of Tommaso's men. Shaking my head, I mouthed 'not her' then turned back to the scene. Everyone was now on their knees, getting zip-cuffed.

"Why are you doing this?" Elena whimpered. "We haven't done anything wrong?"

"Shut the fuck up, El," a male voice snapped. "They have no idea who they're messing with. My dad will get us out of this, no problem. Just keep your damn mouth shut until I get my phone call."

Eagle looked at me as he raised one eyebrow since he was the one holding Axel in his grip. Boy had no idea what was coming of him. Sprocket had Elena, but she was so upset she didn't even notice who he was.

"We've got who we came for, let's move out," Daniel announced as he shoved one of the other guys ahead of him.

Just as they stepped outside the room, shots went off. I couldn't tell if they shot at us first or if one of the men in the hall made the first move. All I knew was Sprocket and I shoved Elena to the floor as Eagle slammed the kid into the wall covering him.

One of the girls screamed, and I saw the guy Daniel had, flinch and sag to the ground as more shots went off. Looking around the room, I noticed a fire escape outside their window. Tapping Sprocket on the shoulder, I pointed. "Get her the fuck out of here. I don't care if you have to drive off. Make sure she's safe."

He looked like he wanted to argue but then looked down at Elena and nodded. I grabbed her face so she looked me right in the face. Wiping away her tears, I used as gentle of a voice as I could while still being heard. "Ellie, look at me."

She did as I asked then her eyes went wide. "Uncle Picasso? What are you doing here? They told me you were *dead*."

"They lied, I've come to take you home, baby girl. Your mom is on her way to meet you in Jersey, but we need to get you there first. Sprocket's going to take you out the back and get you somewhere you'll be safe," I explained, holding up a hand. "Don't argue, Ellie. Now is not the time or the place."

More gunshots went off, making her flinch but accept what I was saying. "Be careful. This whole floor is men who work for his dad. He's not a good man."

"I'm well aware of who his old man is. Now go," I urged, pushing her to Sprocket.

Swiftly, Sprocket cut the ties and they hurried across the room in a crouch keeping out of site. Eagle kicked out Axel's legs and dropped him to the floor next to me. "Might as well try to keep the shit alive," Eagle muttered.

"You stay back here with him. I'm gonna head toward the hall to see what the fuck is going on," I said, but when I tried to move, he grabbed my arm. "Don't fucking get shot. It hurts like a motherfucker."

Rolling my eyes, I gave him a thumbs up—*brothers*. Someone had shoved over a wooden bookshelf across the doorway, giving us some cover to hide behind. Army crawling up to Daniel, I peeked over the wood and spotted five guys, two on one end of the hall, three on the other. It was just the right angle that we had to lean out of the room to make a shot which left us wide open to being picked off.

"Got any bright ideas?" Daniel asked.

"Not good ones, but I know one will do the trick," I answered with a sigh. "Void." He looked at me from where he stood on one side of the door frame. "Think now might be a good time to roll over a present?"

Void grinned at me as he holstered his gun and plucked out one of the grenades I knew he had in his pocket. He pulled the pin, held it for a second with the safety clip release then chucked it down the hall toward the three men.

"Fire in the hole," Void announced, ducking and covering his ears.

Everyone in the apartment dropped to the ground as the explosion went off, rattling the whole building. Void popped back up and whipped out another one in the opposite direction before falling to the ground. "Fire in the hole... again."

Another booming concussion shook the floor under us. Screaming could be heard throughout the building as people realized a war was happening on the top floor. I vaulted over the bookshelf, Void right behind me, ready to shoot in either direction if they survived. When the dust settled, all we saw were bodies, but I wasn't going to trust it until I checked.

Keeping low, I darted down the hall to where the three men lay bloody and mangled. It appeared holding the grenade for that second meant it exploded in the air lessening the damage to the lower floor.

"Void, you clear?" I yelled.

"Swiss cheese over here. I think we're good," Void answered. "Still think we need to check the rooms to make sure no one comes at us from behind."

I gave him a thumbs up and waited for two of Daniel's men to join. There were ten apartments, but it seemed only six people were living on the floor. The other rooms had what looked like the makings of a drug production layout. Bricks of coke or heroin were stacked on a counter with scales and other items needed for distribution. It looked like this was more than just a well-guarded apartment where his son lived. Seemed Axel might be more involved than we'd originally thought.

Stepping back into the hall, I spotted Void with Axel having a heart-to-heart as he was dangled over the railing with nothing but air between him and the ground. "Now listen to me, you little piss ant. What I want to know is if your old man has more people in this building or just this floor?"

"I'm not fucking telling you anything. You're the cops. You can't do this to me," Axel argued, his voice a little garbled with Void's hand around it.

"Oh, for fuck's sake, wake the hell up. We ain't no cops," Void muttered. "Now tell me what I want to know so we can make sure you leave this place alive. Seems your usefulness is still required, so don't make me tell my woman I had to kill you."

"Why the fuck would I care about helping you with your bitch?" Axel said, then tried to spit on Void.

Eagle lunged forward as I bolted in their direction, but Eagle managed to grab the kid just as Void released his hold on him. If Eagle hadn't caught Axel's arm, he would have been splattered on the tile below.

"Fuck, fuck, fuck, I don't want to die. Please don't let me go," Axel begged, panic written all over his face. "I didn't think he was really gonna drop me. I'll tell you whatever you want to know, just don't drop me."

Void grunted as if he was satisfied with the sheer terror in Axel's voice, then helped Eagle pull him over the railing and back to the hallway. Standing there looking at the three of them, my heart in my throat, I realized Void knew Eagle would catch him. The crazy fucking bastard made a move like that, trusting Eagle would step in.

"You fucking crazy bastard," I blurted as I slapped him upside the head. "Dax would have had your balls for pulling a stunt like that."

"Wait, did you just say Dax," Axel demanded. "As in Two Tricks?"

The three of us looked down at him questioningly. "What's it to you?" Void asked.

"She... she's y-your w-woman?" he stuttered. "Oh, fuck me, he was telling the truth."

Confused, I stepped forward and squatted in front of this sack of shit so we were closer to eye level. "While that is absolutely the right response to have, care to fill me in on what the fuck has you pissing your pants?"

"That guy of hers... Jeff, the enforcer we snatched in LA. I think that's what he said his name was. He told me that she would find me and kill me for taking out one of her people. That she's a bloodhound, and no matter how careful we were, she'd find me," Axel explained.

We all knew how hard Dax took Jeff's death, being one of her top enforcers who worked with Brian. In everything else that had happened, we knew it still nagged at her. She hadn't run down his killer, but it seemed karma was on our side.

"One thing you should know about our woman," Void said, crouching and grabbing the kid's neck again. "She never forgets a slight and all those stories I'm sure you've heard of her… she's worse, especially when it comes to those who harmed her inner circle of people. You've done it twice, killing one of her men and taking family. I bet you wish we'd let you drop."

A shrill whistle sounded from below. "We gotta go, times up," Daniel hollered.

Void grabbed the kid and chucked him over his shoulder, and hustled down the stairs with Eagle and me right on his heels. Let's hope things went as well for Dax and the others.

Chapter Twenty-Five

Cameron

Reaching over, I pulled Dax's hand away from her mouth. I didn't think there was much left of that thumbnail and when she noticed, then she'd start picking at her bottom lip. Once she started that nervous tick, it was almost impossible to get her to stop.

"Beautiful, you're killing me with all this nervous energy," I murmured into her ear.

She let out a sigh and yanked her hand out of my grasp to run it through her hair. "You know this whole waiting shit drives me crazy."

"You handled it out in the quarry just fine, *loba*," Cognac pointed out.

"That's because we were outside, and I didn't have to be cooped up in a car parked on a side street lurking near our target's house," she snapped. "Why did we have to get here so early?"

Magnus shifted in his seat to look back at her. "Oh, I'm sorry if my need to be prepared has set you on edge. We still need to drive another ten minutes down the way, but they live in a gated community, so it's not like we could hide out there."

"Listen, Thing One, you don't want to pick a fight with me right now because I'm more than willing to make it happen," Dax shot back.

"Knock it off, both of you," Wes barked. "I need to finish this program so we can get in the side gate and avoid the guard at the front entrance."

"I thought you had that settled?" Jaxson asked, peering over his shoulder to look at the screen.

Wes shoved him back into his seat and continued working. "Yeah, well, when we drove by the front, I noticed the sign for the security company was different, so I looked it up. They switched two days ago, and I was working off what Tommaso gave us. Now I have to alter it slightly."

"Gee, isn't it a good thing I got here so early and did a test pass out front," Magnus said, looking at Dax in the rearview mirror with a smug expression.

She lunged forward, but I caught her and pulled her onto my lap. "Settle down, beautiful. Soon enough, you'll get to have your claws in the man who really deserves them."

Grumbling under her breath about chopping off dicks, she settled into my hold.

"Got it," Wes announced. "We can head on over now."

Magnus turned the key, and the SUV rumbled to life. For this mission, we didn't have any extra people. It was just the seven of us to get this done. Everyone agreed having a smaller party infiltrate was smarter since it was in a neighborhood, and it would draw unwanted attention. Diego's house backed up to the golf course right at the eighteenth hole. The plan so far was to leave the car in the golf course parking lot since there wasn't much security other than a gate closing off the entrance. Once there, it was a matter of getting across the course to the back of Diego's home, where he had plenty of security.

As we pulled up to the gate, Wes used the garage door opener he programmed, and it started to retract back on its rail, opening the way for us. Magnus found a spot that was deeply shadowed by trees keeping it hidden from any security checks. Not like there were many reasons to sneak onto a golf course in this kind of neighborhood. It was farther than I thought it would be to the house, but any other option we tried just didn't get us to a place where we could sneak up on security.

Dax pulled out her gun, screwing on the silencer, as did Jaxson, ready to pick off those we could. All of us could shoot, but when you needed someone who could hit with only a second to aim and make the choice. Diego's backyard had dense privacy bushes that concealed the first floor of the mansion he lived in.

Our intel had told us his wife and children would be home as well, so we needed to keep on the alert. No one had said it yet, but the chances of anyone in this family making it through the night were slim. This was one enemy we couldn't have coming to bite us in the ass later on, seeking vengeance.

Jaxson went left with his brothers and Dax went right with us, following a few paces back. Since Dax was small enough, she army crawled under the bushes as we kept going to the break in the row. A metal gate blocked our way, but seconds later, Dax was there picking the lock to let us in.

"How did you get through so fast?" Cognac questioned.

"Seems they didn't think people would crawl and didn't put the fencing all the way through. Bastard is just asking for someone to break in and overthrow his whole operation. Good thing it's us and not someone else who would have torn the trees down," she commented as she led the way through the backyard.

A guard turned the corner of the house and spotted us, but Dax had already pulled the trigger, hitting him right between his eyes. He dropped like a sack of bricks with only a small grunt coming out of his mouth instead of the alert he was going to give.

"Drag him away from the house and off to the side in the shrubs. The longer we can keep our presence quiet, the better," Dax whispered.

I grabbed the man under his armpits and hauled him away to the large flowering plant of some kind and heaved him in the middle of it. In the daylight, you would be able to find him, but at night, with no lights, it was good enough.

Dax picked off two more guards, one on a balcony of the second floor that had just stepped out and another out by the pool. Cognac took care of the one by the pool, tossing him in and letting him sink to the bottom with the help of a lawn chair. Taking one last look around, Wes headed for the back door. Using whatever technology wizardry he had, he got the door open with a beep and a flash of green light. Turning the handle, he pulled it open enough to make sure it was unlatched, then signaled for us.

Oddly enough, getting into the house was the easy part of the plan. Once inside, there were fifteen bedrooms and five other various areas for people to be using. They had live-in staff on top of the security, so there was no telling who could be in which room and at any given time. The answer to that problem was solved when Harper made the discovery of the panic room in the basement. Now, all we had to do was alert them to our presence when we wanted them to know about it.

The sound of glass shattering and a gunshot had us all whipping around to find Dax in the main entrance with a mangled chandelier on the floor before her. "Oops," she commented with a grin.

Men started to shout and feet clomped to investigate the sound. The three of us spread out, moving through the rooms picking off the guards one by one as they put all their focus on where the sound was coming from. We'd figured there would be five to seven guards outside and probably only three to five inside. What we didn't know was if he had men stationed close by in case of an emergency. This was a calculated risk, but our hope was the other attacks would have used up those men.

"Report, what the hell is going on down there?" a voice asked from a walkie-talkie.

Reaching down, I unclipped it and responded, "There is a woman here. It seems she's all by herself, but she's demanding to see Diego."

"Did she give you a name?" the voice asked.

"Don't ask stupid questions. Just shoot the bitch," Diego snarled. "Hold her off long enough for us to reach the panic room. We'll take the back stairs."

Seeing they were just handing me all the information we needed on a silver platter, I decided to go for gold. "I think we're gonna need backup. She's already taken out the guards outside."

There was no response, so either they didn't have one, or they were dead. The Wright brothers had entered on the other end of the house, figuring we could work toward the middle. Shrugging, I tossed the radio to the side and started to search the rest of the house. This was the one thing the FBI trained me hard on was how to process a scene and not get shot doing it. So far, the rooms were empty until I reached what I believe was a study of sorts. A woman sat in an upholstered chair, reading a book and drinking wine. When I entered, she looked up at me with dead eyes, then went back to what she was reading.

"If you could shoot me in the side of the head, then I'll still be able to have an open casket funeral," Mariana commented.

Frowning, I lowered the gun slightly. "You want me to kill you?"

"Oh, I've been dead inside for so long I'm not quite sure why my body insists I keep living. To me, this is a blessing. I will finally be able to make it all end. I would have done it myself, but it appears I'm just not that strong of a woman," she shared, glancing up at me set her wine down. "Would it make it easier for you if I tried to shoot you? That way, you can say it was in self-defense."

I wasn't a good man, even if I was an FBI agent. Everything I'd done was for Dax to protect her, ensure that she was safe however I could make her. While I didn't have a problem taking out this woman, there was something that held me back.

"Tell me, if we killed Diego, your children, and anyone else who would come after us in retaliation, would you be one of those people?" I asked.

Mariana let out a heavy sigh. "Pity, I thought for sure you were a man with low to no morals. Seems I won't be free after all from this torturous life. If it's not Diego, it will be Marco. He will want his property back now that it's not doing him any good here."

That had my attention. "You know Marco personally enough he would have so much control over you?"

She let out a bitter laugh gulping more of her wine down. "I'm the bastard's little sister, a pawn in his game to be placed where it will best serve the Tesoro Cartel and the man who wants to be king of it all."

"Unfortunately, you will have to live a little longer, but I promise when we have what we need from you, I'll personally see to it you'll get your freedom," I said, backing out of the room and locking the door from the inside before I shut it.

Holy fucking shit, we have Marco's sister who landed right in our laps. The woman was broken enough that she would tell us whatever we wanted to know in hopes her end would come sooner. I mulled over the many questions we might be able to have answered because of this chance encounter.

Finished with the first-floor sweep, I decided to head back to the main entrance and found a few more dead bodies and Dax chilling on the couch, munching on mixed nuts out of a crystal bowl. When I gave her a disapproving look, she offered it to me. "Want some?"

"No, Dax. Shouldn't you be, I don't know, dealing with Diego?" I questioned.

"He's not going anywhere anytime soon. He's in this panic room. The bastard didn't even take his wife or kids with him, just saved his own ass," she said, popping another nut into her mouth. "After dealing with the Mad Dogs, I feel like this was so much easier or maybe because it was better planned?"

I reached out a hand for her. "Come on, let's find the others and get this over with."

"Wes is in the basement, and I think the triplets are clearing the second floor," she shared. "Might as well head to the basement since that's where they will meet us when they're done. They have what we need to get through the door into the panic room once Wes has disabled all the security."

"So I found a surprise that we will be taking with us," I mentioned as we headed for the basement. Dax cocked a brow at me, waiting for me to continue. "Seems that Diego's wife, Mariana, is actually Marco's little sister, who he uses to make profitable deals. She's fucked in the head, but I think there's a chance we can get some helpful inside information from her."

Dax came to an abrupt halt. "She's what? How did Wes miss that major piece of information?"

"My guess would be that since he didn't want just anyone to know the connection, he kept it secret. Possibly even changed her last name or left their mothers, something like that. No one knows much about Marco's family outside of him and his father," I reminded.

"Sounds like an incredible Marco thing to do," she grumbled. "Come on. Now we need to move faster if we have to get two people out of this alive."

The basement wasn't really a basement to normal people's standards. It had a wine cellar, movie theater, and bar with a seating area. The panic room was near the wine cellar, which was smart, I suppose because I would want to grab a few bottles to drink as I waited for all hell to come after me. To my surprise, the triplets were already down there working on how to get through the door.

"We can't use that. It will blow the whole goddamn house up with us in it," Magnus argued. "Where are the plastic explosives that we can pinpoint to where we need them?"

Ghost all but pouted as he dug through a bag and handed him a brick of something that looked like clay. "You always have to take the fun out of everything, don't you, Maggie?"

Glaring at his brother, he got to work molding the explosive material around the door hinges and the center of the door where the vault lock was.

"What was your first idea, Ghost?" I asked because I was far too curious to know what else he had in mind over using explosives.

He perked up at being asked and grinned at me. "Rocket launcher, I feel like it had to do some damage to the damn thing if it can take out a tank."

Dax burst out laughing and yanked the man into a hug. "Fuck, you have some of the best ideas, Ghost, but Magnus is right. We need to be able to walk away from this." She released him and stepped back, clapping her hands with an idea. "I know. Once we get everyone out, you can use it to blow up the place. Then it will cover our tracks, and no one will know who's alive or dead searching through all the rubble. It will make my surprise at the fight even better."

"Oh Dax, you delightful little pixie, you," Ghost gushed, shoving her shoulder. "That's a brilliant idea and makes lugging it all the way over here worth it. I forgot it when we first made the trek. Then I remember we had to get into this thing and thought it was the better option."

"How you're still alive is astounding," Wes muttered as he clicked away on his laptop. "That should do it. All the feeds have been looped to cover our entry and everything that's happened since entering the house. So that won't tell the authorities anything or Marco if he should decide to investigate."

"So boom time?" Jaxson asked, holding up the detonator.

"Why don't we step out of here first so we don't get blown up?" Wes suggested. "Maybe you can pick out a nice wine to bring home to Harper."

"Fuck, you're so smart. It's not like he's going to need it," Ghost said as he headed out to do just that.

Shaking my head, I moved into the bar area, giving plenty of space between me and the explosion. Jaxson looked at us and grinned. "You might want to cover your ears."

Doing as he suggested, I watched as he gave a three-finger count down, and the ground shook, almost knocking me off my feet. A bright flash of light came from down the hall, ensuring us that it had indeed gone off. Working with Dax sure was far more exciting than the FBI ever was. God, I was so glad she forgave me enough to keep me around. We still had things to work on but wasn't that part of relationships, always working to improve?

Musings for another day, now it was time to collect our prey and settle the score that had been a long time coming.

Chapter Twenty-Six

Dax

The door to the safe room lay on the ground, bent and scorched from the explosives. Inside was a swanky sitting room with everything a person could possibly need to spend time comfortably inside. There was even a toilet and sink available if the need should arise. Finally, my eyes settled on Diego De León sprawled on the floor, having been knocked on his ass from the blast.

"You are a hard man to find," I commented. "Here I am stopping by for a visit, and I have to demolish an incredibly lovely panic room. Gosh, it makes me think you didn't want to see me, but that can't be the case, not after you practically invited me to come."

"I did no such thing," he spluttered, his words thick with his Latin accent. "You're the one who broke into my home, coming after me."

Coming to a stop right in front of the man, I looked down at him. "No such thing? Oh, Diego, they didn't tell me you were losing your memory in your old age. How frustrating that must be for you. Here let me jog it for you." I offered, taking a seat in the other armchair that was still upright. "Should we start with how you've been trying to cut me out of the business since the day I got started? Oh, then there is the fact you blamed me for killing a son I knew nothing about just to get my people not to trust me. Hmm, I feel like I'm forgetting something. Ah yes, the assassins were a nice touch, but the real clincher was the fucking with family."

Diego slowly picked himself up, brushed off his clothes, and righted the chair so he could sit, ignoring the six men with guns trained on him. "You started it all when you cut off access to Mexico along with any ports on the West Coast. It was bad for business having to bring it all the way around into the gulf or New York itself. The customs are so much stricter, and I had to bribe the whole customs office here. Taking you out was the smart thing to do, but like a cockroach, you just won't stay dead."

"Oh, am I supposed to apologize for that?" I asked, pressing a hand to my heart like I was truly worried about offending him. "Goodness, I seem to have lost my manners. Let me give it a try."

I sat up straight, cleared my throat, licked my lips, and folded my hands primly in my lap. "I'm so incredibly sorry that you feel so victimized by little old me. My heart is just broken over the fact that you will never be able to beat me. In the end, you're just a sad, old man, who had been led by the balls because Marco didn't think you're man enough to rule your own empire. Seems you needed a good woman to show you how it's done."

Diego's face turned purple with rage as he flew out of his seat to attack me. I didn't bother to sit up. Instead, I grabbed my gun, swung, and hit him in the head with the butt of it. He dropped like the sack of shit he was, falling into my lap. I patted him on the head. "That's a good boy. You sleep for now. We need you to be well rested for your performance tomorrow night. It's going to be a real showstopper."

Shoving him off my lap, I stood and faced the guys who were all trying to stifle their laughter.

"Sorry, did I miss something?" I asked, cocking my head.

"Oh fuck, *loba*, that apology needed to be recorded and saved for all time. I've never heard someone sound so sincere as they verbally obliterated a person with an apology before. It was priceless," Cognac said, giving it a chief's kiss of approval.

I bowed low with a flourish. "Thank you, thank you. I'll be here all weekend."

"Okay, but here's the real question," Wes said, looking at the man at my feet. "Who's carrying his ass back to the car?"

"Ah yes, and we need to swing by the sitting room on the first floor and grab his wife," Cam interjected.

Jaxson's jaw dropped open. "Dude, I know you have some weird fucked-up history with Dax, but you shouldn't be talking about another woman like that. She might love you, but if you step out on her, she'll kill you, I have no doubt."

"Do you think I would announce it to her and all of you if I were going to cheat on her?" Cam asked, giving Jaxson a deadpan look. "Besides, the only reason I give one flying fuck about that woman is she's Marco's sister."

Now everyone had matching shocked expressions. "Okay, yeah, that's a good reason," Jaxson admitted.

"I'll take the rotten bastard," Cognac stated. "It will make me feel better to bash his head into the wall as I walk for all the shit he's put us through."

"Yeah, I would have offered, but I have the rocket launcher," Ghost said, pointing to the duffle bag on his shoulder. "We're still going to blow up the house, right?"

Magnus grabbed him by the back of the neck and dragged him along. "After we all get out."

"I'm excited, not stupid, Mag," Ghost grumbled.

"Just trying to make sure we all get back to our people in one piece," Magnus added as we emerged back on the first floor.

Cam grabbed my arm, drawing my attention. "I'll be right back with her. Meet you by the pool."

I gave him a thumbs up and swiped the dish with the nuts on our way out. They were damn good, and I hated for food to go to waste. Besides, all this double-O-seven spy shit has me hungry. I was so anxious to eat before we left. It took Cam about ten minutes to join us with an incredibly drunk Mariana in tow. She was in a dressing gown of sorts that only rich women seemed to wear and no shoes, not that she needed any, just adding to the strangeness of this whole event.

"How far back should we be for this?" Wes questioned as Ghost lifted the rocket launcher to his shoulder. "I feel like right now we are *way* too close."

"Let's head back into the golf course, then go for it," Jaxson suggested. "That way, if shrapnel comes at us, we can get out of the way or duck."

"How the fuck is this my life?" Wes mumbled as we got a good fifteen feet back from the house.

Ghost got into a wide leg stance, dropped his head to look in the scope, then pulled the trigger. I'd expected more of a recoil, but Ghost hardly moved an inch as the rocket shot out, then there was another burst as the rocket sped up and slammed into the second-story window. The explosion that followed had us all cheering like kids on the Fourth of July. The plume of smoke rose into the air marking our signal to get the hell out of dodge.

Cam had to hoist Mariana up in his arms so we could run without her stumbling over her feet. Our trek across the course was well-lit by the fire that burned behind us. Apparently, a rocket-induced fire spread incredibly fast, but that would keep law enforcement off our trail until we were well enough away. Cognac chucked Diego in the back and shut the door while Cam got Mariana situated in the front seat and buckled in. Magnus didn't wait for us to get seated before he was peeling out of the parking lot. The gate opened for us since we were exiting and off we went into the night with our cartel boss and his wife.

Fuck, I had the best life. Let's hope once this was all over, I wasn't too bored with no one attacking me or trying to kill me. On second thought, it was probably better not to put that into the atmosphere.

Tommaso had a secure place where we could keep Diego for the day. It wasn't as fancy as his panic room, but it had a toilet, sink, and cot for him. We left him water and a few protein bars in case he got hungry when he woke up. I might be planning to kill him in ten hours, but that was no reason to deny him the basics every human deserved. Even mass murderers got a last meal before the needle. It seemed only fair, well as fair as I was willing to be.

Mariana was tucked away in a motel with guards in New Jersey so we could keep her close but not too close.

Eagle and his crew were putting Axel in a separate location, not wanting to risk having him and Diego in one spot. Magnus had called Harper to check in, and she reported that everyone was fine. Their job had gone as well as could be expected, and they were finishing up their loose ends. This meant we could all head back to the apartment and know everyone would be coming home safe and sound.

I'd put all those emotions aside during the job, but now relief flooded through me, knowing that all my men were safe. When we got back to the apartment, I knew exactly how I wanted to celebrate, and it had nothing to do with keeping our clothes on. After fights like this, it drove my already healthy libido through the roof, and right now, as we drove back, I felt like an addict who needed her fix.

Cognac was sitting next to me, and I grinned, knowing he would let me tease him and enjoy it. I slid my hand to his thigh, letting it pause there a moment before resting it right on his cock. He grunted as I rubbed it slowly with a good amount of pressure to make sure he got the point. The look he gave me out of the corner of his eye told me he got the message loud and clear. While tactical pants were thick so they protected you, it didn't block me from knowing just how into this idea of mine he was.

His hand snaked under my shirt, and he managed to pop the button on my pants, allowing his hand to slide under them. Cognac knew my feelings on foreplay well, so when he went right for gold, I had to bite my lip to stifle the moan when two fingers speared me. Not one to back down from a challenge, I tried to pull the same move, but he had a belt on, blocking me from just getting past the button. It would make too much noise to remove the belt, so I went for plan B. Tugging down his zipper, I groped around until I got a handful of cock.

Not bothering to get past the boxers he wore, I started to rub him with a little less pressure. Didn't want to rub the damn thing raw, then I needed him to fuck me senseless when we got the chance.

A tongue flicked the shell of my ear, making me shiver. "Don't forget you owe me from last time, shortcake," Wes whispered in my ear. "I was a team player and didn't grumble when you were too worn out to handle all of us at once, but this time, I'm going to get my time with you."

Fuck, these men were going to be the death of me before I could get them to fill me with their cocks I so desperately wanted.

We pulled up to the apartment building, and Cognac scooped me up in his arms, not bothering to wait for anyone else. Wes and Cam darted into the elevator right behind us as Cognac set me on my feet only to yank open his belt and free his cock. Spinning me so I was plaster against the wall of the elevator, he jerked down my pants so my ass was revealed and slammed into me.

"Oh, fuck yes." I groaned.

Because of our height difference, the only thing keeping me where he needed me was the pressure of his upper body, hands on my hips, and cock in my pussy. He thrust into me deep and slow, making every stroke count to its maximum potential. Wes and Cam stood in a way that helped to block anyone from the security cameras seeing more than they should. They would clearly know what we were up to, but this was no free porno for them to whack off to.

"You like that, *loba*? Having me take you here in this elevator because I couldn't wait another second to feel your pussy clenching around my cock?" Cognac murmured into my ear. "Think you can tease me like that and not suffer the consequences or is this exactly what you wanted?"

"Oh God, yes, this is what I wanted," I cried as he sped up his movements. "Yes, fuck me, fuck me right into the wall, Cognac."

My Latin lover did just that, granting every wish I had, wrapping his arm around my waist as he pummeled into me. Just when I thought an orgasm was going to hit me, the doors opened as we reached our floor.

"Tuck your legs up, *loba*. I'm not going to pull out of you as we leave here so I can bend you over the table and fuck you till you scream so loud the triplets are jealous," Cognac informed me.

So I did as he asked, and he held me to him securely as we left the elevator and moved into the apartment. Each step had him sliding in and out of me in such a way it edged me into madness. Wes got the door open and stepped aside for Cognac to carry me in and do just what he promised. My nails bit into the wood of the table as he hammered into me with no mercy, his own grunts filling the air around us as I begged for him not to stop.

The orgasm I'd been on the verge of having exploded through my body, making me scream out my pleasure as Cognac fucked me right through it. "Fuck yes, make me come again," I begged as he leaned back slightly and spit on my ass so he could sink his finger in, sending me right into another wave of ecstasy. "Goddamn fucking hell," I swore as my whole body started to twitch, trying to deal with the endorphins flooding my system.

He thrust in twice more and allowed himself to come as he draped over my back, kissing along my neck. "*Loba*, you fuck like a goddess, you know that, right? I think the whole building heard you screaming as you came around my cock," he said with a chuckle as he slowly pulled out of my pussy.

Panting, I took a moment before I stood, unsure if my legs would hold me. When I looked up, I found the others sitting in the living room, eyes full of heat, and Void was already stroking his cock. *Oh, tonight was going to be fun.*

"Who's next?" I asked with a grin.

Before anyone could make a move, Wes grabbed my hips and spun me around to face him. "I thought I was clear back in the car, shortcake. This time I'm not waiting for my turn, you're mine right now, and the others can just sit there and watch as I fuck that perfect pussy of yours."

"Bring it on, Westie, show me what you got," I taunted.

Gripping the bottom of my shirt, he ripped it up the front so he could get it off me easier. Tonight I'd worn a sports bra because I could keep an extra magazine of bullets there for emergencies. Knowing this, he removed the clip before yanking the fabric up over my head, leaving my chest bare. Since my pants were already around my ankles, I just needed to get the boots off, and I was buck-ass naked.

While I stripped, so did everyone else, sending clothes flying around the apartment. I was impressed that Eagle was so focused on me that he didn't care about the mess, or maybe it was because it wasn't *his* space.

The feel of leather wrapping around my neck had me pausing. "You ready for me, shortcake?" Wes asked as he urged me forward toward the couch. "I want you on all fours in the middle of the ottoman with that tight ass of yours in the air."

I did as directed, feeling the tug of the belt as I positioned myself as requested. Wes got settled behind me, applying tension to the belt, causing me to lift my head so my back was arched, and I could see the guys all sitting around us.

"What do you say we put on a little show for your men? Let them see me take you while they have to wait, stroking their rock-hard dicks as I take my fill from you," Wes continued as the head of his dick slid up and down the entrance of my pussy, getting it slick with my wetness and Cognac's cum.

When he finally slid into me balls deep, my eyes rolled back in my head. I was still hyper-sensitive from coming with Cognac that it sent shockwaves through my nerves. He started out with a steady pace as if he was warming me up, but that wasn't what I wanted. I started to push back into him, trying to speed up the tempo. The belt tightened, and I gasped, knowing it would be the last breath I could take for a bit.

"Not tonight, Dax. I'm the one in control of what's happening here, and you're just going to have to take what I give you," Wes informed me as he used his other hand to slap my ass, leaving behind a warm burn of pain. "Now, be a good girl and be grateful for what you're given."

With a grunt, he shoved my head down, so it was on the ottoman as he changed up the angle. In this position, he got *so* much deeper and hit that spot deep inside that almost no one could find, but when they did, you lost your fucking mind. The belt loosened enough for me to breathe but with limited supply, giving me the perfect euphoric feeling as my body protested the lack of oxygen. Wes ruled my body as he pounded my pussy, giving my ass a slap every so often to keep it pink and the sting to keep me from coming too fast.

When I was getting close, and I knew he was too, he yanked me up, so I sat back on his cock. He used his hand instead of the belt to choke me as he thrust up, making my pussy clench as my voice came out in garbled tones. I knew when this orgasm hit me, I was going to pass out, but I didn't give him the signal to let up on his hold. Instead, I leaned into the feeling as my vision started to tunnel. Every nerve ending was heightened with the adrenaline that my body was sending out to tell us something was wrong, but that was far from the truth. Nothing could be more perfect than the man I'd trusted with my life countless times, held it in his hands.

His hips started to falter, and he hugged me close as he came inside me, sending me into a tailspin of my own. Wes's hold on my throat loosed just as I let out a cry as I shattered from the orgasm. Just as I predicted, the added shock of coming sent me over the edge, and I blacked out with a smile on my face.

Chapter Twenty-Seven

Dax

"Dax?" Wes called as my eyes fluttered open to see him leaning over me. "You good, shortcake? Why didn't you tell me I was choking you too long?"

As he talked, my mind tried to tell me something else was going on, something that felt heavenly. Then it registered that while I was passed the fuck out, someone was feasting on my ravaged pussy and ass. Lifting my head slightly, I found Cam between my legs, where I now lay on the couch. His eyes met mine as he continued his efforts, and I just flopped back, letting him do as he pleased.

"It's fine, Wes. I knew exactly what I was doing. Pushing it to the edge like that makes the climax *so* much more intense. That's why I blacked out. Not because of the no air part of things," I assured him, reaching out to stroke his cheek. "That was fucking amazing, by the way."

He leaned in and kissed the fuck out of me, needing to reassure himself that I was alright. I let my fingers slide into his hair, holding him there so I could take what I needed as well. Breaking the kiss, I cried out as Cam slid his tongue into my pussy, lapping at it, clearly not at all bothered by the fact two other men's cum was in there.

"You good to keep going?" Wes asked, glancing at Cam, ready to tell him off if I said no.

I booped him on the nose, drawing his attention back to me. "I believe you're the one who called me out for not being able to handle all my men at once. Two down, five to go, and I'm thinking going for an airtight moment might be fun."

"Airtight?" Picasso asked, brushing a hand down my arm only to bring it back up and swirl a finger around my nipple.

"Mm-hmm, think about it for a sec," I challenged. When he still looked confused, I chuckled. "A cock for each hole, plugging them up makes you 'airtight.'"

Understanding flashed in his eyes, quickly followed by hunger to give it a try. "Then I claim that mouth of yours."

"I want her pussy this time since I got it all nice and clean," Cam announced.

"Seems I'll claim her ass then," Sprocket said as he took Weston's spot next to me. "Do you want to be on your back or stomach?"

As I thought about that, Cam got to work lubing up my ass. I wasn't going to question where he got the lube but knowing him, he probably packed it. "If I'm going to have one in my mouth, then I think stomach, better angle for deep throating and all that."

Cam moved to the chaise part of the couch, giving us more room to work with. Reaching out for me, I crawled over and straddled his hips. "I have to ask, do those piercings add to your pleasure as much as it does for me?"

"Oh beautiful, I didn't get it done for me even though they do offer some added stimulation. This was all about your pleasure, and I can tell from the excitement on your face it was well worth it," Cam answered, kissing me deeply as I sank down on his pierced cock.

Each and every rung of the ladder hit so perfectly that I almost came right then and there. Shuddering, I rested my head in the crook of his neck, taking a few deep breaths. "Holy fuck, those are amazing."

"We're just getting started, little rebel," Sprocket reminded me as he used his fingers to ensure I was loose enough for him. Then inch by delightful inch, he filled me.

A hand combed through my hair, encouraging me to lift it, and I found Picasso looking down at me with so much love and heat in his eyes. Picasso wasn't a man who was going to fuck me into a wall. No, he liked to own me in a different way when we were together. Yet he was willing to find his place amongst all these alpha men who like to run the show when we fucked.

"Open that sassy mouth of yours, spitfire," Picasso instructed.

Licking my lips, I offered myself to him and he shifted closer, so I didn't have to strain getting to him. The three of them started off at an easy pace. Even though I was primed and ready to go, it was still a lot to coordinate three people that worked best. Cam and Sprocket found their alternating rhythm while Picasso matched Sprocket's tempo. My mind was lost in the haze of pleasure, overloaded with sensations. Between the three of them, I came twice before they found their completion. I swallowed Picasso's cum down as he trapped my head to his body, grunting his release. Then he freed me to breathe once more as he moved back, pulling out of my mouth.

Sprocket sped up, roaring as his fingers bruised the skin on my hips as he came. This was quickly followed by Cam, who pulled me down so he could bite deep enough into the skin between my neck and shoulder that he broke the skin. We both came at that moment, the pain and pleasure doing me in as he knew it would.

Last time, I'd made the rule he couldn't make the others uncomfortable with his penchant for knives and blood play, but this time I hadn't bothered. Eventually, they were all going to see that side of him, and apparently, they were going to get a taste of it now. The feel of Cam's tongue lapping over the wound as he tasted my blood was oddly intimate.

"To taste you again after so long makes everything worth it," Cam whispered in my ear before placing a soft kiss over the bite. "I will never be able to tell you how grateful I am that you took me back after I failed you that day."

Sprocket kissed down my back as he pulled out, oblivious to what was going on between Cam and me. Once he moved off me, I sat up so I could look down at Cam, his eyes searching my face as if he was worried he'd see something that told him I was upset. Instead, I cupped his face and kissed him, tasting the tang of blood on his tongue.

This wasn't something I would allow just anyone to do, but it was right for the two of us. Our souls were bound with blood and pain. No matter how I fought the connection, it was never going to leave, so I might as well just accept it. We were different people now, but in a way, we'd grown up and become an even better match.

"I love you, Cameron Black. I always have, but I wasn't willing to admit it to myself, let alone you, after what happened," I answered. "We weren't ready for the love we had for each other, but now we are. So let's leave the past where it lies and try to move forward."

"Couldn't have said it better, beautiful," Cam agreed, giving me another kiss as he sat up with me still in his lap. "Well, Eagle, Void, where do you want her?"

Void walked over and plucked me out of Cam's arms. "Little demon, I think you could use some fresh air, don't you think?"

Confused, I let him shift me, so I was clinging to him like a koala as he stepped out on the small balcony that looked out over the city. The summer air blew around us, ruffling my hair as I rested my head on his shoulder. The night sky was pitch black and with the city lights, we couldn't really see the stars I knew were up there. The sounds of cars honking and people shouting settled me, having been away from the city feel since meeting the guys and spending time out on the compound.

"Now, Eagle and I are going to hold you between us as we fuck you out here," Void explained as he shifted me to slide his cock into my well-used pussy. "I want the world to know who owns this body of yours and it's us. No matter what else happens, that is a truth that will never change. You belong to the seven of us, little demon."

Eagle stepped up, kissing my neck as he felt for the entrance to my ass. He slid in easier now that Sprocket had loosened me up, making me sigh at the fullness I could never get enough of. I leaned back into Eagle as he brought his hand up to play with my tits. Being an exhibitionist hadn't been a kink I'd dabbled in since leaving Cam, but it seemed to be one these men enjoyed under the right conditions.

"That's it, little hellcat. Let us take good care of you," Eagle murmured. "We'll fuck you so good that you'll fall right to sleep. I know you haven't been getting enough rest with all the worries going on in that brilliant mind of yours."

I hummed my agreement as they started to move slowly, taking their time as if we had nowhere else in the world to be but right here, at this moment. Void dipped his head to take one of my nipples in his mouth, leaving the other for Eagle to play with. My moans were swept away on the breeze as my men fucked me with love and devotion, soothing my body after being ravaged by the others. This was exactly how every orgy should end, a reminder that with all that happened up until now, it was love that pulled us all together.

Void paused when he saw the mark on my neck from Cam, but I cupped his face and pulled him to me for a kiss. "It's fine, big guy," I murmured. "This is something that might happen from time to time, but I've allowed it."

Void grunted and pulled me to his chest as he sped up his thrusts. Eagle caught on and moved to match his speed, sending me flying into a screaming climax that might send the cops running if they could hear it. The feeling of being sandwiched between these two powerful men as they took what they needed from me was addicting. I might be able to bring crime lords to their knees, demanding respect, but for these men, I would happily allow myself to surrender to their wishes. In the end, it always brought us moments like this, filled with love and trust, something I never thought possible in my life. Together we came clinging to each other as we moaned, panted, and shuddered as we climaxed.

Boneless, I had to rely on Void to keep me from falling out of his grasp while Eagle withdrew. Void didn't bother to pull out of me. Instead, he carried me all the way to the bedroom cock still inside me as we curled up to sleep. "Rest, little demon. The real battle starts tomorrow."

The guys let me sleep for as long as I needed, doing everything to ensure they didn't wake me. So when I woke up finding myself alone in the bed, I sat up confused, then looked at the clock. It was well past noon and the black-out curtains made it feel like dusk. Sliding out of bed, I groaned at how sore my body was after handling all seven of my men last night. Fucking worth it, but damn, I needed a shower and some coffee before I could walk right again.

Clean, dressed, and ready for what this day might bring, I headed out to the living room, where most of the guys were watching the NBA draft. Wes was in the kitchen cooking something that smelled amazing, and Cam was out on the patio talking to someone on his cell phone. His expression told me that whatever was going down wasn't good.

"Ah, look who finally woke up," Wes commented, leaning over and giving me a peck on the lips. "Coffee's hot and been waiting for you."

"God, just when I didn't think I could love you more," I said, heading to get the go-go bean juice. "Who's Cam talking to?"

"Someone from his local office. I think it might be his supervisor asking about what the hell's going on," Wes shared. "I'm guessing they didn't love the fact Diego's house got blown up."

I flinched at that. I hadn't once taken into consideration what kind of backlash that might have brought. Cam was good at getting out of lots of things, but that might be a wee bit hard to explain.

"Fuck, maybe that was a bad idea," I commented as I took a sip of coffee. "Pretty sure what's going to happen tonight isn't going to help either."

Wes moved whatever he'd been cooking off the burner and turned to face me. "You know the moment he chose you over everything else, he couldn't stay with the FBI, right? He's milking it for as long as he can, but it's not going to last. He either needs to quit or find another way to remove himself from them before he gets locked up."

"Even if he did get locked up, it would be simple for us to get him out," I reasoned.

Wes cocked a brow. "Yeah and living a life as a wanted fugitive would make this so much easier."

I opened my mouth to say something, then realized he made a good point and shut it. Turning to look out at Cam on the patio, I knew Wes was right. Siding with me meant that eventually, he'd have to give up everything he'd earned so far.

I knew he wouldn't give two shits about it, having made it clear he did everything for my benefit.

"Hey," Wes said, drawing me back to him. "This is a worry for another day. You need to eat. Then we're heading upstairs to meet with Tommaso, Betta, and the triplets to run through what's going down tonight. We knew you needed sleep, but if you didn't wake up soon, I was gonna have to get you up."

Nodding, I took the plate he handed me and headed to the living room to eat while the guys talked around me. Sports was not my thing, so it was easy to tune out and run through the plan I'd cooked up in my brain for tonight. Now that I for sure had all the pieces I needed, Betta just had to follow through on her end, and this would be it for the De León Cartel.

Stuffed full of yummy food and another cup of coffee in my hands, we headed up to the triplets' place. I found Harper and Betta chatting while Tommaso was going over something with the guys. Papers were strewn everywhere on the table, and it seemed they'd been at it for some time.

"Are we late?" I asked.

Magnus looked up and smirked. "You know not everything is about you, Dax. Tommaso, here, hired us for some help hunting down some guys he knows are going to cause trouble in the new De León Cartel."

"Oh, so you're keeping the name?" I questioned.

Tommaso shrugged. "I mean, it is my real last name and proves that I deserve to take over. Since they already took out my half-siblings who were direct rivals last night, I'm feeling more secure. There arc just a few of the older generation I know won't accept the change, and I plan to nip it in the bud before it causes a problem."

"How pragmatic," I commented, then turned to the girls. "What power play are you two planning?"

"Oh, nothing much, just how Betta can use her last night as one of the four to make a splash," Harper shared. "So, do we get to hear what this secret plan of yours is?"

"What fun would that be if you knew? This is one thing you're just going to have to watch and be amazed."

Harper frowned, not liking that I wasn't going to tell her, but if she knew, I had a feeling she'd talk me out of it. Harper might have toughened up a lot in the last few months with the triplets but not enough to see the benefit in what I was about to do.

"Then why are we even meeting?" Betta asked. "If you aren't going to tell us the plan, how can we prepare for it?"

"Whoa, ladies," I said, holding up a hand to fend them off. "I didn't say I wasn't going to tell you everything. There are some parts I want to keep for maximum impact." Turning to everyone else, I decided to get this meeting started. "Anything about last night we need to share?"

Cam cleared his throat and raised his hand.

"We aren't in school. You can just talk," I said with a sigh.

He just grinned and gave me a wink before he started. "We have Diego's wife, Mariana, in a safe house and plan to take her with us when we leave. I discovered that she's Marco's biological sister, and I got the feeling she's more than willing to share her knowledge with us."

"Ah, well, we found out that Axel is one of the men who kidnapped and killed Jeff," Picasso shared.

That had my attention. I set my coffee down and walked over to him. "He admitted it?"

"Yeah, said Jeff warned him you would hunt him down and make him pay for killing one of your people," Eagle added. "After that, we made doubly sure he was safe so you could kill him properly."

I nodded and started to pace as the plan I had started to build turned into something more. "Okay, good. Did Elena get back to Gabby?"

"Yup, they are safe, back home. We told them to stay at the compound just to be sure they were protected," Eagle explained.

"Tommaso, did you have a grand entrance planned?" I inquired.

He frowned and shook his head. "No, do I need one?"

I flashed him a grin. "Oh, yeah, you do, and I have the perfect opportunity for you to really drive home everything you've been telling me. If you want this partnership between you and me to go off without a hitch, then you'll have to trust me when I call you up to the ring tonight."

"Yeah, I can do that," Tommaso agreed. "If I'm going to pick a side in this fight, then might as well not be shy about it, right?"

I clapped my hands together, smiling like a fool. "Tonight is going to make such a splash, and no one will see it coming."

"Walk us through what you can, little demon, so we can keep up," Void requested, so I grabbed a pen and flipped over one of the maps for something big enough to draw on.

I carefully explained as I drew, watching them all realize what I was going to pull off. I was sure they understood the part I was keeping to myself, but I didn't want to jinx it. This was risky as fuck, but dammit, it would be good to finally pull one over on Marco if this worked.

Chapter Twenty-Eight

Dax

The energy in the underground fighting ring was electric. The bleachers they had held about three hundred people and were packed. Then there were the box seats above that, protected by bulletproof glass, where the more important members of the criminal world sat. There were women in bikinis and heels selling shots, food, and themselves for the right price. When I say this place would have fit in ancient Rome with how debauchery was running wild, I wasn't kidding. Men fucked right there in the bleachers, not giving a shit who was watching.

The fights had started by the time we arrived at nine since Void and I weren't supposed to go on until ten. Or so they thought. We'd managed to smuggle in Diego and Axel with Betta's help since she made it clear we needed our own space to ensure no fighting happened before the ring match.

Up on electronic scoreboards were the odds and bets people were making for each fight. These beginning ones weren't as profitable as what they already had put down for Void and me. Too bad for them, they were never going to see a penny of it if they bet against me. I was just vindictive like that. I still needed to look the part, so I had on tight black shorts and a sports bra. Harper managed to braid my hair tight to my head, so if I had to fight, no one could grab it. I hoped the knife that was strapped to my thigh would deter them, but I didn't trust anyone in here who wasn't one of my people.

Knowing people would want to see me around, I headed out into the main area going for the bar. A double shot of whisky sounded perfect right now. The bartender spotted me and ditched the person who was trying to order to assist me. "What can I get you?"

"Whisky, make it a double," I answered.

"On the rocks?" he asked.

"Nah, just make it the good shit," I said, handing him over a twenty.

The man he'd ignored walked over to me, pissed as all hell. "Listen, you little bitch, I was ordering."

I leaned on the bar and looked up at him. "Who do you work for?" I asked.

"What?"

"Sorry, let me try again slower. Who. Do. You. Work. For?" I tried again.

The man's face turned red at the question. "I don't work for anyone. I'm the leader of the Seven Snakes gang in Baltimore."

"Ah, I see," I said, nodding my head.

"Here you go, Tricks. Good luck with your fight tonight," the bartender said, giving the gangbanger a telling look.

Mr. Snake realized what he said and backed up off me. "You're Two Tricks?"

"I know, it's the height. Everyone assumes I'd be taller, but you know what they say, 'the bigger they are, the harder they fall.' I feel like keeping it low to the ground helps me with that problem," I shared, saluting him with my shot before tossing it back. "Damn, that hit the spot. Well, Mr. Snake, I hope you bet on the right person. Otherwise, this is not gonna be your night."

"What do you mean by that?" he hollered after me, but I just kept walking.

I joined my guys in a section they had set aside for us to watch the fights if we wanted to. Some of these guys were actually pretty good, but some were just ruthless and would take any shot they could get in. Every fight ended with one of them dead, making Harper turn green and hide in Jaxson's arms. We'd tried to tell her she didn't want to come to this, but she refused to be put on the sidelines again. Hopefully, now when we said that, she'd listen.

"It's about show time," Void said loudly into my ear to be heard over the roar of the crowd.

I nodded and signaled to Sprocket and Cam, who were going to escort our guests to the stage when I needed them. Void and I carried only knives like we promised, but all my men were strapped even if it was against the rules of the fight club. Betta had gotten us in without being searched just for this advantage. This was supposed to be neutral ground, but not tonight. I was going to declare war on the bastard who'd been playing this cat-and-mouse game. He wanted me to attack. Well, he was gonna get his wish. Let's see if he liked it as much as he thought he would.

"Ladies and gentlemen, crime lords and ladies, the event you've all been waiting for is upon us," the announcer called over the loudspeakers. "We are going to start off the fights with Two Tricks herself against the opponent of our choosing. The rules are simple, whoever survives using only knives and fists wins."

The whole place went wild with people cheering, screaming, and whistling. Taking that as my cue, I headed up front and climbed the steps to the cage. One of the attendants handed me a microphone. It wasn't part of the original plan but was part of what I had Betta pull off for me.

I tapped it once to make sure it was working and grinned when I heard the sound echo through the speakers. "After all these years, I felt like it was only right that I should formally introduce myself. What's up, fuckers? I'm Two Tricks, Queen of the Hidden Empire, pleased to meet you all... well, most of you. Some of you I know are just assholes."

That got a chuckle out of the crowd. "I know we had a whole thing planned out where my man, Void, and I fought a whole bunch of guys you picked out, but I decided to make a few changes to the agenda."

The crowd started to talk amongst themselves and a few started to boo, demanding their bloodshed. I signaled to Cam, who brought over Axel and shoved him up the stairs into the ring, locking the door.

"Shut the fuck up," I snapped into the microphone. "I wasn't done telling you what the changes were. There is still going to be blood, death, and mayhem, just not the kind you originally had in mind. Anyone know who this kid is I have in here with me?" I asked.

There was more talking but no real answers until someone shouted out, "That's one of Diego's kids."

"Ding, ding, ding, we have a winner," I announced, raising a hand, then turned to face Axel. "Now, Axel, would you like to take a guess as to why you, of all people, are here with me tonight?"

Axel's face was pale and he was shaking. "I... I... I killed one of your people and sent him back to you with a note blaming you for my half-brother's murder."

"That's part of it. There's one more bit that you forgot to mention," I encouraged.

He frowned, then decided to take a guess. "Um... you talking about the bitch we used for blackmail?"

My hand whipped out, slapping him in the face. "Now, I know her uncles, Eagle and Picasso, explained this to you. They are my men making their family my family, so if that's the case and you manipulated, lied, and used their niece to spy on us, what does that make her to me?"

"Y-your niece?" he guessed.

"How the fuck have you survived this long being this stupid?" I asked.

Axel just gapped at me like a fish. Groaning, I grabbed him by the shirt and kicked out his legs, dropping him to his knees before addressing the crowd. "While this idiot might not be the mastermind behind what happened, I'm using him to make a point. You fuck with my family or my people I've put under my protection, I will hunt you down. No one fucks with what is mine. You do and you won't live long enough to regret it. I promise you that."

Grabbing his hair in one hand, I pulled back his head and slit his throat in one swift move. A surprised gurgle was all that could be heard from the kid as I dropped him to the floor. I waved my knife at Sprocket, who dragged a thrashing swearing Diego up into the ring. Diego spotted his son on the ground and looked up at me. A string of words in Spanish flew at me, followed by a wad of spit that missed and landed on the mat before me.

"It's so good to see you again, Diego," I greeted.

Moving forward, I grabbed his arm, shoving up behind his back as Sprocket let him go. I shoved the man toward the center of the ring and dropped him to his knees like his son. Only Diego might be older, but he was a fighter. He swung out with his other hand clipping me in the jaw and whipping my head to the side. I turned back to face him and slammed my elbow into his face feeling his nose crunch under the assault. This had him sprawling on the ground in his son's blood.

Which to me, only seemed fitting for how shitty he was to leave his whole family in the house as he saved himself.

Picking up the microphone from where I'd dropped it, I got down to business. "I'm not even going to ask if you know who this is because I know you do. You guys want me to get down to the meat of the matter? Here it is. Diego had been gunning for me since I came up in the world. I was happy to let him do his business if he left mine alone. Unfortunately for him, he couldn't do that. Now, here we are on the brink of a world war among criminal leaders. You placed bets and made choices on where you stand in this fight. Tonight wasn't just about seeing me fight or possibly die at the hands of one of your goons. Nah, it's far more than that."

I took a moment as the room fell silent, having gained everyone's attention. "Tommaso, would you join me, please?" Shock filled the room as he stepped up and walked over to me. "If you don't know who this is, Tommaso is Diego's firstborn son of his first wife, who had ties to the Italian mafia. As such, he is the next in line to take over his father's business. Recently, Tommaso has also become the leader of the Italian mafia in Boston with the blessing of the motherland. So I wanted to ensure you all knew two things."

Reaching behind Tommaso, I pulled his gun I knew was stashed there and pointed it at Diego. I noticed one of the video cameras was coming in closer over the netting of the cage to get an unobstructed view. Shifting, I looked right at the lens as I spoke the next bit.

"The De León Cartel is now under new leadership," I announced, pulling the trigger and hitting Diego right between the eyes. "And the Hidden Empire fully supports Tommaso as the rightful heir to the De León name and all that it brings with it. This is war, and I've made my move just as all of you have here tonight. Those of you who bet on me to win or to lose, I know who you are. If you're smart, then I would be certain not to get in my way if you value your life. I'm not sitting back anymore, I've stepped out of hiding, and I'm not going to lose."

Stepping closer to the camera, I squared up, knowing that on the other side of that lens, Marco was watching. "Play time's over, Marco, and I'm coming for you next. When we meet in person, this is how I'll greet you."

Lifting my gun to the camera, I watched as it zoomed in and pulled the trigger sending the bullet right into the lens, shattering it into a million pieces. Just like I was going to do to his whole kingdom.

Just you wait, Marco. I'll find you wherever you're hiding.

To be continued in Our Tricks

About Author

Elizabeth is an International Best Seller, originally from Illinois but now living in sunny Phoenix, AZ. Elizabeth has been writing for nine years and started out in YA Fiction but recently found herself loving the Reverse Harem genre. Like her favorite books, Elizabeth loves to write about strong women of all varieties. Not all strength is flashy or apparent at first glance—some lies just under the surface.

Don't Miss Out!

Be the first to know what is coming next by following Elizabeth's social media! You never know when or what will be coming next!

Website: ElizabethKnightBooks.com

Facebook: Elizabeth Knight's Unicorn Queens

Instagram: elizabethknightauthor

TikToc: elizabethknightauthor

Newsletter: sign up here

Also By

Omegaverse
Knot All Is Lost: Part 1

Knot All Is Lost: Part 2 - (October 2022)

Caprioni Queen

Book 1 – Glitter & Guns (October 2022)

Hidden Empire Series

Book 1 - Two Tricks

Book 2 - Three Tricks

Book 3 - Four Tricks

Book 4 - More Tricks

Book 5 - Our Tricks (October 2022)

Hidden Empire Novel

Harper's Renegades

Omega Assassin - Complete series

Book 1 - Dual Nature

Book 2 - Hidden Nature

Book 3 - Perfect Nature

Hope Series - Complete series

Book 1 – Hidden Hope

Book 2 – Claiming Hope

Book 3 – Defending Hope

Book 4 - Obtaining Hope

Mercenary Queen Series - Complete series

Book 1 – Birthright

Book 2 - Dragon Queen

Book 3 - Forgotten Throne

Book 4 - The Final Battle

Elementi Series - Complete series
Book 1 - Discovering Synergy

Book 2 – Refining Earth

Book 3 – Liberating Water

Book 4 - Taming Fire

Book 5 - Rescuing Air

<u>Some Kind of Luck</u>

Book 1 - The Trouble with Luck (co-write)

Book 2 - Tough Luck (Written by Ali D. Jensen)

Book 3 - Stroke of Luck (Written by Elizabeth Knight)

Book 4 - Just My Luck (Written by Sinclair Kelly)

Book 5 - No Such Luck (Written by Letty Frame)

Printed in Great Britain
by Amazon